* * *

The Accidental Vigilante

The Accidental Vigilante

The Innocent – The Evil – The Vigilant

Robert Sterling Hecker

ROBERT STERLING HECKER
P.O. Box 1292
Covington, Louisiana 70434

www.RobertSterlingHecker.com

ISBN-13: 9781518768750
ISBN-10: 151876875X
Library of Congress Control Number: 2015917880
CreateSpace Independent Publishing Platform
North Charleston, South Carolina

Cover Design: Kris Taft-Miller
Content Editor: Ruthann Raitter
Line Editor: Cristy Bertini
Publishing Consultant: Linda F. Radke, Five Star Publications, Inc.
Editing Consultant: Douglas Glenn Clark

Printed in the Unites States of America

To Polly and Lance

Appreciation

Mike E. Cahn
Retired SWAT Team Commander
New Orleans Police Department

To the police officers, sheriffs, federal agents, child advocacy groups, and all who dedicate their lives toward protecting, rescuing and saving our children from abusers, molesters, and those who would do harm to our most innocent, a heartfelt thank you.

Chapter 1

Jeremy Porter couldn't believe his good fortune. After a year of lousy treatment by his colleagues and supervisors and stuck as a patrol officer on the night shift, the rookie cop was being promoted. The Child Abuse Section may not have been the most prestigious or coveted assignment in the New Orleans Police Department, but it gave Jeremy hope. He might finally be able to improve his reputation, do meaningful work in the community, and best of all, save his crumbling marriage.

"Hey, Powder Puff. You've been transferred. Turn in your gear at the end of your shift tonight and report Monday morning to your new assignment."

Lt. Floyd Bayless delivered the surprising news with a hint of disgust in his voice during roll call as Jeremy stood with the other uniformed officers. He was dumbstruck and didn't know how to react. Was it a cruel joke the lieutenant was playing? He waited for the punchline, but there wasn't one. Not a word. Not one hushed insult or taunt. Not even Brock Suggs, a burly loudmouth who had made his life miserable since day one of cadet training, could muster a hurtful quip.

Slowly he began to realize it wasn't a joke. His big break had arrived. He didn't know how it had come to be, and he didn't give a damn. All that mattered was that his short, unimpressive police career was transformed.

It was perhaps the biggest break of his life, aside from marrying Sandy, his wealthy and gorgeous wife. Standing in the blue forest of roll call, he couldn't wait to tell her the miraculous news, and if truth be told, find his way back into her spoiled, tempestuous heart.

Jeremy spent the weekend in a bliss-filled daze and on Monday morning, he turned the ignition of his Aston Martin without a second thought about its display of wealth. As a cadet, he found that the fancy car had caused him all sorts of trouble and poisoned any chance of being treated like everyone else. Now he didn't give a damn. A man in his position could drive whatever the hell he wanted. He felt exhilarated as he headed towards the Second District, the same location he had worked as a patrol officer.

His exuberance was tempered a bit when he arrived at the parking lot to find hordes of media personnel setting up equipment and clogging the entry. *What the hell is this?* He'd arrived early to get his bearings and now he was maneuvering around reporters who refused to give right-of-way. After he finally found a spot to park, he strode purposefully toward the building, ignoring shouting techies and dodging snakes of cable that slithered on the parking lot. As he entered the district office, a couple of uniformed officers deferred to him and the show of courtesy lifted his spirits.

But anxiety finally took hold when he stood on the polished floor of the lobby and stared up the stairs that would lead him to the second floor and the Child Abuse Section. To ready himself, he replayed the weekend's events in his mind: the relief on his wife's face when he told her he was promoted and the smile she forced at the sound of his new title, "Detective Porter."

Together they went on a shopping spree that resulted in a full closet of finely tailored suits, shirts, and silk ties. Jeremy stood in front of a long line of floor-length mirrors in the dressing room, staring at his reflection. The suit hung perfectly on his slender frame. He adjusted his cuffs and ran a hand through his light brown hair. His sapphire blue dress shirt was a perfect match to his eye color. He never thought of himself as particularly handsome, but it was funny how a $1000 suit could boost a man's confidence. He smiled at his reflection. For the first time since Jeremy announced his intentions to be a police officer, Sandy invited him to bed that evening. The sex may not have been the most passionate, but it sure beat the hell out of the spare bedroom he had languished in for the past few months. It was gratifying to be a married couple again. Perhaps the transfer would help steady the rocky marriage.

"Hey, Powder Puff, it's called a staircase. Just take one step at a time. Like this, ok?"

The crewcut police officer took baby steps, smirked, and then dashed to catch up to his patrol car partner.

Jeremy felt his face burn at the encounter with yet one more asshole from the academy who had decided to make him the butt of every joke. God, how he loathed that nickname. It stuck to him like a stench. Then a different feeling warmed him: he was wearing a designer suit, not the blue uniform; and he was now considered a detective. *Fuck you*, he thought, *and fuck you, Brock Suggs and Lieutenant Bayless.*

As he began his ascent, Jeremy's mood changed again. Grinning, he remembered the crayon drawing his little girl had left him before Sandy drove her to school. Across the top of the manila folder in blue, unskilled script, Kayla had written "Detective Daddy." He had so much to live for: a beautiful wife, a great kid and—

"Coming through!"

Halfway up the stairs, a plainclothes officer carrying an unwieldy cardboard box nearly collided with Jeremy.

He steadied the box and stared at Jeremy. "Hey," he said. "You must be Porter."

Jeremy found it refreshing to hear his actual name. "Yeah, that's me."

"Nice threads, Dude."

Jeremy smiled but felt the hot blush return. He realized he looked like a corporate executive compared to this guy, who wore wrinkled, gray dress slacks and a poorly chosen necktie that hung low with a loose, indifferent knot.

"I'm Roy Farmer, the guy you're replacing. Congratulations, Man." He offered a hand under the box and Jeremy shook it. "I've been promoted to sergeant and transferred to the Sixth District."

"Congrats to you, too. That's great."

"Yeah. Couldn't get out of there fast enough, frankly," he cocked his head toward the second floor. "Don't stay too long, Man."

Jeremy cocked his head to one side. "What do you mean?"

"No, no, don't get me wrong. It's a good move up for you. Tons of work and nine-to-five. Nice. But it … oh, hell, don't listen to me," he said as he rolled his eyes. "Shut up, Farmer."

"No, no. I'm all ears. Tell me."

Farmer lowered his voice and scanned the ground floor for eavesdroppers.

"I'm just saying, it can get to you. This type of work, I mean. Know what I'm saying?"

Jeremy wasn't sure that he did, but he nodded anyway, a veteran talking shop with a fellow detective.

"Besides that, I'm afraid this shit is going to blow up one day."

Jeremy was a little surprised by the statement. "Blow up? What do you mean?"

Farmer shrugged his shoulders and adjusted his grip on the cardboard box before heading down the stairs. "Ahhh, I talk too much. You'll figure it out. Go save the world, Porter. Good luck to you."

"And you."

Jeremy watched him walk down a few steps before he stopped and turned back. "Oh, here," he said as he balanced the box on one leg and dug into a frayed pocket with his free hand. He pulled out a single key on a small chain and tossed it to Jeremy. "Key to the office. Just tell Tanner I gave it to you, okay?"

A passing of the baton. Access was an aphrodisiac. Jeremy shivered with excitement. He was on his way.

There were other offices along the dimly lit hallway, but Jeremy's new port of call was the first door at the top of the stairs. A water cooler and trash can flanked the entrance. The lettering on the door said: Child Abuse Section.

Jeremy took a deep breath and pushed open the door. The room looked more like a giant storage closet than an office. Overstuffed filing cabinets lined the gray, faded walls and the empty desks of former detectives were now covered with old newspapers. The trash cans were filled with take-out bags, candy bar wrappers, and empty paper cups that threatened to spill over onto the matching gray, faded floor. Sgt. Greg Tanner was standing in the middle of the room perusing papers in an open folder. Judging by the sheer size of his new supervisor, Jeremy knew the candy bar wrappers must belong to him. Except for the firearm barely visible on his belt, the man's pullover golf shirt and khaki pants gave the impression that he had just finished eighteen holes.

"Morning, Sarge. I'm Jeremy Porter, new transfer. Wanted to get in a little early." His words dwindled into silence.

Tanner didn't speak until he had finished reading the materials he held. Then he turned, looked Jeremy up and down, and frowned.

"Okay, first of all, I gotta say you're a little overdressed for this assignment. Next time, wear casual clothes, unless of course you're thinking of running for mayor."

The sergeant pointed his double chin to the smaller of two desks arranged in a way that made the office feel cramped. "That one's yours."

Jeremy nodded and moved closer to the dented, gouged metal workspace that would look shoddy even in a tawdry secondhand store. He was a long way from his position as resident information technology pro—otherwise known as an overpaid trouble-shooting PC dweeb—at the furniture mega-corporation Sandy's father had founded. Curtis McGuire was affluent beyond compare and politically influential. His money didn't just talk; it could put someone in a chokehold. Jeremy wondered if his new assignment had been a favor with strings attached. His mind flushed when he heard his superior curse.

"Fuck!"

The ill-tempered sergeant had pulled electronic equipment from a tall utility cabinet, causing an avalanche of tangled cables, accessories, and a plastic cylinder of disposable wipes. He kicked the junk aside and hastily began setting up a video camera on a tripod that he pointed toward a steel-gray chair he'd placed in front of his own desk.

"All right, Rookie, you picked a damn fine day to get started," he grunted as he bent over to pick up some of the mess. "The patrol guys just picked up a perv who—"

"A what?"

"A perv. A child molester suspect. Why else would I get here this early," he asked as he threw some of the tangled cables on top of the cabinet. "The perv kidnapped a six-year-old girl. He kept her for over three days, and since she's still alive, it's our case. She's in critical condition. And if she had been found dead, guess what? The case would go to homicide. Lucky them. Anyway, the suspect wants to make a confession so they're bringing him up here. You get to sit in on his little performance to learn how this works. But keep your mouth shut. I'll do the Q and A. I don't tolerate interruptions. You get me?"

"Of course. I want to learn." His eagerness was betrayed by the trembling in his hands. Kayla was six. Memories of her smile and laughter were quickly clouded by sordid images of a little girl, a victim traumatized by an abuser. Tanner's voice pulled Jeremy from his thoughts.

"....okay, we have a few minutes, so I'll give you a brief rundown of this place."

Jeremy struggled to concentrate as he learned that the division was overworked and understaffed. The office once had eight detectives, but was now down to two. They were simply told, "Do what you can. More with less."

Tanner moved to a row of file cabinets and pointed a swollen finger as he explained that their contents were strictly confidential, especially the one labeled ED. Jeremy shook his head to clear it.

"Wait. ED?" he asked.

Tanner's eyes narrowed. "No, it doesn't stand for erectile dysfunction. You got a dirty mind or something?"

"Uh, no."

"Yes you do. We all do. Extremely Dangerous is what ED is. And I'm not kidding, get me?"

Tanner turned to finish cleaning up the mess while spouting statistics, recidivism rates of about seventy percent for the average child abuser, but nearly ninety percent for the ED variety of perverts who were currently out of prison and living the good life.

"They're what? They're not—why aren't they in prison? I mean, do we check up on these guys?"

Sergeant Tanner turned and sneered at Jeremy's naiveté.

"We don't have *time* to check on anybody. That's not our job anyway. Let the probation and parole people do that, even though they're more shorthanded than we are. Maybe they check one or two a month ... maybe."

Maybe? Jeremy struggled to smother his outrage as he gazed at the posters of missing children taped haphazardly on the green walls.

"Hey, there are hundreds of names in ED. There'll never be enough detectives to cover all that. If you want to spend your off days keeping track of these perverts, go right ahead. I'm sure probation would appreciate it."

The burly officer moved to his desk, picked up a thick manual, and let it drop on Jeremy's desk with a loud thud. "This is your playbook, Pointer."

"Porter."

"Say what?"

"My name, Sir. It's Porter."

Tanner eyed his new cohort suspiciously, then nodded. "Just start reading when you have time. You won't have much. Learn on the job, one perv at a time."

Pivoting to his own desk, Tanner pulled a key from a drawer and tossed it to Jeremy.

"That's your key to the office."

Jeremy remembered the key that Roy Farmer gave him. "Oh, no, that's okay. I have—"

"Hey, make sure you always lock the damn door when you leave," Tanner commanded and pointed again emphatically at the file cabinets. "That stuff's super confidential. Protect it. We don't do casual around here, Pouter."

Jeremy flinched and Tanner's eyes flashed with impatience. "What!"

"Uh, Porter. My name is Jeremy—"

A loud knock at the door interrupted their conversation.

"We're here," the voice echoed from the other side of the door. "You ready, Tan?

The sergeant's face darkened as he grabbed the doorknob and he looked over his shoulder at Jeremy. "Your lucky day. Welcome to Pervertsville, Porker."

Chapter 2

Maybe this is what it feels like going to war, Jeremy thought. *If only I had more time to train before being tossed into battle—into a world of mayhem and the unknown.*

When the patrol officers brought in the suspect, Jeremy's soul began to burn like dry brush.

Sergeant Tanner took documents from two cops—one the shape of a fire hydrant who was almost as wide as he was tall, and the other, who looked like a sign post standing next to him. Tanner greeted the handcuffed suspect before directing him to the chair in front of the video camera. The guy was a corpulent, middle-aged, white male with thinning hair and a three-day beard. He wore a filthy, unbuttoned, plaid short-sleeve shirt over a ribbed wife-beater that did not flatter his fat, sweaty gut. Baggy, urine-stained pants led the eye to shoes with cut-out toes. Naturally, the man smelled like a sewer and when his vile body odor drifted over to Jeremy sitting on his desk a couple of feet away, he felt his nostrils burn and his stomach turned sour.

Innocent until proven guilty. Bullshit. All Jeremy saw was a horrible person, a subhuman specimen, a child molester who had preyed on a fragile six-year-old girl and made her his sex slave. The perv turned and the two men locked eyes. Depravity stared back, until Jeremy had to turn away. This was his new reality.

What had ever made him think that police work was for him? He knew the answer, of course. It loomed in his thoughts like a gaudy commercial on a big-screen TV. Joe Doode. Crossing paths with the hero cop who risked his life to save a battered woman had made Jeremy feel emasculated and empty. Having it all, he realized, could be synonymous with having nothing. Determined to earn some self-respect, he had made a radical decision to redirect his life.

Now he wondered if the decision was the right one.

* * *

It seemed like a lifetime ago when the image of being a police officer had first entered Jeremy's mind. It had started when he was twenty-six years old and entrenched as an information tech pro for one of his father-in-law's furniture stores.

It was a hot June day in New Orleans, just another day at the office for Jeremy and Sandy. As Jeremy looked over documents at his desk, he heard a commotion near the front door. When he looked up, he saw a woman running through the store, frantically asking for the ladies' room. He could tell even from a distance that she was very upset. The woman turned and looked at the front door before sprinting toward the restrooms.

As everyone focused on the woman, the front door opened again and this time a huge, middle-aged man entered and glanced around the store. When he spied the woman running toward the restrooms, the man raced after her and yelled, "Don't you run from me, Bitch!" The man was obviously very angry about something.

Everyone gathered at the office window to watch as this situation unfolded. As the man screamed at the top of his voice, customers quickly scrambled out of the front door. Jeremy and Sandy gathered with other employees at the window near the office door. Mr. McGuire walked from his office and asked what was going on. When he was told, he instructed one of the secretaries to call 9-1-1.

The woman had locked herself in the ladies' room. When the man reached the restroom, he growled, "Open this door, now!" When he realized the woman was not going to comply, he stepped back and began kicking the door. The man was holding in his hand what appeared to be a knife.

The interior of the store was now completely empty, other than the enraged man who continued to kick the door. The door started breaking away at the hinges. It would only be a matter of seconds before he would get his hands on his victim.

"Shouldn't we do something?" Jeremy asked Mr. McGuire.

Mr. McGuire shook his head. "No. Store policy says we cannot get involved."

Jeremy felt helpless. He realized that even if he ran to assist the woman, the man was a monster, standing about six feet, five inches tall, weighing close to 250 pounds, and obviously quite capable of crushing Jeremy with one blow.

"Where are the damn cops? Mr. McGuire uttered, hoping to make sure everyone knew that this was a police matter, that no one should try to be a hero, and most importantly, that no one should violate store policy.

The door was now hanging by a hinge. The man grabbed the bottom of it to clear it from his path. He yelled, "You're dead, Bitch!" As he threw the door to the side, the woman tried to run out but the suspect grabbed her by her dress, threw her to the floor, and grabbed a fistful of her hair.

Just then, a young New Orleans cop raced inside. Everyone pointed toward the ladies' room. The officer sprinted toward the restroom and could see the man sitting on top of his victim, holding her head still with his left hand, and raising the knife with his right hand. The officer lunged at the man as he was about to stab the knife into the woman's heart. The officer knocked the suspect from atop the woman and the two of them landed on the floor in a violent struggle.

Everyone watched nervously, hoping the officer would survive the attack. The officer and the suspect rolled around the floor, yelling at each other. "Drop the knife!" "Fuck you!" They continued to roll over each other, neither man giving in. The crazed man was obviously bigger and stronger and refused to relinquish his weapon.

Finally, the officer got the upper hand as he landed a few more blows to the suspect's head. Completely out of breath and bleeding from his arms and hands, he managed to get his handcuffs out and placed them on the suspect. The suspect, also out of breath and bleeding from the face and head, groaned in pain.

The officer went to care for the victim who was still lying nearby on the floor. As it turned out, this was a domestic dispute that turned extremely violent. By this time, several other officers had arrived to assist, although the emergency had subsided. Another officer took the woman out of the store towards a waiting ambulance, but not before she tearfully expressed her gratitude to the officer who saved her life.

Another officer took the handcuffed suspect out of the store and put him in the back of a police car. The emergency unit began administering first aid to the injured: the officer, the suspect, and the victim. After a few bandages were applied, the officer went to check on the victim. She asked for some water. The officer walked back into the store and noticed a group of employees still huddled behind the locked office door. The officer told them that they could unlock the door and then he asked for water.

Three ladies in the group all raced to the refrigerator to get bottles of water. As he headed back outside, he turned and told the group that he would need to get their names before they headed back to work.

After the officer left, Mr. McGuire turned to the group and said, "I'll provide the officers with the information they need. You all need to get back to work."

When the officer returned a few minutes later with his sergeant to obtain the witness information, he saw that Mr. McGuire had sent everyone back to their desks, although most were still in earshot of the conversation.

"I would like to speak to everyone who witnessed this incident," the officer said.

Mr. McGuire stood. "I am the president and CEO of the company, I can give you what you need."

"No, sir. I need to speak to everyone individually."

Mr. McGuire was not accustomed to anyone disagreeing with him. He was taken aback by the officer's response. "If I saw the same thing as everyone else, why the need to tie up all of my employees?" he asked.

The officer clenched his jaw and took a deep breath. All of the employees', including Jeremy's, eyes widened as they pretended to work while listening to the exchange.

"What is your name, Sir?" the officer asked.

"Curtis McGuire, and I am president of this company!"

"Mr. McGuire, I just made an arrest in your store in the presence of several witnesses. The suspect was armed with a large pocket knife and I had to use force to subdue him. As a result, the suspect sustained some minor injuries and now there is a very good chance that he or his lawyer will claim that I used excessive force. Therefore, I need everyone who saw what happened to provide me with the necessary information for this police report. Is that clear, Sir?"

Mr. McGuire stared at the officer for a few seconds and in a contemptuous tone said, "Very well, Officer, please do your job but I just want you to know that Chief Hendricks is a very good friend of mine and I may need to speak to him about this."

"You certainly have a right to do that, Sir," the officer replied in an equal tone before making the rounds and interviewing a total of seven employees, taking the names and addresses of each. When the officer interviewed Jeremy, he asked, "Where were you standing during the incident?"

"With the others." Jeremy began to have an empty feeling inside and hoped the officer would not ask many more questions, but no such luck.

"When the suspect was kicking down the door, did you or anyone else move toward him?"

Jeremy was now embarrassed and reluctant to relive his inactions. He searched for an appropriate answer to the question. *How do you explain allowing a woman to get assaulted and simply doing nothing to help her?* As he pondered his answer, the officer looked up from his notepad, unaware that Jeremy had begun to question his inactions. Jeremy realized the only thing he could say was that he was going to intervene, but Mr. McGuire had a company policy against getting involved with situations such as these. As soon as he murmured those words, he wished he could take them back.

The officer sensed his embarrassment and quickly tried to put Jeremy at ease. "Probably a wise choice, Sir. The suspect was armed with a knife and we would strongly advise against anyone intervening. That's *our* job."

That didn't make Jeremy feel any better. He stared at the officer's nameplate. His name was Joseph Doode. Jeremy felt he was in the presence of an American hero—a cop named Joe Doode. Jeremy couldn't help but notice that Joe Doode had five medals across his chest above his badge. He wondered how an officer so young could have already earned so many medals.

After Officer Doode and his sergeant got all of the information they needed, he made a point to thank Mr. McGuire for his cooperation in front of all of the employees. Mr. McGuire tried to save face, "You are very welcome."

Jeremy continued to wrestle with what happened that day as he drove home. He thought about what he should have done, and what he had *not* done. He tried to convince himself that the officer's comment was correct. It simply was not his place to intervene. He could have easily been killed had he done so. Although it was a reasonable decision, he was not convinced.

He sat down to dinner later that evening, but he didn't have much of an appetite.

"What's wrong with you tonight?" Sandy asked as she poured herself a glass of wine.

"Just thinking about the incident today."

She dismissed his concerns with a wave of her hand. "No big deal, the cops arrested a nut ... time to move on."

Jeremy knew she wouldn't understand why he was wrestling with the issue, but in order to avoid a pointless discussion, he simply said, "Yep."

Late into the night, Jeremy couldn't sleep. He knew if that cop had arrived ten seconds later, he would have witnessed a man murder a woman and would have done nothing to stop it. He lay there thinking about how mundane and scripted his life had become. His only real accomplishment in life was that he was a good father. He could never be a Joe Doode. After several hours, Jeremy finally started to doze off, but images of the hero Joe Doode continued to invade his thoughts.

* * *

"All right, Charles, you're here because you want to help yourself out a little and give us a statement, correct?" Tanner wanted to be sure the suspect was at ease and had not been coerced, so they could get a confession on record without delay.

Now Jeremy was living the reality of being a cop: coming face-to-face with the scum of the earth, Charles Stevens.

The suspect slurred something unintelligible.

"Those cuffs are probably a little uncomfortable. Stand up and I'll put them in front."

The suspect stood and while his wrists were freed, returned a cold, vacant gaze to Jeremy, who squashed an urge to kick the smelly freak in the balls. *Get your fucking eyes off me, shitbird.* Instead, the rookie detective reached for the handbook on his desk. *Perverts for Dummies.*

Tanner stepped outside the office with a paper cup, stopped the door with his foot, and leaned toward the water cooler. He returned and placed the full cup in Charles' hands. "All right, here we go."

That was the cue for the arresting officers to leave the room. When the door latch clicked behind them, Tanner turned on the video recorder and the formalities began.

"This is a statement being taken from Mr. Charles Stevens, white male, age 52, residing in Lot No. 15 of the Swenson Trailer Park, New

Orleans, Louisiana. Those present are Mr. Stevens, Detective Jeremy Panter—"

"Porter."

Tanner expressed annoyance with a steely stare. Jeremy didn't care. He was far more intrigued by the new feelings of defiance and disgust that roiled in him.

"Those present are Mr. Stevens, Detective Jeremy Porter, and myself, Sgt. Greg Tanner. The statement is being taken and recorded in the Child Abuse office in the Second District police station."

After reading the suspect the Rights of an Arrestee and noting the date and time, Tanner asked, "Mr. Stevens, are you ready to begin?"

The suspect nodded.

"Now I need a verbal answer, yes or no."

"Um, yes."

"Thank you. Explain how you met and kidnapped the victim, a six-year-old female child."

"Well I seen this little girl playing in the trailer court down the street, so I noticed she was by herself, kinda, so I—"

"What do you mean by 'kinda?'" Tanner interrupted. "What does that mean?"

Charles smiled in a way that was not friendly, spittle at the corners of his mouth, an arrogance that did not befit his current position in life. As if he had a credential.

"It's like, you can tell when a kid is lonely. They can even be around people but they, it's like, you know?"

Statements delivered as questions. Jeremy's stomach tossed, his patience was spent, and the confession had only just begun.

"Okay, so this little girl was 'kinda' with people or—what?"

Charles Stevens now seemed to be channeling his memory, entranced by the recollection of the horrific event.

"She didn't have no friends, and the couple of adults—I knew they wasn't paying her no attention."

"How did you know?"

"They were down the road a piece. Gabbing sluts."

"Only two women were in the area?"

"Lonely kids need love! I knew I could give her the love she needed."

Jeremy squirmed. Visions of Kayla swirled in his head. Imagining the horror this little girl went through made his eyes water.

"Then what?" Tanner asked.

"I stop and ask her a couple of questions. She seems like a friendly little girl so I tell her I live in the next trailer court over ... and ... then I says, I says, 'I got a bad back. Can you help me with my groceries? I got ice cream and stuff.' So she gets in my truck and I drive to my trailer. She comes inside but I can tell she's scared."

"How sensitive." The muttered cynicism made Jeremy feel exposed. He glanced at Tanner trying to get his attention to let him know that something was wrong. His hands began to shake. *Should I interrupt for a restroom break?*

Tanner ignored him and pressed on.

"So I try to calm her down, but she tries to run out, goddamnit, and I got so mad..." Stevens grimaced, his hands tightened into fists and pounded his thighs, as though he was trying to resist his personal demons of hair-trigger temper, entitlement, and maybe belittlement.

"So I shove her in the bedroom. She's so young, but I thought I could get her to satisfy me like my wife never could, and that bitch left me, so fuck her, but ... So I undressed the little girl and I was real nice, I wasn't tearing at her clothes or nothin'. I told her she could put them back on. I just wanted her to know—"

Jeremy's blood was boiling. He wondered how Tanner could listen to this shit without emotion. He tried to imagine Kayla forced to perform fellatio—an act she could not possibly comprehend. What would such a vile act do to a child?

The perv continued and Jeremy tried to block out the intricate details of the abuse described in a matter-of-fact tone intended to make the attack on the little girl seem normal. A day in the life.

"Then finally I wanted her to suck—" Jeremy let out an intentional cough interrupting the comments. He couldn't listen to another word.

Tanner was obviously aggravated and gave Jeremy a stern look.

Stevens continued. "She wouldn't do it, so I hit her a few times. They were just slaps. I didn't punch her or anything."

"But the report says there are numerous contusions on her face and lower body, Charles," Tanner noted. "Her jaw is broken, her lower lip torn open, and she might need surgery for a fractured eye socket."

"I only spanked her."

"Hard?"

"She was disobeying."

"Disobeying a stranger?"

"I needed her to calm down. I was giving her affection, she needed my love, but she—"

Jeremy felt as though his body had been invaded by a giant, toxic greaseball.

"She what?" Tanner prodded.

The perv was sitting on something; even Jeremy could tell that and he wasn't so sure he wanted to know what it was.

"She's lucky."

"What do you mean?"

Stevens shook his head, got that weird grin on his face again, the putrid sense of superiority. Expert witness to perversity.

"Where she was going—if the cops didn't interrupt and take her from me—she was next."

"I don't follow."

"I suppose you are searching my laptop?"

"We have a search warrant. Police are at your trailer now."

The perv was smiling, something buzzing in his head. He gulped his water and crushed the paper cup. Jeremy saw Tanner's eyes flash to high-alert.

"Tell me what's in the laptop, Charles."

"I can't."

"Why?"

"I'm dead if I tell you."

"You're not exactly living the high life here, buddy."

Charles Stevens shook his head emphatically, as if responding to an inner voice.

"Do something to help yourself, Charles. Tell me about the—"

"You won't break the code! I don't care how smart you guys are. He's smarter."

"Come on, you're not making any sense. Who's smarter? What code?"

"She's lucky she's already in the hospital. She'd be with him by now!"

Tanner leaned in, knowing that something bigger than a solo act of abuse might be in the cards. Short questions now, nothing too direct, circling his prey with the hope the guy would just pop and spew his poison.

"With him? Who are you talking about?"

Stevens was shaking, but not from fear. The person he spoke of seemed to excite him. His tremors seemed more like—

"Hey, keep your hands on the table, Charles."

Jeremy saw the perv rubbing what looked like a growing erection pushing against his piss-stained pants.

"Hey! Talk to me. Who are you talking about here?"

"She was gonna be the next s-s-star of a—"

"Of a what?"

Stevens tilted his head back and shut his eyes tight. "Watch her suffer. Suffer you little bitch. Listen to her scream..."

Imagining Kayla with this monster, Jeremy's urge to vomit was overwhelming. He couldn't listen to another disgusting sound. Unable to control himself, Jeremy screamed. "You disgusting piece of shit!"

Tanner reached for his firearm as Jeremy lurched to his feet and shoved his desk away to make space for an escape.

Stevens spun, frightened by the outburst.

"Sit down, Porter!" Tanner commanded.

But Jeremy was already darting forward, cutting a path between the sergeant and the perv, tripping on the camera cable and rocketing through the door before bending over the trash can and heaving his guts. The propulsion was loud and sloppy and shot past the container onto the tile floor. Even when he had nothing left in him, the new detective continued to retch as the smell of vomit choked him and made his eyes water.

"Jesus Christ, Porter." Tanner stood over Jeremy for a moment, returned to the office, and shouted into a phone requesting a sanitation crew. "Bring a wet mop and pail!" The door opened again but Jeremy still couldn't stand. He nodded when the sergeant barked, "Stay out here. Don't come back in. When you're cleaned up, go home. I'll carry you on sick leave."

Jeremy groped for the water cooler, feeling faint and utterly defeated. His face and the front of his clothes were a stinking, sopping mess. He didn't have a handkerchief, so he yanked out his shirttail to wipe his mouth. Feeling another wave of nausea gathering in him, he groaned. It came fast, folding him over before he could get to the trash receptacle. Only spittle shot out of his gaping mouth.

Fast footsteps echoed in the hallway. Jeremy felt a hand on his back and another on his arm, stabilizing him before he fell on his face.

"You okay, Man?"

"Easy does it."

The two patrol officers did their best to revive him. But all Jeremy could do was nod and wave them off, too humiliated to look them in the eyes or even thank them.

Disoriented, Jeremy didn't see the men's room down the hall. He yanked off his silk tie and tossed it into the trash bin, then pulled off his jacket and wore it over one shoulder like a matador's cape, partly masking the mess on his shirt. He gargled a sip of water, spit into the bin, and began the long journey to his car.

Oh, shit. He'd forgotten about the media crews in the parking lot. Now he knew why they had gathered. Perv arrests are big news. He raised his jacket over his head like a tent, then ducked behind vehicles before dashing to his wheels.

In his car at last, he felt safe but stupid. The scent of the leather seats fought for but never really achieved dominance over the vomit. He found a fast food napkin in the console and pulled down the vanity mirror attached to the sun visor. He did not like what he saw.

Sandy's voice and glorious images of the weekend—goodwill sex, cooking on the patio grill, and playing with Kayla—made his head ache.

The man in the mirror was talking. *You fucking loser. You blew it! You're done.*

Chapter 3

Jeremy's friends were green with envy when he told them he was getting married. "You struck it rich, Bro!" "Hit the lottery!" "How'd you do it, Man?" His wife-to-be was a hot, hoity-toity, New Orleans aristocrat, and her picture was always in local lifestyle magazines.

Half a dozen years earlier, Jeremy had been a college student looking for part-time work. He had been offered a position as a clerk at a swanky country club. Why not? On his pay and middle-income background, he'd never in a million years be able to join. But after graduation, he had been promoted to a full-time job, and his perks included the use of the facilities.

He loved checking-in, bantering at the front desk, and answering the phones because he was good with people and had a photographic memory for names and faces. And, because he had played tennis his entire life, he was occasionally invited to fill in as the fourth man in a doubles match, glad-handing with the rich and notorious. It didn't hurt one bit that the first time Sandy McGuire saw him, he was dominating a crew of middle-aged players who wore knee braces and argued line calls as if they were at Wimbledon. After slamming an ace, he looked up to see the rare beauty glancing his way, absolutely striking in a tennis outfit that clung to an incomparable figure. Her long, blonde hair was perfectly coiffed into a high ponytail, her tan skin shimmered in the sunlight, and her eyes were the color of the sky. Awestruck, deaf, and dumb, he didn't hear his irritable doubles partner complain. "Hey! Are we here to play or what? Serve it up!"

Before the end of the match, Jeremy learned that the blonde was the daughter of furniture magnate Curtis McGuire, a multi-millionaire who enjoyed poolside cocktails far more than racquet sports. Reading his mind, one of the crusty members of his foursome chuckled and advised, "Sorry, Kid. She's out of your league."

Another added, "Actually, she's out of this world. If I were thirty years younger—"

"You mean, 130 years younger?"

More jousting followed, a war of words, each man boasting triumphs of a very distant past. Jeremy smiled and donned sunglasses so that he could secretly watch Sandy's every move.

In the days that followed, the young man asked so many questions that his amused co-workers began to report sightings.

"Saw your gal at the mall yesterday. Lordy, that skirt was short."

"Hey, Miss America is playing on Court 3. Does she ever actually sweat?"

He tried to act uninterested, but he was obviously crestfallen the day he saw a Ferrari stop in the circular entrance area. The muscular, handsome man in the driver's seat beamed and then leaned over to kiss the woman who slipped into the car. Sandy held the smooch way beyond the norms of appropriate public display of affection.

"Who's the lucky guy?" Jeremy asked anyone who could answer.

The gal behind the reception desk smirked, "Her fiancé. He's a linebacker for the New Orleans Saints."

"NFL, huh?" His heart dropped below his low-cut tennis socks.

"Yup. N-F-L, as in No Fucking Luck," she snickered.

But a month later, Jeremy opened the *Times-Picayune* sports section and learned that Mr. Hotshot had been traded to the Chicago Bears. *Out of sight, out of mind. Game on,* he smiled.

The next time Sandy appeared, he was ready. He all but stalked her as she wandered from the gym to the juice bar. After she was served, he approached casually, though in fact he had practiced exactly what he would say to her.

"Hey, how are you?"

"Fine, how are you doing today?"

She was friendly, noncommittal. She wasn't shocked that a mere mortal would speak to her. *So far, so good.* Jeremy began his prepared comments.

"I work the front desk and see you come in all the time. Just wanted to say hi and introduce myself. I'm Jeremy."

Sandy accepted his hand. The silk texture of her fingers and palm, the intoxicating scent....

"Oh, I know who you are. But you always seem so busy up there at the desk."

"Yes, yes."

"So many responsibilities."

"Well—" He shrugged. Modesty becomes a man.

"I didn't want to disturb you by introducing myself."

Jeremy hadn't expected to hear that. He groped for a reply before blurting, "Disturb me, please!"

Sandy's smile—pearly white teeth behind full, shapely lips—made him tipsy. "Well, all right then. Next time, I will."

"Be a pest."

Her laugh suggested that she was genuinely tickled. She tossed her long blonde hair, and cooed, "Oh, boy, be careful what you wish for."

He could have left right then. Mission accomplished. He'd made contact with Planet Sandy. But as she signed her ticket for her beverage, he was aware of other men staring, ogling, and probably pining to replace him. Dare he be bolder?

"Hey, you know, I was wondering ... would you like to get a coffee or something sometime? I mean, more than a coffee if you want ... I mean ... you know. . .actual food would be okay, too ... something to nourish our ... or ... I mean, maybe you don't have time, but . . ."

Garbling his words, he felt as if he were dangling from a precipice. He'd reached too far. Her rejection would send him to oblivion.

"Sure, give me a call. Do you want to put my number in your cell?"

Jeremy ripped his phone from its belt holster like a cowboy drawing a pistol. "Ready when you are."

He was good at data entry. Computer science was his college major. Three seconds—done.

"All right, then," she said. "Well, I need to get going but give me a call, okay?"

They shook hands again and she turned to go. She took two steps and her phone began to chirp. She stopped, pulled it to her ear, and then spun around. "It's you."

Jeremy grinned. "Just wanted to make sure you gave me a real number. I'll try not to be a pest."

She searched his face, a smile of appreciation slowly dawning. "Call me later tonight. Promise?"

So began the relationship. Jeremy was so proud of overcoming his shyness and pursuing the girl of his dreams. They were married a year later and had their baby girl nine months after the wedding. Sandy's father seemed to like Jeremy from the outset. Sure, he would have preferred Sandy marry someone with similar prestige in the community, but he also recognized that Jeremy idolized his daughter and believed she would always be able to control things within their family. Mr. McGuire realized Sandy was a strong-willed, opinionated woman and Jeremy's somewhat passive personality was probably a good match for her.

The wedding was fabulous. While Sandy assembled eight bridesmaids, Jeremy actually had a hard time finding eight close friends to be his groomsmen. The two closest friends he had joined the military shortly after high school and seemed to drift away after they left town. As it turned out, Jeremy had to call on some of Sandy's friends and relatives to round out his eight groomsmen Nevertheless, the wedding was a success, especially when Mr. McGuire gave the couple a new home for their wedding present. Jackpot!

Jeremy and Sandy went to Europe on their honeymoon, compliments of her parents. Upon returning, Jeremy accepted a job at Mr. McGuire's largest furniture store as the store's IT director. Sandy was also employed at the store as sales director. Jeremy majored in computer science in college and quickly realized that there was no other company that would start him at the $150 thousand salary he made at the furniture store.

In addition to giving Jeremy and Sandy their new home, he also gave them a brand-new, red Aston Martin DBS Coupe, valued at roughly $275 thousand. On his first day at work, Jeremy recalled Mr. McGuire introducing him to everyone as his son-in-law, which gave him immediate celebrity status.

Sandy got pregnant on their honeymoon and took a leave of absence a few months after they returned. Jeremy was living the American dream. At twenty-two years old, he had a $150 thousand salary and a beautiful wife and child. They lived in an extravagant home in the New Orleans Garden District. Employees in the store addressed Jeremy as Mr. Porter. He had it all … or so he thought.

Growing up, Jeremy always tried to please his own father. His father was a Baptist minister and kept tight reins on Jeremy, giving him a curfew all the way through high school. Mr. Porter insisted the family attend church weekly and sent Jeremy to a small Christian school. He did not allow his son to participate in any contact sports but did permit him to play tennis. It was probably a good idea since Jeremy was a small-framed man, five-feet, eight-inches tall and weighing only 160 pounds. Jeremy was a good tennis player, not quite talented enough to make the college team, but he did participate in the intramural leagues. Jeremy's father eventually retired from the church and developed early signs of dementia. Jeremy's mother spent most of her time caring for her sick husband.

Jeremy never had a strong circle of friends. He didn't consider himself a loner, but his few friends were those from his church or the intramural tennis teams. Jeremy sometimes surmised his life was scripted by his father, but tried not to dwell on it too much. After all, he was married to a beautiful woman, had a terrific income, and now a baby daughter. As an adolescent, Jeremy always thought that once he was an adult and away from the tight reins of his father, he would be able to spread his wings.

However, he often wondered if instead he allowed himself to simply continue having someone control his life, and that someone was now Sandy. Sandy called most of the shots—who they went out with, where they went on vacation—and usually involved only her parents in the important family decisions. But Jeremy was quite flexible and patient. He seemed to accept his somewhat subordinate role in the relationship, especially since he enjoyed the finer things life had to offer.

His station in life probably hit him the hardest when, after he found out Sandy was pregnant, he brought home a book of names for the baby. Sandy told him that she and her mother had already picked out boy and girl names. Although Jeremy thought this was the time he needed to put his foot down, he blew it off and the matter was never again discussed. The baby was given the name Kayla—a consensus of Sandy and her parents. Nevertheless, Jeremy adored his little girl and was thrilled that she looked just like him—with beautiful, blue eyes, fair skin, and light caramel brown hair. He would often leave work early to pick her up from daycare to spend more time with her. He loved seeing her little face light up when she saw him waiting at the door. "Daddy's here!" she would squeak and run towards him with her ponytail bouncing on her shoulders. Jeremy was the model father.

* * *

On the drive home from the police station, Jeremy stripped off his soiled dress shirt and wore only his v-neck undershirt when he dropped his suit jacket at a dry cleaner.

In the shower, he scrubbed his body raw before realizing that the odor that repelled him was in his nasal system, or maybe in his memory. Clean clothes and a strong dose of after-shave made him feel better. Maybe he could smooth things over with Tanner. He would offer a heartfelt apology along with the claim that he awoke that morning with a touch of the flu. He could only hope Tanner would understand and give him another chance.

The news reports also gave him incentive. Pacing and restless, he turned on every television in the house to watch the coverage of the Charles Stevens arrest. The report cut between the mayor's press office, "We expect a statement soon from the mayor and police chief." He made mental notes about the case and began to rethink his distasteful time with the scumbag as a fateful brush with fame. He participated in a confession and his name would be etched on the arrest register. And if Curtis McGuire had indeed pulled strings to make the promotion happen, the furniture magnate would know that he'd done a good thing. His son-in-law: New Orleans crime buster.

Later, Sandy flew in with a bag of groceries from a gourmet market and stopped in her tracks when she saw him. "Home early? Nice! God, how I hated that night-shift crap." Then her attention darted to the enormous flat-screen TV. "They got that monster. I heard it on the radio."

"Yeah. I sat in on his confession."

"What? You arrested him?"

"No, no, I—"

"That's amazing. On your first day!" She was over-the-top flabbergasted.

"No, Sandy, listen, I was there when they brought him in. Don't make it seem like *I* did everything."

Her eyes flashed and then narrowed with intrigue. "So humble."

"Yeah ... maybe a little."

"I like that. The strong and silent type."

More affection took them to the kitchen, where he unpacked quinoa pasta, organic veggies, and artesian water, and learned that Kayla had gone home with a friend after school.

"I think they should castrate the bastard."

"Or behead him."

"Same thing," she said, then jerked her head toward the TV on the marble-top island. "Hey, look! It's you!"

Horrified, Jeremy turned to face the damning image. Behind an on-camera news reporter, partly obscured by men in blue, Detective Jeremy

"Powder Puff" Porter could be seen in the district parking lot shielding himself with a designer suit jacket before ducking out of sight. The sequence repeated, underscored by an in-studio newsreader.

"Now that's impressive."

"Huh? What is?" Jeremy's mind flipped through a dozen excuses he could offer.

"Avoiding publicity after all you did?"

If only it were true. He couldn't bear deflating Sandy's enthusiasm, especially considering the cold war, tantrums, and threats that followed his announcement that he wanted to leave his lucrative job with the family furniture enterprise to be an NOPD street cop.

* * *

After the Joe Doode incident at the furniture store, Jeremy tried to put it all behind him and again immersed himself in his work. He also tried to stay busy by playing an occasional game of tennis and spending more time with his daughter.

A few weeks had passed and Jeremy was still thinking about Joe Doode and how awesome it would be to feel like a hero, even for a few minutes. He went to his desk and typed "New Orleans Police Department" into his computer's search engine. Jeremy wondered what it would be like to be a police officer. He looked over the NOPD web page, and more specifically sought out applicant information. Just for a moment he pictured himself in a New Orleans Police uniform.

For the next thirty minutes, Jeremy read the web page from beginning to end. Thoughts of becoming a police officer continued to race through his head. However, he knew very well this was not going to be a topic for discussion with Sandy or anyone else, for that matter. He knew that Sandy would be adamantly opposed to his even considering being a cop, but Jeremy couldn't let go of the idea. He began to dwell on the possibility—did he even have the ability to do that type of job? He thought of the honor and prestige of being one of New Orleans' finest. He thought of the pride, the integrity, and the high esteem from the community. He imagined how great it would feel to help others and serve the public. He even thought maybe he could be another Joe Doode.

Without mentioning his idea to anyone, Jeremy sent in the initial application. A few days later, forms arrived in the mail informing him that he needed to take a series of tests. It was time for him to come clean. After dinner, he found Sandy sitting on the sofa, drinking a glass of wine and watching television. Jeremy had already put Kayla to bed. He picked up the TV remote and looked at his wife. "Do you mind if I turn this off? There is something I need to talk to you about."

Sandy frowned as she could never recall Jeremy beginning a conversation in that manner. "What is it?" she asked with annoyance.

"Sandy," he said, "I'm going to ask you to support me in a decision I've made. A career decision."

Sandy lifted an eyebrow. "*Career* decision? What's wrong with the job at Daddy's company?"

He bumbled through his response with phrases like "it's not fulfilling" and "I need more out of life" before finally confessing that he'd applied to the New Orleans Police Department and would be taking the Civil Service test to determine if he was fit to be a police officer.

"A *what*? Are you out of your fucking mind?"

Yes, it was crazy, he admitted. But he wasn't happy being a computer nerd in the family business. He even brought up the frightening incident in the flagship furniture store that had brought Officer Joe Doode into their lives. "I saw a man with courage and incredible purpose in life, and I—"

"He almost died that day, Jeremy!"

"That's true, but this is something I've given a lot of thought and—"

Furious, Sandy jumped to her feet. "You make a decision like this without even discussing it with me?"

Jeremy had seen Sandy angry before but never quite like this. He had tossed a ball into a nuclear beehive. She stomped aimlessly around the house throwing things, knocking over lamps, and swiping at small appliances.

Finally, she returned to where he sat and screamed, "How dare you do something like this and not give a fuck about my opinions or feelings? If you want to stay married to me, you'll pick up that fucking phone tomorrow and cancel your stupid test! That's it! I don't want to talk about this anymore!"

The lady of the house then stomped into their bedroom and slammed the door behind her. A moment later Kayla awakened in her room, crying. Jeremy went to his daughter and soothed her with white lies. "It's nothing. Mommy gets angry sometimes. Go back to sleep, Sweetie."

He woke the next morning on the couch with a lower back cramp and a lot more hell to pay.

The climate at home continued to be icy, and Jeremy and Sandy did not discuss the NOPD job. Jeremy tried his best to calm the waters. He took Kayla to school and picked her up, allowing Sandy to have free time to spend at the gym. He knew Sandy wasn't going to change her mind. After all, she had never lost an argument with Jeremy. But, Jeremy was determined to continue with the process. It was something he just had to try.

One evening, Jeremy decided it was time to give Sandy an update.

"So, I took the police test," he stated in a most apologetic manner.

Sandy's only reply was silence and a steely glare before she started toward the bedroom. As she reached the bedroom door, she turned and yelled, "Jeremy, for the last time, you need to drop this idea and come to your fucking senses!" With that, she slammed the door behind her.

* * *

Now, standing in the kitchen with his adoring spouse who believed he was a brand new, yet successful detective, Jeremy decided to keep his mouth shut. He'd go to Sergeant Tanner early the next morning to apologize and try to smooth over his indiscretion, so life at home would continue its upward trend.

"Thanks for all your support, Hon. I know this last year has been—"

His words trailed off. Once again, he was drowning in the undertow of her stunning beauty. Her baby blue eyes held him in high regard as her long manicured finger traced his lips. This much should be said for the spoiled, bewitching daughter of Curtis McGuire: when she calmed down and forgot about status and other shallow measurements of worth, she could be disarmingly humble and decent.

"I was wrong to say those awful things. I was wrong to stand in the way of my husband's ambition to make a difference." Her lips grazed his mouth and then her warm, sweet breath tickled his ear. "I love you." Jeremy hadn't heard those words since he mentioned his intentions of joining the NOPD.

Seconds later, she cursed. "Damn!" Jeremy tensed. Her phone was chirping and he recognized the ringtone.

"Hi, Daddy. Yeah, I'm at home—alone with my detective."

"I suppose he shared the news of his being transferred back to the night shift."

It was excruciating to watch her joy spoil so completely. Disbelief at first, then outrage spiked with a toxic kick of supposed betrayal. She shrieked and threw her phone onto the mosaic tile floor, shattering the voice of Daddy.

"You lasted one fucking day on the job, you lying bastard!"

Other insults followed, and fists, too. But the shrill attack didn't keep Jeremy from registering one basic truth: if Curtis McGuire had been alerted to his disastrous first day, his father-in-law surely had something to do with the unexpected transfer to Child Abuse.

"Sandy, *Sandy*, I can explain."

No, he couldn't. Not really. When would his lousy luck change?

Not anytime soon.

Chapter 4

When his cell phone reception died, McGuire realized what he had done and called his beloved daughter on her landline in the gorgeous home he had bought for her. He called five times before she answered thirty minutes later.

"We need to talk."

"We just *did*, Daddy."

"Sandy, listen to me. Come over to the house. Cool off. Daddy wants to talk."

Sandy must have been desperate to get out of her own home because she immediately agreed.

Later, as daughter and father sat in the study, McGuire began his lecture.

"Sandy, I know you are totally against what Jeremy has been trying to achieve—"

"Achieve? Like what? I *hate* what he's doing and he's a screw-up. He's destroyed our marriage, and I don't know if I want to be married to him anymore, especially if he goes back on that fucking night shift."

McGuire scratched a balding spot on the crown of his head. He realized the situation was much worse than he had imagined, though he should have known.

"Sandy, sweetheart, sometimes we need to let our spouses pursue their own ideas about life."

"Oh, please, Daddy. Jeremy, a cop?"

Curtis grinned. His gem of a daughter was caustic, combative, impossible, and so quick.

"Jeremy loves you very much, and he's a good father to Kayla."

"I wish he were a better husband."

McGuire knew what was coming next. In a preemptive strike, he said sternly, "The last thing we need in this family is a divorce. Give Jeremy some space. You're being too hard on him. He never really found his self-confidence earlier in life. I mean, consider his upbringing … nobody taught him to dream big."

He watched his daughter for a wary moment and wondered if he was getting through. "Let him go through this disappointment, this process. It might actually help him find that confidence that all men need."

"Daddy, he doesn't have the balls or the temperament or the aggressiveness to be a police officer. Jeremy couldn't hurt a fly with a flyswatter."

McGuire couldn't argue. "Okay fine, he's a bit of a—"

"Wimp."

"Sweetheart."

"Tell me I'm wrong."

McGuire suppressed a laugh. "Honey, I truly believe he will come to realize that this type of work is not for him and he will come to his senses. And yes, in case you are wondering, I'll hold his position at the company. I'll willingly take him back, if that's what he wants."

"Wants? He *wants* to be Joe Doode."

"Who?"

"That cute cop who saved our asses when the abused lady ran into the store. Remember?"

McGuire did. He had needed to humble himself before a mere police officer who was doing his job—and doing it very well. He'd hire that guy in a minute.

"Sandy, will you listen to me? If you stop Jeremy from pursuing this, he'll always wonder what might have been. Men hate that. He'll withdraw."

"Then I'll kick his ass out of my house."

McGuire paused. "Honey, please. Let's give it a little time."

Sandy, for once, was silent. As she stared at her glass of Jamaican iced tea, she actually seemed to contemplate her father's advice.

Sensing her indecision, he spoke.

"Why don't we support him in this endeavor, at least for the time being? Let's see what happens, and see how it goes. I like Jeremy, which is saying a lot for a dad with an only daughter. And I love you. I do not want to see this marriage fail."

She reached out and placed her hand on her father's strong, aging paw and whispered, "Okay, Daddy, I'll back off. But—"

McGuire put his other hand on hers. "It's going to turn out fine, my darling. I read people pretty well. In due time, our Jeremy will ask if he can come back to the McGuire enterprise."

He said all this with complete conviction, even as he recalled the events that led to Jeremy's unlikely recruitment by the police academy.

* * *

Jeremy was at a crossroads. For the first time in his life, he was going off script and he was paying dearly. The easy way out was to simply tell Sandy he changed his mind and was dropping the idea, but he couldn't get the notion out of his mind.

It had been several weeks since Jeremy completed all of his Civil Service tests and his background check, but he had not received any calls or mail from the police department. He knew the academy was going to start a new class in two weeks. Maybe he was worrying about nothing—maybe they wouldn't accept him and the entire situation would resolve itself. He sat at his desk at McGuire's Furniture Store and pondered his future.

A few minutes later, Mr. McGuire walked into Jeremy's office and pulled up a chair. "How is it going, Son?" he asked.

"Okay." Jeremy felt uncomfortable. He was applying for another job while continuing to work for Mr. McGuire.

"Have you heard anything from the NOPD?" Mr. McGuire asked.

Jeremy was hesitant to answer and murmured his response, "Oh I, uh, took the test a few weeks ago and I ... am just going to see what happens, but I ... haven't made any definite plans ... I guess."

Mr. McGuire realized Jeremy was in an awkward position with his pending departure so he quickly changed the subject. "How is my beautiful granddaughter?"

"Oh, she's great!" Jeremy brightened and filled his father-in-law in on Kayla's schoolwork and activities.

As Mr. McGuire walked out of Jeremy's office, he remembered his lunch engagement. "By the way, I am having lunch with your future boss today," he said pleasantly.

Jeremy quickly turned from his desk to look at him. "My future boss?"

Mr. McGuire smiled. "The chief."

* * *

Mr. McGuire was on the city's law enforcement committee. The committee had interviewed candidates for the vacant police chief's job. Eventually, the committee recommended hiring Morris Hendricks. Chief Hendricks enjoyed a huge pay increase and was quite indebted to Mr. McGuire and the others on the committee. It was only natural that Chief Hendricks made sure he kept a close relationship with Mr. McGuire.

Mr. McGuire often invited Chief Hendricks to lunch and the chief always complied. As the two gentlemen dined in one of the city's finest restaurants, they spoke about a variety of subjects. Mr. McGuire enjoyed these lunch gatherings with the chief. It allowed him the opportunity to drop a few hints about a favor or two he may need.

"My son-in-law has applied to your department," Mr. McGuire mentioned casually between bites of his crab salad.

"Oh, really," said Chief Hendricks, surprised that a family member wouldn't work at one of the McGuire's Furniture Stores. "We have an academy class starting in a couple of weeks. What's his name?"

"Porter. Jeremy Porter."

Chief Hendricks put down his fork and immediately picked up his cell phone.

"Frank, this is Chief Hendricks, how are you?"

Capt. Frank Chetta was the director of training and in charge of the department's police academy. "Fine sir, how are you?"

"Frank, don't we have an academy class starting up in a couple of weeks?

"Yes, Sir. October first."

"Frank, check to see if you have a recruit by the name of Jeremy Porter in that group."

"Hold on, Sir and I'll check." After a few seconds, Captain Chetta reported, "He is not in this class. Does he have an application with us? Would you like me to check his application status?"

"Yes, please."

"Please hold for a minute, Chief, and let me check on that."

It suddenly dawned on the chief that Mr. McGuire's son-in-law may not have made the cut, which put him in an awkward position since he made the call directly in front of McGuire, and now he was going to have to provide some type of explanation, not knowing that McGuire would have been perfectly happy if Jeremy had been rejected.

Captain Chetta returned to the phone and stated in a serious tone, "Uh, Chief? He was classified as marginal and we had an ample number of acceptables."

"Have we ever hired from that group?" Chief Hendricks asked, deliberately avoiding use of the word "marginal."

"Uh, yeah . . ." Captain Chetta responded in a somewhat hesitant voice.

"Let's just give it another look, what do you think?"

Captain Chetta was no fool. He knew that in not so many words, Chief Hendricks was telling him to hire Jeremy Porter.

"We sure will, Sir," Captain Chetta responded.

"If it works out, can we squeeze him in the upcoming class?"

"Always room for one more, Sir," pacified Captain Chetta.

The chief didn't detect the disdain in Captain Chetta's voice, nor could he see Captain Chetta shaking his head in disgust in the academy office.

Chief Hendricks hung up, smiled at Mr. McGuire, and picked up his fork. "Looks like your son-in-law was stuck in some red tape, but we're going to see what we can do to get him in the next class."

Mr. McGuire realized Chief Hendricks believed he was doing him a huge favor and he didn't have the heart to tell him otherwise. "Well, that sounds fine," he responded.

* * *

Captain Chetta scribbled Jeremy Porter's name on a scratch pad and walked out to his assistant's office. He handed him the note and said, "Pull this guy's folder from the marginals and add him to the academy class."

He read the note and gave the captain a puzzled look.

"Friend of the chief's," Captain Chetta said mockingly.

The assistant shook his head. "Okay, but it's a little late to send him an acceptance letter."

"Just call HR and let them know we are adding one more recruit to the class. Ask them to make the official job offer. If he accepts, they can tell him when to report." Captain Chetta shook his head and walked back to his own office. "Fucking politics!"

With that two-minute phone call from the chief, Jeremy Porter would be hired and accepted into the New Orleans Police Academy.

Jeremy was sitting at his desk later that afternoon going through some reports. Although he had not received any official notification, he had come to believe he was not going to be accepted by the NOPD. He really wasn't sure where he came up short, but he had resigned himself to the fact that his destiny was to eventually take over the reins of the McGuire furniture empire—not a bad runner-up prize.

At exactly 3:04 p.m. on September twenty-first, Jeremy heard his cell phone buzzing on his desk. He picked it up and saw "New Orleans Police Department" across the screen. Jeremy thought this was the call letting him know that he had been rejected. He was already in the doldrums so he was hesitant to answer. How would he handle the rejection? After the fourth ring, Jeremy answered.

"Hello?" he said in a somewhat sour tone as he anticipated the news.

The voice on the other end asked, "Is this Jeremy Porter?"

"Yes, this is Jeremy."

"Jeremy, this is Ms. Richards at the NOPD Human Resource Division. I'm calling to offer you the position of police officer for the NOPD. Do you accept the offer?"

Jeremy sat stunned. He was speechless. He stared straight ahead without responding.

"Mr. Porter? Are you there?" Ms. Richards asked impatiently.

"Uh, yeah, I'm here, uh . . ." Jeremy stuttered. He wished he had more time to absorb the question, perhaps to run it by Sandy one more time, but he knew he had to respond. This was it. Jeremy Porter had to make a decision now.

"Yes, I uh ... accept the position."

His mind was spinning as Ms. Richards explained that he was to report to the police academy on October first at 7:30 a.m.

"Is it a problem for you to give your employer less than a two-week notice?" she asked.

Jeremy thought for a moment. Would this be an excuse for him to delay the process until he could discuss this with Sandy? "No, no, it's okay." he answered.

What had he done? Although Sandy knew about the NOPD application, Jeremy made this vital and final decision on his own, which was totally out of character for him. For the rest of the afternoon, Jeremy sat in his office on an emotional roller coaster trying to come up with the best way to approach Sandy with the news but he could not successfully figure out how to quell her Irish temper.

Jeremy picked up Kayla from daycare and headed home. Luckily, Sandy had not arrived yet, so he had a little more time to gather his thoughts. She walked in a few minutes later and smiled when she saw Kayla. "Hi, Baby," she said as she kissed the top of her head. Her smile faded when she looked at Jeremy. She could read him like a book. "What's wrong?" she asked.

"NOPD called me today and offered me the job," he said in a low, apologetic tone. Sandy stared at Jeremy with a look of disdain and asked, "And *what* did you tell them, Jeremy?"

"Please don't get angry Sandy, but I just feel a need to do this."

"That's fine. You go save the fucking world, Jeremy Porter. Kayla and I will be just fine."

"Do you want me to fix supper?" Jeremy asked.

"Not hungry, you all go ahead," Sandy said angrily as she retired to the bedroom.

The next morning Sandy didn't mention anything about the job until she was about to walk out the door. "So when do you start?" she asked.

"October first."

Sandy shut the door without any further comment.

Jeremy went to work and looked for an opportunity to speak with Mr. McGuire. Finally, mid-morning, Jeremy asked if he could speak to him in his office. Jeremy entered and tried to find the right words to use.

"As you know, I uh ... applied with NOPD and uh, they called yesterday." Jeremy paused, waiting for a response.

Before he began a follow-up comment, Mr. McGuire smiled at him. "Jeremy, you go out there and be the best cop on the force!"

Jeremy was relieved that he didn't have to endure giving Mr. McGuire a long, drawn-out explanation and simply said, "Thank you, Sir. Thank you."

"Now since you start on the first, go ahead and start closing out your office and let me know if you have questions about anything."

"Thanks again, Sir." Jeremy was somewhat surprised that Mr. McGuire knew the start date. "Did Sandy tell you the start date?" Jeremy asked, hoping that Sandy had softened her position enough to speak to her father about the matter. Mr. McGuire quickly put that notion to rest as he answered with a chuckle, "I'm friends with your chief."

This wouldn't be the last time that Curtis McGuire became involved with Jeremy's career at the NOPD. After Jeremy had been languishing on the night shift for a year, Curtis had another meeting with the chief.

Chapter 5

Jeremy Porter's unusual transfer to detective in the Child Abuse Section began when Curtis McGuire invited Police Chief Morris Hendricks to the country club for lunch. The setting was relatively discreet and quiet. McGuire wanted it that way because he and the chief were not as close as they had once been and it was time to patch things up.

Over a fine meal of fresh-caught seafood and iced tea, the men made small talk until the strain of muttering nonsense was unbearable. Finally, McGuire broke the polite stalemate with an apology.

"Morris, my daughter was wrong to speak to you the way she did last year. I should have interceded immediately. I asked you here today so that I could apologize. I hope you'll believe I'm sincere."

The chief was a gracious man but he wasn't stupid. The movers and shakers in New Orleans rarely apologize for anything. Hendricks wondered what road McGuire might be trying to pave with the mea culpa. He wiped his mouth before responding. "It wasn't your fault, Curtis. I'm a father, too. Our children have minds of their own, right?"

The men shared knowing smiles.

"And, let's face it, Sandy had a point. I didn't like the way she handled it, but what happened during the graduation ceremony was personally distasteful to me as well," Hendricks added. "It wasn't fair to your family and certainly not to your son-in-law. We didn't find the cadet who was responsible, but we sent a *no tolerance* message to the entire graduating class."

During the ceremony, when his name was called, Jeremy had risen from his seat and proudly climbed the steps of the stage to accept his Peace Officer Standards and Training certificate. The usually enthusiastic audience had groaned and then hushed after reading a paper sign attached to Jeremy's rear belt loop: *I am a rat*.

Sandy, appalled and outraged, had dropped her camera into her bag and begun to seethe. When the ceremony ended, she had rushed to Hendricks and unleashed a loud, foul-mouthed tirade.

Over their lunch, Hendricks and McGuire both noticeably relaxed after their candid exchange. Second helpings were served, followed by a rich assortment of desserts, including beignets, which sweetened their talk. As he stirred cream into his French Roast coffee, McGuire returned to the subject of the mistreatment of Jeremy.

"I spoiled my daughter. There's no going back on that. But Jeremy, the son of a Baptist preacher, was unassuming and never expected much working for me. He was a joy to have on staff at the company, always polite, and frankly, some days I enjoyed his company more than Sandy's."

Hendricks chuckled, powdered sugar dusting his lower lip. "Wish I could say the same about my son-in-law. If only I could have him arrested for loitering."

More laughter further repaired their bond. The road had been paved. McGuire moved ahead swiftly. "Jeremy has been stuck on the night shift for over a year and it's causing serious marital problems. Sandy is home alone with their daughter, and they don't see much of each other, and when they do, they argue. I'm worried. I know Jeremy has to wait his turn to rotate to the day shift, but considering the incident at graduation, which I have to believe unfairly tainted his standing . . ." McGuire shook his head, seemingly helpless. "Morris, is there anything that can be done?"

Okay, there it was, the request for another favor laid out on the table. Hendricks poked at it with an imaginary fork. Should he acquiesce as he had done a couple of years back by interceding when Jeremy failed to pass his Civil Service exam? It wasn't for lack of intelligence that the young man had been rejected; it was a matter of EQ, or emotional quotient. Did he have the right mix of smarts, savvy, and sensibility to survive on the streets of New Orleans? Maybe. But he was assessed as marginal.

On the flipside, the chief could certainly decline to help by revealing what he knew about Jeremy's performance during training. The preacher's son had gotten himself in trouble from the very start. He was reprimanded for driving his car in a reckless manner, fell behind with physical training, and he'd filed a complaint with the academy staff, alleging that he was being bullied by Brock Suggs, the cadet who was rumored to have set up the "rat" prank. With no proof, no one could be punished, so a sharp "No Tolerance" message was delivered to the graduating class. But something stank, all right, and Hendricks never quite got to the source of the dispute.

The truth was inconvenient but simple: Porter was considered an oddball—not a bad person, but a bad fit. Perhaps he should be convinced to resign. But if that happened, Hendricks knew he would have to contend with the political ramifications. Curtis McGuire had close ties to the mayor, who eighteen months hence would decide whether to extend the top cop's appointment.

Feigning deep concern, Hendricks sat back in his chair, sighed, and then offered some reassurance. "Let me check on a few things and get back to you."

The train wreck was thus set in motion.

Hendricks returned to his office, not at all pleased that he would have to put some pressure on Dexter Reed, the Second District's captain. After all, fate had already taken a bite out of the man's ass when Hendricks initiated a reorganization plan after he took office. The goal was to decentralize investigative services that were all in one building downtown. Child Abuse was sent to the Second District, adding one more burden for an already beleaguered ranking officer.

He mulled, then dialed.

"Dexter."

"Sir."

Not exactly a warm reception. Hendricks inquired about the status of Jeremy Porter and invited an assessment of the rookie's performance. Reed pulled no punches.

"From what I hear, the kid's a wimp, a complainer. It was hell trying to match him with a field training officer. Nobody trusts him. The guys are convinced he's a rat, and let's face facts, I can't push back against a whole platoon. If you've got a bad apple, you toss it, you don't keep it in there and taint the whole bushel."

"So you're saying—"

"I'm saying the truth hurts, but it is what it is. And it's no secret why Porter is even on the job. Everybody else had to *earn* the appointment."

Hendricks' ears burned. Nobody on the force, to his knowledge, had specifically pointed at him, but any suggestion that favors had greased Porter's hiring and advancement hit home. The chief was already under fire for instituting his unpopular reorganization plan, which was seen as a move made solely to allow the department to avoid promoting division heads to captain at a higher pay grade. Critics cast the chief as a heartless administrator—"Hatchet Man Hendricks"—willing to cut budgets to please politicians.

"Okay, Captain, I know you can't ignore majority opinion. But now let's get to the facts. Has Porter misbehaved, or have there been any negative incidents since teaming with his FTO?"

"Nothing reported from field officers. But—"

"But what?"

Reed hesitated. He'd already delivered a bitter harvest.

"At one point, Porter asked to be transferred so that he could ride with another cop. Joe Doode. A kind of mentor thing. Frankly, I was annoyed. We can't have rookies reassigning themselves."

"Of course not. But what came of that request?"

"Nothing. He never got back to me to formally make the request."

A long silence. Hendricks had hoped Reed would be a little more cooperative and collegial. Now the chief was going to have to force another change.

"Dexter, aren't we promoting one of your detectives soon?"

"Yes, sir, Detective Farmer is moving up to sergeant, Sixth District."

"What about transferring Porter to Farmer's old position?"

Stunned, Reed searched for a respectful way to say "No fucking way."

"Well, it would be unusual, wouldn't it? Jumping over other candidates who have been waiting and, as I've already said, have earned that opportunity."

Hendricks had no more time for diplomacy. He closed the conversation with a crisp order. "Let's give him a try. If he doesn't work out, we'll move him."

"Yes, Sir."

The chief hung up only after promising himself he would not forget Reed's slightly sarcastic tone towards the end of the conversation.

Lieutenant Bayless was dumbstruck when he received the typed memo: *Effective Monday, Officer Jeremy Porter will be transferred to the Child Abuse Section, filling the position vacated by the promotion and transfer of Detective Roy Farmer. Please notify Porter tonight during roll call.*

Sgt. Greg Tanner was next in line to hear from Captain Reed. The phone chat was blunt.

"Greg, I am transferring Jeremy Porter to your office."

"Who?"

"Porter," he repeated impatiently. "Jeremy Porter. He'll start Monday morning."

"But I thought we were going to interview officers on the waiting list. I'm short-handed. I don't have time to train some numbnuts."

Reed was too irritated to explain. *Fucking politics!* He hated his job some days. "Change of plans. You're getting Porter. Make it work."

* * *

It all came full circle Monday afternoon when Tanner requested a meeting with Reed. The sergeant took a chair in front of his captain's desk and threw a dart.

"Porter is not going to work out."

Reed chuckled. "Come on, Greg. He hasn't even finished his first day."

"I sent him home this morning."

Reed straightened in his chair. "What?"

"The guy doesn't have the stomach for this kind of work. He almost ruined the Stevens confession when he blew his groceries. I even tried getting nicey-nice with the scumbag, but he shut down and now he's lawyered up and we'll probably never get it out of him."

"Get what out of him?"

"The stuff he kept hinting about. There's something on Stevens' laptop. Something else is going on here. It's more than just the little girl. He might be working with—"

Reed rubbed his bald head with the heel of his hairy hand. "I should have been notified immediately."

"Our techies are searching the laptop."

"No, I mean Porter. You send him home without—"

"Captain, believe me, I'm trying to be the good soldier here. I thought about this all day before coming in here but Child Abuse is too important."

"It's not your decision, Greg!"

"This is why I'm here, Captain. I mean, how the hell did that rat—"

"Don't start with the 'rat' crap. I've heard enough of that bullshit."

"I'm saying, somehow this guy jumps other officers who can help us in there?"

"I know, I know."

"Look, Captain, I've lowered the crime rate in this division for the past two years."

"Let's not go there. I know how you lowered the crime rate."

"I'm just saying, Porter would never go along with—"

Reed didn't want to have to notify Hendricks of his decision to lose Porter. He regretted that he'd sounded like a wise-ass on the phone last week, and now he couldn't immediately go back to the chief and, after one lousy day on the job, say "Sorry, just didn't work out."

He also couldn't have a fuck-up working in the Child Abuse Section. The public was outraged by the Charles Stevens case, and the media, including national news outlets were beginning to question how the NOPD was handling child abuse cases. The mayor was being hounded, and worse yet, Reed had been told that the little girl may have permanent damage. They couldn't tell reporters and civic leaders, "Oh by the way, to serve and protect the community, we've promoted a weak-bellied male runway model to the Child Abuse Section."

"Can we get Farmer back," Tanner begged, "For a couple weeks, until we figure this thing out?"

Reed knew that wouldn't work. The Sixth District captain was thrilled to get Farmer and needed him badly to fill a leadership void. He also didn't want Porter's demotion to flash like lightening through the department grapevine. And it would.

"And, Captain, there's something else." Tanner added hesitantly.

"What is it?"

He lowered his voice before continuing. "We could never trust Porter to go along with the downgrade program. He got all hot and bothered when I—"

Reed put his hand up to quiet him. "No. We don't talk about that here."

"I'm sorry, but when I gave him perv statistics—"

The captain stood abruptly. He stared down at Tanner and hissed. "Not in here! Walls have ears, Sergeant." He paused a long moment before speaking again, this time in a normal voice. "It sounds like you're saying Porter is not a team player who understands and accepts necessary procedures in this section."

"Yes, that's it, yeah, that's all I'm trying to say. We cooperate around here. That's the way it's gotta be."

"Of course. I understand." Reed sat behind his desk and bit the bullet. "Okay. Look, Greg, keep this to yourself for now."

"But—"

"Until tomorrow. Then as soon as Porter comes in, send him to me."

"He'll be here early, I bet."

"Maybe we can give the guy a week of sick leave or—"

"But I need help in here."

"You need the right kind of help. We'll figure it out. I just want Porter out of the picture for a few days until I can break the bad news to Hendricks." He lowered his voice. "It was *his* decision, Greg, not mine. Some kind of fucking payback, I bet."

But Hendricks already knew about the disaster. He had learned while congratulating the patrol officers who brought Stevens in and escorted him on the walk of shame in front of TV cameras at the intake center.

"Too bad what happened to the new detective," Officer fire hydrant had said.

"Yeah, doesn't look like he is cut out for child abuse." Officer sign post added.

Call it damage control, but that very moment the head of police was dialing a certain New Orleans bigwig to distance himself from the inevitable: *I did what I could, friend, but just so you know, your son-in-law's transfer is going to be revoked.*

Chapter 6

When Jeremy entered the Child Abuse office the next morning, the first words he heard were, “We need to go see Captain Reed.” He’d been nervous driving in and now his knees were knocking. Tanner hadn’t even let him sit at his desk so that they could have a private talk about what had happened the day before—just a tense grunt and that chin again, pointing toward the door.

Shit. The speech he’d rehearsed began streaming through his mind like a teleprompter but it was of no use now, unless the captain would give him a moment to plead his case. Fat chance. He knew how Reed could be. He’d gone to him once for guidance. It was after graduation.

That first night of roll call the rookie cops were assigned to field training officers. Jeremy caught a beady-eyed, thick-headed veteran named Dave Pichon.

“You’re riding with me tonight.”

“Okay. I’m Jeremy Porter.” He held out his hand to shake but could tell his teacher did not want to shake the hand of a rat.

“Meet me in the parking lot after you sign out a Taser in the storage room. Tell Sarge Finnegan you’re with me.”

For the first hour or so in the field, Pichon said nothing, but the car radio was busy squawking emergency calls. Finally, Jeremy asked why they weren’t responding.

"Sit tight, Kid. We're a report-writing car, they'll call us if they need a report somewhere."

Nice to know. Jeremy was eager to learn more but Pichon was the bard of short, stingy answers. Clearly, he did not like his new partner and didn't want to communicate any more than he had to. It went on like that for several weeks. Jeremy wrote a few accident and cold crime reports but was so bored and felt so isolated that he wondered if he should diplomatically ask Captain Reed for help changing FTOs. Just the thought of it put his gut in knots. He dropped the idea until a coincidence inspired him to make a change.

Late one evening, the patrol car approached fire and police vehicles parked in front of a smoky building. Emergency lights painted the chaotic scene in garish primary colors. Officer Pichon slowed down, took one look, and cursed.

"Can't we help?" Jeremy all but begged.

"Not our beat. Sixth District. Let them deal with it."

But as he felt the car pull away, Jeremy saw a cop being pulled along the sidewalk by medical personnel. "Wait," he shouted. "I know that guy!"

The rookie was out the door before an angry Pichon could fully stop.

Jeremy ran through the street and reached the opposite curb just as Officer Joe Doode was lowered into a seated position, trying desperately to take gulps of fresh air. An EMT pulled an oxygen mask over his face, patted his back. "Easy does it, Officer. Easy now."

"What happened?" Jeremy asked.

"Apartment fire. This officer learned a kid was trapped upstairs so he went in. Smoke inhalation." More pats on Joe's back. "Take it easy, Guy."

Before he could ask, Jeremy heard crying and further down the street saw a female cop hand off a young boy to his relieved mother. The kid was coughing but otherwise apparently unharmed. Jeremy recognized the Hispanic officer from training: Luisa Olvera had the wide-eyed look of a rookie under duress, and she was wired.

"Luisa."

"Hey, Porter. What are you doing here?"

"Driving by. What happened?"

"My FTO and I came up on this fire and when he heard about the kid he just started running."

"Damn. So Joe Doode's your field trainer, huh?"

"Yeah. You know him? Great guy. Luck of the draw."

Jeremy was envious. "Did you go in, too?"

"Nah. He wouldn't let me. Said it made no sense to risk two lives." Olvera shook her head. "How could he think so clearly with all this shit going on?"

Jeremy's mind began to buzz with memories of Hero Joe, wrestling a knife-wielding brute to the floor of the McGuire furniture sales area. Jeremy's crystal clear memories of his first encounter with Joe Doode were interrupted by Pichon.

"This is why we stopped, so you could gab with another rookie? Let's go, we're not needed here."

Officer Olvera shot a knowing, sympathetic look at Jeremy and excused herself.

"Sorry, Dave, but I owe my life to the officer on the curb over there. I couldn't rush past without seeing if I could help."

"But you can't. He'll be fine. Now let's go."

Jeremy ignored Pichon and walked over to Doode, who had lowered his oxygen mask.

"Joe, how are you feeling?"

The officer, still coughing, stared blankly, shrugged. "I'm okay, I guess. Thanks."

As the EMTs helped Doode rise and move toward an ambulance, Jeremy followed.

"I know you probably don't remember me. I'm Jeremy Porter. We met at my family's furniture store when you answered a domestic violence call."

Jeremy's heart leapt when he saw a glint of recognition in Doode's eyes.

"Yeah ... yeah, I remember. But you weren't a cop then, were—" Coughing bent him over and an EMT gently pushed Jeremy away.

"Come on, Officer, give this guy some space."

"Sure. Sorry. I'm sorry." Jeremy felt stupid. Pichon only made it worse.

"A lot of good you did. Get in the freaking car."

The rookie obeyed orders while recalling the final words Doode had spoken to him two years before after the furniture store arrest had concluded. *Let me know if I can help you with anything.*

Before reaching the patrol car, Jeremy had made up his mind to speak with Reed about being assigned to a different FTO, not realizing that all he would get would be another black mark in the eyes of his superiors.

* * *

Jeremy followed Sergeant Tanner out the door and down the stairs to Captain Reed's office. The secretary told them it would be a few minutes. The wait stretched to ten, with neither man speaking.

"Captain Reed is ready for you now."

In the office, Reed gestured to a chair. "Have a seat." He avoided eye contact until both men were in their chairs. A moment of silence only made Jeremy more nervous. It was like waiting for the firing squad to pull their triggers.

"Porter, we gave you an opportunity to work in Child Abuse, but we realize that you are not ready for an assignment like this. Sergeant Tanner described the incident yesterday when you lost it during the taking of a statement from a suspect. If you didn't know then, I'm sure you know now, this was a very high profile case and we had a suspect who abruptly stopped his confession due to your disruption. Not good."

It was obvious to Jeremy that Captain Reed had carefully prepared his comments.

"We realize that it takes time to adjust to a new assignment, and to develop a strong stomach for the kinds of assignments the Child Abuse Section catches each week. Unfortunately, with only two people in that office, we simply cannot wait until you develop a harder shell." Reed could see the disappointment in Jeremy's face. "In retrospect, it's not your fault. We should have chosen someone with more experience handling sensitive and often troubling interactions with this sector of ... of the New Orleans population. So Porter, effective today, I am—"

Jeremy stood. "Sir ... I don't mean to sound disrespectful, but all I'm asking for is another chance. I mean, after one day? Is that fair? Is that ..."

Jeremy wanted to say more but his throat caught and tears burned his eyes. He put his head down until he regained his composure.

Sergeant Tanner and Captain Reed exchanged glances before Jeremy continued.

"Sir, what I'm trying to say is ... this isn't only about me. I have a ..."

He didn't dare say the word *wife*. After visiting with her father the night before, Sandy had returned home with a cooler head, if not exactly a forgiving heart. "I'm done getting emotional about this," she'd said and then dropped a couple bombs.

"Jeremy, I will never ever get over the fact that you ventured into this police fantasy without consulting me. And to make matters worse, you ended up on the night shift, leaving Kayla and me home alone. I hope by now you realize it was Daddy who got you the detective assignment. Yeah. And you fuck it up on your first day. Okay, maybe it wasn't *all* your fault, but maybe you're just not cut out for police work. So this is it. No more night shift. Do whatever it takes to get your day-job back, because you can't count on Daddy bailing you out again. I'm pretty sure he's all out of favors. And I want a husband who's home at night."

There wasn't much more to say. Husband and wife retreated to separate beds and Jeremy barely slept as he pondered how to gain control of his own life. His entire marriage had been dictated by his dearly beloved—vacations, outings with friends, holidays—and now she was wielding divorce like a club, only too eager to bring it down on his head. For a moment he stood before the captain in silence, trying disparately to hold back his tears and find the right words.

"Sir ... I really want to do right by everybody involved. You, Sergeant Tanner, and the Child Abuse Section. I'll study. I'll work extra, on my own time. I'll even help the Probation Department. I'll make a difference. Really, I will. Please hold off before ... you know."

Reed had a heart, but he didn't have much patience for interruptions or sob stories.

"Officer Porter, while I can appreciate your offer, your display of emotion today may be more proof that you are simply not suited for this kind of—"

"Sir, please ... *please* ... I can't lose this assignment."

Reed pulled back, stunned that he was cut off again. Tanner was outraged—he spoke through his teeth.

"Porter, you don't interrupt a commanding officer."

"Sorry."

Reed took charge. "He's right, Porter. You're out of line."

"Sir, all I've ever wanted was a real chance to succeed as a police officer. So far that hasn't happened. Not at the academy or field training with Dave Pichon, and not in the Child Abuse Section. What do I have to do to get a fair shot?"

"It's not our fault you have no aptitude for the work. Many are called, Porter."

"But few are bullied and mistreated, Captain."

"You don't follow rules. That's the problem here."

"Sir, I do follow the rules such as keeping my mouth shut. For too long. Much too long. Can you honestly say I've had a fair chance to prove myself?"

Reed and Tanner shared a look of incredulity. How dare a rookie....

Jeremy didn't care. He had too much to lose to sit in silence. He was desperate to save his marriage.

"Listen, Porter, this is no different than the last time we met. You wanted to run the show then, too. You wanted to choose your own FTO."

"I respectfully requested a change because I did not feel I was getting the kind of training a rookie deserves and needs. For four weeks, Officer Pichon barely gave me the time of day."

"Did you file a complaint?" Tanner challenged.

"What good would that have done? In training I was called Powder Puff, and then labeled a rat! No wonder Pichon didn't like me, and when I went to leadership for help all I got was more grief."

Jeremy returned his attention to Reed. "When I came to you, Captain, to discuss my FTO assignment, I believed I would benefit from a mentor who had high standards and would treat me like a human being. In my opinion, at the time Officer Joe Doode was my best chance."

The night after witnessing the effects of smoke inhalation on his hero, Jeremy had gone to Lt. Floyd Bayless at roll call and requested a meeting with Reed.

"What for?" Bayless had asked.

Jeremy had hesitated, hoping to keep his talk private. "I want to discuss a transfer."

Bayless rubbed his dark mustache and looked up at the ceiling. "Porter, you aren't even out of field training! How the fuck are you planning to be … you know what? I don't care, go ahead. But if I were you, I'd limit your talk to the transfer issue."

Jeremy knew what the lieutenant was implying: complain about the name-calling and hazing that had gone on throughout training and had continued to the platoon, and things would only get worse.

That first meeting with Reed had been short. Initially, the commanding officer was unreceptive to the transfer request. When Jeremy suggested that he might be able to broker a personnel swap, the captain eventually softened and said he would consider it only if his district received a quality cop. "Someone we *want*. Fair enough?"

Yes, it was fair. Only later did Jeremy realize he'd given the captain a convenient way to get rid of him.

Now, facing heat from both Reed and Tanner, Jeremy was begging to be retained. This was not lost on the captain, who was shrewd enough to keep hammering on the Doode request. He wanted to know why, after all the negotiating, nothing had come of the exchange between the two districts.

"I recall giving you leeway at our first meeting, Porter, despite my misgivings. You had your shot. Why didn't you come back to me with a solution?"

This time it was Jeremy who felt blown back. Flustered, he shifted in his chair and stared at the floor before answering.

"Several weeks after our meeting, Joe Doode left police work for a job in the private sector." Jeremy still felt the crush of the unexpected turn of events but cleared his head and pressed on. "Sir ... all I'm asking for is another chance to work Child Abuse. I ... I really think I can do this kind of work, and I think, you know, my computer science skills could be—"

"I don't need an IT," Tanner interjected. "I need a detective who can hold his lunch and carry his workload."

"But I have ideas. Organizational stuff that could help—"

Tanner exploded. "Excuse me, Rookie, but when I need you to tell me how to run my department—"

"Okay, Greg."

"—I'll be ready for the funny farm! The gall, Captain."

Reed allowed the sergeant to express his ire and pace for a moment before laying down his edict.

"Porter, my decision is final. You'll have a couple more days of sick leave to sort through your feelings. I know this is disappointing. But effective today, I am transferring you back to your platoon on the night shift. Report for duty Thursday evening."

He heard the death sentence but was thinking of Sandy and how divorce would affect his relationship with Kayla. He felt gutted and faint.

"Yes, sir."

"One more thought, Porter."

Already on his feet, Jeremy turned to face the captain.

"Learn to get along, Son."

Grim and bitter, he nodded and reached for the door. Then Tanner spoke.

"I need your key."

The final affront. Access denied. The former detective dug into his pocket, found the key, and handed it to his nemesis. "Will that be all, Sir?"

Chapter 7

Two nights later, when Jeremy returned to Second District roll call, the avalanche of ridicule and sarcasm immediately began. First there were snickers and side-of-mouth taunts from various officers. Then Lieutenant Bayless, calling out the names of all those present and ready for assignment, stopped when he saw "Porter" on his list.

"Hey, Powder Puff, that was the shortest transfer in the history of the New Orleans Police Department. Did you even last twenty minutes?"

Predictably, it was Brock Suggs who performed a caricature of vomiting with sound effects. The jarhead moaned and retched until the men and women in blue convulsed with laughter.

"Get him a bucket!" one cop yelled.

"God, it stinks in here!" Another whined.

"We're gonna need a mop!"

Jeremy stood in his usual spot in the back row of the lineup and watched grown men carry on. Even Dave Pichon—a real comedian—got in the act.

Only one patrol officer didn't join in. The African-American officer stood tall and stared straight ahead. His name was Leslie Scott and he was six feet of pure muscle. If he wanted to, he could have silenced the jeering fools with one hard look. Nobody messed with Leslie, a former special services and Iraq War vet. Jeremy was ashamed to admit that he wished the man he considered a friend would stand up for him.

Fight your own battles, he admonished himself. Then he heard the familiar voice.

"Very funny, Brock."

Leslie was a chiseled work of art; not an ounce of fat on a body that was a remarkable fusion of power and agility. Suggs had beefed up lifting weights, and bragged about his bench press. But by comparison, he looked like a superhero-shaped helium balloon, the kind that floats overhead during holiday parades. When Suggs heard the voice, his wide grinning mouth began to deflate.

"*Really* funny," Leslie continued. "Almost as funny as the time Officer *Porter* here kicked your ass during defensive training at the academy."

"I slipped."

"On what? Your tongue?"

Suggs flinched, then shrugged. "What's your point, Scott?"

"Whenever you're ready for a rematch ... let us know."

Us. That one word changed the temperature of the room.

* * *

Brock Suggs took a disliking to Jeremy the first time they met in the academy parking lot. Maybe it was the red $275 thousand Aston Martin DBS Coupe. Jeremy thought nothing of driving the exquisite car to training because his mind was filled with big plans: he'd decided to become el numero uno, the number one trainee in his class. He was going to be the next Joe Doode.

On that first day, he parked his car and joined the other recruits, mostly men but also some women, who had gathered near the entrance of the training facility. All were dressed in white pullover shirts and dark slacks. Some smoked, while others held steaming Styrofoam cups of coffee. When he introduced himself, most of the guys just nodded and stared at the Aston Martin. That was when Jeremy realized all the other cars in the lot were pickup trucks or rusty Ford and Chevy compacts.

"Nice car."

He turned and offered a hand. "Oh, thanks. I'm Jeremy Porter."

Brock Suggs ignored the handshake. "Never drove one of those before. You don't mind if I take it for a spin, do you?"

Jeremy hesitated. *Weird request. Pushy.*

"Just around the block."

Maybe this was a useful way to show that he was just one of the guys. No big deal, it's just a car. He handed over the keys. "Okay."

As Brock walked toward the car he invited a buddy to join him. When the two yucked it up and cast glances over their shoulders, Jeremy began to feel queasy. He looked over to a Hispanic woman for reassurance. Luisa Olvera offered none.

"Are you sure you want those dudes driving off in your car?" she asked.

Before he could answer, the group heard screeching tires. In unison, the young men and women jerked their heads, mouths agape, as the sporty automobile disappeared around a corner while the engine roared and squealed.

Olvera gave Jeremy a look that said "I told you so."

For the next ten minutes, the group could track the path of the car by sound only—tires screeching and burning rubber, and RPMs pushed to upper limits.

When the Aston Martin reappeared, Jeremy ran forward to inspect it for damage. Without a word, Brock tossed him the keys as he and his chattering passenger strode toward the building. Relieved, Jeremy swore *never again*. Unfortunately, the vow came too late.

Before being dismissed for lunch, the recruits were introduced to the assistant academy director, Lt. George Klein, a trim man of medium height, who opened his remarks with an angry question.

"Who is driving the red Aston Martin?"

All eyes went to Jeremy, who slowly raised his hand.

Klein ordered, "Stand up, Son."

The trainee obeyed. Maybe Klein was a car buff and wanted—

"We received several complaints from neighbors who said you were driving recklessly this morning, squealing your tires, making sudden stops, accelerating without regard for the safety of others. Listen up. We do not tolerate that type of conduct around here. And you shouldn't need even ten minutes of training to understand why. We're here to serve and protect, not to endanger and destroy. You've embarrassed the academy. Therefore, I'm putting you on notice, Son. If I receive one more complaint about you or your driving habits, *you are gone*. Is that understood?"

Jeremy was stunned and his mouth was dry as stale bread. He couldn't find his voice to respond.

"I said, do you under—"

"Yes. Yes, Sir," he squeaked.

And so began the days of terror, mostly but not exclusively orchestrated by Brock Suggs. Misunderstandings and administrative mistakes haunted Jeremy in the early going, such as his misspelled nameplate. *Powter* quickly became *Powder* before morphing into *Powder Puff*. His attempts to befriend other trainees were rebuked. He was slowly edged out of the inner circle and treated like a strange, unnecessary appendage. He mostly kept quiet, for fear that being outspoken might provoke more derision, and soon he found himself ostracized and spending breaks and lunch hours alone. Usually, he hopped in his car and grabbed sandwiches at local eateries. Tired of fast food, he decided to pack meals and relax in the usually empty academy break room. One day he discovered the quiet, reclusive Leslie Scott, deep in thought, and chewing slowly.

"Mind if I join you?"

With a pinch of sarcasm, Leslie replied, "You don't need my permission to be here."

It couldn't quite be called a friendship, at first. Jeremy was careful not to push. Leslie tolerated his questions with short, civil answers. When real trouble arrived, the conversation and relationship grew.

Jeremy had kept up quite well with the rigorous physical training at the academy. His slender, resilient tennis body could handle long-distance challenges and sprints. His weakness was hand-to-hand combat and gun retention. When paired with cadets he didn't have the bulk and physical authority to overpower, he had no experience with martial arts or other methods of self-defense to draw on.

Leslie, on the other hand, was a superstar whose military training prepared him to quickly dispose of all competitors. He was quick as a cat and when necessary, could deliver ultimate force at lightning speed. Instructor Reemer praised him often.

"Did you see that? Watch Scott's technique—and then copy it! The best I've seen in years. Anybody know why?" When no one responded, Reemer chided. "Come on, people, what have I been repeating every damn training day?"

"Uh ... he uses only the amount of force necessary to overcome the resistance?"

"Bingo! Excellent, Tran. At least one of you guys has been listening. But now let's talk about another type of situation. Help me demonstrate, Scott."

Leslie stepped forward as the instructor explained that there may be occasions when an officer finds himself in severe danger. "The assailant gets the jump on you and you're pinned, let's say, and can't utilize the standard equipment to back him down. No firearm, no Taser, you're in a life or death struggle"

The grim truth of police work sucked the bravado out of every guy in the gym.

"So what do you do? Take control—by any means necessary. Do whatever it takes to save your life. You hear me? *Do whatever it takes to save your life*. Pick up a hard object, bite, kick, twist, and shout. Do anything you can to defend yourself. But remember. When it's all said and done, you'll have to explain your actions to your supervisors ... and maybe a grand jury."

Those words hit home to the cadets. The complications and dangers of the job were beginning to sink in. Make split second decisions to save your life, but your actions better be completely justified or your career and perhaps your freedom will be over.

Instructor Reemer tried to answer everyone's questions about what amount of force is justified. To stop the barrage of questions, he decided to spontaneously attack Leslie Scott as an illustration to always be ready. Instructor Reemer placed Scott in a chokehold. Scott seemed to get weak and appeared on the verge of blacking out. Scott twisted, maneuvered, and suddenly wiggled free. Scott flipped the instructor and pounced, pinning Instructor Reemer to the floor. Instructor Reemer was helpless and patted the mat to surrender.

"Good work, Scott. I know I don't have to ... worry about you ... out there." Struggling to catch his breath, the instructor then scanned the faces of his other students and asked a sobering question. "But what about you guys? Huh? Are you ready? Listen to me ... when the time comes—and it will, believe me it will—do whatever it takes to survive!"

The workout that followed was exhausting. As the cadets spread out over the mats, the instructor called out pairings and then changed them in a snap, creating a mass attack of danger that confounded the cadets and put them all on edge.

Toward the end of the chaotic drill, Brock Suggs saw an opportunity and went rogue. Pretending to be an aggressive criminal, he came up from behind Jeremy, locked his muscular arms around the slender man's torso, lifted him high, and slammed him to the mat as he let out a victorious roar.

"Always be ready, Powder Puff!"

Jeremy couldn't respond. Breathless, halfway off the mat and lying on his side, he felt a sharp pain stab and travel through his ribs and chest. He was all but paralyzed when Reemer glanced over and shouted, "All right, all right, Suggs, knock it off before somebody gets hurt. Class dismissed."

In the locker room, Jeremy's every move made him wince. He showered and dressed as best he could without complaint because he knew what was at stake. Reporting the injury might lead to a medical discharge just weeks before graduation and the last thing he needed was to be labeled a rat.

Yet his limited movement in the following days of hand-to-hand combat endangered his dream. The instructor was constantly on his ass, scornful and demanding.

"Oh, Jesus, Powder Puff, my grandma can do better than that! Fight for yourself. Fight!"

In the lunch room, Jeremy confided to Scott that he likely had fractured a rib. "I'm fucking sick of the bullying. If I don't heal soon, I'll fail physical training and won't graduate. Should I go to Lieutenant Klein and tell him what Suggs did?"

Leslie said, "I wouldn't do that. Gut it out, and in a few weeks you'll be in the field with the rest of us."

"But I'm lousy at self-defense. And now with the injury I might fail."

"Stand up."

"Huh?"

Leslie was already towering over Jeremy, pulling the student to his feet.

"Go for my throat."

"What?"

"Just do it."

Jeremy attacked and Leslie easily swatted him aside.

"See? I have no strength. I should carry my tennis racquet in class!"

Leslie grinned, a rare occurrence.

"The strongest guy doesn't always win," Leslie said. "All you've got to do is get the enemy off balance. Suggs has upper body muscle but he doesn't work his legs. A man needs a foundation to carry all that weight."

The military vet began jabbing at the tennis amateur and explaining how to deflect thrusts of strength.

"You don't beat power by colliding with it. You seize the momentum and guide it, so your opponent basically destroys himself. Even if the guy is smaller than you, why waste energy? Suggs lifted you up and threw you down. You can't let that happen."

"But I didn't see..."

Leslie looked thoughtful for a moment. "You watch football?"

"Sure."

"Watch the great quarterbacks. They don't always see the pass rushers but they sense when they are closing in. They sidestep, they move, and they avoid the big hit."

"How do I learn to sense someone getting close if I don't see them?"

"How about if your life depends on it?"

Jeremy smiled. "Wow, you really have a way of getting your point across."

The training resumed. Pain continued to pinch Jeremy's every move as the two men relentlessly pushed and punched, knocking aside tables and chairs, squashing egg salad sandwiches and a bag of potato chips. Leslie called out instructions and encouragements, and by the end of lunch, Jeremy was astounded by how little was needed to alter outcomes. He began realizing his body was an asset, not a liability.

Unfortunately, one lesson was not enough. The next morning at physical training, the instructor pulled Jeremy aside.

"Lieutenant Klein wants to see you."

Jeremy felt like he was walking the plank of a pirate ship as he headed down the hall for his meeting.

The frowning lieutenant sat behind his desk, perusing an open folder.

"Porter, what's going on? You were doing pretty well, but recently your PT grades have dropped to unsatisfactory. You're on the home stretch of your training. This is no time to lose sight of your goals."

Klein was blunt, assuring Jeremy that graduation was out of the question unless he made significant improvement in the coming weeks. Jeremy nodded or answered, "Yes, Sir," throughout the lecture and yet seemed strangely remote.

"Porter ... do you fully understand what I'm telling you? You seem distracted. Don't you want this for yourself? Don't you care?"

Of course he did. But he was mulling over how he could defend his poor showing without filing a complaint.

Annoyed with the unsatisfactory answers, Klein shoved a single sheet of paper across the desk.

"All right. Please sign the warning notice and then get back to class."

Jeremy grabbed the pen but hovered over the signature line without marking it. Instead, he made a snap decision. He might regret it later, yet in the moment, he could think of no other way out of his predicament.

"Sir ... there is one problem I've hesitated to mention."

"Oh?"

"I don't want to get anybody in trouble, but I am being humiliated and harassed by another recruit. I have broken ribs and... "

"Who is it?"

"Sir, I would prefer not to give any names. I was just hoping perhaps you could have someone look into the..."

"Porter, I know how to handle this. What's the cadet's name?"

When Jeremy returned to the gym and revealed what had happened in Klein's office, Leslie was silent and stern. For all of the harassment Jeremy endured, he couldn't blame him for speaking up but knew there might be repercussions. Then he shoved his student to the mats. "Let's practice the standing arm-trap move again."

Moments later the instructor called out, "Suggs! Lieutenant Klein wants to see you. Double-time it and get back here fast!"

Jeremy was sweating and panting from his workout when Suggs returned and deliberately shoulder bumped him and whispered, "You fucking rat."

The harassment worsened in subtle and obvious ways. Suggs and his cronies would surround Jeremy in the locker room or shower but say nothing. Or they'd trip him up during the strenuous workouts and mumble "rat" under their breaths.

Meanwhile, the lunchroom mentoring continued and Jeremy's improved performance in hand-to-hand classes won mild praise from Reemer.

"Better, Porter! Better."

Yet as the training drew to a close, Jeremy was not convinced he'd done enough to pass. In a final series of performance tests, he was confronted with one opponent after another, all of whom seemed to hold a grudge. He fared well in most encounters, but before Instructor Reemer could conclude the competition, a voice called out.

"Let me try."

Brock Suggs sauntered to the center of the mat, his eyes as dark and focused as sniper scopes.

"All right, Suggs, let's see what you've got," Reemer said. "And, Porter, I know I've put you through your paces today. Just do the best you—"

Suggs didn't wait for the "go" signal. He attacked with a speed and ferocity that made Jeremy yelp. The cronies snickered. Reemer stepped aside. Leslie calmly watched as Jeremy caught Suggs in an arm trap, bent back his wrist, and then followed through with a smack to his aggressor's face.

Suggs cried out and slammed onto his back like he'd been shot with a high-powered rifle. His agony and horror were obvious as he gingerly examined his limp wrist.

"You broke it. You broke my fucking wrist, you cocksucker!"

Jeremy didn't respond, still in shock from the speed of the assault, and the muscle spasms that stung his upper torso.

Instructor Reemer rushed to assist Suggs.

Leslie, unsmiling, merely nodded at his student. It was against his honor code to gloat.

But Jeremy couldn't resist. The months of harassment, the injustices, and the marital problems his career change had created all mushroomed. Seizing the moment, he expressed concern for Suggs and then crouched for a closer look at the wrist. It was beginning to swell.

"It ain't broken. If I wanted to break it, I would have. You'll be fine... *Powder Puff.*"

"I'll kill you, Porter. I swear, I'll—"

"Can it, Suggs," ordered Reemer, who was carefully probing the injury. "You've got a bad sprain, no broken bones."

"But—"

"Hey! You attacked. Porter defended himself. End of story."

* * *

Leslie Scott's show of solidarity during roll call was only a momentary boost to Jeremy's spirits. Lieutenant Bayless restored order, announced assignments for each patrol team and then, dodging the offensive nickname, barked, "Porter, as you know, we only work teams, two-officer units on the night shift. Since you are the odd man out, you're assigned to the front desk to assist Sergeant Finnegan. You'll be in charge of the supply room. Inventory officer. Anybody needs equipment during the shift, they come to you. Don't fuck it up."

The disdain and titters that followed made Jeremy's heart implode. He didn't relish partnering with another asshole like Pichon, nor did he want to sit at a computer for the foreseeable future. As the police officers marched into the night, Jeremy kept his mouth shut—complaints had gotten him nowhere—and began the long walk to his latest dead end.

Chapter 8

The entrance to the Second District building led to a spacious alcove where the front desk was located. Jeremy stopped before entering. He knew enough about the basic functions of this position to anticipate stacks of police reports written earlier in the day. They'd need to be segregated into types of crimes and then bundled. A host of other mind-numbing administrative tasks would follow.

He sat and rolled behind the PC and began scrolling through data in an attempt to familiarize himself with the workload.

"Hey, get out of my chair."

Sergeant Finnegan, a pimpled cipher in blue, limped forward, cramping the space behind the desk and making it awkward for Jeremy to comply.

"Oh. Sorry. I was just trying to—"

"How about trying to stay the hell out of my way?"

"Okay. I'll move." He tried to keep his tone even, but did not entirely succeed. "Anything else I can do to help tonight, Sir?"

"Yeah. Get your butt where you belong. Your chair is out in the hallway by the inventory room. You got extra Tasers for when the guys discharge theirs. Make 'em sign for it when they grab a new one. And you got other supplies in there, too. Understand, Office Depot?"

Great. A new nickname. Jeremy looked at his watch and stifled a groan. It was only 10:37 p.m., an eternity until his shift ended at 6:00 a.m. the next morning. *At least I'm not on the twelve-hour rotation*, he thought.

The supply room was not much more than a glorified closet with a lockable door. He stared at the contents with all the excitement of a corpse and then sat. From his new position, Jeremy watched Finnegan swivel in his chair and grab a remote. Seconds later the television that sat on the desk began to chatter. The man's indifference to his job added to Jeremy's woes.

"Fucking a-hole."

Thankfully, Finnegan was possibly deaf or determined to mindlessly serve his term until he could collect his pension. It was a waste of energy to discipline a deadbeat.

Humble yourself, Porter.

Yet that's basically all he'd done since entering the academy. Hell no, since marrying the rich man's daughter. Just get along, Jeremy. Be nice. Your Baptist minister dad was the perfect example. Never reveal what you really feel. *Just smile, Office Depot.*

This new position was just a way for Bayless to justify denying Jeremy street patrol. Taser traffic wouldn't be heavy because cops used the electroshock device only once or twice a month. Basically, he'd have to sit through his shift hoping an administrator would request a ream of paper or, wow, even more exciting, more ink cartridges! This was the first step towards convincing Jeremy Porter to sign a letter of resignation.

With so little to do, Jeremy couldn't help but replay his fight with Sandy. After his meeting with Captain Reed, he decided to drive to the furniture store, hoping she would contain her anger and be more forgiving with other people around. He knew he had made a big mistake as soon as she saw him enter.

"What are you doing here?"

"Can we go to your office, please? I want to talk."

She'd granted his wish, but as soon as she closed the door behind them, the rant began.

"I hope you're happy, you sonofabitch."

"Sandy, wait."

"You've fucked up our family with your stupid cop nonsense. Jesus Christ, a cop? When will you admit—"

"I spoke to Captain Reed. I tried to get another chance."

"Why would they give *you* another chance? You're a fuck-up! I can't do this anymore. I want you out of the house. I'm filing for divorce."

"What? You're going to split up the family because a career choice went bad?"

"You can't even admit you've made a mistake. You think you're the next Joe Doode. Admit it, you're not capable of being a cop. You are a wimp. I know it and obviously the police department knows it. You've ruined us. I've had enough!"

"But we have a family. I mean let's think of Kayla."

"I don't love you anymore! Can't you understand that? And I'll let you know when you can see Kayla."

"You can't keep me from seeing my daughter over this."

Sandy came close with verbal daggers, lowering her voice while ramping up the intensity.

"Jeremy, you are a loser, a total loser. Get your fucking stuff out of our house, today. Don't be here when I get home from work."

It was nearly 2:00 a.m. when Jeremy rose from his chair by the supply room. He couldn't take it anymore. He was restless and angry, still aching from the implosion of his marriage, with nobody to talk to or confide in. He could request help from the police psychologists, but he knew that would just create more havoc for him. He'd never dig out if "lunatic" was added to his other nicknames.

He peeked into Sgt. Couch Potato's alcove. "I'm going to lunch. Or breakfast. Whatever."

Without turning, Finnegan raised a hand to give his blessing. Then the phone rang and he was forced to lower the volume on his favorite show, *Wife Swap in Baton Rouge*. Feed your mind, Finny.

"Sergeant Finnegan here. Yeah. Uh, huh. Okay, okay, but here's who you should call... "

The man's gruff voice followed Jeremy as he continued down the hall. Since riding shotgun with Pichon, he no longer packed a lunch so he'd have to go out for a sandwich. He reached into his pocket for his car keys as he passed the staircase that led to the Child Abuse Section. He stopped and stared into the darkness of the second floor. He wasn't sure what was worse, recalling the sight, sound, and smell of Charles Stevens, or suffering regret. If he'd been able to survive his first interview with a child molester, he would have a career, a purpose in life, and a proud wife.

He cursed and turned toward the parking garage, then abruptly stopped. He opened his palm and stared at the keys spread in a circle. One was tarnished gold and looked older than the others. He'd put it on his ring after Roy Farmer tossed it to him. He'd forgotten about it when Sergeant Tanner and Captain Reed revoked his transfer to Child Abuse.

Down the hallway Jeremy could hear the melodrama of TV voices. In the opposite direction, he saw no one. With the old key held firmly between finger and thumb, he ascended quickly and soundlessly on rubber soles. He slowly climbed the stairs.

The hallway was pitch black at the top of the stairs. Perfect. But when Jeremy made his move toward the Child Abuse door, overhead lights snapped on. *Shit*. Sensors. Probably a cost-saving installation. But who knew?

Fuck it. He was sure there were no video cameras mounted on the walls. And maybe the lock had been changed. If only. His key easily slid into the slot and a mere twist of his wrist turned the dead bolt.

What's the plan here, Porter? What the fuck are you doing? he asked himself.

He didn't have a clear answer, just an urge to have another chance, to prove that he could overcome his frailties and serve his community. He looked over his shoulder one more time, sucked in a deep, fretful breath, and then heard voices downstairs.

"Hey, Fin, where's your new inventory officer? I need a Taser."

The booming voice echoed through the hallway below and up the staircase.

"Yeah, very funny, Kosinski," Finnegan said. "Help yourself and then shove it up your ass."

Laughter and heavy footsteps were followed by the clatter of an exterior door opening and shutting. Heart pounding, Jeremy used the commotion to enter Tanner's kingdom. A moment later, the hallway lights went out and he was stranded in total darkness. As his eyes adjusted, he took a tentative step and whacked his knee against the corner of the desk. *Fuck!* He hobbled while fumbling for the flashlight app on his cell phone. The illumination panned the file cabinets until it found ED.

Run, Jeremy. Get your ass out of here before somebody catches you.

He stepped forward, opened the top drawer, and began flipping through files. Although many police resources were now paperless, hard copies were preserved in some sections because it was easier to read and review than digital documents. Jeremy started at the beginning of the alphabet, pulling several folders before moving to the photocopy machine that, gratefully, was asleep but had not been shut down. He startled when the copier awakened to his touch, and then opened a tattered folder and began his chore. Only half a dozen pages spit out before production stopped. *What the hell?* He gently pulled out the paper tray. Empty. His anger flared but was quickly cooled; the setback was actually a blessing.

Inside the utility cabinet where the video equipment was stored, Jeremy found two reams of paper and a stack of manila folders. Excellent. But then and there he realized the materials would need to be replaced, otherwise Tanner might begin to notice that his supplies were dwindling and suspect a break-in. Jeremy's mind raced through the possible consequences—the domino effect of one unlawful act—in a hasty attempt to cover all bases in the event that he was ever questioned. Internal voices argued for and against his stupidity. He knew he was making a typical small-time crook's mistake: *nobody will ever know.* Yet he couldn't stop himself, and to justify his rash decision, he recalled what Tanner had said before the Stevens confession. *"There are hundreds of names in ED. There'll never be enough detectives to cover all that. If you want to spend your off days keeping track of these perverts, go right ahead."*

"Done deal, Sergeant," he said as he turned to his superior's desk. "That's exactly what I'll do."

But first he had to resolve how to manage his paper trail. He brightened when the perfect solution came to him. He'd simply go downstairs and request more paper and folders from the 'inventory officer'.

An hour later, the rogue cop had copied fourteen files. His stomach rumbled from hunger but skipping a meal had been worth it. He gathered his project under his arms like an innocent schoolboy's books, and slowly began his descent down the stairs and out the door to his car in the parking lot. He had returned to his storage closet to explore his supplies when he heard a shoe dragging against the shiny floor.

"Hey, Office Depot. When did you get back?"

"Been here awhile, Sir. Minding the store."

Finny grunted. "Yeah, sure. Hey, an officer dropped by after you left. Needed a Taser. You blew your first chance at being a good inventory officer."

Jeremy turned and smiled pleasantly. "Oh, sorry, I'll take shorter lunch breaks."

This seemed to annoy the sergeant. "What are you smiling at?"

"Nothing. I just want to do a good job as inventory officer."

"Just watch the desk, Rookie. I gotta take a piss. But don't touch anything. I don't want you messing things up. Understand?"

"Whatever you say."

Finnegan shot another hard look at Jeremy, trying to read his mind.

"Are you actually thinking of staying on this job, Porter?"

"Sure, why not? This inventory job may have some long-term benefits."

"Benefits? What benefits are you going to get by sitting in this hallway every night?"

The surly sergeant shook his head and limped away.

"*You'll find out one day, you deadbeat.*"

Jeremy pulled out his cell phone and opened a digital notepad. He tapped in a date and the quantity of paper goods he had used upstairs. He would replace them once Finny had returned to the desk and then jot the time so that he never forgot what he had or had not done.

Anxious, contradictory feelings were also expressed in his diary:

Each month I'll remove one predator from our streets.
But I can't keep entering an unauthorized area.
I'm doing it so our kids will be safer. Think about Kayla.
I'm in deep shit if I ever get caught.
I'll be asked to return as detective when they see what I've achieved.
Not if they arrest me first.

Recording his movements and decisions became a habit that, in the coming weeks, would help keep him partially sane while also rendering him insanely vulnerable to prosecution.

Chapter 9

After clocking out Friday morning, Jeremy ordered a big breakfast and two large coffees at a drive-thru restaurant before heading to his new home, a room at the Heraldson Hotel. He'd booked his lodgings on the day Sandy told him she was filing for divorce. At first he had no idea where to go, so he left the furniture store, found a secluded area to park, and cried his eyes out. The weight of his failure had crushed him. After the sobbing had subsided, he sat for an hour, drained and lost. When a police cruiser sped by, he remembered a hotel where NOPD officers worked off-duty details.

In the lobby, Jeremy introduced himself to the presiding cop and showed his identification.

"Hi. I'm Porter from the Second District. Think I can get a room for a few nights?" The officer was from another district and didn't know Jeremy. Maybe that's why he was so friendly and helpful.

"Sure, the hotel isn't full. Just show your ID at the desk and they'll give you the police discount."

"Cool. Appreciate it."

"Enjoy your stay. And stay out of trouble, my friend."

The cop's joke came with a pat on the shoulder and for one brief moment, Jeremy felt embraced and accepted by the blue brotherhood that had mostly rejected him.

He hauled in the clothing and belongings he had tearfully retrieved from his former home, and then made arrangements to rent a car. His black Chevy Cruze was a far cry from Sandy's Aston Martin, yet it felt suitable and right. He'd eventually have to find a way to buy his own car and rent an apartment—all on a rookie policeman's salary. It dawned on him that he needed his job more than ever. He liked the idea of supporting himself again. No family money, and no gnawing guilt or embarrassment of riches.

In his room, he sprawled on the bed eating and eagerly perusing the files he had copied. The accusations in each case were despicable and gut-wrenching. Jeremy was once again astonished that these men were all out of prison and walking the streets with little or no scrutiny. He was shocked to see that eye-witness complaints about the suspicious actions of several of these individuals had gone without any follow-up or investigation.

As he sifted through the material, a simple plan began to develop. First, he created a grid of the current addresses of all fourteen abusers. Then he prioritized by rating each suspect from "most" to "least" dangerous. Three multiple offenders took top honors, so they would be the focus of Jeremy's initial surveillance. Each afternoon he'd dedicate several hours following a suspect to determine if he displayed suspicious behavior. And if he did?

Determining the appropriate response was more complicated than he had expected. Would an anonymous tip to NOPD work? Not if immediate action was needed. Jeremy stared at his police credential and reminded himself, *I'm a cop. If I have to make an arrest to save a child, I will.*

A thrill ran up his spine. Finally, he had a purpose. His work would matter. Yet despite his newfound mission, Jeremy struggled to keep his heavy eyes open. Before draining his second cup of coffee, he conked out for five hours of deep sleep.

When he heard the Amber alert, he thought he was dreaming.

Jeremy sat up in bed and discovered a television broadcaster reporting breaking news. He forgot he had turned on the set before crashing.

"The boy is thought to have been abducted from the St. Charles Street area... "

He stood and approached the TV. *When will this shit end?*

"... Benito Jackson is eight years old with short, dark, cropped hair and thought to be wearing a New Orleans Pelicans basketball jersey. A person of interest is being sought after witnesses told police they saw him driving in the area shortly before the Jackson child was abducted. He is a thin-built white male, with deep pock marks on his face, driving a late model white SUV."

Jeremy's heart sank. What if the missing child had been Kayla? What would she be feeling and thinking right now? Do abducted children immediately understand that they are in danger? He had the urge to report for duty to help in the search.

He quickly changed his mind. At least police were aware of Benito Jackson's abduction. What about all the other innocent children who were being stalked right now by men like Charles Stevens and the others in the files he had photocopied? His mission was to track them down and try to stop them. The Amber alert added urgency. He knew he would never obtain official approval to track child molesters. He had to go out on his own and he had to begin *now*.

After a fast shower, he grabbed several case folders and exited his room.

Moments later he shoved his way back in and hurriedly searched his pile of belongings before finding what he was looking for. It was heavier than he remembered as he lifted it from the bottom of his temporary closet.

More than a year ago, during the family gathering following his academy graduation ceremony, Mr. McGuire had asked Jeremy to join him in his study.

"I have something I want to show you."

As Jeremy entered the room, he saw his father-in-law unlock a wall safe and pull out a hand-crafted wooden box that contained an immaculate handgun that looked brand-new.

"Jeremy, my father gave this to me some forty years ago. I'm pretty sure he wanted to encourage me to take up his interest in competitive shooting. Unfortunately, I was never bitten by the bug to be a sportsman. In fact, I don't recall ever firing this pistol. It has remained untouched all these years, just taking up space in my safe."

The furniture titan handed the gun to Jeremy, who was truly in awe of its beauty. Clearly, this was of the highest quality, the best money could buy, not a garden-variety handgun. Later, he would find documentation in the box that verified the pistol was a 1943 Colt .38 Caliber, chrome plated, US Army issue. In other words, a true treasure.

"I know our department uses semi-automatics, but this ... my god, just the *feel* of it. It's like ... it's like the Rolls Royce of handguns."

McGuire smiled. He genuinely liked Jeremy and appreciated the unselfconscious wonder the younger man expressed when handling and experiencing the finer things that came with wealth.

"I want you to have it, Jeremy. You're the only one in the family who is trained to use it and will treat it right. I bet my own dad would approve of my bequeathing it to you."

"Sir ... uh, I mean—"

"I like it when you call me Curtis."

"Yeah, yeah, I know," he grinned, nodded. "It's just that ... I just want to say that I know my decision confused you at times and maybe even made you think I didn't like working for you. But I did. You were a very generous boss. And an even better man for trying to understand my need to ... *do* something with my life."

The men embraced, patted shoulders.

"You know, my father told me this gun was very unique and would be considered a treasure one day. It certainly is a beauty. Perhaps you can find out what it's worth," McGuire said.

"I already know." Jeremy gripped the handle, felt its impeccable balance and weight. "It's priceless. Thank you, Curtis."

Sitting in the hotel room, he tried to calm his tremors. *This is important police work. I should not go into the field unarmed.*

Nor should he walk through the hotel lobby bringing attention to himself with iron strapped to his thigh.

He stripped off his pants, found another pair that was baggier. He positioned an ankle holster, inserted the Colt, and walked around the room for practice. It was a bit clumsy, but he'd adapt.

His father-in-law's gift would be his off-duty firearm.

* * *

It didn't take long to realize how difficult surveillance would be. That first afternoon, Jeremy wasted hours parked outside a middle-class residence with no sign of his multi-offender. He returned the following morning after finishing his police shift, hoping to trail the guy driving to work or doing errands. No luck. So he drove to a new neighborhood where the next name on his list lived.

Several days passed without the slightest clue as to what each suspect was up to. Did these guys ever get out of bed? Or had they left for the day before he could get to their neighborhoods?

For that matter, was child molestation a crime of convenience or impulse, or were there prime times for perversion? Before- and after-school hours came to mind. But Jeremy had no way of catching criminals in the act if he couldn't first locate them. He considered canvassing the area and asking questions of residents, then rejected the idea. Since he was not officially assigned to the task, he didn't want to draw attention to himself. He thought about approaching Tanner and offering to volunteer his time, but quickly remembered that the guy dumped him after one lousy day.

A week had passed and Jeremy nearly exhausted his initial case load without spotting one pervert or observing anything akin to criminal behavior. Refusing to give up, he fell into the routine of using his lunch break to copy more files, accumulating dozens so that he would always have a name and neighborhood to trace.

Other matters also demanded his time. After a week at the hotel, he found a two-bedroom apartment closer to Sandy and Kayla, who he insisted on driving to school each morning. Initially, he intended to decorate the spare bedroom for his daughter. When Sandy balked at overnights, Jeremy made the room his operations center. He organized the folders, put maps and photos on his walls, and then installed a bolt lock so that visitors couldn't casually stroll through the premises and discover what he was up to. Long hours were spent studying the patterns and characteristics of pervs and reading pages he had copied from the manual Tanner tossed on his desk that first and last day.

Finally, his due diligence began to pay off. Richard Peabody was weird from the first sighting. He'd often peek out from behind window shades and curtains, as if paranoid of neighborhood traffic and noise, or maybe hoping to catch an eyeful of local kids. Also, it appeared that he chose from an assortment of wigs and optical wear before leaving his home for aimless, late afternoon tours of distant sections of the city. He'd hide his fashion statements under a floppy hat, which he'd remove once he began to drive.

On his third afternoon of surveillance, Jeremy sensed something different as soon as Richard left his home. He jogged to his car which was parked curbside as if late for an appointment and drove directly to an elementary school with a large, fenced-in playground. Peabody circled the block a couple times and slowed on his third pass when young children started pouring out of the entrance gate. The perv's green Ford Focus came to a stop near two little girls who were standing beside the curb. Richard lowered his passenger-side window and began talking to the children. One girl stepped closer as she listened.

With no adults in the vicinity, Jeremy decided to pull in behind the Ford at a discreet distance. Next he propped up his cell phone on the dashboard and touched the start button on his video camera. The conversation continued until the little girl glanced at Jeremy's Chevy, inadvertently alerting Richard, who peered into his rear-view mirror then sped way. The girl looked startled.

Jeremy pulled up to the girls, rolled down his window, and held up his badge. "Don't be afraid. I'm a police officer. What did that man say to you?"

The little girl looked at her friend, who blurted, "He lost his puppy and asked me to drive around with him to help him find it."

"But I told him I couldn't because I don't get into cars with strangers."

Jeremy thought of the child who had been seriously harmed by Charles Stevens. If only she had been so aware.

"Good girl. You did the right thing. Is your mommy coming to pick you up?"

The other girl began hopping in place and pointing. "There she is!"

"Okay, girls. Be safe."

The Ford Focus turned right at the intersection but Jeremy didn't follow. He assumed his car had been made by the perv and maybe the guy even recognized it from his neighborhood and quickly made the connection.

Jeremy took an alternative route, betting dollars to donuts that Richard Peabody would take evasive action before returning home. After parking around the block, Jeremy strolled through the scrappy area of one- and two-story clapboard homes set close to the curb. The streets were cracked and pockmarked with irregular repairs but they were wide with scant foliage, so Jeremy had a good view. North Rendon, which was Peabody's street, was one way and so was Dumaine. The perv would need to pass the intersection if he intended to park in front of his house.

The inclement weather darkened the skies but couldn't hide Jeremy. He felt exposed, like a loiterer, so he walked toward the "For Sale" signs that stood in narrow strips of lawn and took photos, recorded addresses, and pretended to call the realtors, as though he were a potential buyer. Forty minutes later, the green Ford puttered past and pulled to the curb.

Now what? Richard Peabody had not broken any laws, although technically he had violated his probation by lingering near school grounds. Lost puppy? Bullshit. The bastard wanted one thing only: to lure a little girl into his car.

To avoid being noticed, Jeremy considered waiting until nightfall before approaching the house, but that would waste hours of precious time. Maybe it was enough that the cloudy weather threatened rainfall and made everything look darker than normal for that time of day. *Make a move, Porter,* Jeremy told himself. *Let him know you're watching him.*

His heart pumped double time as he walked toward the house.

Chapter 10

The one-story home was at least a half-century old and in need of a paint job, if not a complete makeover. The roofline sagged, the breeze could be heard whistling through warped window frames, and the unkempt front lawn was a catch-all for refuse. Richard Peabody apparently lacked a green thumb.

Standing on the tiny porch, Jeremy glanced in every direction in search of passersby or neighbors. The street was barren. With barely a plan in mind, he knocked on the door. Richard opened the door, but only enough to size up his visitor. He wore no glasses or wig, betraying close-cropped brown hair and gaunt facial features.

"What do you want?"

The man's gruff, aggressive voice and physical stature were more intimidating than Jeremy had anticipated. He swallowed before speaking.

"Did ... uh, by any chance ... you lose your puppy?"

"I don't have a fucking dog!"

The door slammed shut.

Flustered, Jeremy gathered himself before knocking again. No response. He knocked harder. When he heard footsteps marching toward the door, Jeremy put his hand on the identification folder in his back pocket.

The door swept open and Peabody stepped forward, mean, impatient.

"I told you, I don't have a fucking—"

Jeremy held up his police ID, silencing him.

"Police officer!"

The perv changed his tone and his eyes began searching the street.

"What do you want?"

"We need to talk, Mr. Peabody."

"How do you know my name?"

"Everybody knows your name. In this neighborhood and on the child molesters' registry. You're famous. Maybe someday you'll have your own show, like Charles Stevens."

He didn't know why he had invoked the minor celebrity's name. But he noticed Peabody flinch when he heard it.

"You can't just barge into a man's home."

"I'm not barging. I knocked on your door and you slammed it in my face using foul language. Do you have trouble managing your anger, Richard?"

Peabody took another furtive glance at homes across the street. "All right. Come in, if you want. Hurry up, I'm busy."

"Thank you."

As soon as he crossed the threshold, Jeremy knew he was probably violating police rules and regulations by conducting an off-duty investigation without making the proper notifications. There was no turning back now.

"What's this about? I got rights, you know."

Jeremy took a quick look through the comfy but tawdry front room. A hallway bisected the structure and probably led to a bedroom or two in the rear, and an adjacent kitchen that likely had a back door—an escape hatch.

"Richard, when's the last time you spoke to your probation officer?"

"I don't know, a few months back."

"A few months? Aren't you required to have regular—"

"I don't have to answer all these questions."

"You're right. Maybe I should go now and mention Baldwin Elementary School to Probation. Sound like a good idea, Richard?" Jeremy felt in command, and he liked it.

"You can't prove anything."

"Yes, I can."

Jeremy pulled out his cell phone and played the short video he had recorded earlier.

"Is that little girl a family member, Richard? I don't think so. But she did mention something about your missing puppy dog."

Beads of sweat formed on Peabody's forehead and his mouth quivered. Jeremy pressed with another question.

"Who else is here? Anybody in the back?" Jeremy asked.

"No. Nobody."

Jeremy stepped toward the hallway for a quick look and noticed the glare of a computer screen illuminating the nearest room. When he turned back, he could tell Peabody's fear had kicked up a notch. Call it instinct, that raw moment when something flashes and a man knows, *he just knows* that he's got something and must act—immediately.

"Turn around and place your hands behind your back."

"What?"

"It's protocol."

In seconds, the handcuffs snapped around Peabody's wrists.

"Are you arresting me?"

"No. It's policy. Just stay calm."

He guided his prey into the bedroom where he saw the computer screen. He sat Peabody on the edge of a frayed day bed, then moved to the card table that held the desktop PC. He wanted to check recent history to determine if Peabody had visited child pornography sites and possibly downloaded imagery. He soon realized he needed some cooperation.

"I need your password, Mr. Peabody."

"No."

Jeremy swung around and stared at his prisoner.

Richard repeated, "I don't have to give you my fucking password."

"I'm hearing some anger again, Mr. Peabody. Are we going to have an ugly incident here?"

"How would you feel? Somebody just barging in—"

"We've already gone over that. I was invited into your residence to—"

"Yeah, and then you barge into my personal space."

"Oh, is that what this is?"

"I sleep in here."

"What else do you do here?" He looked directly at the computer screen. "Is this a personal space, too?"

Peabody pouted. "I'm not giving you my password."

"Okay. I get it. You type in the password and I'll avert my eyes. Fair?"

"Yeah, like I can do it backwards."

Jeremy instructed Peabody to stand. He unlocked one wrist, guided the man's arms forward and then quickly clamped the cuff again.

"I don't know why I should have to do this."

"A search warrant is easy to get. Probable cause. Cops will search the whole place. You want them looking through your wig collection?"

The perv walked to the computer and typed in the password only after waiting for Jeremy to turn away.

"Thank you for your cooperation. Please sit back down on the bed."

Jeremy's search quickly brought results: websites strewn with images of naked children and blogs that extolled the virtues of man-child sex. Richard hadn't erased his recent history from the browser because he'd probably been online when Jeremy arrived.

Finding incriminating files in the computer was another matter. He tried several keyword searches before opening the folder options window and then clicking the "view" tab. He knew the menu that appeared could be configured to show whatever might be hiding in possibly incriminating folders. In the subsection of the checkboxes, he clicked "hidden files and folders" and then, "show hidden files and folders," which would show actual locations of Word documents. A whole new and lurid world appeared on the screen. Jeremy lowered his body into the folding chair.

There was not enough time to open each file, so Jeremy ran a search for images by typing in *.jpg. He was startled by what he found. His computer science skills were a big help, and yet Tanner had been scornful when he suggested that he might offer special services to the Child Abuse Section.

"Do you have any other hobbies, Mr. Peabody?"

"What do you mean?"

Jeremy didn't answer. He'd clicked a shortcut link on the desktop that took him to a curious portal that refused entry. With each attempt, the PC made a funny thump sound.

"What's this, Mr. Peabody? It needs a password or some kind of special code. How do I get in?"

Fingers flashed across the keyboard as Jeremy tried every hack trick he could think of. Absorbed in his work, he cursed to himself when he failed to break the code.

Shit. Let me in, you bastard.

Richard Peabody, who had grown more tense with each discovery Jeremy made, had a revelation. He cocked his head and looked at Jeremy with fresh eyes.

"Let me see your badge again."

Jeremy's eyes were still on the screen. "What?"

"Are you sure you're a cop?"

"Why wouldn't I be sure?"

"Maybe you want to steal my stuff. Maybe—"

"I need your cooperation here, Mr. Pea—!"

Jeremy turned in time to see Peabody raise his cuffed hands overhead and bring them down hard. He shoved his hand between skin and steel, felt the cold handcuffs smash his fingers against his throat, fell out of the flimsy chair, and landed with his back flush against his assailant's chest. Peabody, breathing hard, tightened his grip. The rookie cop twisted like a fish and savagely kicked out his legs, toppling the table and sending the PC crashing to the hardwood.

He'd lost all feeling in the fingers wedged against his throat and knew Peabody would choke him to death if he didn't get some leverage. With his free hand, he swiped ineffectually and tried gouging Peabody's eyes. In return, he felt Peabody's chin push firmly against the top of his head. The pervert's hot breath burned his ear and spit-filled grunts moistened his hair. He was beaten. He began to blubber and moan. He'd soon die from strangulation by a sex offender who had tried to seduce a little girl with a false puppy story. His body might never be found.

Like a kid in the midst of a tantrum, he kicked his legs against the wall, in an attempt to rock free. All he got for his effort was a hamstring spasm—and a peek at the Colt .38 strapped to his ankle.

Jeremy knew from the angle of his body that Peabody was leaning back to get full leverage on his handcuff choke. Jeremy could barely breathe as they rolled to the side. In one fast move, he bent his knee and felt the butt of the pistol. He was able to get it unsnapped and slid it from the holster without Peabody noticing.

When the cuffs tightened even more against his neck, he whipped the gun upward until the barrel found the hard surface of the pervert's skull. He got off two shots.

Jeremy's head snapped back as Peabody recoiled from the bullets, then the man's body crashed sideways to the cold, filthy flooring.

Ears ringing from the gunfire, Jeremy wiggled free of Peabody's arms and felt oxygen return to his lungs. His hair and clothing were soiled with blood and human tissue.

What the fuck have I done?

Then he froze. Someone must have heard the shots. Maybe they called the police. Would he hear squad cars soon?

He panicked and ran to the front room to peek out the window. No movement outside, but the skies had darkened and a light rain had begun to fall. *Should I call this in? How will I explain being here? Looking through stolen files? I can't call it in. I just can't.*

When he returned to the bedroom, he didn't bother checking for a pulse. The guy was dead as nails. But Jeremy's hands shook as he removed the handcuffs from Peabody's wrists. *Leave nothing behind.* He knew he had to get the hell out and run for his car, a rental he would exchange as soon as possible.

How am I going to explain this? How the fuck am I—?

Shaking, he used pillowcases to wipe his face and clothing and eliminate fingerprints on the computer, keyboard, and chair.

Get out, Porter. Get your ass out of here.

Fortunately, all the shades and curtains were drawn in the secretive man's home, so Jeremy could return to the front door without being seen. He decided against leaving the premises that way and retreated through the hallway to the back of the house. The kitchen, gratefully, included a door to a small backyard that was surrounded by a wooden fence. The rain was now thick and fast, a decent cover for his escape.

Run, dipshit. Go now.

But he returned to the bedroom and began a frantic search for Peabody's wig collection and floppy hat. The closet had everything, including a baggy raincoat, which he pulled on.

Still, he wasn't ready to go. What about the body? He couldn't use his cell phone to call it in.

Jeremy grabbed the receiver from the wall phone in the kitchen and began to dial, then stopped, dialed again, and hung up. What would he say? *I just shot a pervert who tried to kill me after I illegally entered his home and discovered—Oh, and by the way, I'm a cop. Christ, Porter!*

Jeremy ripped a sheet of paper towel from a roll with a flower print. He wiped clean the telephone hand receiver, which he then dropped and let dangle on its coiled cord. Then he covered his fingertip and dialed 911. He heard the dispatcher answer, "911. What is your emergency?" But there was no need for him to explain because by leaving the phone off the hook he knew a police cruiser would be sent to check out the residence.

Thunder yowled and startled Jeremy as he opened the back door. He wrapped the raincoat around him, did a belly roll over the rickety fence, and landed on his feet in the neighbor's yard. Lights illuminated the interior of the home but he saw no one and could only hope and pray that nobody saw him. Even if they did, all they'd see was a raven-haired man in a floppy hat and raincoat.

Once on the sidewalk, Jeremy resisted the urge to run like hell, then realized it was pouring down rain and so picking up the pace was natural. At the end of the block he could see his car parallel-parked next to the curb up ahead. He began to sprint and then slowed when a police cruiser appeared and turned down Peabody's street.

Be cool, Porter.

He unlocked the black Chevy and made sure the raincoat completely covered his body before he got in. The floppy disguise was awkward but he kept it on until he was out of the area. Then he pulled off the hat and wig, located a dumpster behind a grocery store, and ditched them. Before driving to his apartment, he felt a chill ripple through his body.

What the fuck have you just done to yourself, Porter?

Chapter 11

Officer Leslie Scott was grateful for the rain. It helped keep people indoors and out of trouble so the day had been fairly quiet. As his cruiser idled near the entrance to Adry Cleaners, his eyes were heavy and he wished he could nap. He had agreed to forsake his normal day off with Second District and work overtime to help out another platoon that was short-handed. That meant it would be nearly ten days between his last and his next days of rest.

He sat up straight in the passenger seat when he saw Officer Willmer dash out of the shop, his newly cleaned and pressed uniforms sheathed in plastic. He opened a door to the backseat and hung his clothing, then took his place behind the steering wheel.

"Thanks, Scott."

"No problem."

"Needed to pick this up before they closed for the day"

"I get it."

"You about ready for dinner?"

Before Leslie Scott could answer, the dispatcher interrupted on the radio. The officers were instructed to visit the 900 block of North Rendon Street to check up on a 911 caller.

By the time they arrived, the rain had subsided. They approached the small, rickety house, with Willmer taking the lead. He knocked on the front door and Scott stood to the side and rear of him. A protective, defensive posture.

No response. Willmer knocked again.

"I'll take a tour of the perimeter," Scott said.

"Sounds like a plan."

The windows were curtained until Scott reached the kitchen. He pulled himself up and peered through the glass and over the sink toward a narrow hallway where light from another room spread. He called to his partner.

"Willmer, I see a light on and the phone is hanging off the hook."

"On my way."

Scott lowered himself and jogged to the back where he found the door. He swept the narrow backyard, now in shadow, before knocking and turning the knob.

"Back door unlocked." He pushed it open and called, "Police! Anybody home?"

Willmer came close, peered over Scott's shoulder, and saw the dangling phone.

"Yup. We better go in."

Before they made their move, Willmer pulled the radio mic from his shoulder and called for supervision. A green light was quickly granted.

Both drew their handguns as they walked the short distance through the galley kitchen toward the light. Scott saw it first.

"Definitely a struggle, computer and office supplies on the floor and—oh, shit. Man down!"

"Got your back."

Scott entered while Willmer covered the dark back bedroom, then shifted his focus to the front of the house.

"Blood everywhere. Gunshot wounds to the face and temple."

Willmer pulled at his radio again. Despite lack of vital signs, it was protocol to request an emergency medical service unit. He also defined the crime and requested a homicide team.

"Signal Thirty. I repeat, Signal Thirty."

The response was a deluge. Minutes later the neighborhood pulsed with cruiser lights and the chaos of discovery. Cops warded off curious pedestrians and questioned neighbors until homicide detectives and crime lab technicians arrived and began to inspect and prowl the scene and outer environs.

A violent struggle was evident, yet no weapon was recovered. Shoe prints not evident inside were traced in the tawdry grass from the back door to the fence and into the adjacent yard, where indentations suggested an escape around the side of the house and, presumably, onto the cement sidewalk that, unfortunately, was washed clean from the downpour earlier.

Leslie Scott quickly found the name of the victim on a stack of unopened junk mail. He held up a letter from Probation and Parole. "

"Richard Peabody."

Willmer looked confused. "What?"

"The dead man's name."

"Ah. Good eye. Let's talk to some neighbors."

While moving from one curious face to another Scott wondered what had provoked gunfire. Had the homeowner walked in on a crime in progress, a robbery? When the onlookers gave him no substantive information, he knocked on some doors until an elderly black man answered.

"Ain't surprise me none. Happen sooner if some folks got they wish."

"Sooner?"

"Man a pervert."

"He had a criminal record?"

The man guffawed. "Nice way o' saying he done bad things wid the chil'ren. Don't worry me no more, my kids is all grow'd. But I be talking over the fence about it."

Scott pulled out his notebook. "With who?"

The elder pointed to the homes set close on both sides of his property and mentioned names further down the street—families that were angry that a registered sex offender lived nearby.

He questioned several other residents before returning to Peabody's home. When he entered the bedroom, Detective Telly Gikas was kneeling beside the dead man's body.

Gikas studied the deceased. "Victim has bruises and cuts on both wrists."

Scott had also noticed and wondered about the abrasions.

"Detective," Scott offered, "according to the neighbors, the victim had a history. Apparently, a child molester. They tell me he is a multiple offender."

"Sayonara, shit bird," muttering to no one in particular, the weary investigator stood. "Does it even matter who killed this douche bag?"

Scott hesitated before asking, "Could it be a revenge killing?"

"Could be. But if this guy is a child molester, the list of his enemies could be very long."

"One of the people I interviewed was pretty hot about him living here."

"That doesn't surprise me. Who is it?"

"This guy Krawley, five doors down. He even organized a protest to pressure Peabody to leave."

"Yeah, they want the creep to move to somebody else's neighborhood. Jesus," Gikas said, staring at the list of people Scott interviewed. "What's your name?"

"Leslie Scott."

He dangled the piece of paper. "This is helpful. Thanks, Officer."

* * *

The police radio static put Jeremy on edge as he sat on the rim of his old porcelain bathtub treating his neck wounds. Every time he heard "Signal Thirty," he cringed. Although he was off-duty this night, he was certain that at any moment a swarm of cops would burst through his apartment door and arrest him. He killed a man. Self-defense, to be sure. But how the hell was he going to explain his reason for being in Peabody's home?

He had started an investigation without approval based on files he had pilfered from Child Abuse.

Jesus Christ ... what have I done? All I wanted was a solid arrest of a child molester. Yeah, and a little praise for good police work. He was sure no one would believe his story. *I should have stayed at the scene, taken my chances, explained why the fuck I was there. Showed them the video. Too late now. Shit, shit, shit!*

Thoughts of spending the rest of his life in prison, and Kayla, his darling Kayla who had drawn Detective Daddy with crayons, were agonizing. He jumped up, went to the living room, surfed the television channels, and paced while waiting for the evening news.

He was the lead story.

"Oh, fuck."

"New Orleans police are investigating a homicide that occurred earlier this evening in the 900 block of North Rendon Street.

As the newscaster continued, footage of crime lab techies and detectives at Peabody's place made Jeremy want to vomit.

"....The man's identity is being withheld until notification of next of kin. Police encourage anyone who may have witnessed...."

"Oh, great. Here we go. Somebody must have seen an asshole in a floppy hat."

"....or has information about the homicide...."

"It's a *justifiable* homicide!"

"....to call crime stoppers at the number shown on the screen...."

He lowered his head and buried his face in his hands. As the public information officer continued to blather the usual nonsense, he continued to whisper to the empty room, "It's a *justifiable* homicide."

Chapter 12

Sleep did not come easy for Jeremy. He battled torrents of anxiety and bloody, horrific imagery. He'd been at death's door and couldn't shake the notion that he could have, or maybe should have, died at the hands of Richard Peabody.

In the middle of the night, he abruptly rose and went to the war room where he began writing an exact record of what occurred during and after the Peabody incident. Also included were the photos he took of the bruises and scratch marks on his neck. The only difference between his detailed work and an official police report was that he was not able to request a report number from dispatch.

When he finally surrendered to exhaustion, the gray gloom of pre-dawn had begun to lighten his windows. By the time the sun was in full command of the sky, several hours had passed. The apartment was quiet and still until the sex fiend avenger shot upright and grabbed for his cell phone.

"Oh, shit!"

He was late. Kayla needed a ride to school and ...then he remembered he had called Sandy the night before, claiming he was ill and didn't want to share his flu bug with their daughter. It was the right move. He could have hidden his neck wounds with a high-collar jacket, but he feared he would not be able to hide his agitation and fear. His soul felt disheveled, upturned, and off-kilter. A look in the mirror would likely reveal a blurry man out of sync, distracted by an inner demon.

By sitting upright, he established that he had fallen asleep on his not-so-comfortable couch, newly purchased from a store *not* owned by Curtis McGuire. He would need breakfast and coffee soon, but more than anything, he needed news and it did not take long to find it.

The TV brightened as a man named Norm Krawley, surrounded by what looked like a group of supporters, faced a throng of television cameras. He was self-righteous, probably talked too much for his own good, and didn't hide his disgust for the now deceased Richard Peabody. Jeremy knew he must be talking about the sex offender because he recognized the North Rendon neighborhood in the background—clapboard siding, the sky defaced mostly by telephone poles and sagging cables, and residents of all different ethnicities.

"Oh, yeah, like I killed the bastard and then just strolled home waiting for the cops to show up. Grow some brains, People. The man was a pedophile. We didn't like him. We didn't want him near our kids, but this is crazy."

The men and women behind Krawley nodded and called out in agreement.

"Tell 'm, Norm."

"We're with you."

"Got what he deserved."

Several reporters asked questions all at once. Krawley looked annoyed, waved his hands as if he were a magician wanting it all to disappear.

"Yeah, yeah, yeah. We organized, we protested. Who wouldn't? We have crimes in this neighborhood that never get investigated. Cops who don't give a damn. You wouldn't protect your kids when you learned a sex offender just moved in next door?"

"Mr. Krawley, the victim also reported that his tires had been slashed and bricks were thrown through his window," a blonde, coiffed reporter said.

"So? What's that got to do with me? I don't carry knives or throw stones. I use my voice, my rights as a citizen. I—"

"Then who would kill him?"

The question chilled Jeremy's soul.

Krawley's patience was ripped open. "Now I'm supposed to be Sherlock Holmes?"

His supporters pushed forward, shouting and jabbing fingers at reporters, incensed that their law-abiding neighbor should be suspected by the media.

The live broadcast shrunk to a corner on the TV screen as the newscaster repeated basic information.

"Today, police revealed last night's homicide victim as Richard Peabody, age forty-four, a convicted child molester who had lived in the area for less than a year. He'd filed complaints about threats and property damage as recently as last month and complained police had not…."

During his surveillance, Jeremy had observed Peabody regularly peeking out his window and now he knew why. The guy apparently felt besieged, and yet continued his search in adjacent areas for woeful children he could woo into his car. Jeremy again felt the urge to vomit yet simultaneously understood that it was nothing to be ashamed of. Most normal human beings would have the same response.

Anger suddenly burned in him. If he'd been trained, and been given time to read through prior cases and police reports, he would have been prepared to confront the morbid reality of child abuse and the dead, repulsive eyes of Charles Stevens.

He flipped channels and discovered more interviews. Some churchgoers offered prayers for the misbegotten soul of a troubled man, while others did not hide their relief that Peabody could no longer do harm. Still, more voices complained that law enforcement should keep tabs on the many multi-offenders who roamed New Orleans' streets with impunity.

For the first time since the struggle with Peabody, Jeremy felt his burden lift. He spoke out loud as if Reed and Tanner were in the room.

"Are you listening to this? Those people would thank me if I told them what I've done. I'd have their full support. So why the hell don't I have yours? Why couldn't you give me another chance?"

A familiar voice turned Jeremy back to the television. Police Chief Morris Hendricks stood before a podium addressing a slew of reporters at a downtown press conference. He was smooth and imperturbable.

"We share the community's outrage at these recent events and know more must be done to keep our city safe. But let me remind you that it is not the duty of the New Orleans Police Department to track sex offenders who have been released from prison. Probation is charged with that responsibility, and we're in full support of their excellent efforts, given serious personnel and budget constraints. We will find the murderer. That is *our* job."

Hendricks paused, looked down at his notes and then, before continuing, and for dramatic effect Jeremy assumed, slowly moved his eyes over the audience, left to right.

"Yet there is something else I believe may be brewing in some sectors. Members of law enforcement sense an impatience and possibly the urge by some citizens to take action, to literally take the law into their own hands in a potentially calamitous and tragic attempt to rid their localities of alleged—yes, *alleged*—criminals. Not every offender who has served time is a *repeat* offender, and so I—"

"Oh, come on." Jeremy recalled the high recidivism percentages quoted by Sergeant Tanner. "He was a predator!"

The polished Hendricks finished his remarks but Jeremy was not listening. He moved to his war room, unlocked the door and entered. Photos and maps with landmarks of previous crimes were pinned to the walls, photocopied files and his laptop sat on the desk ready to assist their master.

Hiding everything that was now in plain sight would have been the smart move. But Jeremy rejected that idea when, to his surprise, he felt his core reverberate with pride. Later he would tell friends that it was as if the angels of purpose and righteousness were fluttering around him.

His misalliance with crime was a gift—a momentary, elevated, fucked up occurrence that told him, *you have a mission, a calling. Carry on.*

And so, while this was not the time to select his next surveillance subject—he would need events to play out before he could determine how to move forward—Jeremy nonetheless took stock and made decisions.

First, later that day he would return his car rental, and then choose another vehicle at a competing firm. Better to change the style and color of his ride as much as possible in the coming weeks.

Second, he would study each folder learning the habits, mannerisms and traits of child molesters. He would learn their characteristics, sites they visited and how they stalked their prey.

Finally, he would treat this war room as his refuge. Before entering, he would shed all fears and doubts and leave them outside so that within these four walls he could experience the pure, unparalleled grace of order and calm.

Chapter 13

Lieutenant Bayless called for attention at roll call before he began reading messages to the platoon. As was his habit, Jeremy took a position in the back row, virtually invisible to the other officers who, as usual, paid him no attention. He'd wanted to call in sick but quickly realized that would draw suspicion.

Earlier, when he entered the locker room to change into his uniform, he was a spastic hive of nerves. His hands shook as he quickly buttoned his NOPD top and strapped on gear. He feared comments or questions about the raw abrasions around his Adam's apple. His boots, usually easy to tie, gave him trouble and offered only one respite: while sitting and bending over his feet, no one would notice his angry red neck and ask, "Hey, what happened to you?"

The bland bellow of Bayless started with a couple reminders about training sessions, burglaries, and robberies, and descriptions of individuals who may have participated in those crimes. Then he veered into territory that made Jeremy want to disappear. He felt conspicuous, even though he understood that nobody gave a damn about an inventory officer.

"A homicide in the First District occurred last night. The victim died in his home as a result of two gunshot wounds to the head. The victim, one Richard Peabody, was a convicted child molester and registered sex offender."

The solemn silence didn't last long. Brock Suggs disturbed the peace with his crude comedy act.

"Awww, too fucking bad. Somebody did us a favor."

Jeremy's stomach tightened and his teeth clenched. His hands shook so much he shoved them into his pockets.

But a few officers laughed nervously as Bayless continued, "The wanted subject is unknown and at large at this time."

"Hey," Brock shouted, "If anyone catches the *wanted subject* anytime soon, bring his ass to me. I'll give him a blowjob. Nice work, buddy."

Laughter and agreements shook the dignity of police formality. Jeremy stayed silent, still as stone, until he realized his reserve might actually give him away. He forced a smile and pretended to chuckle. He let his shoulders shake as if he were trying to contain his mirth. But in reality, he was hurting. He was surrounded by fifteen skilled, armed officers who were duty-bound to find the murderer—a rat named Jeremy Porter.

Nothing seemed humorous anymore.

Even so, in a flash of irony or arrogance, he wished he could confront Brock in front of everybody and say, "You owe me big time, Asshole."

Bayless had heard enough horseplay.

"Hey, knock it off. And show some respect. One of our own, Officer Leslie Scott, answered the call and was praised by detectives for his thorough work in the field. Good job, Scott."

The news made Jeremy shake even more. He felt the odd, illogical sensation of being exposed, as if Leslie would know his friend and self-defense protégé had been in the room where the crime occurred. He looked down and away for fear that others would wonder why he appeared so startled.

"And one more thing. Memo from Captain Reed. This child abuse thing—the Stevens case and now this Peabody situation—beware of the agitation it's causing in the city. Report any group or individual who seems a little too fired up, a little too aggressive. Any questions? All right, then. Officer Suggs, I need a minute. Everyone else—dismissed."

As the blue platoon dispersed, Jeremy lingered and noticed that the lieutenant and Suggs enjoyed a casual bond that seemed to stem from family relations or social circles.

"You all right?"

Jeremy spun and looked into Leslie Scott's concerned face.

"Hey." They shook hands. "Yeah, it's just sometimes Bayless and Suggs…"

"Yeah, so unprofessional. They had to be desperate to promote Bayless to lieutenant.

But I was talking about your neck. Looks painful."

"Huh?" He moved his fingers across the abrasions. "Nah. It's just—"

"What happened?"

He'd rehearsed several answers to the inevitable questions, but now found himself improvising.

"Kayla. My daughter. You know, horsy-back rides. I won't let her use a rope next time."

"Ah. Bucking bronco."

Jeremy forced a laugh. "She is stronger than I thought."

Scott chuckled and Jeremy felt his nerves relax. He decided to risk a question.

"Hey, but I was surprised to hear—why were you at the crime scene last night?"

"Oh, yeah. First District needed help and I could use the overtime, so we got the call."

"Uh huh, uh huh."

"Messy scene, man. Stuff knocked all over the place. Lots of blood, of course, and … I don't know, something was just … weird."

"What do you mean?"

"Well, kind of a stupid thing to say, actually—it's a crime scene. Everything is weird."

Jeremy took precautions to sound as casual as possible. "Yeah, but, you mean, what, you noticed something stranger than usual?"

Scott looked over his shoulder, suddenly paranoid. It gave Jeremy a chance to glance at Brock Suggs, who was laughing along with Bayless.

"Let's get out of here," Scott said. "I'll walk you to your station."

In the near-empty hallway they walked and kept their voices low as Leslie Scott grappled more with a feeling, an intuition, than anything material, such as hard evidence.

"First, somebody had to call 911, right?"

"Right."

"Okay, we'd assume it was the victim. But when? It had to be *before* he was shot, right? Sensing danger, he runs for the phone."

"That's what I'd do."

"Me, too—if I'd had the chance. But if that happened, Peabody probably would have been pursued by the killer. They struggle in the kitchen—he drops the phone after dialing."

"Makes sense."

"But the dispatcher didn't hear anything like that and the kitchen was neat as a pin. And, Jesus, after he was shot in the face he couldn't have made it across the hallway—oh, sorry, right in the middle of the home there's a short hallway between the bedroom and the—"

"Any witnesses?"

Leslie looked a bit surprised by the interruption. "Not yet, not that I know of. But the detectives are canvassing the neighborhood and checking to see if anyone has surveillance cameras."

"So, no description of the perpetrator?"

"No, didn't you hear the roll call message?"

"Yes, but I thought maybe someone mentioned something at the scene."

"Anyway, as I was saying—"

"Did they lift any prints?"

"Well, crime lab did their usual thorough job, prints, DNA. Hopefully, they will get a match."

"But, no witnesses, huh?"

That caused an aggravated stare from Leslie. "You just asked me that. Are you okay?"

Jeremy gulped and felt blood rush to his face. *Shut the fuck up, Porter.* He stared at Leslie, helpless, trying to stay calm and recover while feeling sweat bead on his forehead.

"Yeah, sorry, I mean, I just wonder if I'll ever be able to help with a case like that."

"As I was saying, not much space in that small area of the house."

Relief filled Jeremy's lungs as his friend began to walk again and proceed with his story.

"All right, so there's *one* issue. And I assume homicide detectives will figure it out."

"What's that?"

"Something they seemed to ignore."

Jeremy's body was like one of those hot/cold muscle compresses. His temperature spiked and crashed, depending on what Leslie reported.

"Uh huh?"

Jeremy's mind raced as Scott described the crime scene: the toppled table and computer, the crushed folding chair, the victim's body. It was as if he was witnessing a playback of the event. He saw Peabody wrap the handcuffs around his neck and drag him down. Then he watched as his body twisted and his legs kicked out and nicked—

"The wall, low, just above the molding, there were all these marks," Scott said. "Like a repetitive motion. Kicking maybe. Desperate kicks, I'm thinking, the dark marks the sole of a rubber shoe might make, because the drywall surface, I mean it was painted, but—"

"A light color?"

Shut your mouth, Porter. Jesus.

"Exactly, so the markings were easy to see and there were some indentations."

Scott slowed as they came close to Jeremy's inventory closet, as if to stay beyond the aural reach of Sergeant Finnegan's kingdom. The television was already jabbering some shallow nonsense, likely another episode of *Babes on the Bayou*.

"So you're saying....?"

Leslie grinned. "Yeah, good question. What the hell am I saying?"

Jeremy returned the grin, grateful for a moment of kinship.

"It's just that the position of the body ... I mean, shit happens, but ... Peabody couldn't have made those marks."

"Why not?"

"How?"

"I don't know. I'm not a detective ... anymore."

"Okay. Let's say that at some point he was on his back, kicking the shit out of that wall."

"Struggling."

"Right."

"Just a possibility. But even then he still couldn't have been the one who made those marks."

Jeremy was afraid to ask why, but he did anyway, and the observant Leslie Scott had an answer.

"Because he was wearing these big shit-kicker boots. Size twelve, Man. The dude was enormous."

Jeremy shook his head, remembering. "I know."

"You knew him?"

"No, no, I mean, I'm agreeing. Boots that size...."

"But when I ran it by the detective, you know, just trying to contribute and learn and—"

"Right."

"Nothing."

"What do you mean?"

"He shrugged it off. Nothing they could make sense of or trace. But, shit, if Peabody didn't make those marks, then who the hell did? The murderer, obviously, or...." He shook his head, more confused than assured of anything. "Something weird was going on. It's not what it seems. I hope we drag the perp in just so we can ask, what the fuck? And I haven't even mentioned the victim's wrists."

The image of handcuffs jolted Jeremy. "What about them?"

Scott paused and stared at Jeremy, as though something new was rolling around in his head. Perhaps something troubling. He finally answered.

"Why? I just want to know *why* the marks? I mean, they were fresh. How'd they get there?

"So you are thinking—"

"I don't really know. It was such a bizarre scene. I hate to say this but part of me feels like maybe the pervert got what was coming to him. I can't help but wonder how many kids' lives this scumbag ruined. It's crazy, but I almost feel empathy for the killer."

"Yeah, I know what you mean."

"But I'm a cop, so empathy or not, the guy is a murderer and needs to be brought to justice."

"Yeah, I guess so." *But he isn't a murderer.*

"Well ... gotta go. Have a good night. Hope your neck wounds heal quickly."

"Oh, it'll be fine."

Jeremy was impressed that his buddy had thought so deeply about the crime. Leslie had absorbed details *before* EMS and everybody else showed up. That meant he kept his cool and had a perceptive, logical mind that was not easily misled. And despite rank and seniority issues, he wasn't afraid to engage with more experienced personnel. The man had a bright future. Then Jeremy had another darker thought. During the conversation, he had made multiple blunders, all but blurting out incriminating information. *Stupid, stupid, stupid!* He'd also left a lot of DNA at the scene. Then his mood brightened.

First, Powder Puff was the last guy anyone would suspect of murder. Even better, in a flash he realized NOPD did not have his DNA on record. Call it dumb luck, but because he was accepted into the police academy very late in the process, administrators had to rush Jeremy through the paperwork. In their haste, they had neglected to request the DNA samples that all the other recruits had submitted three weeks prior to the first day of training. They would find no trace of him in their DNA data bank.

Regardless, he gave himself a thrashing for all the clumsy questions he'd asked his friend, and then made mental notes:

> *Think like a cop. But start behaving like a criminal and keep your mouth shut. And pray to the gods of justice that you are never chased down by someone with the talent and unwavering curiosity of Officer Leslie Scott.*

Chapter 14

Lt. Frank Styles was not happy. As supervisor of all homicide investigations, he preferred to see progress in the early hours of any major crime. If too many days passed without fresh discoveries and new leads, he began to feel the burden of another cold case, which he feared would make his already gray hair turn white or fall out. Not good for his track record, and not good for community relations.

That's why he called in Detective Calvin Vuong, the homicide investigator assigned the Peabody case. Both men sat at a long meeting room table reviewing reports from the coroner and the crime lab. Spread out over the flat surface were a slew of crime scene images.

"Calvin, this one troubles me."

"Don't they all?"

The corners of Styles' mouth wrinkled in what would serve as a smile. "Yes, my ulcers are acting up again. But this one ... we're a few days into this and all we have is some speculation about Norm Krawley, the so-called community activist."

"Yes, Sir, that's correct. And, unfortunately at best, I think Krawley is a well-intentioned loudmouth. He has a solid alibi for his whereabouts that day and evening."

"And now he has a burgeoning television career. Why do people love the camera so much?"

"Yes. He'll have his own talk show soon."

Styles enjoyed Vuong's understated humor.

"But what about an accomplice, maybe a member of his neighborhood watch group?"

"We've interviewed everyone on his email list and whoever contributed funds or attended a rally."

"Funds? They are a nonprofit?"

"In their dreams. They weren't well organized and when they were snubbed things pretty much fell apart."

"So not enough money to....?" Styles felt foolish even fielding the subject.

"Hire somebody to do the deed?"

"Well, in a city that's still recovering from Katrina, even Krawley's paltry treasury chest might have attracted a taker. But, nah, there's no indication."

"A rogue member, taking things into his own hands?"

Vuong shook his head, not so much dismissive as sympathetic to his superior's grasping at straws.

"That's the problem. A rogue player comes out of nowhere, damage is done, but nobody saw it coming and he leaves no trail."

"He. The murderer would have to be a *he,* I suppose. Not a mother of a victim, or—"

Negative. No need for Vuong to remind Styles that Peabody was an imposing figure who regularly lifted weights in his spare bedroom.

"Is there nothing fresh?"

Vuong leaned forward and opened a folder.

"A woman came forward this morning. On the afternoon of the murder, her daughter was approached after school by a man in a car—a green car just like Peabody's. But the kid said the man wore glasses and a floppy hat, had blond hair. Peabody's hair was brown."

"Huh."

"But the girl said he was a big guy, so... "

"Disguise?"

"Yeah, detectives found wigs in a closet when they searched the guy's house. But here's the odd thing. The man suddenly drove away and another man, also in a car, a black car, spoke to the girl and said he was a police officer."

Styles looked up from his files. "What? Somebody from Probation?"

"We spoke to them. Nobody was trailing Peabody from their department."

"But did the guy who claimed to be a cop—"

"He didn't fit Krawley's description. So we may have another player in the field."

Styles bit his lip and sat back, quiet for a moment. He didn't like the heat he was catching from Chief Hendricks, but it wasn't the first time he'd been pressured for results.

"Thinking out loud," he began.

"Please."

"The cuff marks on the wrists ... could they have been caused by handcuffs similar to police issue?"

"Yeah, possibly," Vuong said. "They were probably metal cuffs, not plastic zip ties, because of the way they cut into his skin and the width of the wounds."

"Are you telling me our killer may be someone inside the law enforcement community? Maybe an ex-cop who dealt with child molesters, maybe had a traumatic event as a kid?"

"We can't rule it out, Sir, especially with this new witness, the mom with the little girl."

"And it might answer why the perpetrator called 911. I mean, who does that? Who else would know we'd send a car when no one responded? It's like he wanted the body to be discovered."

"Good point."

"But *why?*"

The question hung in the air until Styles asked for suggestions.

Vuong explained that the crime lab had lifted some prints and partial prints but most likely the perpetrator wiped down everything before escaping. And while DNA was recovered from under the victim's fingernails, no matches had been made thus far in the DNA bank. Finally, the coroner's report suggested that the way the cuffs dug into the victim's wrist, the murderer probably pulled the victim around while cuffed.

"Sadistic bastard," Styles said.

"Yeah. Speaking of which, the victim's mother identified the body at the morgue, and oh, what a piece of work she is. Is there a statute of limitations on lousy parenting?"

"God. Imagine that. Anything else?"

Vuong quickly scanned his notes, bobbing his head as he checked off incidentals.

"Obviously, we are checking Peabody's cell phone to see who he called, texted, and so forth.

And to confirm, I'll have the DNA tested against police samples to make sure our perp isn't an active-duty officer. That'll be easy. Everybody on staff is now required to provide DNA."

"Pray to God we don't get a match."

The two men rose, nodded, and exchanged knowing smiles. Styles was first to the door.

"Oh, one more thing," Vuong said. "Peabody's computer had a lot of kiddie porn stuff, and other sites we'll check out. No surprise there. But there was one portal we still can't figure out how to open."

"Well, what are techies for?"

Vuong chuckled. "Yeah. But the funny thing is, remember the Charles Stevens case?"

"Who could forget?"

"The same kind of portal is on his laptop, too."

Chapter 15

The long, boring nights as inventory officer gave Jeremy way too much opportunity to worry and conjecture. Each time he heard heavy footsteps in the hallway, he was sure a team of homicide detectives was coming to arrest him. He assumed his days were numbered.

His respite from the anxiety was picking up Kayla after finishing work at dawn. His routine was to have a satisfying breakfast at a nearby restaurant, scour the local newspapers, and then head to his former home.

He parked at the curb and approached the house. Before he could knock, Sandy opened the door.

"You look like shit," she said.

"Ah, thanks. Nice to see you, too."

"I'm serious. Your eyes are all bloodshot and—" He tensed as she leaned in and scrutinized his neck, which was on the mend and mostly hidden under a high, buttoned collar. "What the hell happened to your neck? Are you sure you're okay to drive?"

"I made it this far, didn't I? I'm fine. I work for a living, remember? Graveyard shift."

"Daddy!"

Kayla appeared, her backpack snug against her small body. Her sweet sound, her joy at seeing him always chased away the gloom.

"Hey, love bug, let's go or we'll be late."

Jeremy took his daughter's hand, nodded to Sandy, and headed toward the street.

"New car?"

Jeremy stopped. "Huh?"

"Weren't you driving a black Chevy?"

He wanted to slap his forehead. *Stupid.* His choice of the eye-popping, cherry red Chrysler was too dramatic. It shouted, "Hey, look at me!" Yet he had been uncomfortable with muted grays or shades of blue, because they fit within the spectrum of his previous ride. He couldn't risk familiarity with witness testimony.

"Oh. Got a better weekly rate on this one."

"Looks nice for an *American* car. When are you going to buy something?"

His weary smile was effortless. "When I have time. Renting is easier for now."

In the car, Kayla was talkative. She pulled drawings from her backpack to show Jeremy, and complained about the loud boys in the back of the classroom. Daddy nodded, grinned, kept his eyes on the road, and then made the mistake of asking about the weekend.

"Oh, it's so cool." She bounced under the constraints of her seatbelt.

"Cool? What's cool?"

"Mommy and Mr. Ray are taking me to the beach."

"Who?"

"Mr. Ray. Mommy's boyfriend, silly."

Jeremy felt his insides crash like an avalanche. The pain of loss rumbled so deeply he almost pulled to the side of the road to put his head down. It took all the will he could muster to pretend he knew.

"Oh, right. That's nice."

"It will be so much fun. I like Mr. Ray. He's funny. It's like having two daddies."

Questions did back flips in his brain. *What does he look like? His full name, please? What does he do for a living? What kind of car does he drive? How long has Mommy been seeing him?*

The day Jeremy's transfer to detective was revoked, he'd visited Sandy in the furniture store. He'd asked for a chance to make things better, but she exploded, "I don't love you anymore! Can't you understand that?"

He did now. Sandy may have already had another man in mind or didn't waste any time finding someone.

Kayla's school appeared before Jeremy could find a diplomatic way to explain why he had no intention of sharing his daddy status with Mr. Ray. He jumped out of the car and kneeled to hug his little girl as though it was the last time. As Kayla ran toward a group of giggling girls, fear and then acceptance ravaged him. If he had to spend the rest of his life in prison, maybe it was good that his daughter had an alternate dad.

Chapter 16

As he drove to his apartment, Jeremy summed up what he had just learned. Clearly, Sandy had moved on, and likely without hesitation or remorse. Now it was his turn. He couldn't just stand still, paralyzed by the fear of arrest. Sitting at a long stop light, staring at nothing, he considered his options and made up his mind: *I'll put away as many predators as possible before I'm discovered.*

After a long stretch of broken sleep—spooked by voices in the apartment building and street chaos—he awoke in the early afternoon and went to his war room. The first order of business was to review the police report he created after the Peabody incident. He needed to learn from the mistakes he'd made after entering the man's home. Revisiting his notes was also a way of remaining objective and clear-headed in the event of an arrest. In a sense, the report was his defense for pulling the trigger.

But now Jeremy realized there was a darker reason for keeping record of his actions: he might not survive the desperate violence of another Richard Peabody; or for that matter, the gnawing anxiety that was rotting his nerves and conscience. By leaving behind as much information as possible, the police and his family would understand his choices.

Jeremy made a fresh list of priorities and for the next week searched for the sick overachievers. When he didn't make contact within a few days, he moved to the next name.

Over a week later, his red Chrysler was parked under a generous cluster of deciduous trees on Cleveland Avenue near the home of convicted child molester David McDougal. The vantage point provided shade and a clear view of the two-story, double-occupancy, faded teal clapboard home.

He opened a briefcase and studied criminal reports while remaining aware of movement in his peripheral vision. He hoped the activity would make him look like a businessman who had merely pulled to the curb to catch up on a little work, rather than a cop staking out a location.

The boredom was getting to him, though. He considered moving on to his next pervert but reminded himself this was only his second day on this watch.

Several hours later, a thin, white male exited the residence and hopped into a white Sport Utility Vehicle. Jeremy glanced down at the file photo and knew he had a match.

Jeremy followed at a distance and was eventually led to City Park where a school picnic was in full swing. *Here we go again*, Jeremy thought. *All the world is a playground for a pervert.*

McDougal circled the park area, sometimes slowing to a crawl. He appeared to be searching for a victim—maybe a loner kid who could be lured further away from the crowd. No chance. School staff and chaperones kept their flock in a tight circle.

Next McDougal drove to a movie theater and looped his way through the parking lot—up and down, back and forth—but no prey was visible.

Finally, the perv traveled to a supermarket and parked in the lot but didn't get out of his car. A short time later, a woman parked nearby and got out of her car with two young children. Jeremy watched as McDougal casually followed the family into the store, grabbing a shopping cart for cover.

Jeremy quickly caught up, lifted a hand basket from a stack, and mimicked McDougal who tossed a few items—sweets, mostly—into his cart. It was evident that he was stalking the hen and her chicks. When the little boy lagged behind, that was McDougal's queue to hold up a package of cookies and tear it open.

"Do you like these?" he asked, popping one into his mouth.

The boy wasn't sure if he should speak to a stranger. He looked down the aisle for his mother, but she had rounded the end and disappeared.

Still chewing, McDougal held out his hand and said, "C'mon, let's go find your mom and ask her if you can have a few. God, these are good."

Near the opposite end of the aisle, Jeremy was amazed by what he was witnessing: the solicitation was so bold, in a public place, where others might see and remember. He kept his distance, pretending to be a frugal shopper, and then tensed when the boy appeared ready to accept McDougal's hand. *Run, kid. Run.*

"I better go ask my Mom"

The boy turned and briskly walked away. McDougal dumped the cookies into the cart and appeared to curse. He looked up and down the aisle, eyes wide, as if to weigh his options. Jeremy made a move to leave the aisle, as if indifferent to the little drama. Next he heard the fast clicking of heels coming toward him. McDougal had abandoned his groceries and was walking hurriedly toward the exit. Jeremy set down his basket and followed.

The perv drove erratically, hastily taking several turns, one on a red light, before finding Scott Street, which intersected with Cleveland Avenue.

Jeremy let the man park his SUV and enter his dwelling before parking his own vehicle down the block. He checked his 1943 Colt revolver on his ankle before exiting the car, striding to the porch and softly climbing the wooden stairs where two entrances awaited. He didn't want to knock and possibly make his presence known to the neighbor, so he tried the button on the frame and heard it chime inside.

McDougal's mousy nose sniffed through the barely opened door. "What?"

"David McDougal?"

"Maybe. Who wants to know?"

Jeremy held up his police badge. "We need to talk. *Now.*"

The man, who, for a time had seemed so at ease in the grocery store, was now unable to control the nervous twitches that jumped between his lips and eyes.

"What's this about?" he asked.

"Why didn't you finish your grocery shopping?"

A mixture of fear and outrage washed across his face. "I haven't done anything," he complained, as the door opened wider.

Up close, Jeremy noticed pockmarks that were deeper and much more prominent than McDougal's mug shot suggested. They stirred a memory from somewhere.

"I disagree. You didn't pay for your cookies. Were you unhappy with the product you sampled?"

"Oh, yeah, now I see. Trying to get me on some bullshit charge—"

"Did you or did you not pay for the—"

"I don't have to answer your—!"

McDougal tried to slam the door but Jeremy had already imposed his body into the open space, forcing the perv to stand back.

"I can come in and talk, or you can make some more noise so all your neighbors wonder what's going on. What's it going to be?"

McDougal's face looked like a slot machine at a casino as his eyes shifted and tumbled. In a burst of frustration, he threw up his hands and walked away.

"All right, come in."

Jeremy closed the door behind him. "Who else is in the house?"

"Nobody."

"Live alone?"

"I'm going to call my probation officer!"

"Okay."

Jeremy watched McDougal paw a phone from a table, then hesitate. Saliva dripped from the open corner of his mouth.

"You can't remember the number, can you? You didn't bother putting it in your contacts. When's the last time you had a little chat with—"

He jabbed the air with the cell. "You know, you know, I mean, I'm really upset because you have no goddamn right following me around and harassing me and—"

Hyperventilating, McDougal put his hand against the wall to steady himself. The pockmarks turned blood red.

Jeremy waited, then asked, "That little boy in the store ... didn't want the cookies, did he?"

The child molester's face turned pale.

"Where's your computer, Mr. McDougal?"

"Now wait a minute...."

"Probably in your bedroom, right?"

"It's in the shop. It crashed, okay?"

Jeremy let his shoulders droop and looked away as if deeply disappointed.

"Dude... and don't tell me I need a warrant. According to probation—you can check the next time you call in—police have a right to view the contents and viewing history on the PC or Mac of a registered sex offender." He raised his ID again. "Got it?"

"Upstairs."

"Lead the way."

The staircase gave Jeremy a bird's eye view of the orderly downstairs living area. The second floor was equally well-appointed and tastefully decorated. Neat and clean, everything in its rightful place, like somebody's mother lived there.

McDougal's bedroom pulsated with another vibe. The man-boy cave exhibited an erotic nude male sculpture and fine black-and-white framed photography that blatantly expressed his sexual predilections.

"I'm an art collector."

"I can see," Jeremy said.

"Is that a crime?"

"Time will tell."

Jeremy reached for his handcuffs and discovered that he'd left them in his car. *Damn it!* So he stood at an angle over the computer and kept a close eye on McDougal, who paced and then leaned against an antique chest of drawers.

The search history revealed numerous boy porn sites and desktop files with bland titles were stuffed with imagery, exotic man-boy fiction and links. He looked over at McDougal, placed one foot on the chair in front of the desk and leaned in for deeper examination. He was aware that the new position exposed his ankle holster and Colt .38.

On the PC screen he spotted a familiar portal. *Aha.*

Boing. That annoying sound when a command was denied rang out. Jeremy tried to hack his way in but got nowhere. Each attempt was met with "Wrong user name or password. Please try again."

"What's the password for this?"

"I don't remember."

"Don't bullshit me or we'll be here all night. Is that what you want?"

"I want you to leave."

"Not until I've—"

"It's not fair! I'm not hurting anyone. Subscription sites aren't illegal, are they? What kind of porn do *you* like, Mr. Fucking Policeman?"

Jeremy stood and stared at McDougal, taking note of the near-hysterical response. It was too familiar. *What's with these guys,* he thought. *What sets them off like that? Stevens, Peabody, and now this asshole.*

"Are you going to cooperate or do I need to place you under arrest?"

"For what?"

"For starters, trying to entice a minor in a grocery store."

McDougal placed his hands on his head and his eyes began to water, "This can't be happening."

"Just calm down and give the damn password."

McDougal placed his arms on the top of the chest, his head resting on his wrists, He blurted, "Emperor!" Then in a meek, beaten voice he added, "Everything uppercase, except the first and last letters, then one underscore and the letter 'X'."

"Uppercase?"

"Yes," he choked, now weeping, "and ... and ... an exclamation point. But it will change next week."

"Huh?"

"Only the symbols after eMPEROr. Precautions."

Jeremy hit enter and watched the screen open up like the Kingdom of Oz with an emerald green smoke screen that soon dissipated and revealed two app choices:

Rehabilitation for men convicted of child abuse
ENTER

Afraid he would forget the password in his excitement, Jeremy tossed a pen and pad of pink Post-It notes, to McDougal, barely glancing towards him. "Write it down for me."

"What?"

"The password! Then bring it to me."

Jeremy clicked the rehab link and was directed to what appeared to be a foreign-based website.

"Shrewd. Very shrewd," he said to himself. "Man oh man… "

"What. *What?*"

"Deterrence. These jokers know stateside police won't bother jumping through hoops to investigate a site that's overseas. Even big-city budgets can't cover the man-hour cost to chase garbage through places like Nigeria or Russia. But me? I've got all the time in the world."

He heard whimpering, but was unconcerned as he tapped the "View" app. When it didn't oblige, he tried several more times, unaware that McDougal's right hand had slid down and began to open one of the smaller top drawers of the chest.

"Hey, why won't this open? And bring me the password."

When McDougal didn't reply, Jeremy turned and discovered a Sig Sauer handgun pointed in his face.

"You see, the thing is, I gave you a chance," McDougal said, now cold and still, both trembling hands gripping the weapon. "You could have left me alone. But you're like all the others, aren't you? Cold, inflexible."

"David, listen—"

"Don't 'David' me. I die or you die."

"That's ridiculous. Why do you have to—"

"Get away from the computer. Move!"

Jeremy had no choice but to back deeper into the room, away from the door. McDougal held the gun with one hand and began tapping the keyboard and moving the mouse with the other. "I should have deleted it. Sloppy. Precautions, David! Precautions."

"So, are you here about the boy?"

"What boy?"

"Don't play dumb with me."

Benito Jackson. It all came tumbling into place—the faint, nagging memories, breaking news. He shook his head, incredulous.

"Couple weeks ago. The Amber alert was you. Pockmarked face, white, late-model SUV. But the Jackson boy was never found."

McDougal turned pale.

"Where is he, David?"

The perv shook his head. "They'll torture me."

"Who will?"

"None of your business."

"Just tell me where Benito Jackson is and—"

"I've already turned him over."

"What do you mean? To who?"

"He's gone, for crying out loud! Are you dense? Are you so fucking stupid—"

"He's dead. Is that what you're saying?"

McDougal's expression was fervent and wide-eyed. "He's immortal. He is with the Emperor."

"Who is that?"

"You don't want to find out."

"Maybe I do."

"You will need to go to Russia."

"How does a kid get taken to Russia?"

"With the transport team."

"How the hell does that—"

McDougal jabbed the Sig Sauer at Jeremy. "Take the holster off of your ankle and slide your gun over here. Now."

Jeremy considered his options but found them lacking. He unholstered his gun and kicked it across the floor, only to realize he'd been duped. McDougal scooped up the Colt, then threw his own weapon onto the bed.

"Mine doesn't actually have bullets—it's kind of a sex toy—kinky, huh? But I bet yours is loaded. You're pretty fucking stupid for letting me open a drawer."

"I didn't come here for a shootout."

"No shootout. I'm the only one with the gun now."

"Listen, David, don't do anything stupid. Please."

"Shut up, I need to think. Just shut up!"

McDougal began taking deep breaths. His hands were trembling with his finger on the trigger. Tears now flowing down his face.

Jeremy promised to walk away and not report the incident; then promised leniency for his help in finding the boy. His voice rose to a hysterical pitch as he cautioned against homicide when, by comparison, a prison sentence for downloading kiddie porn would seem like a long weekend at a health resort.

The mention of incarceration was a mistake.

"You still don't get it, do you?"

McDougal began shaking uncontrollably, his composure deteriorating fast. Jeremy reached his hands out, gesturing, reasoning, begging, then reflexively pulled them back to protect his face from being blown away. He could only imagine the headlines: "Cop Killed by His Own Weapon."

"I am not going to prison! *Ever*. Not for that!" He jerked the Colt toward the computer.

"Emperor? It's just more porn, right?"

More disgust twisted McDougal's face. "The film, you idiot! The *film*!"

"Just calm down. I don't know what you mean."

McDougal shook his head. "Fucking Cops."

"David, please put the gun down. Please."

"Shut up. Just shut the fuck up! My head...fuck." McDougal raised the gun to his head.

"Wait! Just tell me what's going on. I can help you, if—"

This time someone would hear. It was only one blast, but it rang and then echoed like a bell tower, or so it seemed to Jeremy who was knocked to the floor, his ears aching from the toll.

Oh, shit! Oh, shit!

A good cop, a Joe Doode, would have noticed the subtle change in tone and intent. In an instant, McDougal's facial expressions had gone from despair to sublime arousal as he quickly swallowed the barrel of the gun and pulled the trigger.

Jeremy didn't need to look—he knew the man was dead. He fell to his knees and began to curse himself.

"No, no, no. Jesus Christ."

He carried on, until loud knocking at the front door interrupted. When he heard the woman's voice, his teeth began to chatter.

"David? David, are you all right? Open this door, David!"

Chapter 17

The body had fallen against the chest of drawers. Brain tissue, blood, and fragments of skull dripped down the aged, oiled face of the antique sculpture.

"David? David!" The woman's voice was shrill.

Jeremy crab-walked to McDougal and discovered the body had tilted and then fallen on top of the Colt .38. He had no choice but to lift the dead weight bare-handed and retrieve the gun. He stuffed it into the waist of his pants, then pulled out his shirttails.

"David, if you don't come to the door—"

"Jesus, lady," Jeremy growled. "He's not coming to the fucking—"

He opened the top drawer, fingered a pair of boxer shorts, wiped the handle, and moved to the PC.

"We have an agreement, David. If you don't speak to me right now, I'm going to get the key you gave me and I'm calling the police. Do you hear me?"

Go on, do it, lady. Jesus.

He heard a frustrated shriek, clumsy footsteps pounding the wooden porch, and the squeaky opening of the opposite door.

Good, Jeremy thought. If she dialed the police, he wouldn't have to repeat the Peabody 911 fiasco.

The keyboard needed the most scrubbing. As he hastily performed that task he tried to recall everything else he might have touched. Wireless mouse, desktop, chair and—*oh, fuck.*

He spun and searched the floor before reaching under the bed. The pen and pad of Post-Its he'd tossed to McDougal would be smeared with his DNA. But where was it?

"I'm coming in, David. You hear me?"

Shit, shit, shit!

Jeremy dashed down the staircase as he heard the key slip into the front door lock and turn the bolt. Sprinting toward the back of the first floor he found a TV room with a La-Z-Boy chair, and behind the drapes, a sliding glass door. With McDougal's boxers covering both hands, he flipped the lock and yanked the handle sideways. It refused to budge.

"David?"

The lady was inside and making noise with a clumsy search, likely intended to warn David that she had arrived. *We have an agreement.* Jeremy wished he could put her under an interrogation lamp and squeeze her for everything she knew about her neighbor.

He yanked the slider again; still no movement.

"David, are you back there?"

Jeremy flipped back the drapes seeking a hiding place and discovered a broom pole lodged in the bottom track rail between the door and frame. He pried it free and opened the door. A breeze caused the drapes to billow as he slipped through the narrow opening and found himself on a stone patio.

"I'm coming upstairs, David. Okay?"

God, she must be dense, Jeremy thought. *When will you realize the fucker is—*

The scream startled him, even though he had braced for it. The lady's voice curdled, whooped, and then abruptly went mute. Jeremy assumed she had vomited.

Across the backyard, he saw the backs of homes on the other side of the residential block. He took a step toward it then froze as fast, heavy stomping made the staircase inside the house creak. Footfalls also thundered on the front porch and Jeremy knew the lady was flying back to the safety of her own home. He didn't wait to hear her scream into the phone, "Oh my god, oh my god, please send help! My neighbor shot himself!" He made his move.

Before he made it a short distance to the house behind McDougal's, he heard sirens. Another neighbor must have already called. He pulled the hood of his jacket over his head, took a quick turn, and found solace on the sidewalk on the opposite side of the block.

As he reached his Chrysler, he was fairly certain that the emergency unit and at least one police cruiser had reached the home because the sirens mimicked the lady's voice—an aching swoop and then silence.

As he turned the ignition he searched his surroundings, looking for witnesses to his escape. He saw no one on the street as he began to roll but that didn't mean he hadn't been spotted. Stupid cherry red car.

Distracted, his mind reeling, Jeremy yelped when two teen-aged boys on bikes swept past his windshield. He stomped on his brake, screeching his tires. They sneered and shouted.

"Watch where you're driving, fuckhead!"

He slowly crossed the intersection, rolled down a window and heard more sirens. They marred an otherwise pretty, sunny day. Too sunny. He wished someone would turn off the lights so that he could disappear.

He shouted at nothing and pounded the steering wheel.

Why didn't you take his gun!

Then with equal vehemence, he realized it didn't matter.

Once police realized the firearm left at the scene had not been fired because it was unloaded, they would know a second gun was involved. An intruder's gun. That's when they would classify the crime as a homicide.

He parked in a dark corner of his building's garage and took the stairs to his apartment. He stripped and turned on the shower. After toweling off he wiped down his Colt, unlocked the war room, and turned on his police radio.

The voice on the radio squawked, "Signal Thirty, Signal Thirty." They were all over it. Detectives and crime lab techies would search the premises and if they could locate the bullet and analyze it, they would determine the same gun had been used in the deaths of two child molesters. That would mean Inventory Officer Jeremy Porter would be wanted for not one, but two murders, though he had not yet been identified.

Barefoot and shirtless, he raced to the kitchen, still sweating from the hot shower. He ripped open a can of beer, then another. He gulped them both, hoping they would steady his hands as he sat down in the war room to write his police report. It was the only way to calm his mind and regain his focus. *Every fucking detail of McDougal's activity. Write it down. Now, Porter.*

The length of his reportage kept growing, page after page. When he finally had exhausted his memory, he rose to grab another beer then stopped and fell back on the chair. *What was it—write it down—what was it?*

He jotted the word:

Emperor

Gratefully, the suffix quickly bubbled to the surface:

_X!

The next challenge was upper/lowercase:

Emperor

No. Doesn't look right. Imagine it scrawled on the Post-It. He didn't give me the fucking—

That's when he realized the spelling was wrong. He corrected it, sat back, and tried to reconstruct the conversation, the defeated timbre of McDougal's voice.

eMPERor

Yes. No. McPervert said first and last letters.

eMPEROr

Bingo.

eMPEROr_X!

Got it!

Victorious, he stood, growling and shaking his fists at the ceiling. He stopped and flopped back into the chair when he recalled McDougal saying the password would change next week. That only gave him a few days to locate the website. The Deep Web, he assumed, where you don't just type in a name and dot com. And—

Wait a minute. I can't access a child porn site on my own computer. How would it look?

Jeremy believed he would eventually be found out. As a result, police would confiscate and explore his laptop. Thanks to his lousy reputation, they might make a case that he was a member of the club: *Powder Puff the Pervert.*

The local library had computers. And there was the Internet Café on Toulouse Street in the French Quarter, where he could buy a week's pass. He knew the coffee would be good. Or maybe he would just hack into Sgt. Tanner's computer.

Chapter 18

"New car?"

The question shot across the well-lit parking area and felt like an accusation to the jittery, defensive Jeremy. He spun before closing the door of his gray Toyota Corolla.

"What?"

"Hey, hey, Porter, it was just a question."

Ofc. Luisa Olvera approached, eyes sparkling like stars in the night sky. Since they'd met as recruits, he'd always thought she was pretty. But he was a married man and didn't dare ask about her status, although he was tempted to visit her Facebook page. Now, an hour before roll call, her long, dark hair not yet twisted into a tight bun, she was wearing a simple print skirt, blouse, and canvas sneakers. She was the embodiment of femininity. He wanted to swoon into her arms and babble all of his secrets.

Perhaps that said more about his mental state than his libido. He couldn't nap, food was unappetizing, and reels of bloody cinema—a double feature—incessantly arrested his mind.

"Hey, what are you doing here?"

"Nice to see you again, too."

"No, I meant—"

"I'm teasing. I asked for a transfer. This is my first night."

"Why Second District?"

"Well ... you remember Joe Doode, right, my FTO? When he left police work... I don't know. Nothing felt the same. He taught me so much."

"Familiarity breeds contentment."

"Or resentment," she charmed with a smile, nodding toward Jeremy's Toyota. "New?"

"Oh, no. No, it's just, uh... " His hand was twirling.

"A car?"

He grinned. "A rental, actually."

"What happened to the Aston Martin?"

Jeremy cringed. Luisa was the one sensible person he'd met that first day of training. She couldn't believe he'd tossed his car keys to Brock. If only he hadn't.

Luisa apologized. "Sorry. That sounded mean."

"No, fair question." He closed his door and walked with Olvera toward the district building. He wondered how much he should say. *Something,* he thought. *Uncork the bottle.* "Sandy and I ... my wife ... we're divorcing. So...."

"Oh. I'm sorry."

"I haven't said anything. You know, it's ... it's like a bad dream. I'm still trying to wake up. Or, I mean, I woke up. She has a new guy."

As they walked in silence, he felt the hurt and anxiety rise in him like flood waters and feared he could no longer contain them. Sandy's demand that he move out was painful enough—to be replaced so quickly only revealed that the relationship may have ended sooner than he had thought. Now add two dead bodies and the ineptitude responsible for the mayhem, he seemed to be fulfilling her low opinion of him. If only he felt loved and respected. Would any of this have happened?

Luisa sensed his turmoil. She patted his upper back, and let her soft, caring hand linger. The touch uncorked him. He turned away to hide the rush of tears, but Olvera grabbed his upper arm and he swung back, like a door on hinges, wrapped his limbs around her and buried his face in her shoulder. If she was alarmed, nothing in her body betrayed it. She held his embrace by rising on her tiptoes, whispering, "I'm really sorry."

* * *

At roll call, Jeremy stood next to Leslie Scott, afraid to be within an arm's length of Olvera. The memory of her breasts pressing against him, her tender hands and cooing lips lit fires in him. He shook his head clear so that he could concentrate on everything Lieutenant Bayless said, though only one item in his lengthy list of messages truly mattered.

"Signal 30 victim was a white male, David McDougal, age forty-four, residing in the 4500 block of Cleveland Avenue. Victim died from a single gunshot wound to his head."

When Bayless ended by saying McDougal was a convicted child molester, humor and laughter erupted among platoon members.

Officer Scott used the noise to share information to the platoon. "They thought it was a suicide at first. The lady next door said he'd threatened suicide on several occasions. Then they realized the gun at the scene hadn't been fired."

Jeremy agonized about Scott's comments. He glanced at Olvera and was pleased that she was looking his way. They nodded, professional, but their eyes revealed something more personal. He turned back focusing his attention on Scott.

"So the investigating officer called in homicide, crime lab, all that. I think they are getting a little nervous about this. Two convicted child abusers murdered inside of a month. Is it a coincidence or something else?"

There was a silent pause among the group. Jeremy wondered if they could hear his heart pounding, and see his nervous twitch and locked jaw. He did his best to keep a poker face.

Bayless finished his comments and excused the platoon, giving Jeremy a moment to recover. He stole a glance at Olvera who had hooked up with her patrol partner, and then returned to Scott.

"Hey, how did you get that additional info from the uh ... from the ..." Jeremy couldn't bring himself to use the word.

"Homicide?"

"Yeah."

"I called the detective earlier. Ever since I made the Peabody murder scene, I have developed a strong interest in these cases. You know, I just want to learn as much as I can."

"So, no identity on the suspect?"

"Don't think so."

"The lady they interviewed, she didn't see anyone?

"No but they said she practically fainted during the detective's Q and A."

"How come?"

"She realized the killer may have been in the house when she was looking for McDougal."

"Why do they think that?"

"Sliding glass door in the back of the house, it was open a crack."

"So?"

"So the lady said the victim always had a dowel in the floor track railing. You know, to stop break-ins?"

"Oh."

"But it was on the carpet under the drapes. It had to have been removed by somebody from inside."

"Maybe McDougal let somebody in."

"Back door?"

"A male prostitute he didn't want anyone to see?"

Scott brooded. "How did you know he was gay?"

Flustered, caught dead to rights, Jeremy groped for words, excuses, a magic wand to make everything disappear.

"Is he? *Really?* Actually, what I meant was...."

Yeah, what did you mean, dumbass?

Jeremy yearned to share with Scott all that he had learned in recent weeks. His hours poring over dossiers and crime reports had made him a walking encyclopedia of traits and patterns, though not necessarily a good cop. He had begun to believe he could spot a child molester in a line up or at a crowded social event. It was like a sixth sense.

"I meant ... the day I was in Child Abuse, Sergeant Tanner mentioned that some of these guys are ... charismatic? So maybe he preferred to sneak someone in through the back door?"

It was a lie. But it seemed to work.

"I suppose. Anything's possible."

The hallway was still bustling as platoon members caught up with buddies or reviewed orders for the night. Jeremy had racked up so many blunders, he had an urge to run to his inventory closet and hide. Yet Scott wasn't ready to part.

"So maybe McDougal lets somebody in, a teenager, young adult ... we don't know ... but somebody he doesn't realize is ... gunning for him."

Jeremy was stunned. "What do you mean?"

Scott kept his voice low.

"Look, I'm going to tell you something ... probably everybody's going to know this by the end of the week. But hold it close for now, okay?"

"How do you know all this stuff?"

Scott didn't particularly like interruptions. He was methodical, needed time to work through complexity one step at a time. It seemed to Jeremy that his friend grappled with the question and then decided to ignore it—for now.

"Listen, just before roll call, ballistics confirmed that the bullet found in McDougal's skull matches the bullet that killed Peabody. So the Homicide Division now believes—"

Jeremy felt strangled by the tension. What else had Homicide discovered? And how soon would he be arrested?

"—that we have a person out there who has a vendetta against child molesters. They're calling him the Pervert Vigilante."

Chapter 19

As he drove through the district, Leslie Scott found it difficult to keep his mind on his patrol duties. The evening had been momentous, though the day had not started out so grand. To his surprise, he'd received a call from headquarters asking him to meet with the supervisor of homicide investigations long before roll call.

"Is there a problem?" he had asked the administrative secretary.

"I was told to call you. That's all I know, Officer."

"I'll be there. Thank you, Ma'am."

The ambush happened about 5:30 p.m. just as he was about to enter the Homicide office. An officer seemed to be waiting for him. "Leslie Scott?"

"Yes."

"Follow me, please."

"But I was told to—"

"No worries. Homicide has been notified that Commander Watts would like a word with you first."

Confused and growing concerned, Scott followed the officer into a nearby conference room where they found Watts, an African-American man pushing sixty. The gray in his temples did not in any way diminish the energy and fortitude he exuded.

"Officer Scott." They shook hands. "I'm Jeffrey Watts. I apologize for the confusion."

"Yes, I must admit I am a little confused."

"I would have brought you to my office. But to mesh schedules and make these changes more fluid—"

"Changes, Sir?"

"Please. Sit."

The table was far too big for the two of them. The accompanying officer remained on his feet.

"This is your last shift as a night patrol officer."

"Oh?"

"You look worried."

"Surprised. Has my work in any way been unsatisfactory?"

Watts suppressed a laugh, a glint in his eyes. "No, no. I've simply come to the conclusion that night shift is no place to waste a man of your talent and dedication. They're a bit short tonight, so I need you to go out one more time. Then you'll take a couple days to reorient your body clock before joining the Special Operations Division."

Scott was humbled and elated. SOD was the premiere assignment in the NOPD. It was the unspoken goal he had worked for since being recruited.

"I'm ... I'm grateful. Overjoyed. Thank you, Sir."

"It's our gain. Your military record is exemplary and you've brought that same mentality and work ethic to your patrol responsibilities. You'll be trained to join SWAT and help us with all the toughest, most critical maneuvers in New Orleans. Congratulations."

Scott was allowed to ask a few questions before Watts apologized and cut the meeting short.

"A lot is happening quickly, Leslie. So I need you to follow my assistant back to Homicide. But I promise we'll have another chance to speak.

"Thank you, Sir."

Watts' assistant smiled but kept to himself as he led the way back down the hall. He opened the door for Scott and spoke to the secretary.

"Officer Scott is ready to see Lieutenant Styles."

The woman who had called earlier rose from her chair and wagged a finger at Scott.

"Well, well. And here you thought it was bad news."

They shared a laugh before Scott was ushered into the office of Lieutenant Styles, where he was surprised to be greeted by ten other members of the department.

"Thanks for coming in early, Officer," Styles said. "Congratulations."

The others apparently all knew what had just happened. They applauded lightly and offered nods of approval. Scott believed he might be dreaming.

"I know you have a long night ahead of you, but Commander Watts has agreed to let you join the special task force I've assembled to look into two recent homicides of sex offenders. Detective Gikas recommended you. Said you did great work at the scene of the Peabody murder."

Gikas nodded from across the room.

"I'm honored. Thank you, Sir. And thank you, Detective."

Others in attendance included detectives and SOD members, male and female. Also present was Sgt. Greg Tanner of Child Abuse, who handed out packets of information as Styles continued his comments.

"I've invited Sergeant Tanner to sit in, to guide us with his knowledge of this population. But he has a department to run and he's short-handed, so all of you will be doing the heavy lifting. Scott, do you know Detective Vuong?"

"No." Scott reached across two other officers to shake hands. "Good to meet you, Detective."

"Appreciate your help."

"Calvin has agreed to lead this group and report to me as needed. Now, everybody take a look inside your packets."

The lieutenant warned that the information was strictly confidential and not to be shared with media or even other officers in the department.

"Folks, there has to be other witnesses out there. Both killings happened fairly early in the day, though rain may have provided cover for the Peabody escape. We're going to canvass these locations again. Ask questions. Don't be deterred if somebody says, they already told police everything they know."

Skimming through the data, Leslie Scott raised his hand.

"Yes, Scott."

"Wasn't the McDougal shooting ... I mean, I heard the McDougal shooting was determined as unclassified."

He felt a rustling in the room. Obviously, the others knew something he did not.

"Good question. But before I answer, I must stress once again that everything we share here is confidential. Got it?"

"Of course."

"Ballistics has just informed us that the same gun was used in both shootings. More importantly, the lab came back and confirmed the suspect's DNA was found at both scenes. So as far as I'm concerned, we have a serial killer out there."

Vuong added, "We're calling him the Pervert Vigilante."

Nodding, Styles went on. "Our job is to find the guy and book him. We'll let the district attorney sort out the rest."

Scott felt other questions percolating, lots of them. He was reluctant to pester the lieutenant, so he turned to Vuong.

"Excuse me, Detective. I know I'm the new guy."

"That's okay."

"Well, I've been studying these incidents and—"

"Folks, listen," Styles said sternly. "We've got to get out in front of this thing before a third incident. Let's not waste time. We need to move forward now."

Scott apologized, embarrassed. He noticed Gikas grinning.

"I don't mind questions," Styles said. "But listen first, and let the others in this room bring you up to speed."

"Yes, Sir."

The lieutenant addressed the entire room. "And realize there's more at play here than meets the eye. First, when the ballistics info becomes public—and it will, sooner than we want—the department will catch heat. Lots of heat. Social media will light up like fireworks and newscasters local and national will nail us to the cross. Suddenly, we got panic in certain neighborhoods. See what I'm saying?"

Nods, quips rippled through the room. A peremptive strike was the best plan. Vuong sprinkled a little more gas on the flame.

"Keep in mind, the Peabody thing ... we still have lots of unanswered questions. It's a strange crime scene. We still don't quite know what happened, I mean *how* it happened."

"With a gun." The voice was Gikas' and the cynicism was thick.

"Also, the kick marks on the wall... " Scott shut up when Styles turned to him. A tense silence ensued.

"Well tell us! What about the markings?"

"They don't match the type of shoe the victim was wearing. Obviously, there was a struggle, but what kind of struggle? Was Peabody winning, then the tables turned on him—literally? What was the fight about? Why did it end in murder?"

Styles pounced. "Exactly. *Exactly*. See how you're shaking your head, Officer? It's a mystery. We don't have answers. We *need* answers, folks. Now if there are no other questions ... dismissed."

Sitting in the police cruiser, remembering the moment made Scott cringe. After the glory of meeting with Watts, he'd felt stupid in the task force meeting, like he'd blown it. Rookie shit. His mood improved as he replayed what happened next, outside the lieutenant's office.

Detective Gikas had pulled him away from the others, looking up with a salacious grin that cut his face at an angle.

"Good questions Scott, but the lieutenant prefers the new guys to listen first."

"Looks like he got annoyed by my questions."

"Don't worry about it. He needs you. *I* need you. We want you to ask questions. That's why I'm here."

"Thank you, Detective."

"And loosen up. In private call me Telly or Gike."

"Okay. Thank you."

"But never shithead. I don't like shithead. I take it personal."

"Well, I would, too."

"I bet."

Telly Gikas winked and moved them both further away and lowered his voice.

"Now look, here's the real reason Styles is all hopped up. By the end of the week the Audit Division is going to release a report that is going to bring a lot of heat on the department."

"For what?"

"We got a lousy record on sex crimes, forcible rapes, and especially child abuse cases."

Scott was speechless.

"Yeah. Tanner won't be named, nobody'll be named 'cause it's ongoing, but he's part of it."

"Tanner?"

"That's why he's sitting on the sidelines. Styles doesn't want him attached to our righteous little task force."

"But what did he do?"

"Do? No, it's what he *doesn't* do. No follow-up on many incidents. Downgrading crimes. All to manipulate the stats and show the public that crime is going down. But he is just a pawn in this chess game. This all starts from the top. Hendricks was brought in to lower the crime rate. Tourist industry was getting real nervous. So he was under enormous pressure to show crime on the decline. Maybe too much pressure. Tanner, Reed, they play the game but when this shit breaks, I expect the mighty will survive and guys who manipulate the stats will take the fall."

"Are you saying we neglected victims and allowed some perps to go free?"

"That's exactly what I'm saying. There were many complaints that were filed away without any follow-up. It's all about lowering the stats to make it appear Hendricks was reducing crime."

"That's outrageous."

"Yes it is, and this audit is about to explode. Some will be scrambling for bomb shelters or their lawyer's offices.

"So the last thing they needed was a vigilante to expose them?"

"Yes, and once it breaks, it will be interesting to see if the mayor keeps Hendricks around."

"Gotta love politics."

* * *

In the cruiser, Scott pretended to be listening as his patrol partner chatted. The radio cackled like a hoarse fan at a baseball game. In truth, he couldn't shake news of the audit. It was deeply troubling because it made him distrust the department's leadership.

The dispatcher calmly called out details of an auto accident, several injuries. "That's ours. Here we go," declared Scott's partner.

Scott flipped on emergency lights, tightly gripped the wheel, and cut through traffic with the authority vested in him by the City of New Orleans. As the car picked up speed, one worry about the task force still nagged at him: he'd been told to keep everything confidential, yet he had disobeyed.

He whooped his siren, chasing motorists to the side of the street. Partner grumbled, "Get the freak out of the way, boneheads."

He wasn't sure why he'd felt the urge to share the ballistics findings with Jeremy Porter. He also wasn't quite sure why he'd befriended the man at all. He hadn't particularly liked him, he just hated bullying. He'd seen hazing that he'd considered heinous in the military. Wolf packs preying on individuals. He realized that Porter endured more harassment than most anyone could withstand. Disgraceful.

Ahead, Scott could see two damaged automobiles at odd angles in the middle of an intersection. A bloody body draped out the front passenger door window.

Suddenly, Scott knew what was troubling him. Over time he'd come to realize Jeremy had more spine and smarts than generally assumed. He liked that. But recently something about Porter was strangely out of sync —in disarray—like the aftermath of an impact.

Scott ran toward the crushed car. An ambulance shrieked in the distance.

Chapter 20

Jolted. That's how Jeremy felt after reading the headline on the newspaper that was spread across the counter of the breakfast joint.

'PERVERT VIGILANTE' STALKS NEW ORLEANS

Forcing himself to act natural, he sat, ordered food, and read every word of the article. Jeremy shouldn't have been surprised—he knew it was coming. The shock was more about how quickly things were changing. Originally, the mission was to trail pedophiles and alert police to suspicious behavior. Simple. Now, two homicides later, law enforcement was onto him.

A roving waitress poured coffee. Eggs, potatoes, and toast arrived next.

The previous night Jeremy had sneaked into Tanner's office to use the computer to search the Deep Web. But the talk with Leslie Scott had unnerved him. He didn't hack the PC and fled after photocopying only a couple files.

Throughout the night he'd had to suffer Sergeant Finnegan, who had turned as chatty as a schoolgirl, bragging that he'd seen it coming before anyone else.

"I knew there was a vigilante after the second homicide. Something wasn't right. I knew it. I could *feel* it. Same gun, same killer. I've sat in this chair too many years."

Sat. If he'd been any good as a cop, Uncle Finny would have been transferred upstairs, not sent out to pasture where he could sit on his ass, trade barbs with vets, and fall asleep watching mindless reality shows about celebrities that nobody gives a shit about.

"You ask me, the guy's doing us a favor. Put him on salary. Undercover."

That was the funny part. Jeremy was now receiving the thanks and praise he had yearned for. The only problem was all his fans assumed he was a killer and would not defend him in court. Nor would he be accepting a lifetime achievement award anytime soon.

Sipping his third cup of mud, no sugar, killing time before picking up Kayla, Jeremy's stomach was a snake pit of slimy, reptilian movement. His mind bounced like a pinball machine, ricocheting from one thought to the next. It was time to talk with Sandy.

He weighed the pros and cons, finally concluding that he had to tell someone or he'd burst. Maybe there was a way out. He'd kept meticulous notes. The McGuire family could afford the best legal defense in New Orleans. Curtis would want to save face, maybe even defend himself. Did the Colt .38, his gift, make the mogul an accomplice to the crimes? If Jeremy stopped now, he might have a chance.

"Check, please."

When Sandy opened the front door, Kayla rushed out and headed for the car.

Sandy was tense. "You're a little early, aren't you?"

"Am I?" He turned to watch Kayla get into the car. "She seems ready."

"She waits for you."

"That's because I'm her daddy. Right?" He let that hang in the humid morning air. "Look, after I drop off Kayla, can I come back? We need to talk."

"About what? No, I've got to get to work."

"Okay. After work, before I head in. I'll meet you near the store."

"Why?"

Over Sandy's shoulder Jeremy was sure he saw a shadow disappear into the back of the house. His wife saw him staring.

"Look, this isn't a good time. I'm ... we're ... packing tonight, heading to the Bahamas tomorrow morning."

"You're taking Kayla out of school?"

"No, are you nuts? She'll be with my parents. You won't have to pick her up."

"When were you going to tell me all this?"

"I'm telling you now."

"*We're* packing tonight? What's that mean?"

Her mouth opened, dumbstruck, he pushed past and headed for the kitchen.

"Excuse me, are you Mr. Ray?

Sandy chased after him. "I didn't invite you in."

Jeremy found Ray standing behind the island, placing a pod into the coffee machine. He was well-built and could have been an athlete, except he wasn't. Later, Jeremy would learn his replacement was in retail, men's clothing, and that he and Sandy had met at the gym. Initially the flirting between the two was innocent, but following the separation, their relationship developed well beyond the level of innocent flirting.

Jeremy was now face-to-face with Mr. Ray. Sandy slid between the two and began making all kinds of noise, the usual stuff: profanity, screeching indignation, and threats.

Jeremy let her tug and beat on him, a moth batting at a screen door. He remained still, staring down Mr. Ray, who to his credit held the gaze. Silence replaced hollow demands. He knew he was overstaying his welcome. He stayed a little longer.

"Background check."

Sandy frowned. "What?"

"Any man, a stranger, who lives in the same house with my daughter needs a background check."

"That's ridiculous. He doesn't *live* here."

"Could have fooled me."

Even cool and collected Mr. Ray began to overheat.

"Whoa. Hold on, Jeremy."

"It's called precautions."

Sandy squealed, "Get out of here now!"

Jeremy looked from his wife's disheveled hair to her lace nightie and continued.

"Full name, please."

"Coulter. Ray Coulter."

"Spell it." Jeremy waited. "Thank you. Street address."

"Wait a damn minute."

The Pervert Vigilante pulled out his police ID. "You're spending time with my daughter, Mr. Coulter, I trust you understand my concern."

"Jeremy, you need to leave now." Sandy snarled.

Ignoring her orders, Jeremy continued. "Street address?"

A moment later, when he was sure he had delivered a sufficient scare, he walked out of the house. Behind him, he could hear Sandy's bare feet stomping behind him. She grabbed his arm and tried to contain her tantrum in the presence of her daughter.

"You son of a bitch."

"And you have a pleasant day, too."

As he drove away, he glanced in the rear view mirror. He watched Ray place his arm around Sandy as they returned to the house, what used to be his house. Although he felt a sense of satisfaction, he pondered, *Did I just close the final chapter of my marriage?*

On the drive to school Kayla asked, "Daddy, why do you keep changing cars? I liked the red one." He cringed, forced a smile, and tried his best to savor the sound of "Daddy."

Chapter 21

Creeping through the alley was not exactly his style. But Jeremy had thought better of forcing himself through one more front door, this time in an apartment building where a dozen urban dwellers might hear or witness trouble. If he could locate the apartment of Eric Dietz from the rear, maybe he could make a more graceful and surprising entrance.

The low rung of the iron fire escape was tantalizing and possibly his only hope. If he stood on the dumpster, took a leap of faith, and pulled himself up to the first landing, he might have a chance.

He had been on his way to the Internet café on Toulouse in the French Quarter to do some online research when he decided to swing through Dietz's neighborhood. It was convenient and might save time later if he checked it out for surveillance. The gods had been with him. As he passed the building up ahead, he saw a lean man in worn jeans and a faded t-shirt walking down the center of the street toward his car. He matched the file photo.

Although he was not able to spend the usual amount of time reading through Dietz's folder and court documents, he was fairly certain he fit the profile of an active predator. Jeremy's suspicions were quickly confirmed when Dietz went into trolling mode, slowing near the entrance of a school. Just like Peabody and McDougal. *Jesus.* Dietz stopped his pickup truck—probably a construction guy of some kind— got out, and immediately engaged a group of boys. One kid seemed upset. It looked like Dietz tried to reason with him, then had a hissy fit, grabbed the boy by the arm, and dragged him into the truck.

What the fuck? Jeremy was stunned by the brazen act and realized he would have to pursue. He was witnessing an abduction and had no way to contact police without jeopardizing his identity.

* * *

As he stared up at the fire escape, he yearned for legitimacy. He should be calling in for backup, medical, as well as manpower. Instead, he wedged one shoe into an indentation low on the dumpster, grabbed the handle on the fold-down top and—

"Going someplace?"

The voice was quiet but sharp. Jeremy's mind went to work inventing an excuse. He chuckled as he climbed down. "Well, actually, I was—"

Jeremy put on a smile as he turned, but his face went blank when he discovered Eric Dietz moving fast and raising a ball-peen hammer. He fell against the brick wall of the building and caught the assailant's wrist. They struggled, kicking and gouging, each seeking an edge.

"Why are you following me?"

"I'm not!"

"Bullshit. I saw you before I made it to Timmy's school."

"Where's the kid?"

"I'm not telling you—"

"I'm a cop, asshole! Tell me where the kid is!"

Dietz backed off, still holding the hammer high. "Prove it."

Out of breath, Jeremy yanked his ID folder out of his back pocket and flashed it to Dietz.

Both men panted from exertion. Dietz finally asked, "What the fuck is going on?"

"Dude ... come on ... you're a registered sex offender. You just abducted another victim. Where's the boy?"

"You dumb shit."

"I don't think so."

"*He's my son!*"

The earth fell from under Jeremy and the sky was out of reach. Floating, he tried to comprehend the confusing news.

Dietz continued. "How did you find me?"

"How do you think? You've got a file, a police record."

The angular, muscle man grit his teeth and tore at his hair. "When will this end? When will it fucking end?"

From above a small voice called down.

"Dad ... are you okay?"

Jeremy followed Dietz's eyes to the third floor. Timmy, pale and frightened, leaned out the window.

"Sort of. Yeah. I'm okay, son. This man's a policeman. He ... he was trying to protect you."

Timmy's voice cracked. "Then why's he fighting *you*?"

Dietz stared upward, silent, aching. "We're coming upstairs, Timmy, 'kay? Don't be afraid."

Once they were in the spare, clean apartment, Jeremy was taking no chances. He checked every room and then began his talk with Timmy, a condition he demanded before entering.

"Why were you arguing with this man, Son?"

"He's my *dad*." Like that answered everything. And it did, kind of.

"But something made you mad."

"Grandma said I could go to my friend's house after school."

Dietz piped in, "And I thought I was supposed to pick him up. I'd left work early and ... money is tight. I lost my cool."

Jeremy asked, "What do you do?"

"Carpentry. Freelance. No construction company will hire a...." Tears began to well up in the eyes of a very tough man. "Hey, buddy, how 'bout you watch some TV. This officer and I need to talk in my office. You gonna be okay? Huh?"

"Yeah."

"Get some snacks. I got the bean chips you like."

"Thanks—but keep the door open."

"That's a good idea. Sure."

Dietz led them into a tight pantry reminiscent of Jeremy's inventory room. The landlord probably listed this place as a two-bedroom and hiked the rent. The space included shelves, a file cabinet, and a desktop PC. Closing the door would likely have suffocated both men.

"Look, Timmy's mom ... she's not in the picture any more ... she was an addict. She wanted a divorce and made up all kinds of shit about me abusing Timmy thinking she'd get full custody and a big settlement."

"To buy more—"

"Smack. Brown sugar. I served some time. Christ, like swimming in a portable toilet. My life was ... then, you know, what do you call it, those college kids who dig up shit and try to get you off?"

"Innocence Project? Maybe Loyola?"

"Right. They do good work. God, Jesus Christ Almighty, they actually got me out. Overturned. Victory, right? But things took a turn for the worse."

"Why?"

"The judgment was never wiped clean. I kept calling the college, but students move on, professors retire. I was lost in the, you know, whatever, and the cops wouldn't do shit."

"Who'd you call?"

He pointed to his file cabinet. "I got names. The Child Abuse department, then lieutenant so-and-so, and captain somebody. All the way up the line. Time and time again. I called and called. But nobody called back. They don't give a shit if my life is fucked hell to high water."

Timmy appeared at the door, chomping bean chips. He offered the bag. Jeremy accepted to be friendly—just like a perv, he realized: establish rapport.

"What if I'd killed you, man?"

The man's forearms were thick with blue bulging veins. He could have snapped the inventory officer in two.

Pinball again. Jeremy's brain was playing fast and loose. He had ideas. Too many ideas. His ass could be grass by tomorrow. How dare he dig a deeper grave. He just couldn't stop himself from saying—

"Maybe I can help clean up your record. I know how the Child Abuse Section works. But I'm going to need your help."

Dietz was wary. Who could blame him? "What kind of help?"

Jeremy pressed on, "There is something out there, Eric. I'm not exactly sure but we need to find out."

Fuck it. Kids' lives are at stake.

"How good are you on that computer, Eric?"

Chapter 22

Leslie Scott didn't need a couple of days to orient his sleep schedule. He wanted to get a head start on his task force assignment. So the day after his transfer was announced, he visited the neighborhoods of the two deceased child molesters.

Cleveland Avenue was first. Scott had driven a generous circle around McDougal's duplex and noted landmarks and even traced possible escape routes the Pervert Vigilante might have used. All this was assuming the guy hadn't parked in front of the crime scene. More likely than not, he'd hoofed it to an automobile and driven away, unnoticed.

Since Scott arrived roughly at the same time of day as the murder was reported, he drove the grid observing patterns and rituals—traffic and people—hoping something would jump out at him. Nothing did, until …

The officer stomped on the brakes as a peloton of cycling teens sped by—carefree and arrogant—as if they owned the streets. Scott glared as he waited for a second platoon of kids, lazier than the first, to slowly clear the intersection. He sat, thinking, until a car behind him honked. Following a hunch, he turned the corner and began to trail the bikers.

Kids just out of school, he figured. Laughing, riding no-handed, competing with each other. They were like a flock of birds, swooping in formation, parting, and then regrouping to take command of the road, ignoring angry motorists. A mile later, thinned out yet still raucous, the cyclists surged toward a small neighborhood market and stopped.

Scott parked and waited until the boys came out of the store gulping sodas and ripping open bags of junk food. He approached while they loitered near the entrance, pushing and taunting each other with profanities. They all looked up when his shadow cut across their faces.

"Which one of you is the leader of the pack?"

Scott wasn't in uniform, but he'd clipped his badge to his belt. He would have commanded their respect, regardless. The group's cocksure attitude shrank to a whisper.

"Relax, gentlemen. Nobody's in trouble. At least I hope not." He chuckled, showed his perfect white teeth. "But I was wondering ... maybe you guys can help me solve a crime."

All eyes popped, voices and 'tude perked up.

"*True Detective*!"

"*NCIS*!"

Laughter, jousting. Scott had won his audience.

* * *

During his drive to Peabody's North Rendon locale, Scott had wanted to call it in. A red car, American built, had almost wiped out a couple of the cyclists' buddies on the day of the murder. Could be nothing. Hell, *he* had nearly crushed a couple of them, too.

But the driver of the car was wearing a hoodie on a bright, sunny day. Why? And he seemed spooked after hitting the breaks, looking around, afraid to move through, the amateur detectives reported as they washed down barbecue potato chips with canned sugar and caffeine: everybody loved their drug of choice.

He held off calling Detective Vuong with the hope of having a little more to show for his effort.

After cruising by Richard Peabody's former place of residence, Scott parked halfway down the block and took his time approaching the small, tidy home. The front door opened before he got there.

"You again."

"I knew you'd be happy to see me."

"Oh, yeah, after you made it sound like *I* killed the perv?"

"Not me. *You*. I just took notes."

Scott usually didn't care for wisecracking banter. But in his first encounter with Norm Krawley, he'd found the man to be voluble and brassy, so he countered with his own jabs of sarcasm. It was the only thing that seemed to slow the blabbermouth down.

Krawley came out instead of inviting Scott in, and jabbed a finger toward the crime scene.

"See anybody down there anymore? Hell, no. All gone. They'll never come back. Unless, of course, somebody shoots Jesus Christ."

"He's already dead."

"He's back, my friend. Saw him at the barbershop last week."

The banter was a litany of complaints. Try as he might, Scott couldn't get Krawley to relax and rethink the evening of Richard Peabody's murder.

Annoyed, he listened to ten minutes of grumbling before realizing Krawley was delivering more than initially thought.

"Norm, you mean, that's why you organized your neighborhood watch group?"

"Hell, yes. Peabody was just another pain in our ass. Sorry, not literally. He never got anywhere near me. But damn right we didn't like him and didn't want him here. We squawked because it was just one more slap in the face. Police hadn't done anything for years. Now they dump a sex freak down the street?"

"Were you ever interviewed?"

"Hell, yes! TV reporters heckled me for days."

"No, I mean from the police department. Maybe somebody from ... the Audit Division?"

Krawley was thoughtful, finally. Or suspicious. His eyes narrowed and he pursed his lips.

"You trying to get me in trouble again?"

"I never got you in trouble in the first place."

"Sheesh. *You guys*."

"So they did contact you?"

"You make it sound like *I* did something wrong. I told them I reported suspicious activity to the police several different times but nothing, I repeat, *nothing* was ever done."

Det. Telly Gikas wasn't blowing smoke. A smack down was coming soon, and loud civilians like Norm Krawley, while not named, could take pride in knowing that someone, finally, was prepared to grease the squeaky wheels.

Chapter 23

Sergeant Tanner sat at his desk fuming. He'd pulled some strings to get a sneak peek at the Inspector General's audit. Even the title page made him angry.

REPORT OF INQUIRY
DOCUMENTATION OF SEX CRIME INVESTIGATIONS

It was as if someone had invaded his space and spied on him. Not everything in the report would focus on the Child Abuse Section, yet Tanner was sure there would be enough to fry him. A demotion might be coming, and that would screw to hell his pension.

Before he turned the page, he vented, as though defending himself in court. *I got no budget, no staff, they send me shit help, guys like Porter, who are dumb enough to want in when vets all want out—the sooner the better.* Retirement now seemed like Paradise Island: a hazy fantasy somewhere in the middle of nowhere.

The executive summary of the audit also felt invasive, like bed bugs crawling around in his underpants. Eighty-seven sex crime-related reports were examined and the actions (or lack of action) of several unnamed detectives were under scrutiny. A graph showed the types of complaints that had been largely ignored:

Signal 42, Rape
Signal 43, Simple Rape
Signal 80, Indecent Behavior with a Juvenile

Child molestation was also among the neglected categories.

He was tempted to slam shut the ten-page document after the summary revealed that only twelve percent of more than a thousand sex crime calls included supplementary material which would have detailed further investigative efforts. But he couldn't help himself. In a rage that veered toward panic, Tanner flipped to the back and read the conclusion.

> "The widespread failure to submit supplemental reports and discrepancies between reports and other factual data is proof that there was no effective supervision of the detectives over a two-year period. The neglect of these cases resulted in many offenders not being arrested or prosecuted. Victims, including abused children were abandoned. The report recommends that the appropriate agency conduct an investigation to determine if the lack of follow-up investigations was simply ineffective police work or done intentionally."

There it was. He wouldn't survive. Shoddy procedures meant that Sgt. Greg Tanner would be exposed as indifferent, incompetent, and possibly facing criminal indictment.

Not to mention, since this Pervert Vigilante guy showed up, it was common knowledge that the sergeant couldn't walk through the corridors without being heckled by some wise-ass in blue.

"Looks like somebody out there is doing your job for you, Tanner." High, sissy laughs always followed, echoing everywhere. *Oh, yeah, big joke. Fuck you!*

He pushed back the chair and stood. He would lawyer up—fast—and document, as best he could, discussions with Captain Reed, who had admitted that the demand of accepting incompetent personnel started at the top. Hendricks was at fault. His association with Jeremy Porter's father-in-law and other money men could easily be proven. Politics.

But his defense wouldn't start and end there. Systemic rot was the core threat. Tanner was only dealing with the shitty, soiled cards he had been dealt. *Think you can bring me down? Well, you're all going down with me!*

He pulled at the cell phone that was snapped to his belt, hidden under a roll of belly flab. He texted a buddy he had planned to meet later at the driving range. *Sorry. Can't make it. Working late.*

In a hasty swoop, the sergeant clawed the audit report and lurched toward the photocopy machine. He lifted the lid that protected the glass copying surface and cursed.

Face down was a document that apparently had been used earlier. Some doofus had left it there after making a copy. Probably the new guy. He would jump his ass in the morning.

Goddamnit, this is how important material gets lost. Do I have to do everything around here?

Tanner swiped up the paper and froze. It wasn't a memo or some certification reminder. Its corners were marked with a numerical code that matched documentation in the file cabinet marked ED—Extremely Dangerous.

"What the fuck's going on?"

He opened the appropriate ED drawer, searching for the hanging file sleeve that matched the paper he held. When he found it he noticed the contents—unlike the other files—were jostled and unkempt, as if they had been tossed in a rush. It was stuffed with too much shit to ascertain if documents were missing.

Yet Tanner wasn't stupid. ED had been penetrated by an unauthorized sneak who likely wanted to bring him down.

But who? The list was long.

Chapter 24

Det. Calvin Vuong brought the coffee from a local café because he knew Lieutenant Styles had refined tastes and couldn't bear the district's rot-gut brew. Styles removed the plastic lid on his bittersweet chocolate latte, inhaled the holy fragrance, sipped, and went blind as the steam rose and fogged his reading glasses.

"Oh, god, that's good."

Vuong grinned and then refreshed his mouth with sweet iced coffee. Simple pleasures.

"Okay, Calvin, whaddya got?" Styles asked, wiping the froth from his upper lip.

"I call it a one-gun, two-car theory."

"Intriguing. What the hell does it mean?"

"Ballistics tells us that the same gun was used in both perv deaths, right? And now we have a DNA match from both crime scenes. So we know the same person committed both crimes."

"Okay, but why the two-car theory?"

"After the Peabody death we had a mother come forward. You remember. We were pretty sure she nailed our vic, who had solicited her daughter on the day of his death. But the girl also mentioned a second man in a black car—"

"Who claimed to be a cop."

"Right. But our new man Leslie Scott—"

"I thought we told him to cool his heels for a couple days."

"The best never rest."

Vuong wanted to say "the beasts never rest." Officer Scott was that rare, quiet talent who stalked truth; he had a tireless, unquenchable thirst for discovery.

"And he called in his findings—with apologies."

Styles laughed. Vuong's dry humor was its own late day pick-me-up.

The detective explained how Scott spent time in the McDougal neighborhood and found witnesses who may have seen the murderer's car.

"Great," said Styles. "We have another link between the two crimes."

"Well... "

"Oh, boy." The next sip was warm and momentarily soothing.

"The second car was red, and the first car was—"

"Black. Do we know make and year?"

"Both probably American built."

"And so...?"

"We're thinking rental cars. Changing the vehicle color and brand for each incident would make tracking more difficult."

"Damn right."

"We're asking for cooperation among the major car venues."

"Why just the bigger firms?"

"Volume. Easier for our guy to get lost in the data. We're looking for short-term rentals that began before the murder dates and were returned on the day of or soon after. Actually, we're starting at the end—the returns—and then will trace back to the rental. We'll expand from there."

"Good job." The coffee had sufficiently cooled so that Styles could swallow a generous wash of heavenly chocolate, milk, and caffeine. "What else?"

Vuong was prepared, yet couldn't help but feel eroded and a little weary from the questions all commanding officers used liberally. *Whaddya got? What else? More, more, more.* The engine of law enforcement fed on the elusive octane of evidence.

"DNA samples from police personnel."

"Yes?" Styles asked hopefully.

"Samples all negative."

Styles grimaced, stared at his throwaway cup. He was sitting in one more drab room with table, chairs, and nearly naked walls that he wouldn't remember and that wouldn't remember him. This was his work, his career and, on some days, his regret.

"Cal ... why do I feel disappointed and not relieved?"

Vuong hesitated, realizing he was witnessing himself in another ten or fifteen years: burnt out, keeping count of questionable victories, resentful of any road that leads to nowhere.

"Because you are understandably... "

"Flawed."

The detective liked Styles, despite the Catholic obedience to commandments and rules that were deliciously out of reach.

"I was thinking more like frustrated because we haven't narrowed the field."

Styles took a deep breath and sighed. "Yes."

Both men let the silence spread. Styles swallowed one last taste of confection that was now cold in his throat. Vuong noted that the melted ice in his beverage had diluted satisfaction.

"Cal, we are going to collect new DNA samples from everyone in the NOPD. No exceptions. I'll ask Hendricks to send out a memo. Just need to make sure no one slipped through the cracks."

Chapter 25

Jeremy hated the wait. It had been three days since Eric Dietz had agreed to help launch a risky plan. The impulsive decision steered his mission in a new direction. But the bigger, broader implications might save his ass—if he could break the case before he was arrested. That's why his chest burned with anxiety. *Time.* He knew it was melting as fast as a cheap candle. His talk the previous day with Leslie Scott had confirmed as much.

After changing into civvies following another boring night on the job, Jeremy exited the district building and found his friend waiting near the parking garage. Like everyone else, he had heard through the grapevine about Leslie's new assignment. He wondered why he hadn't been told the day it happened, when the men had talked about the Pervert Vigilante after roll call.

"Hey, Jeremy. Have time for a coffee before you pick up Kayla?"

"Sure. Kayla's with her grandparents for the week."

Scott would start his afternoon shift later, so they walked to a nearby joint and ordered food with their morning Joe.

While stirring sugar into his black coffee, Scott asked, "How's it been going?"

Jeremy didn't feel particularly talkative. What could he say without stupidly, unconsciously divulging something incriminating? "I'm okay, I guess."

"You sure?"

"Yeah. Why?"

"You look like shit, Man."

Jeremy smirked. "You sound like my wife. Uh, I mean my *ex*-wife."

"What?"

Squirming, Jeremy forgot that he'd never revealed his marital fate. Only Luisa Olvera had been told, and she promised to keep it a secret.

"My wife wants a divorce."

Scott looked genuinely shocked. "So it's over? Papers filed and all that?"

"No, not quite. But ... the writing's on the wall. She wants what she wants, including a new boyfriend."

"Jesus. *Already*?"

"I'm thinking it started once I got sent back to the night shift ... the fuck-up with Child Abuse and ... I guess I shouldn't be surprised. But I love her and can't imagine going through the rest of my life without her, despite her bad temper. I can only hope that by some miracle her heart will soften and she will let me back in. I'm determined to do everything I can to get this marriage to work."

Plates of food were served. Both men reached for condiments, salt and pepper. They dug in, hungry for an excuse to move to a different topic of conversation. Finally, Scott broke the silence.

"You're not yourself, Man. Now I guess I know why. You getting any sleep?"

Jeremy shrugged. "I catch a few hours here and there. Trying to figure things out. Personal projects and—" *Shut up, Porter.*

"Career change, you mean?"

"Might have to, the way things have gone."

"Don't do anything rash. You haven't been given the chance to show them what kind of cop you can become. Top drawer, I think."

"You and nobody else. But thanks. *Really*. And congrats on Special Ops. You must be excited."

Scott nodded, pursing his lips in humility.

"Why didn't you tell me?"

Jeremy could tell the question was unexpected. Scott apologized without actually offering an explanation.

"I should have told you the other night. But your deal, what you've had to put up with ... it's wrong. That Bayless. What a helpless jerk. He should have put the hammer on Suggs and his dogs months ago. He is a poor excuse for a supervisor. But ... actually ... there's something else going on. I wanted to tell you."

It was coming. Jeremy felt his spine straighten. Hold on. Here it comes.

"You know about my transfer, but I was also asked to join the task force."

"Which task force?"

"The Pervert Vigilante task force. They've been keeping it quiet … for now … but not for long."

Jeremy fought tremors, felt his stomach tighten. He put down his fork, reached for his coffee cup but didn't lift it. Couldn't. A task force. All gunning for *him*.

"When we find this Pervert Vigilante guy I won't know whether to shake his hand or shoot him." Scott paused, grinned, then nudged Jeremy out of a stupor. "Dude, come on, you can't appreciate a little black humor?"

He couldn't laugh. Tried to, but really only wanted to scream, *It's me! I'm your guy. Can't you see that?*

"Anyway ... Chief Hendricks is catching hell. Media hounding him. He wants this thing cleaned up fast. A few people think it may be a cop or former cop."

Everybody in blue knew their DNA had been checked against evidence. But Jeremy hadn't worried because he had never been asked for a sample. Not only had the academy screwed up the spelling on his nametag, but his last-minute recruitment—father-in-law calling in a favor, he now knew—apparently meant some basic steps were skipped. He wouldn't be implicated.

Then Scott set off a dirty bomb.

"Styles is so sure it's an inside job that he's ordered a new round of DNA samples."

"What?"

"Yeah, the first search was negative. So he's ordered new samples. Everybody. No exceptions. Even Hendricks. The janitors. The secretaries. The—"

Jeremy's hand began to shake. He tried to lower his cup into the saucer but his hand went into spastic contractions. The cup dropped from his hand. Coffee spilled across the table and onto his lap.

"Fuck!"

Jeremy shoved off from his counter stool. Scott startled.

"What? What's wrong?"

The Pervert Vigilante struggled to explain. He stuttered nonsense but wanted to run. Other diners were staring. He stared into space, envisioning himself in handcuffs, the walk of shame to the booking center. Kayla would be taunted at her school: *your dad's a killer.*

Quietly, Scott reached out, urged his friend to sit down. "Come on, I'm sorry. I've been talking shop and you ... you got a lot going on. I'm sorry about Sandy. I didn't know."

Jeremy shook his head and sat. "No problem. Not your fault. I guess I'm just ... exhausted."

"Women, huh? Damned if you do, and damned if you don't."

It was the first time the two men had ever come close to discussing the topic. Luisa Olvera's face and the memory of her body pressing against his made him feel lonely. He shook it off, waved to the waitress for more coffee. Then he decided to probe.

"What makes Styles so sure?"

"We don't have to talk about this shit."

"No, that's okay. I'm curious."

Scott swallowed and wiped his mouth on the thin paper napkin. A stain of ketchup and Tabasco smeared like lipstick.

"Well, I can see his point. The little girl nailed Peabody soliciting at the school. Then she told her mom that a second man pulled up and claimed to be a cop, right?"

"Anybody could say that."

"But why bother saying anything?"

"To calm the girl?"

"Okay. But then the 911 call after the murder. Guy must have known something about common procedures."

"Or maybe he has a family member who—"

"That's a good idea, too. See? You think without prejudice. I like that. But McDougal—"

Just hearing the name made Jeremy stiffen. He couldn't bear any more revelations.

"We just found out that a woman complained to a grocery store manager that a man of his description tried to lure her boy with some cookies—and then later that day McPervert is dead. I'm pretty sure the mother didn't go stalking that dude. Somebody, *somebody* knows how to find these guys, track them and observe offensive behavior, and then ... bang! Instant justice."

Jeremy nearly jumped off his stool again when his phone rang. He could tell that his friend took note of his jittery grab for the Android.

"Sorry. Gotta take this."

"No problem," Scott said.

Jeremy walked toward the men's room. Eric Dietz wouldn't call this early unless he had something.

"Porter, I got a response from Emperor, or whoever the hell he is. Can you come over?"

Chapter 26

Dietz was grim as he led Jeremy through the small apartment to his computer in the pantry. He sat, opened his email, and pointed to one message.

"It says my application has been accepted but now I have to put up a thousand bucks to view the film. And it's not a purchase, it's a rental. Once I view the film, I have to agree to delete it."

As a tech pro, Jeremy found the process intriguing. "Interesting how they're handling this."

"Interesting? What's so interesting? I'm not putting up money to some website in Vidnoye, Russia."

"I know. I never asked you to spend any money."

During their first encounter several days ago, Jeremy had showed Dietz the website because he realized the man's conviction for child abuse, although apparently revoked, could be useful. The online club that attracted Peabody and McDougal accepted applications only from men who could prove they were registered sex offenders. The sales pitch, if it could be called that, was sly. Whoever Emperor might really be, he understood the perverts would necessarily protect each other and the site and by joining, they were entrapped. That was one reason both dead men had been so nervous about sharing passwords.

After digging around on the site that apparently emanated from Russia, Jeremy finally had found an application for English-speaking people.

"Here's how it works," Jeremy had explained. "The application asks for lots of info, like where were you convicted, who was the victim, how much time you served, name, address, case number, etc., etc."

"I thought you said you could help clear my record," Dietz had said.

"I believe I can. But to do that I need your help taking down a child abuser—maybe more. I know you're not eager to revisit all this shit, but these guys are shrewd. They must actually do a background check to avoid being infiltrated by cops. That's why I can't apply. Only convicted offenders are allowed in."

"This is crazy. What exactly am I applying for?"

"We won't know until we get in. But two men associated with this site have already died because they... " Jeremy was about to out himself as the Pervert Vigilante, so he put the brakes on.

"What guys? And how do you know they died because of this?"

"I'm privy to the police investigation, and I once worked in the Child Abuse Section." *Once*. "Look, don't do it if you don't want to. But I promise to clear your record if we can prove you went the distance to help stop child abuse."

"But it says Rehabilitation for Convicted Child Abusers."

"Yeah, and that's a crock of shit."

"And I'm not an abuser."

"But you have a criminal record that says you are."

Jeremy guessed that the only reason Dietz hadn't blown his stack was the presence of his son Timmy in the other room. After a long, tense standoff, Dietz unlocked his black metal file cabinet, reached for a fat folder that included his court records and case number, and began filling out the application. Meanwhile, Jeremy was battling doubts. Would it have been better if they'd set up a separate computer? Maybe not, because they still would have needed the personal details to enter the site. Dietz paused and pointed at the screen.

"What's this?"

The last paragraph of the website's agreement stated that any violation of the agreement and breach of confidentiality would result in "serious consequences."

Jeremy remembered the paranoia pouring off Peabody and McDougal.

"Sounds like they want to scare off ... intruders?"

Dietz stared hard at the screen, then hit *Enter*. "Fuck 'em. How much worse can my life get?"

* * *

Three days later, the application had been approved but the men hit another roadblock: money. It was Jeremy's turn to step up.

"I'll pay. We've come this far... we can't stop now."

From his jeans pocket, Jeremy pulled out a folded stack of fifty and one hundred dollar bills. He'd withdrawn a substantial amount of cash after Sandy threatened divorce. He feared she might try to lock him out of their joint account, so he always kept money on hand. It helped with the car rentals and other things, though on some days he questioned if he really wanted the green so that he could disappear on a moment's notice.

He was embarrassed by the effect the money had on Dietz, a guy who was struggling to pay the bills and support a son who loved bean dip chips. The man's eyes opened wide and a palpable envy took hold.

"Here's a thousand." As he counted out c-notes, he had a second thought. "And here's another five hundred."

"For what?" Again, suspicion tightened the conspirator's face.

"For helping me."

"But—"

"It's okay, keep it. I'm paying for our expenses. Need to make a deposit before we—"

"No."

Dietz, angry about so many things, muttered as he typed in his credit card number. "Probably a scam. And we just blew a thousand bucks."

Once he tapped *Enter* on his keyboard the screen opened like an old-time movie theater. Red velvet curtains opened and allowed access to the entertainment. The titles were written in Russian but it was obvious what the next step must be: Dietz moved his cursor over the only live link—Пуск—and an amateurish video that was poorly lit began. After titles rolled, a hulk of a man appeared in a black hood and cape. The camera followed him as he entered and slowly moved around the room. Then he turned and spoke, his face shrouded in shadow.

"I am Emperor."

Jeremy wondered why the guy went through the pretense of building a Russian portal with a foreign font and content but performed in English. *Because the site is meant for American clientele, dumbshit.*

The camera panned across the room to where a frightened young boy sat naked in a chair. His hands and ankles were tied down, but the close-up clearly revealed that his slender, six-year-old body was trembling uncontrollably.

"Holy shit."

"What?" Dietz said.

"It's Benito Jackson."

"Who's that?"

He's immortal. That's what McDougal had said after Jeremy demanded to know where the boy was.

"He was kidnapped last month—Amber alert—but never found."

His rage began to build. He wanted to raise McDougal from the dead and pistol whip him.

"How in the hell did they ship him to Russia?"

Jeremy didn't answer.

"Hey ... how'd they get him to Russia?"

"Maybe they didn't."

It was beginning to make sense. Create the illusion that the abusive site was in a distant land, beyond the reach of domestic police. But locate in an American port city and make your misery—and a small fortune—without being detected. McDougal had delivered Benito. But how and where?

Then other memories rushed in: Charles Stevens. That fateful day in Child Abuse. The creep had played coy with Tanner, suggesting he had somehow done right by the little girl he'd abused. *She's lucky she's already in the hospital ... I saved her little ass. She'd be with him by now ... she was next.*

The caped man appeared on camera again and repeated his name in a gruff voice, "I am Emperor." It would have been silly, bad theater, if not for the horror they were about to witness.

In a melodramatic sweep of his arm, the Emperor picked up a wand attached to a cord and lunged at the helpless boy.

Jeremy yelled at the computer screen. "You motherfucker! I'll find you!"

"Now I know what this is," Dietz whispered as tears filled his eyes. "It's a snuff film."

He got out of his chair and stood back from the PC screen.

"A what?"

"You're a cop and you don't know what a snuff film is? We just paid a thousand dollars to watch this piece of shit kill a little boy."

They heard Benito Jackson scream again, as the Emperor ramped up the voltage to inflict more pain.

"I can't watch this," Dietz said.

Yet both men had to watch, to witness the atrocity, to avenge it.

The camera circled on the flailing of the executioner, never revealing the man's face, and then went for a close-up of the power control on his electric wand. The Emperor's long fingernails were filed to perfection with the fore and index nails painted with artistic designs. They slowly eased the lever to MAX, and then the man raised his weapon as though it were a sword. Minutes later, Benito's body went limp.

Yet the vile was not done. From his cape, he pulled a sleek nasty knife that glittered even in the tawdry lighting, nodded to his audience, and then carved his name in the pale, frail chest of his victim. The camera moved close, framing Benito, whose head hung forward, as though the tiny victim was looking down at the dripping blood of—

EMPEROR

Dietz rushed out of the room, slamming through doors. Jeremy heard a howl and then a rush of vomit, but he held his own impulse to void his guts. He was tougher now. No longer a rookie. He seethed with a clarity of purpose he'd never experienced before. His urge to kill the pervert who makes sport of murdering children, he realized, was at its core a profound need for revenge. At any price.

"What do we do? What the fuck do we do?"

He turned and found Dietz leaning on the doorframe, wiping tears and vomit from his pale face with a towel. Jeremy wanted to say something comforting, professional, but exhaustion fell on him like heavy chains.

"I ... I can't think. I have to go home. I've been up all night and—"

"I get it. But what should I do about—" He pointed to the computer.

"Follow instructions."

"Delete it? How will the cops find this monster? I want his ass fried."

"You gave us a way in, Eric. We're closer now. Thank you for your courage."

As he let himself out, Jeremy heard Dietz say, "Call me ... when you can."

Chapter 27

Halfway home, Jeremy changed direction and sped toward Second District. He might make it in time to catch Captain Reed before he entered his office and opened his hectic daily appointment book.

Entering the building, he immediately sensed a buzz. Something was up, but he was too tired to figure it out. Cops huddled in corners, administrators hustled in every direction.

Reed's secretary who was usually cool and remotely polite, was uptight. The phones kept ringing and she had no time for Jeremy or his request.

"So you don't know when he'll be in?"

"Officer, Captain Reed's schedule has been turned upside down. I can't promise—" She yanked the ringing phone to her ear, "Please hold," she said sternly before returning her attention to Jeremy. "As I was saying, Officer, it's very unlikely he'll have time for you today."

"What is going on?"

Another phone line lit up. The secretary needed more than two arms to handle the onslaught. Jeremy left the office and decided to stick around for a few minutes.

He heard the voice first, and then Captain Reed rounded a corner and marched down the hallway with Sergeant Tanner and Lieutenant Styles in tow. Reed barked at the others, their faces red and tight.

Jeremy knew they would rush past and ignore him, so he blocked their path. The three men seized up, like horses frightened by a snake in the grass. They looked puzzled.

"Excuse me, Captain Reed, but—"

"Not now, Officer."

"Sir, all I need is a minute of your time."

Annoyance creased Reed's face. "You still have not learned the basics, have you? Chain of command, Son. Chain of command."

"It's a serious matter I've only just discovered. And I know how packed your days are, so I thought—"

Reed guffawed, rolled his eyes in disbelief, then ordered Tanner and Styles to wait for him in his office. As they strode by, the sergeant gave Jeremy a poisonous look.

"This is highly inappropriate. Not that anything I say will ever sink in with you. Now what's this all about?"

Jeremy had much to explain, too much. He sputtered a moment, then tried his best to piece together the evidence most cops knew about the Peabody and McDougal deaths.

"The icons. There's an icon on each victim's computer, right?"

"Yes, yes, I remember something about icons."

"I believe the icon is a membership site for child molesters that pretends to be a Russian set-up, but—"

"We already know about that Porter, but we aren't about to go chasing after criminals in Russia or Somalia or any other goddamn country. We've got troubles right here. Too many troubles."

"I understand, but what I'm trying to say is that the Russian site might actually—"

"Listen, Porter, let the detectives who know this stuff work these cases."

"But they don't have time!"

Reed growled with an irritation that was startling.

"I don't need you ... *nobody needs you* ... to tell us how to run this district. If you're unhappy, get the hell out and go back to selling sofas. Now stop wasting my time with chatter about Russia, understood? I am ordering you to drop this matter once and for all!"

Reed didn't wait for an answer. He bullied his way through to the door to his office.

Jeremy heard voices, the harried secretary, Styles, and then an inner door slammed. Silence. A moment later he re-entered.

The secretary looked up from the phone, perturbed. Before she could complain, Jeremy put up his hands and whispered, "Please just tell me what the heck is going on around here?"

She dropped the phone and reached under a pile of paper work, then shoved a bound report at him.

"Go ahead, take it. But get out of my office or I'll shoot you with your own gun."

* * *

At home in his war room, Jeremy sipped a big cup of coffee and stared at the report that he now knew was the cause of the uproar he'd experienced at the district.

REPORT OF INQUIRY
DOCUMENTATION OF SEX CRIME INVESTIGATIONS

He made himself read it a second time, though the implications were already obvious: he was alone. No backup. The NOPD would first scramble to cover its ass, make promises to the furious public, and then finally return to its practice of habitual negligence.

Jeremy wanted to know more about Emperor. He could use his computer skills to track the origin of the website to Vidnoye, Russia, and maybe discover additional information. Or maybe it made more sense to notify Russian police. But he couldn't do it without help.

To prompt his weary mind, Jeremy opened his laptop and scrolled through his address book. It didn't take long to find the name he was looking for. Allen Bordes was a former teammate on his college tennis team and worked at the State Department. He was the only college buddy who had RSVP'd and shown up at his wedding.

Jeremy dialed, not expecting to get Allen on the first call. He was correct. An operator transferred his call and soon he heard his friend's voicemail. He left a message then fell into bed with his Android. Sleep came fast.

When the phone rang, he had no idea what time it was. "Hello? Porter here."

"Doubles anyone?"

"Hey, Allen, thanks for getting back."

"No problem. We keep promising we'll get together for a grudge match. I figured that's why you called."

If only. In fact, Jeremy couldn't remember the last time he pulled out his racquets and hustled a game at the country club. After some small talk, Jeremy explained his predicament—sort of. He needed help soliciting the Russian police to track down the owner of an IP address originating in Vidnoye, Russia. NOPD police budget wouldn't cover his expenses.

Allen hemmed and hawed. "Does this have anything to do with the Pervert Vigilante crimes?"

"You actually read local newspapers?"

"Uh, yeah."

Jeremy wanted to sound light, jocular. In fact, he was twisting in the wind, trying to avoid the Pervert Vigilante phenomenon while divulging some of what he knew. He confided the run-in he'd had with Captain Reed earlier in the day, as if that explained the pickle he was in. He didn't like that he'd become so adept at situational lying.

"Look, all I can say is the investigation of those events, you know, gave our tech guys the opportunity to poke around in the victim's computers. They found similarities, online connections."

"I bet they did."

"And that's how the Emperor was exposed. All I'm trying to do is get some assistance before things get even more out of hand."

More silence. Jeremy quashed the urge to rush the net with more pleading.

"Well, normally, this isn't how we do things around here."

"Allen, if it is any solace, nothing about this case is normal. I'm hoping, if I show a little initiative, NOPD will get lucky and nail this bastard."

"It's disgusting. Where do these people come from?"

"From Russia."

"From Hell. I have friends in Moscow. Great people. All right, buddy, I'll tell you what. Let me make a couple calls and get back to you. You going to be in?"

"I'll be here."

"But you owe me dinner, if I can get you hooked up."

"I owe you dinner anyway. Let's do it soon." *Like before I head to prison.*

Jeremy covered his head with a pillow and sank into a sleep that was a garbage disposal of horrific images and strange convoluted narratives. Some faces were familiar, while many others were not. It was as if all the turmoil of the past months had been spliced into a fast and furious snuff film of innocence and good intensions.

This time the phone vibrated incessantly on his bedside table before he could find it. Bleary-eyed, still foggy and disoriented, he resumed his conversation with Allen Bordes.

"Hey, hey. Match point?"

The silence stretched a bit before a woman asked, "Jeremy?"

He sat up. "Yeah, this is Jeremy. Who's this?"

"Luisa."

His mind wouldn't work. He knew he should recognize the name, but—

"Luisa Olvera. I'm sorry to bother you."

"No, no."

"Were you sleeping?"

He couldn't lie, so he laughed. "Yeah, I was, but, hey ... what's up?"

"Jeremy ... I need a hug."

Chapter 28

He wanted to be touched, held, and loved. That was the only explanation he could give for what happened when Luisa Olvera arrived at his apartment. She had asked him to meet her at a restaurant where they could talk. But his fatigue was so great, the ordeal of his secret life so heavy, he invited her over instead.

She was not her usual self when she entered. Tentative and self-conscious, she wandered into the living room, absorbing Jeremy's way of life.

"Nice," she said.

"It's a little ... sparse."

"But you have good taste."

"Thanks. I learned a little at the furniture store."

Luisa declined coffee and sat on the couch, staring out the window. Then she began.

"I need help."

Jeremy was barefoot, dressed in jeans and a button-down shirt that he hadn't bothered to tuck into his pants. He had showered quickly and still felt water in his ears. Concerned, he sat in the soft chair adjacent to her.

"This is not working for me."

"What isn't?" he said.

"Being a cop. I just don't know anymore. I mean, not even Joe Doode could go the distance. At least his guidance made me feel confident, for a while. But now... "

She went through her doubts, the way she felt patrolling at night with her partner, the dismay of being stuck with night shift duties and how it had turned her life upside down. Then she went to the sex crimes investigation.

"Have you read the report?"

"Yeah."

"I'm ashamed."

"It's not your fault."

"But how can we expect the people of New Orleans to trust us anymore? How can we trust our commanders? They won't follow up on rapes and child abuse? It's *inconvenient*? I'm not okay with all this."

"Hey, I hear you."

"And as a woman ... I mean, I feel so disrespected. You know? It's like—" She rose abruptly. "God, listen to me. I know I'm not making any sense."

"Sure you are."

"Really?"

"Women ... kids ... it's like they're all disposable. You're probably afraid your own department wouldn't support you if you were... " He couldn't say the word.

"Exactly. I mean, maybe I'm in the wrong job. Maybe social work or some other way of helping is better for me. Putting on the uniform every night, it's just not ... it's... "

Her arms froze in mid-air, her mouth was open but not moving, unable to summon the words that could express her uneasiness. Then she sighed and was animated again.

"May I use your bathroom?"

"Sure." Jeremy rose, guided her with his hand on the small of her back. "Just down the hall."

"Thank you."

She disappeared from sight, then called back. "It's locked."

He panicked and found her in the semi-dark hallway. "No, it's ... at the end."

"Sorry." Over her shoulder she asked, "What's in there, all your treasures?"

"Don't I wish. Nah. Just some storage."

Luisa closed the bathroom door without another remark, too lost in her own distress to care. And that was good. No more questions.

In the kitchen Jeremy poured cold, fizzy water into a pitcher and added squeezed lemons and grabbed two tall glasses from the cupboard. He was pouring drinks over ice when Luisa returned.

"You're quite the host."

He grinned and shrugged.

"Manners. That's nice."

Jeremy offered a glass but she didn't accept. Instead, tentative again, she looked into his eyes, pleading it seemed, for him to read her mind.

"Thank you," she finally said.

"For water?"

"For understanding."

"Hey ... you helped me the other night. I was a mess. Being a cop ... sometimes it's hard to know if we're doing any good. It is for me, anyway."

"Really?"

"Really."

She stepped forward.

"But you seem so calm, friendly."

Smirking, not looking at her, "I hold it all in."

"Don't."

"Hmm?"

"Don't hold back."

It felt as though he had been lifted off his feet, floating in indecision like the raised hands of the pianist pausing before resolving a chord.

"Could I get that hug now?" she asked.

Dark hair curling at her shoulders, gloss shimmering her full lips ... what man wouldn't want to get close to this woman? He held out a hand, which she accepted, then he pulled her to his body. She tightened the embrace and then looked up at him, reaching for his mouth.

They went rogue. The world and its worries fell away. Kisses deepened as boundaries were overrun. Their move to the bedroom happened in stages of undress.

She surrendered on her back, and then pushed him away when she sensed that he was on the verge. "Make it last. Make it last a long time," she said, and then offered her body in a new position, offered her mouth and her breasts, offered the blind dumb luck of ecstatic consummation.

They lay together under a sheet kissing softly. Then she hopped out of bed and rushed to the bathroom. Upon return, she stopped in the threshold, smiling, providing a chance for him to behold her full, naked shape out of uniform. Dazed, with a crooked smile spreading, he was at peace, briefly, for the first time in months.

"Thank you for your DNA sample, Officer."

She could feel him tense as she crawled back into bed.

"What? DNA?" he said, pulling away.

His worry surprised and concerned her. It was as if he felt tricked. "*Jeremy.* It was a joke. You know we all have to submit another sample, right?"

"Oh, right. There's talk."

"Well, from what I hear, the chief's memo will probably be read at roll call tonight." She did a spot-on impression of Bayless. "Listen up. Memo from Chief Hendricks. All NOPD personnel must deliver a DNA sample by...."

He laughed, which allowed him to feign indifference. "Oh that. Yeah, yeah."

"What'd you think? I was doing undercover work?" She pulled the sheet up and winked at him. "Well, I guess I was *kind of* undercover."

The two lay still, embracing. Jeremy stared upward as Luisa placed her head on his chest. Suddenly, euphoria crash-landed to be replaced by feelings of guilt. *My dear, you just made love to a man wanted for two homicides. A man so conflicted. A man who still loves his wife.*

She felt the tense change in his body. "Thoughts?"

"Yes, thinking of this moment in time. It's wonderful. Thanks for being here." He tightened his arm around her back.

"It's a pleasure, Officer Porter."

He decided then and there to block the conflicts from his mind and welcome any drop of goodness that came to him, before the DNA match brought him down.

Chapter 29

After a business-like greeting late in the day, Allen Bordes ushered Jeremy to his office in the US State Department building on Loyola. Once the door closed, he loosened up. No more need for a show of protocol.

"Holy shit, Man, what have you gotten yourself into?"

Nearly every question Jeremy fielded these days was ripe with irony. *If only you knew.* He had to fight off the urge to confess, to purge his guts. It was natural, he supposed, to want to tell somebody—anybody—about the turmoil his private mission had caused. The only relief he'd experienced since the fiasco on his first day with Child Abuse was his unexpected intimacy with Luisa Olvera. And he even felt guilty about that. If only he could walk away from the mess he'd made and live a normal life. Fat chance.

"What do you mean?"

"Our police contacts in Russia got on this right away."

"That's lucky."

"Yeah. They have nothing else to do over there." He grinned. "What they found is that the location in Vidnoye is an Internet café, of sorts. A signal originates here in New Orleans and is relayed overseas."

"So they can hide in plain sight."

"Kind of. It's like digital ping pong. But the hide-and-seek won't last."

"They've just been discovered."

"Right. Police spoke to a man in the café who claims he knows nothing about the website. He says he was simply hired to set up the relay from our lovely city."

"Bullshit."

"You'd make a good cop," he said with mock seriousness. "Sounds like they're not buying his story and hope to shut him down in a few days."

"Okay, but what about here in New Orleans? How do we find our guy?"

"That's a problem. The ITs can trace the bounce, but we don't have an exact address yet. And it's likely the signal is pinging to a bunch of cities, as well. Finding this Emperor guy could be difficult."

"He'll get away. He'll know we're onto him."

"That's my worry, too. Snakes slither into the grass. Are you keeping this in-house for now or going to the feds?"

The question hit Jeremy like a storm front. His surveillance project that had been started so naively, as an attempt to assist Child Abuse, might soon involve the FBI and possibly other federal agencies. Or *not*. He already knew Reed would do nothing; he didn't have the resources, and the audit of sex crime investigations would consume his focus for days and weeks to come. Yet since his arrival at NOPD, it was common knowledge that commanders often complained that the feds were either too intrusive or stingy and reluctant to commit resources to a global fox hunt. Not even the big boys had the money or manpower to chase every hint of perversion.

The next surge of the storm hit him even harder than the first: he was alone, without any meaningful resources, facing something that was beyond heinous. He had stumbled upon evil, and driving around in a rental car was not going to win the day.

Allen must have noticed his jitters and swirl of anxiety.

"You okay?"

He didn't care anymore that he might be divulging incriminating information. The stress was pulling him apart.

"It's bad enough that these pervs get their hands on kids. All I wanted to do was put some heat on them, keep them in check, possibly make some arrests."

"Hey, you were just following orders, right?"

Jeremy lied again. "Of course. Yeah."

"And now your diligence has exposed something that's much bigger. Take a bow."

"It's too much, Man. I'm in way over my—" He stood abruptly, before he said anything more that could hurt him.

"What do you mean? Your investigation has uncovered the worst kind of human being, and probably a whole child porn trafficking operation. You've done something good here, Jeremy. Give yourself a pat on the back and then hand it over. Let a higher power step in."

Could it be true? He wanted to believe he had done something worthwhile, despite his stupid mistakes and carelessness. He hadn't murdered the two sex offenders, but his actions had certainly led to the violence that caused two deaths. Would he be celebrated or scorned? Set free or imprisoned? His prospects didn't look promising.

The sun on its downward arc spread tossed shadows and sharp spears of orange light through the office window. Bordes came around his desk and put a hand on Jeremy's shoulder.

"You look like you're carrying a lot of weight, Friend."

"Yeah."

"Don't. That's my advice, not that you asked. Don't go it alone."

Bordes slid an index card from his desktop and handed it to Jeremy, who read the name and phone number written in blue ink.

"Randall Hockey?"

"Yes. FBI. We worked with him on a few things. If you decide you want the feds, give him a call. If he can't handle it, I'm sure he'll send you in the right direction. Okay?"

* * *

Jeremy was thankful for Allen's help, but he still felt trapped. The Emperor had to be caught before he could harm another child. Unfortunately, by calling the feds, the walls would start closing in around him as questions were asked about how and where he discovered this information.

By the time he was back in his apartment, he knew what he must do. He dialed.

"Agent Hockey."

"My name is Jeremy Porter. I am a New Orleans Police Officer. Allen Bordes gave me your name."

"Okay. How can I help?"

"I have some information that may involve a child kidnapping."

"Is this an emergency?"

"No, the kidnapping occurred about a month ago in New Orleans."

"Okay, well, that's not my department. But I can have Agent Paul Miller give you a call. He works Violent Crime Squad."

"I'd appreciate that."

"Let me get a little info. Is this your case? You're the investigating officer?"

The question caught Jeremy like a sucker punch. He should have called anonymously.

"Uh ... well—"

"If you're not, who is?"

"No, sorry, yes, I'm your guy. I'm, uh, it's a little unusual. I'm assigned to the Second District but working with Child Abuse on this case."

"Got it."

Hockey asked a few more questions then said he'd hand it over to Agent Miller.

"That's Paul, right?"

"Correct. Thanks for calling this in."

"Sure. Thanks for your help."

Chapter 30

The message popped up from the dark, undetectable dungeon of his computer:

WE HAVE A PROBLEM.

The man sitting before the screen had the choice of "accepting" or "ignoring" the message. He never ignored problems. By micromanaging his domain, he had remained safe while expanding his wealth by providing the unspeakable to a variety of niche audiences. The desecration of young, beautiful women would always be in demand, and pimps in transgender circles had spawned a unique craving among deviants. A new venture was also thriving. Who would have thought that the community of registered child sex offenders could provide such a generous cash flow?

The man used touch screen functions to accept and engage. Voice recognition software created the screen text he shared with a man named Demyan, who resided in the city of Vidnoye, Russia. An app called Dust OFF would automatically erase all correspondence within twenty minutes of its completion, leaving no detectable trail.

"Tell me, Demyan."

"The police."

"Again?"

"Yes. They returned and asked more questions about the relay I have set up for your website. They did not like my answers."

"Why would they suspect you, an honest freelancer struggling to survive Putin's regime?" Text could not capture the droll nuance of the man's commentary.

"The Americans? Could local police have suspicions and alert Russian police?"

"But how could this have happened? Our subscribers know the rules."

"Guessing, but I've discovered that two of your subscribers have been murdered."

The man paused. Very little surprised or unnerved him. This, however, was strange. "Why was I not notified?"

"Your accountant didn't detect the problem until I asked if she had noticed any imbalances or tampering with subscriptions. She discovered payments had been stopped by the banks of three men in New Orleans. I asked for the names and discovered one arrest and two deaths. One of the dead subscribers recently delivered an immortal."

"Send me the names."

The man never took delivery of his victims. He had others perform those duties so that he didn't have to meet with the kind of people who were so low, so entirely beneath his imperial station in life. He ran his hand through his thick mane, which had been curled and coiffed, then stroked his cheek with the two fingernails painted expertly by his personal manicurist. Her artistry had given his murderous hands class and distinction.

He glanced at the screen when the names popped up.

Charles Stevens
Richard Peabody
David McDougal

Demyan typed, "McDougal delivered the kid named Benito. Remember?"

The silver-haired man didn't answer but mulled over the situation. Obviously, by now police had confiscated the computers of the three sex offenders. Although he had paid huge sums to the developers who guaranteed his site and infrastructure could not be compromised by law enforcement, he knew that the apprehension of three hard drives in a rather short period was worthy of his concern.

Demyan typed, "Still there?"

"Yes. Thinking."

"Police threatened to shut me down by the end of the week."

"Can they do that in Putin's free Russia?" Again, the sardonic tone.

"Yes. Once they receive proper documents. They know the signal is going back to the US. I insisted that I knew nothing about this, nothing about videos, I was only hired to set up a relay."

"Your correspondence with my accountant has been destroyed?"

"Yes, of course. We continue to operate in dark mode."

The man looked around his office that overlooked the staging area for the snuff porn he created. The office and small studio area was sectioned off from the otherwise trash- cluttered floor space. The makeshift studio was complete with new furniture, lighting, and camera equipment. The space served his evil purpose very well—a perfect fit for a psychopath. His only complaint was that he had no windows overlooking the sea or fields of poppies, ensconced as he was in a veritable concrete bunker, a former and now defunct foundry.

"Recent subscriptions," the man said. "Anything suspicious or unusual?"

"Only the one I mentioned."

"Which one?"

"A man named Eric Dietz. His records were real, but I hacked deeper and found a mention of Request to Overturn, or expunge."

"What came of it?"

"Nothing. He's still in the books as a molester."

Now he remembered. *The fucker.* He hadn't liked the application, a gut response that he had not heeded. *Money seduces and blinds a man*, he thought.

"Police will be back. Maybe I have a few days."

"Stay with it for as long as you can. I have plans in mind."

"Don't tell me. I never knew what this was all about and don't care to know now. I was just asked to set up a relay for you. That's all."

He understood Demyan was only repeating an alibi in the unlikely event that the Dust OFF app would malfunction and not destroy this conversation. It was the same reason they had agreed to never use his chosen name: Emperor.

"Thank you for your help."

When the screen went black, he sat for a moment contemplating his choices. He turned when he heard footsteps.

Boris and Ahtoh had been loyal followers. If they lacked imagination they made up for it with brute strength and no apparent conscience or moral inhibitions. They were deviants, too, after all. And Ahtoh held the camera for the Emperor while the little victims were tortured and snuffed.

"Gentlemen, we have a problem. I suspect a recent subscriber may have violated his agreement by cooperating with authorities. Needless to say, I cannot be sure. So I need you both to visit with him and ask questions. Contact me once you have his full attention. At that time, I will have further instructions and information. That will be all."

Chapter 31

Luisa Olvera had been right. That night during roll call, Bayless announced the order for DNA, and each officer received an acknowledgement form that required a signature and included an appointment date and time with an independent lab. The lieutenant's words and manner were nearly identical to her improvisation:

> "Listen up. Memo from Chief Hendricks, who orders all NOPD personnel to deliver a DNA sample. No excuses, no exceptions. Get 'er done."

Jeremy went blank, knowing he had four days before his appointment. And then how long before the results would be compared to evidence? With more than 1,200 samples to process, he believed he might have a week, total. Time enough to find a lawyer, create a legal defense. It was bizarre for him to be thinking this way, and entirely necessary: *Get in front of it, Porter. Call Curtis McGuire. You need his bank roll and contacts. He'll understand—unless he disowns you.*

"Officer Porter, are you clear about the lieutenant's instructions?"

Olvera was playing it straight. It felt as if she wanted Jeremy to know that what they'd shared earlier in the day would remain private. Regardless, he couldn't help but whisper his compliments.

"You should do stand-up. You nailed the voice and rhythm."

Barely audible, "What rhythm?"

A glint in her eye made him want to get close again, but any thoughts of continuing the romance would be disastrous. She would be so hurt to know she had a relationship with the Pervert Vigilante. He had to somehow try to create distance between them.

"Call me tomorrow?"

"Yes, of course, Officer. Have a good—"

Her eyes flickered when she looked over his shoulder. He turned and found Brock Suggs, grinning like a jack-o-lantern, which could only mean tricks, not treats.

"Hey, family reunion. Academy rookies make good." Then he looked at Jeremy, put on a sad clown face. "Well, mostly."

"Is there a reason we should tolerate your interruption, Officer Suggs?"

Luisa's voice was a laser with pinpoint accuracy that warmed Jeremy's heart.

"You always could dish it out, huh, Olvera? But just wanted to tell Mr. Inventory Guy here that Bayless asked me to say you don't need to deliver your DNA. We all know you don't have the balls to take down a perp. Have a good night, *team*."

The secret lovers watched the fat-assed Suggs saunter out of sight.

"That man is the most offensive bush league jerk I've ever met."

"I think he likes you."

"He asked me out once, you know."

Taken aback, "*Really*? What'd you tell him?"

"I was tempted to hand him his balls on a clipboard, but he doesn't have any. I know someone who does, though." She paused a moment, peering into his eyes without betraying a hint of their recent history. "You have a good night, Porter."

"You too, Olvera." *Please forgive me.*

* * *

Maybe it was the comment from Suggs. Or maybe it was the futility of ever finding the vile man known as Emperor. Whatever, Jeremy could barely control his itch to return to Sergeant Tanner's office. When the clock showed that he was halfway through his shift, Jeremy called to Finnegan.

"Breaking for dinner, Sergeant."

"Don't hurt yourself."

Jeremy cringed but kept walking. When he was sure the hallway was empty, he quickly ascended the stairs to Child Abuse. As he approached the door, he worried that the audit of sex crime investigations might have altered the way Tanner organized his office. Maybe some files had been confiscated or locked down.

He was relieved to discover the Extremely Dangerous file cabinet was accessible and full to the brim, as always. After his meeting with Allen Bordes, a new plan had emerged. He would scour the files looking for any indication that the perps might likely be drawn to the offensive website, and then go after the exclusive list with whatever time he still had left. He pondered what he would do if he was arrested in the line of duty. Would that help or hurt his case?

At home he had revisited the files of Peabody and McDougal. The Dietz file was an aberration, so he put it aside. But he identified what might be valid common denominators: time since release from prison and age.

As they aged, some pervs mellowed, lost the juice, even if they never actually repented. So he searched in a range of 27 to 43, and only bothered with guys who had been out of the can for about six months. It wasn't scientific, but he reasoned that perverts would initially be afraid of being caught again, so they'd stay away from the life until the urge to prey could no longer be suppressed.

This still didn't address how or when molesters would gravitate to the Emperor's site. Yet if the site admin had been savvy enough to demand police records, and had the ability to hack the court system for verification, it was likely the enterprise had gathered an email list of child molesters and communicated with them in the same manner as any online business that had something to sell to a niche audience. There was one more common denominator: means to pay for the snuff films.

A thousand bucks per pop was heady stuff. So Jeremy searched for single men (no family to support) or indications of professions that likely had created generous incomes before incarceration. Money stalks.

He was so engrossed in his search that he was late returning to his post. Finnegan didn't let it slide.

"You the only one around here who needs a break? Don't let it happen again or you won't be inventory officer anymore. You'll be a test dummy for the Tasers, got it?"

"Yes, Sir." *And please go screw yourself, asshole.*

The TV junkie limped toward the break room with a frozen dinner dangling in a plastic grocery bag. The Italian cuisine would bubble nicely in the district's microwave.

Chapter 32

The following day found Captain Reed in a mood as foul as the season's smothering heat. The long week had included dodging media requests and endless strategy meetings with Chief Hendricks. More time with the chief did not make the heart grow fonder. Upon returning to the Second District building, the captain couldn't shake his annoyance with some comments made by the hatchet man.

"The mayor is very unhappy with the sex crimes investigation audit. But you knew that, Captain. What may surprise you is that he is even less impressed with your response."

"*My* response?" .

"Child Abuse falls under your purview."

"Yes. A change in policy that you chose to implement when the mayor appointed you."

"Change or no change—"

"Sir, my only point is that the audit reflects the performance of the department. No one man should be—"

"Leadership, Captain. That's the issue here. That's the issue Mr. Mayor continues to stress."

Reed cautiously continued his defense.

"It was my understanding that by decentralizing several investigative units we might do a better job of protecting New Orleans."

"Meaning?"

"Meaning I seek support from ... leadership. Every new initiative, like it or not, spoken or unspoken, is on probation. We give it time to prove itself or fail. The failings may be a mixture of execution, personnel—"

"I really don't need a lecture, Captain."

"And I apologize. I'm just a little confused."

"How so?"

"Until the audit report I never received any criticism, blunt or constructive. The general message seemed to say grin and bear it. Do the best you can."

"So your point is that you've done the best you can?"

"With the hand I've been dealt, Sir. In my opinion—"

"Not that I was asking."

"Sorry. I apologize again."

"Accepted. Go on."

"What Child Abuse needs is—"

"Yes, tell me."

"The section needs a commander of its own. The responsibilities are too vast and too critical to the community."

Hendricks stared hard at Reed. The guy was good at that. He could appear affable but deep down he was a player who was good at throwing elbows and delivering body checks. A mixed sports metaphor, to be sure, but an accurate one, because if Top Kick was anything, he was a hybrid social climber.

"You're recommending Sergeant Tanner?"

Hendricks' assumption had caught him off-guard. He was on good terms with Greg Tanner and had no real gripe. But this was no time to back a guy who was front and center in a shit storm. Equally, he didn't want to say anything that sounded negative and might trickle down to the sergeant.

"... I'm making a general statement, Chief."

He heard his secretary's voice before he announced himself. When he came through the door, she looked relieved.

"Oh, here he is," Jane said into the phone. "Please hold and I'll, yes, I'll transfer you."

"Busy morning?"

"That's what I'm here for." Janie smiled. He liked her a lot more than he was willing to admit.

"Agent Paul Miller is on the line. FBI?"

"I'll take it. Thanks."

Reed grabbed his desk phone before sitting. "Hello, Paul. To what do I owe the honor of this call?"

"Hey, Dexter. Following up on an email I received late yesterday. Something about having additional information on one of the kidnappings?"

Reed chortled before inquiring, "What the hell are you talking about?"

The federal agent read the email to Reed, who strangled the handset when he heard, "Called in by NOPD Officer Jeremy Porter, who is working Child Abuse on this particular case. Sound familiar?"

The captain clenched his teeth so hard he would not be surprised if his lovely Janie heard it in the next room. She might also take note of the fist that pounded the desktop as he sat.

"Captain?"

"Yes, yes, sorry, I'm here."

"Anyway, this Porter said you had some information for us."

He sighed, "Jesus Christ."

"No, no. Says here the name is Porter. Problem?"

"Dontcha know. He's a bit of a renegade, an oddball of sorts, which actually sounds like a compliment, but it isn't."

"Ah. So I should just—"

"Listen, Paul, he's not working the case. He's a patrol officer who got a tip about some fucking Russian porn site and wants us to chase it halfway around the world."

"Oh really? Wow."

"You've heard of Curtis McGuire?"

"Yeah, the furniture magnate?"

"That's right. Well Porter is his son-in-law, so we have to babysit the rich kid while he plays cops and robbers. Chief Hendricks put him in

Child Abuse and he lasted all of twenty minutes. I guess he still hasn't gotten the message that he sucks as a detective."

"Oh, boy. Sorry to hear that. Would you like me to call him back and explain?"

"No, no, I'll handle it on my end."

"Sure. I'll just consider this closed for now."

"Thanks. We'll talk to him for the tenth fucking time. Sorry he bothered you guys."

"No worries. Always good to speak with you, Dexter."

"Right back at ya."

Fucking Porter.

Captain Reed prowled his office, snarling, hungry for red meat. He'd gladly chow down on the chain of fools who spoiled his lion's den: McGuire, Hendricks, and Porter.

He yanked open his door. "Janie. Get Lieutenant Bayless on the phone for me, will you?"

"Sure. Everything all right in there? Thought I heard some thunder." The smile. And was that a wink? Was she flirting again?

He swiped the phone on the first ring.

"Floyd?"

"Yes."

"Floyd, listen, just got a call from the FBI. Porter went to them with this fucking Russian porn bullshit. Claimed he's working on the case."

"What!"

"Roll call tonight. Yank this kid's leash. And make it hurt. Issue him an official reprimand. The whole works. Send the message that it may be time for him to resign. I've had enough of this yo-yo."

"Happy to do it. But he's not back in rotation until Monday."

"Oh, Hell."

"Yeah, guy scores a weekend off."

"Okay. But here's the deal. I've already warned him about the chain of command, so I expect you to include that with the reprimand."

"What about Chief Hendricks?"

Jesus, everybody knew. Even Bayless.

"Frankly, I don't give a damn. This isn't daycare."

"Yes, Sir. I'll take care of it."

It was only after hanging up that Reed realized how skillfully Hendricks had avoided the topic of Jeremy Porter earlier. To his credit, the chief had not made a beef when he was informed that Tanner had dismissed the young man from Child Abuse. The captain had waited a couple days before breaking the news over the phone.

"Chief Hendricks. FYI. The Jeremy Porter transfer ... it's not going to work out."

He'd explained the snafu during the Stevens interrogation and Tanner's unwillingness to work with a newbie, and then he'd waited for a reply. The silence stretched longer than the Lake Pontchartrain Bridge.

Finally, Chief Hendricks said, "Do what you gotta do, Dexter."

So he did. But was today's meeting downtown a deferred payback? The chief could pin the audit debacle on Reed as a way of staying tight with the mayor and his benefactor.

Mr. Mayor, Mr. McGuire ... I think maybe the captain's poor leadership tainted any chance Jeremy had of succeeding with Child Abuse. If I'd known...

Reed closed his eyes, rubbed his temples, and wondered if he'd ever get the guts to invite his Janie to dinner. He was well aware of the department's policy prohibiting supervisors from dating subordinates, but hell... if he kept it discreet, who would ever know?

Chapter 33

Bart Johnson was a white male, age 41, who had served six years of a ten-year term for abusing a boy. He'd been out of prison for almost seven months when Jeremy decided to stake out his residence. Nothing unusual had occurred on the first day. But on Saturday afternoon, Jeremy sat up when Johnson strolled out of his home and hopped into a 1998 Ford Explorer.

It was curious how quickly even a self-taught profiler could notice and interpret the mannerisms, habits, and body language of child abusers. Jeremy believed he was much better now at sorting the dangerous predators from the benign souls who, for whatever reason, had lost their taste for the chase.

Jeremy's suspicions were confirmed when Johnson went into a trolling mode. The perv's search for prey was slow, methodical. He'd patiently circle a playground, and then speed off to find another, always slowing as he came close to his hunting ground of choice. Sometimes Johnson would park his vehicle in a playground parking lot but didn't get out. The afternoon wore on and Jeremy was weary of waiting when Johnson pulled his truck into the parking lot of a mid-city baseball field where a game was in progress. This seemed out of character because the players were all young teens.

Yet Johnson was apparently curious enough to leave his Explorer and slowly walk to the entrance gate. He stopped short of going into the high-rise seating area and Jeremy wondered why—until he saw a group of small children, perhaps the siblings of the athletes, playing by themselves behind the stands.

Johnson focused on an extremely active boy in a gray baseball shirt who ran around and then beyond his playmates. With Smartphone in hand, the perv covertly snapped a few photos of the boy and then leaned against the fence and called him over. The child stopped running and moved toward Johnson.

From his Toyota, Jeremy couldn't hear what was being said, but he could guess. *Hey there, I just talked to your Mom. Did you know she is thinking of getting you a new puppy? Do you want to see a picture of him? He is so cute.* He'd have a stock photo of the cutest pup you'd ever want to see and then scroll to a photo of the boy he'd just taken and make a joke. *Oops, there's another one.*

The boy giggled. The perv's spiel must have worked. The two were developing a rapport. Now the boy was staring at Johnson's vehicle as he listened to more sweet talk that would go something like this: *Hey the puppy is in my truck. Go take a peek. But get in and close the door so the puppy doesn't run away, okay? We wouldn't want that, would we? Play with the puppy for a little bit and let me know if you want him. He likes little boys.*

Jeremy's breathing tightened when the boy began moving toward the rusty truck. Johnson hovered, as if not caring what the boy did, when in fact he was eyeing the group of kids and looking into the stands for parents. When he knew he was not being observed, he nonchalantly walked to the truck.

Approaching the SUV and intercepting Johnson was a possibility, but Jeremy held off; he didn't want another father and son situation, like Dietz.

After one more quick look Johnson opened the driver's door, got in, then reached across the passenger seat. When the opposite door swung open, it hid the boy from the baseball field. He climbed in, naïve, unsuspecting. An instant later, the vehicle was on the move.

Calling for help would have been wise, but Jeremy decided against it. A cry of wolf would not only be a major embarrassment, it could send him to prison for the deaths of Peabody and McDougal.

The Explorer meandered back to Johnson's home, where the garage door opened on command from a remote control. Jeremy drove past the address, pulled to the curb, and sprinted back to the residence. As the garage door moved downward, he rolled underneath and stayed on the concrete, where he saw no one. Then the door stopped and reversed direction, clattering like a slow-moving train. From his vantage he saw the infrared safety beam that had triggered the ascent. *Fuck.* He scrambled to the driver's side of the SUV to hide, afraid the pervert might return. When the locomotion finally ended, he moved toward the side-wall exit.

Johnson and the boy apparently had entered the house through a short breezeway that attached the garage and dwelling. A kitchen window gave Jeremy a view of the interior. He was confounded to discover a brown paper bag floating upside down in mid-air. Then underneath he saw the body of the boy and realized Johnson had blinded the kid so that he could not identify the house and street. The boy's hands appeared to be bound behind his back.

His hand went to the doorknob as he leaned over to unbuckle the safety strap on his Colt .38 ankle holster. He entered with minimal squeaking from the hinges and heard the child whimper, "I want my mommy." When he made his move toward the boy, Johnson appeared already armed with a butcher knife. Without a word, he attacked.

Not having time to pull out his firearm, Jeremy countered with the defensive moves Leslie Scott had taught him at the academy. He used Johnson's unruly momentum to throw the perv off balance. He crashed against the counter top.

The move had become natural: side-step and use the subject's momentum to throw him off balance. Johnson fell sideways against the wall with a grunt but held onto his sharp weapon. Jeremy stooped to one knee to pull his Colt .38 from his ankle holster but Johnson was on the attack again. Jeremy dodged the knife, fell, and then scooted on his back into a corner of the kitchen. As Johnson gathered himself to pounce, Jeremy grabbed the handle of his Colt .38, and as he pulled it from the holster he shouted.

"Police! Drop the knife!"

Enraged, the perv ignored the warning. Standing directly over Jeremy, he aimed the knife toward Jeremy's neck. Jeremy fired one shot into Johnson's chest. Stunned, the man took a step backward, stared down at the red paint spreading on his chest, and then toppled forward on top of Jeremy. The boy began to wail.

"It's okay, it's okay. Everything's going to be all right now."

But Jeremy was pinned by the dead weight. He squirmed and pushed until he was free of Johnson's heavy body. With both hands on his revolver he quickly searched adjacent rooms. Not a sound or movement. He spotted a computer but by then the boy was bawling, so he returned to the kitchen, knelt, and tried to calm the child, who was shaking uncontrollably.

"I want my mommy! I want my mommy!"

Jeremy reached for the brown paper bag over the boy's head, hesitated, and then removed it.

He removed the shoelaces that had bound the young boy's hands.

"Son, I'm a police officer. You're safe now. You're safe, okay? I'm a good guy, and the bad guy over there can't hurt you anymore."

"Is he d-d-dead?"

"Yes, but I don't want you looking over there, okay? Now tell me something. Do you know where you live, your street address?"

"Y-yes."

"Good boy."

He patted his pants pocket. "It's in here."

What is?"

The boy pulled out a plastic Dino the Dinosaur wallet. It held a dollar bill, grimy photos, and a business card. Scrawled on the back was a street address and phone number.

"Banks Street, huh? I know where that is."

"I want to go home."

"No problem. Banks is a couple blocks from the playground. Hey, want to see *my* wallet?"

Jeremy grabbed his Police ID and let the boy hold it.

"That's me. I'm a police officer. Will you trust me to take you home?"

The boy nodded, in awe of the badge. "Do I get to keep this?"

He smiled. "Sorry, little buddy. I'm going to need that, at least for a while longer."

* * *

As they exited the garage, Jeremy hoisted the boy into his arms and made small talk to keep the child calm. In the car he finally asked, "What's your name, Son?"

"Elliot."

"That's a nice name. I like that name."

"What's your name?"

Good question. Jeremy wanted to reassure the boy with his real name, but knew he shouldn't.

"Just tell your mommy ... tell her you met the Pervert Vigilante."

"That's a funny name."

"Can you say it?"

The boy struggled with vigilante. They practiced a few times.

As they turned onto Banks Street, he hoped the tinted windows on his Toyota would shield his identity from nosey neighbors. But what did it matter? The DNA was the end of the road. At least he had saved one child.

Then he saw a phalanx of police cruisers and a TV news van clustered down the block. Bad news travels fast. He pulled to the curb.

"Okay, buddy, I'm going to let you out here. I want you to run home as fast as you can and then go right inside, promise?"

"Yes."

"One more thing."

He quickly jotted Johnson's street address on a piece of paper and handed it to Elliot.

"Give this to the police. That's how they'll know how to find the bad guy's house."

"Is he really dead?"

"Yes. He can't hurt you, buddy. He can't hurt anybody."

Elliot started to climb out of the Toyota, then turned to his savior.

"Thank you, Pervert Vigalentil."

Jeremy smiled and tousled Elliot's hair. "Close enough."

The tears were spontaneous. Jeremy choked them back, laughed, then noticed a swatch of blood on Elliot's baseball shirt. It must have rubbed off from his own clothing when he'd carried the boy to his car. Johnson's blood. Evidence. He'd let the authorities figure it out.

"Okay, buddy. Time for you to scoot home."

"Can I hug you good-bye?"

With tears now flowing, Jeremy leaned over and gave the boy a hug.

"Bye, Elliot."

Elliot slammed the car door shut, waved, and began to run. Jeremy stayed long enough to see his new friend race past police officers and head for his front door. Home sweet home.

Jeremy definitely needed a new ride, so he steered his Toyota toward the rental firm as he sped away. He knew his shirt was bloody but had learned from experience to come prepared. With his eyes on the road, he blindly reached for the zip-up jacket in the back seat, unbuckled his safety belt, and slipped on the garment. Thank God it was Saturday. His night off. He wouldn't need to report for duty.

* * *

Amy and Marty Foster had been cheering their eldest son's little league baseball team when the flock of small children appeared. Their eyes were wide and haunted. Amy knew immediately. She could feel it.

"Where's Elliot?"

"Huh?"

"Elliot! Where is—"

That moment of barren, helpless horror was bad enough. But it worsened when the tiny girl in the oversized t-shirt began to cry. "I think he was tooken by a man."

Amy's hysteria caused the umpire to halt the game as parents scattered into the surrounding park, calling for the boy and asking picnickers if they'd seen anything.

Police arrived and tried to assure the Fosters, but onlookers complained and taunted with gripes concerning the news stories they'd read about the sex crime investigations scandal.

"Are you going to actually do anything about this one," one woman demanded.

Another added, "They will probably need a donut and coffee before they start looking!"

The near riot was quelled only after Amy screamed, "Bring me back my son! I want my boy!"

An hour later, in their Banks Street home, Amy and Marty couldn't help but imagine the worst, despite the Amber alert and an APB that spread beyond city limits.

"I can't stand just *sitting* here," Marty barked from the edge of his patterned, overstuffed couch.

Sgt. Greg Tanner, despite his day off, had sped to the Fosters as much to save his job as the life of the child. Both were in serious jeopardy.

"It's better that you're both here, in case Elliot... "

As much as he wanted to be sincere and consoling, Tanner knew the odds. The Benito boy, like so many others, had been lost and never found. He didn't know how many more times he could bear to watch and listen to the grief of adults who outlive their babies. He was about to ask more questions when the front door swung open and Elliott sprinted in as though competing in a relay race.

Amy Foster shrieked at the sight of her son. "Oh my god! Oh my god! *Oh my god*!"

She swept her boy into her arms and then both were smothered by Marty and Elliot's older brother, Rick. Squeals of joy and exhaled anxiety belched from the huddle, until the squashed lost boy began to complain.

"Mom!"

"Where have you been! Are you okay? Where have you been?"

Her cries were so loud police officers on the street ran into the house. The portly Tanner waved them off and then placed his hand on the boy's shoulder.

"You must be Elliot."

"Uh huh."

"Welcome home."

"Thanks."

"What are you holding, little man?"

"Oh yeah. The Pervert Vigalantern told me to give this to you. It's where the bad guy lives."

"The bad guy?"

"Yeah, the bad guy took me from the baseball field to his house and the good guy came in and killed him."

Tanner's jaw dropped as he took the paper, scanned it, and then shoved the information at officer fire hydrant. "Go there now!"

The mother shrieked again. "He's got blood on him. Are you hurt?"

Elliot protested like an old pro. "Mom, I'm not hurt. It's the bad guy's blood.

"Son, I need to ask ... how did you get here?"

"My friend dropped me off. He's a good guy not a bad guy. He saved me. I really liked him. He showed me his badge."

"His badge?"

"He's a policeman."

Tanner felt his chest seize. He'd read about heart attacks and often wondered if it was true that aspirin alone could protect him. Too late now. He pushed through his pain. Or was it exhilaration?

"Son ... think now ... can you remember what kind of car he drove?"

* * *

He could have walked out of the house casually and gotten into his police cruiser. But Officer Fire Hydrant ran instead, knowing full well his speed would arouse the interest of the television reporter, who was blonde and very pretty. The officer was the guy who had arrested Charles Stevens. After the media hullaballoo and public praise from Chief Hendricks, he'd developed a rabid taste for celebrity, even if it was short-lived.

Sure enough, the cutie with the TV crew caught up to him before he could hop behind the steering wheel.

"Officer, what's going on in there? We heard screams and—"

He milked it. His worried eyes shot back toward the house, and then returned and pointed downward as though he was torn. In fact, he only wanted a quick peek at her cleavage before staring directly into her oceanic eyes.

"Come on, you know I'm not the public information officer. We got rules."

She stepped closer. Her voice was rich with suggestion. "*Come on*. Just for me."

"Let's go, Mack!" Officer Sign Post was getting impatient.

Hydrant, the tortured hero, leaned toward her and whispered, "The *Pervert Vigilante* strikes again."

Chapter 34

He almost told her on Sunday. They'd spent the late morning in bed together with the air conditioning on. Luisa was so affectionate and available, the confession nearly oozed out of his pores. I am the Pervert Vigilante.

But he held it in, and when she left his apartment to get some sleep before her shift that night, he was relieved that he'd kept his secret.

In the war room he re-read his police reports, triple-checking that he had not left anything out. The details gave him some sense of satisfaction: the descriptions were objective and professional. He hadn't pleaded his case, but rather let the narrative do its own good work.

His story began to unravel on Monday.

Visiting the independent lab to provide his DNA sample soured any fleeting sense of peace he'd enjoyed during his days off. His saliva was his admission of guilt; it would place him at all three crime scenes. By the end of the week, Lieutenant Styles would have his suspect and order an arrest. Goodbye yellow brick road. And Goodbye to my little Kayla.

The takedown actually began at roll call. He should have seen it coming. The room was too quiet, too still. Voices were subdued and he felt all eyes turn on him when he took his place. He didn't dare share a smile with Officer Olvera.

Lieutenant Bayless entered with a scowl on his face. "Porter!"

"Yes, Sir."

"See me after roll call. I have a reprimand to issue you."

Without pause, the commander launched into his list of messages.

"Lieutenant," Jeremy interrupted, "did you say reprimand?"

"You heard me, Porter."

"For what, Sir?"

Bayless made a show of annoyance, inhaled, and then in a controlled state of righteous indignation began.

"Well, since you ask ... let's start with failing to follow a direct order from Captain Reed. You still haven't learned chain of command, have you, Porter? So let's begin with the violation of chain of command."

"When? Where?" He knew his bluff was useless, but to save face—

"Also, you made a call to the FBI impersonating a detective. We all know that couldn't be further from the truth. You puked up that opportunity in about twenty minutes. And then you tell them you're working a Child Abuse case? Jesus, Porter!"

"No one here would help."

"Help with what? A Russian porn site?"

A few laughs were rebuked with a glance from Bayless. He was in no mood.

"You just don't get it, do you, Porter? Lying to the FBI is a goddamn felony! You are lucky we are not arresting you. So add untruthfulness to the list. And it's about time you were reprimanded for spending too much time away from your post, according to Sergeant Finnegan."

"I may have been a few minutes late but—"

Finnegan stared straight-ahead as if to prove he was untouchable.

"Add failure to devote full-time to duty. Any more questions, Porter? Now do you understand why you are getting a reprimand?"

Chapter 35

When he was released from prison and could finally be with his son again, Eric Dietz built a panic room in a closet. He knew Timmy had been traumatized by his smack-addict mother and the circumstances of his father's sudden disappearance. The space, which could be locked from inside, was softened with cushions and stacks of pillows, and stored a few packaged snacks, comics, and a mini iPad purchased by Grandma. Sometimes Timmy would go there because he liked the privacy and squeeze of the tight dimensions. Dietz knew his boy was there when he heard the knock on the door. It was Tuesday evening.

"Hey, buddy, lock it down for a few minutes, okay?"

"Okay, Dad."

Dietz had told his son that Officer Porter would likely drop by for a short visit, but he was surprised that the cop had come directly to the apartment door. They'd set up a simple protocol to protect his privacy with Timmy and to avoid surprises. One golden rule was *call before arrival,* unless there was an emergency.

Earlier, while still at work, he'd spoken with Jeremy and could tell that something had changed. Porter's tone was flat. He sounded depressed and said he needed to talk. They planned to meet after Dietz picked up Timmy from soccer practice. He and Timmy were home by seven. The carpenter had an inkling of why Porter had called. Since Saturday, the city had been buzzing with news of another pervert death and reports said a sketch artist was working with a boy who claims he was saved by the vigilante. For a cop, Porter seemed overly sensitive, even rattled by these events.

Ever cautious, Dietz opened the apartment door only as wide as the security chain would allow. He found a thick, bearded man. "Yes?"

"Eric Dietz?"

"Who wants to know?"

"I need to speak to you. It's very important. Can I come in?" Boris knew the drill: courtesy first, then escalate.

More cops? Legal harassment? No. Dietz recognized the man's accent and knew it had been a mistake to subscribe to the website.

"I'm busy right now. What's going on?"

"Just open the door. Then we'll talk."

"No thanks. You should leave. Now."

"Sorry. Too late for that."

From the rear of the apartment glass shattered.

"What the hell is going on?"

As he turned toward the sound, Dietz tried to slam the door shut. Boris burst through, snapping the chain, and attacked. Soon a second man, equally menacing, climbed through the fire escape window. He was carrying a gun. The gun was pointed at Timmy's head.

"I told you to lock down!" he yelled to his son.

"I heard noise, I—"

Boris shoved Dietz against the wall. "Ready to talk now?"

"He's a boy, motherfucker. Don't hurt him."

Boris cocked his head, grinned at Ahtoh. "A boy. That's special, eh?"

A fear he had never known, not even during his first days in prison, gripped Dietz. Jolted by the memory of Benito Jackson, he exploded, made one all-out attempt to battle the intruders. His insurrection didn't last long. As he hit the floor, he tasted blood in his mouth, and felt a stream trickling from his brow.

"You violated the agreement, didn't you, my friend?"

Dietz convulsed, strained against the heavy hands around his neck. The barrel of the gun rested on his forehead.

"No, I didn't, I—"

"Ahtoh, this man is lying." Ahtoh pointed the gun at Timmy's face.

"Don't hurt him. *Please*."

"Then don't lie to us. You violated an oath, then contacted authorities."

"No. That's not how it happened." He knew he couldn't protect Jeremy. Only his boy deserved mercy. "Promise me you won't hurt him and I'll—"

Ahtoh slapped Timmy's face.

Stunned, the boy tried to stand tall. "It's okay, Dad, he didn't hurt—"

The gun whipped across Timmy's face with the speed of glinting, metallic light, silencing him. The barrel of the gun pressed against the boy's temple.

Boris continued. "We don't make promises, Eric Dietz, to scum like you. You contacted police, didn't you?"

"No, no. He came to me. A cop. He ... he's working the case."

"What case?"

"The snuff films and those sex offenders you killed."

Confused, Boris looked to Ahtoh. "What's he talking about?" A shrug, then Boris continued. "We don't kill sex offenders. They pay good money for our services—until now. You've fucked it up. Now we got cops coming at us?"

"One guy. Only one guy. He's a loner, an outsider working on his own. I agreed to help so he'd clear my record."

"You fucking asshole!" He beat Dietz, just to vent. "So only one cop knows about us? One! Is that what you're saying?"

"Yeah, yeah. He didn't want anybody else knowing what he was—"

His cell began to chime. The ring tone mimicked the old-fashioned sound of Ma Bell. Dietz had chosen it so that he could easily recognize Porter.

"That's him."

"Convenient," Boris said.

"Let me answer! Please."

Ahtoh ordered, "Let it go to message. Just give us his name. And we'll call it in to our boss."

Boris liked that idea. He dug into Dietz's pocket, snatched the cell phone and heaved it into the next room. It clattered against a wall and went silent. Then he asked Dietz for a name and street address.

"I don't have a—"

More violence. Timmy was crying softly.

"Okay, okay. All I know is Second Street. The McGuire home. Garden District. That's where he drops off his daughter."

"How old is his daughter?"

"Timmy's age."

"Who else lives there?"

"I don't know. His ex, I guess."

"His what?"

"His wife. They're getting a divorce."

"So he won't be there."

Boris didn't wait for an answer. He pulled out his own phone and sauntered to the opposite end of the room. Ahtoh shoved Timmy to his knees in front of his dad. The barrel of the gun swayed between the two frightened faces.

Call back Jeremy, Dietz pleaded. *Work something out so no one gets hurt.*

"You cooperate, you may live. Not so sure of your police buddy."

"Please, can we work this out?"

"You break rules, somebody must pay."

"Please, I'll do anything. Just don't hurt my son."

Dietz could hear portions of Boris' conversation, then the Russian disappeared and didn't immediately return. Clearly, someone in the organization would confirm Jeremy's name and profession. They'd find a street address and then take action. Violent action.

* * *

Holding the phone to his ear with his shoulder and pawing through the files in Dietz's office, Boris spoke to the man called Emperor. Details were passed to Demyan who began his hack of New Orleans city records.

There was silence for a time as the great man waited for information and pondered the possibilities. The Russian thug tapped the speaker phone function, set down his cell, and with free hands he quickly found the folders containing Dietz's conviction. Boring. All public record. He tossed the contents and turned his attention to the PC. A drawer held several small tools, including a screwdriver. He loosened the back of the computer and ripped out the hard drive.

The elegant voice of the Emperor returned.

"This is what we are going to do, Boris. These two men have harmed us, harmed us deeply. They must pay for their deceit. First, do you have the crate in your vehicle?"

"Yes, of course."

"Good. Crate the boy and bring him to me. Then we'll wait a few hours, till after midnight, when they are asleep. Then you'll go get the little girl at Porter's wife's home. Since we'll need to move our operation—fast—I'll treat our subscribers to a grand finale. A spectacle. A double bill of immortals. Then we kiss New Orleans goodbye."

"Got it. But what should I do with Dietz?"

Chapter 36

The Baptist church was empty when Jeremy entered and sat in a pew. He stared at the vaulted ceiling and considered whether he should confess his sins to his deceased father, a preacher whose sad, ascetic temperament had made for a boring childhood. Why bother? It wouldn't change anything. He'd really only stopped at the church to kill time while he waited to visit Eric Dietz.

After the Bayless debacle the previous night, Jeremy had returned home but was unable to sleep. He read the text that Luisa had sent in the wee hours asking what was going on. He didn't answer because he believed his call would spell disaster for her career. Washing away the tarnish of having associated with the Pervert Vigilante might take years.

By mid-morning, Leslie Scott also made contact and left a voicemail: "Need to talk? You've been under a lot of pressure, with the divorce and everything. But what's all this other stuff? I'll help, if I can. Give me a call." But Jeremy didn't.

Later in the day he decided to arrange a meeting with Dietz. Not that it was entirely necessary. In fact, maybe it was wrong of him. But he felt the man deserved to know why he intended to drive to Second District and surrender.

"Jesus ..." He lowered his head into his hands. Three homicides. They sickened his soul.

If only he could turn back the clock. If only he'd listened to reason and held onto his position with the McGuire enterprise. Hell, if he and Sandy had kept their marital vows, he likely would have been groomed for CEO of the furniture enterprise. Too late for that. And the biggest crime of all was the impact his stupidity would have on Kayla. He'd enjoyed being a father, more than he could have imagined. If that had been his only purpose in life ...

He dozed, exhausted from his ordeal, then pulled himself to his feet. Standing at the altar, watching Jesus on the cross, he wanted to say something profound. All he could muster was, "I'm sorry."

During the drive, his call to Dietz had gone unanswered. When he reached the neighborhood he waited nearly an hour, then got restless and began to walk. He stopped when he spotted Eric's truck parked at the curb.

Climbing the stairs, Jeremy dialed one more time, then tapped lightly on the apartment door while listening to the voicemail message. Was Dietz avoiding him? He was about to leave when he noticed a deep gash in the threshold at about knee height. When he stroked it with his finger, chips of paint peeled: fresh wounds, the kind caused by clumsy furniture movers. Sliding his hand upward on the surface of the door he found an indentation at shoulder height, possibly caused by impact. He reached for the knob and the door swung open. The broken security chain dangled from its brass mount.

"Eric? Timmy?"

The floor was scuffed and the small rug he remembered in the entry was gone. He stooped to the hardwood to get a closer look at the damage and discovered fresh drops of blood. He pulled his handgun from his ankle holster.

The kitchen looked normal, but in the office he found the PC ripped open liked a slaughtered pig and court records scattered in heaps.

"Eric!"

A moan barely carried over the sound of street traffic.

He found the carpenter in the bathroom. His arms were lashed around the toilet tank so that his face—a sock gag choking him—hung over the bowl. Even after Jeremy cut him loose, Dietz could barely speak, his body was listless. That's when Jeremy realized his friend's forearm veins had been slit. The man was bleeding out.

"Eric, can you speak? Tell me what happened?"

Sprawled on the linoleum floor, Dietz seemed to be gathering himself, clawing back to consciousness. Jeremy couldn't wait. He needed to call 911, but on Dietz's phone. Where the hell was it? He speed-dialed his Android and immediately heard chiming from Dietz's phone in the next room. He scrambled and found the cell on the floor, fingered the digits, and raced through the other rooms searching for Timmy. As he discovered the panic room closet and a broken window sash, he heard the dispatcher.

"911 Operator. What is your emergency?"

He blurted out the address and shouted, "Send emergency unit—code three—I have a man bleeding badly."

"Code three? Are you a police officer?"

"Just send the fucking unit. Code three—code fucking three!"

He tossed the phone and returned to the bathroom where he grabbed towels, wrapping them as tightly as possible with tourniquets on both arms. He also reached to the sink and opened the tap. He filled a cup with cold water, but Dietz wouldn't sip.

"Took Timmy. Going for Kayla after... " He coughed lightly, drooled blood. "Kayla ... midnight."

"What do you mean? Who did this, Eric?"

There were tears in Dietz's eyes, regret and pain, another impossible fight he might not win.

"I had to tell them everything. They know about you now."

"It's okay. I understand."

"They hurt Timmy. But... " He held up two fingers, desperate to be understood.

"They broke in? Two men?"

Dietz nodded but fought to say more. "Your house. Midnight."

The voice was faint, a flutter of breath, but Jeremy was absolutely sure he heard the words "Save my boy. Please. Save my boy."

Jeremy, fighting back tears, leaned over and whispered into Eric's ear. "Eric, I am so sorry I dragged you into this. You hang in there, Man. I'll find Timmy. I promise."

Chapter 37

His little girl was in danger. That's all Jeremy could think about. He ran out of the apartment, met the arriving First District officer on the stairs, and flashed his badge.

"I'm a cop, Second District. This is my friend's residence. Some people broke in here. He's in bad shape."

The officer took a quick glance at Jeremy's ID folder, "No, problem, Man. We got EMS on the way."

"Fantastic. Thanks."

As the district officer raced in, he radioed dispatch, "Keep EMS on a code three!" Then he turned to ask a couple questions, but Jeremy was gone. "What the hell?"

Jeremy hauled ass to his car, a white KIA Forte LX Sedan. The dashboard clock said 8:55 p.m., which gave him only about three hours to come up with a plan.

Before his hasty exit, he'd gotten Dietz to drink some water. Hydration and cool washcloths on his face helped revive him enough to describe, in choppy segments, the arrogant Russian men who boasted about their orders to abduct both children, Timmy in a crate not fit for a dog. They would come for Kayla after midnight. A snuff film was being prepared for both children.

It was pointless to rush to authorities now and try to explain everything. Maybe they'd be nimble enough to protect Sandy and Kayla but what about Timmy? He'd be doomed. Jeremy owed it to his friend to do whatever he could to save the boy.

After parking at the Second District station, Jeremy grabbed his gym bag from the trunk and strolled in. His first stop was the row of clipboards that hung in the roll call room. All three platoons posted schedules and lists of personnel for each twenty-four hour period. Relieved that a full crew was lined up for the third shift, Jeremy pulled an annual leave form from a tier of shelves, quickly filled it out, and placed it on the clipboard.

From there he walked unnoticed into his inventory supply room, shoved four Tasers into his gym bag, and exited. His final stop was the front desk where he found the second platoon officer checking his watch.

"Long day?" he asked.

The officer suppressed a yawn and smiled. "Caught me."

"No problem. I've been there. Hey, just wanted you to tell Lieutenant Bayless that I need emergency leave tonight. Family stuff. My request is on the clipboard."

"Oh, okay."

"Shouldn't be a problem."

"Nah, they have a full load tonight, don't they?"

"Luckily."

"I'll let him know. You have a good night."

"I'll try."

The wall clock showed 9:20 p.m.

When he arrived at his apartment, Jeremy unlocked the war room and removed a neat stack of police reports from his locked file drawer. He placed them on the coffee table in the front room. All three reports detailed the series of events he'd been involved in, describing how each "perpetrator" had died.

He dialed Special Operations Division, where the PV Task Force was assigned.

"Hello, this is Officer Porter, Second District. Is Leslie Scott working tonight?"

"Yup. He's on the street right now."

"What time does he finish?"

"Midnight."

"Got it. Thanks."

He sat on the couch and remembered how pretty Luisa had looked on her first visit, then quickly flushed his mind of such things. With paper and pen he wrote a letter for Scott.

Leslie,

This is the key for my apartment. The address is 2214 Milan Street. I left an envelope on the coffee table for you. It is very important that you read its contents immediately. Please pick it up when you get off tonight. Thanks. You have been a great friend.

Jeremy

He dropped his front door key in the envelope with the letter, then drove a short distance to the Special Operations office. Before leaving the building he made the desk sergeant promise he would give the envelope to Scott.

"It's very important. A personal matter that needs his attention."

"I understand. No problem."

"Thank you, Sergeant."

No matter what happened later, Jeremy believed that his friend would understand the intentions of the Pervert Vigilante. He needed somebody to speak up for him.

It was 10:10 p.m. when he steered toward his former residence in the Garden District. As he drove, Jeremy dialed Sandy's cell phone. When she didn't pick up, he cursed. He tried the landline in the house and still got no answer.

"Goddamnit, Sandy!"

He would have pulled into the driveway but a black Prius was parked there, probably Ray Coulter's wheels.

In the dark, his eyes panned the neighborhood but found nothing unusual. At the front door he dialed Sandy one more time. When he got voicemail, he began to pound on the door just hard enough to sound an alarm.

* * *

Sandy had ignored Jeremy's first couple of calls because she was enjoying an HBO movie on the plush sofa with Ray. Actually, they'd lost interest in the story after they exchanged soft kisses and warm embraces.

"Need to get that?" he asked.

"I'll call him back later ... Ahhh, that's so good."

But when the front door began to beat like a drum, she pried her body free and jogged to the foyer security camera.

"Shit!"

Ray came up behind her and placed his hands on her shoulders. "Who is it?"

"It's fucking Jeremy. Goddamnit. I should call the police."

"Yeah, they should be here by tomorrow morning." He grinned, but she cursed, so he stopped fondling her. "Just ask him what he wants. You don't have to open the door, do you?"

She considered the idea but decided to answer.

Ray stood behind her as her enamel fingernail touched the intercom. "What!"

"I need to come in, we need to talk, it is very important."

"It's late."

"Let me in."

"Why can't it wait until morning?"

"Because you won't be alive in the morning."

Sandy looked at Ray before answering. "You're threatening me?"

"Sandy, please open the door. It's an emergency."

When Jeremy entered, he pointed at Ray.

"Sorry, but you need to leave. Now."

Sandy protested. "What the fuck, Jeremy? You can't order us around."

"You and I need to have a very private conversation. This is a serious situation." He addressed Ray with a tad more diplomacy. "You'll thank me later."

When the lovers didn't budge, Jeremy tensed, "Sandy, this is urgent, extremely urgent. You and I need to talk in private. Ray, get the hell out of here *now*!"

Ray stepped forward. "Hey, come on, man."

"She's the mother of my daughter. I'm here to protect her. You need to go. And don't be stupid enough to drive around the block and play Superman."

The standoff ended when Sandy, sensing something strange, said, "I'll call you later."

"You sure?"

"I'll be alright."

She made it a point to kiss him so Jeremy could see and know that she was still boss. When her beau was gone, she launched.

"You better have a fucking good reason for barging in like this!"

Jeremy waited for Ray's car to drive off before he answered.

"You and Kayla are in serious danger. And it's my fault."

"What are you talking about?"

"You know about the Pervert Vigilante, right?"

"Yeah. Everybody does."

"It's me."

"What?"

"I'm the Pervert Vigilante." It sounded so stupid, so incredibly ridiculous, he understood her attempt to laugh it off.

"Oh, come on. This is why you interrupted my evening with—"

"Sandy. I am the Pervert—"

"No!"

"Listen to me."

"Get away from me."

"It's not going to help to ignore what I just said."

"Don't touch me!"

Stunned, mouth opened, she seemed to be gasping for air. One loud gasp, then several short sucks of oxygen. She backed away and moved into the house, turned off the television and then threw the remote, as she paced in front of the sofa, trembling and ready to explode. She grabbed fistfuls of her hair.

"Jesus Christ, what have you done to us ... you've ruined my family."

He moved to her. "Sandy—"

She attacked, shrieking and pounding his chest.

"You've ruined us! After all my dad did for you? I hate your guts! I hate your fucking guts!"

Jeremy grabbed her arms, but the force of her rage pushed him backwards, until she spent her last words and collapsed into his arms, weeping.

His watch said 10:37 p.m. Jeremy knew he couldn't wait much longer. He had to make a move.

Chapter 38

"Sandy, I need you and Kayla to come with me. You need to get out of here, *now*."

"You still haven't told me anything! Why would we go anywhere with a killer?"

"I've been exposed. Some very bad people are coming here. They want to bring me down by hurting you and Kayla. I've got to get you somewhere safe."

"But—"

"I'll explain everything later, Sandy!"

His explosion frightened her. "I ... I need to pack a bag."

"There's no time! Get Kayla out of bed. *Move*."

Sandy bundled Kayla in a blanket and the small family ran for the KIA.

The groggy little girl asked, "Where are we going?"

"The electricity went off in the house, Baby, so we're going to spend the night out. Sound like fun?"

Sandy shot him a look, still a mess of emotion, tears flowing, but he didn't bother telling her where they were headed. It wasn't grand, but the Heraldson Hotel would be safe; it employed a couple of police officers twenty-four hours a day, seven days a week. And he knew the desk clerk from his short stay there after he'd been kicked out of the house. The reservation had already been made.

She groaned when Jeremy led them into the room—common verging on tawdry—and laid a sleepy Kayla on the bed.

"It's secure and no one will look for you here. If anything scares you, call downstairs. Two cops are in the lobby. I'll ask them to keep a close eye on this floor and roam the hallways."

"Shouldn't they be looking for you, the Pervert—"

"It's not what it appears to be."

"Isn't that what they all say?"

She was right. The truth hurt. The line between being a cop and a criminal was evaporating but there was no turning back now.

He dimmed the lights and turned to Sandy.

"Jeremy, the whole city is looking for you."

"Right now that doesn't matter."

"Why?"

"Because somebody much worse is looking for you and Kayla."

"I'm calling Daddy."

She pulled out her phone, but Jeremy stopped her.

"No. Not yet. There's another child in danger and we can't do anything that would—"

"Jeremy! Call the police!"

"I am the fucking police!" He flew into a tirade of curses and bitter denunciations. He spat out what he knew of the Emperor, snuff films, Timmy Dietz, and the inability to get his commanders or the FBI to give a good goddamn about any of it.

Kayla stirred and complained. He lowered his voice to a harsh whisper and continued.

"They don't fucking get it. They won't until ... by tomorrow it will all come out."

"God, I'm hoping this is a bad dream."

"It's not."

He kissed Kayla, stroked her hair, then moved to the door. "I'll call when I can with instructions."

"Instructions?"

"I'll let you know when to call Curtis and the police."

"Jesus, Jeremy… "

He tried to put his arms around her but she pushed away, in anguish.

"… I'm sorry. For everything."

Both shed tears and stared at each other, mute as distant stars at twilight.

He checked his watch: 11:19 p.m. As he reached for the door he felt his heart and soul drop out of him with the weight of sandbags.

"Lock up when I leave."

* * *

By the time he made it back to Sandy's house, it was 11:44 p.m. He knew the Russians wouldn't recognize his car, so he parked a few doors down from the residence. Only Sandy's car was visible in the driveway. He sat near the front window peering through sheer curtains. Twenty minutes later he noticed a steel gray van pass the home for the second time.

Many of the Garden District homes felt remote from one another. Not because of the distance, but from the foliage that created layers of privacy. Jeremy sucked in air when he saw two hulking figures enter the gate near the street and quickly find refuge in deep shadows.

Please, God. Help me through this.

Armed with four Tasers, his body armor, and the Colt .38 he had stuck in his belt for quick access, Jeremy moved into a first floor closet near the downstairs bedroom and staircase. He cracked open the door and waited. Moments later, he heard glass breaking in the rear of the house. Soft footfalls came next, and then a flashlight beam bleached the floor.

Only one man appeared, and that was ideal. Jeremy opened the closet door quickly, and at close range shot the Taser. Two small darts flew and spread. One dart lodged in the neck of the intruder. The other dart in the left shoulder. The intruder yelped as his spastic body smashed to the hardwood. The wire conductors that connected the darts to the Taser made for a clumsy retreat into his hiding place. He made it in time to avoid the beam of light that crawled along the floor toward the fallen figure.

"Ahtoh, what the hell?" The accent was thick as dirt.

Adrenaline pumping, desperate to strike, Jeremy charged, but the door jammed against the boots of the first man, smashing Jeremy's forehead against the painted wood.

"Fuck!"

Gunfire sang high and wild. Jeremy was struck twice in the chest. The body armor absorbed the bullets, but the impact hurt. He dropped to one knee, set down the first Taser and pulled out his Colt with his left hand. With a second Taser in his right hand, he opened the door enough to shoot. Darts dug into the second man's chest, sending the scumbag to a hard landing. For good measure, Jeremy squeezed the trigger one more time, sending the bearded one into a temporary state of oblivion.

He quickly approached Boris and bound his wrists with zip ties.

Ahtoh's head rose off the floor. "What the fuck's going on?"

Jeremy scampered back to the closet, retrieved the first Taser and pulled the trigger twice. Ahtoh flopped onto his back, then curled into a dazed ball. His wrists were bound moments later.

A search of both bodies yielded weapons and cell phones, which he tossed into his gym bag. On the floor he also found what felt like a burlap sack. He fingered it as he flipped on a hall light to get a good look at his prey. They groaned and cursed.

Each must have weighed over 200 pounds because Jeremy labored to lift the thugs to their knees. To get their full attention, he waved his Colt in front of their faces.

"Hey! Look at me! Tell me where you took the boy."

Ahtoh said, "I want a lawyer. I'm not talking to no cop."

"Oh, you want justice? Is that it?"

"Goddamn right!"

Jeremy grabbed hold of the connective wire attached to the dart in Ahtoh's neck. The tip was barbed, like a fishing hook. There was a certain process to remove the dart but Jeremy wasn't following procedures on this night. He pulled slowly until the tension threatened to rip a fleshy hole near the man's jugular.

"Feel good?"

Ahtoh cried out. "*Sh-iii-t*."

"There's your justice. Now wise up. You guys weren't looking for a lawyer when you broke in here."

"You're a cop. A *bad* cop. We deserve—"

He sucked air when Jeremy pulled harder on the wires and then reached for the other man's chest. The Taser propellants had easily penetrated the thin black t-shirt, and the conduits hung like the strands of a cowboy tie. Soon both men were howling a tune from a demonic choir's hymnal.

Then Jeremy let go and made a show of being distraught. Tortured, he reached for a hallway chair, slammed it down in front of his foes, and sat heavily.

"Jesus, look at me. All I wanted was to be like Joe Doode. But you motherfuckers ... *your type* ... you've turned me into a raving, fucking maniac. Goddamnit, I ... I ...I want to blow you' your fucking brains out."

Ahtoh glanced at the bearded Boris. Both appeared more frightened of words than weapons.

"You two fuckers break into my house to kidnap my little girl to have her tortured and snuffed ... and you want me to call you a fucking lawyer?" Jeremy rolled his eyes toward heaven, waved his handgun recklessly. "Joe ... speak to me, buddy. What the fuck would you do? What would you do with these scumbags? TELL ME!"

Abrupt, yowling, Jeremy stood, picked up the chair, slammed it down again, and went after Boris.

"Where's the Emperor?"

Wide-eyed, Boris shook his head.

Jeremy repeated the question to Ahtoh, who continued to babble about wanting a lawyer.

"Listen up. One of you guys is going to tell me where the Emperor is. And you're going to tell me exactly how to get there. But since I don't have much time ... let's have a little competition for the honor, okay?"

With both men's' eyes fixed on Jeremy, he popped open the chamber of the Colt .38, Jeremy emptied the ammunition, then loaded only one bullet before closing and spinning the chamber. Only Jeremy knew where the one round landed.

"Wild guess—I bet you guys are really good at Russian roulette. National pastime, eh?"

He smiled, cackled like a lunatic, and then pushed the gun against Ahtoh's forehead and cocked the hammer.

"Okay, you're first. Tell me where I can find the Emperor."

Ahtoh stuttered, shaking his head, pleading for—

To the ears of the two intruders, the click of the hammer was as loud as a cannon shot.

The silence was unnerving, too. It stretched as Jeremy ditched the crazy man shtick for a hard stare that said *I am dead serious.*

He cocked the hammer and pressed the barrel against Boris' temple.

"Where is the Emperor?"

Stinking with sweat, Boris gritted his teeth and closed his eyes as—

Click.

"Interesting. You're both so ... *strategic*. But let's review. Only six chambers in a Colt, meaning only four are left. My advice? Start thinking percentages, guys. This next trigger pull has a twenty-five percent chance of killing you. If that's a blank, the percentage rises to thirty-three and a third, then fifty percent, and then ... nighty-night, Motherfuckers."

Boris finally spoke. "But only one of us will die."

"Oh. Now I get it. You're the *smart* one. Okay. Excellent point. But I have two more guns—yours.

"Motherfucker!" Ahtoh blurted.

"Flattery gets you nowhere, Dude."

Jeremy cocked and aimed the Colt at Ahtoh. He calmly asked the question but didn't bother waiting for a reply.

Click.

Then he looked sadly at Boris.

"Gosh, suddenly I don't like your chances."

"We, we can make—"

"A deal?" Jeremy lurched and shouted in Boris' face. "Here's the deal. *Where the fuck is the Emperor?"* The gun pressed against Boris' temple so hard it moved his head to his shoulder.

Boris realized Jeremy was seconds away from blowing his brains out. His head trembled and tears flooded his dark eyes. Panic slurred his speech.

"Pardon? I'm sorry. I can't understand you … it must be your *accent*. No, no, we have to play by the rules. I'll just pull the trigger so your friend can have his next turn, okay, big guy?"

Boris bawled, accelerated the head shakes, and all but hopped on his knees. Jeremy clamped a free hand on the scared man's throat.

"Listen, I *think* you want to help. But if you pull some bull shit on me ... first, I'll shoot Doofus in the face and then I'll show you torture like you have never seen. *Do you understand every fucking word I'm saying?*"

Fervent nodding, trying to catch his breath. Jeremy backed the gun slightly away from the Russian's temple.

Boris gasped for air, then spat out, "East New Orleans."

Jeremy stared lasers into the man, pulled the cartridge from the Taser and, turning it into a stun gun, aimed it directly at Boris's temple.

"Could you be a little more specific?"

Chapter 39

Jeremy could tell that Boris was exhausted, convinced that the mad man waving the gun was seconds away from blowing his brains out. That's exactly what the Pervert Vigilante wanted. He lifted the burlap sack he'd found after Tasering the thugs.

"What's this for?"

Boris explained that he had planned to subdue Kayla by tossing the rough bag over her head and upper body. Then she'd be easy to carry to the van where he'd lock her in a crate for delivery to the Emperor. Jeremy burned, clenched his teeth.

"I should blow your fucking face off."

Boris hung his head, then begged for mercy.

Jeremy ignored him and dragged Ahtoh into an adjacent bathroom. He Tasered the man's back, then cut the zip ties so that he could wrap the man's arms around the toilet basin and tilt his face over the bowl. Like he'd found Dietz. Then he resecured his wrists and as the man came back to weary consciousness, he crouched down to have one last chat.

"You didn't think my friend would survive, did you? Well he did, and he's going to fry your fat ass in court. Smile for the camera."

Jeremy took several photos with his phone and sent them to Dietz. He doubled the ties on Ahtoh's wrists and ankles and then returned to Boris.

As he sat in the chair directly in front of Boris, a cell phone in the gym bag began to vibrate. A text message arrived with only two dots from an "unknown" sender.

Jeremy shoved the phone at Boris. "Is this him?"

"Yes."

"How do you respond?"

"Two periods means okay.'"

Jeremy had been tempted to jam the Taser against Boris' crotch. But after a long pause he tapped a two-dot response.

"Like that?"

"Yes."

"Final answer?" He raised the Taser.

Boris nodded and Jeremy thumbed the send button.

"The Emperor is now waiting for…."

"….the little girl"

"….to arrive."

"….for a double feature with Timmy."

Jeremy struggled to control his emotions. "Do you have any idea how much I want to hurt you? What is the location in New Orleans East?"

"It's an old industrial concrete building, empty. He leases it."

"Do you know the address?"

"No, but I know it is exactly 1.25 miles past the Rigolets Bridge. You will see an old rusted sign that says East Industries. You turn down that road for about a half-mile and it is the only building there."

"How do you get in?"

"You can't break in. It is a concrete building with a steel door he keeps locked. If he does not see us, he will not open it."

"You better figure out a way I can get in there and quick."

"One chance. Maybe you can fit. If you sneak around back, you will find a ladder against the building. I was installing an air vent because of the foul odor in that place. The vent is loose in the frame because I haven't finished the work. But even if you fit through, it's a two-story drop to the floor."

"Does he have weapons, guns?"

"We have the guns. He has his stiletto and…." Boris didn't finish.

"And what?"

"….his cattle prod."

Jeremy buried his fury, pulled Boris up, and shoved him out of the house into the McGuire driveway. The elite neighborhood was asleep as Jeremy guided Boris into the trunk of his car. Before closing the trunk, Jeremy looked at Boris one more time.

"Let's review. I won't just kill you if you get this wrong, right, Boris?"

"Yes."

"As in, you know I'll keep you alive as long as I possibly can before you die a painful, horrid death?"

"I get it."

Jeremy reloaded his Colt .38 revolver and set out toward the Rigolets Bridge.

* * *

The area was considered New Orleans but was mainly fishing camps—a sprawling, neglected area of the city due to nonexistent street lighting and deplorable roads. Scattered about were desolate manufacturing plants set back off the Chef Menteur Highway. Jeremy remembered the thruway had been closed recently due to unusual icing and hazardous road conditions. On this humid, suffocating night, that would not be an issue. Still, the Pervert Vigilante had to jolt himself out of a weird tourist mentality as he took in the vast stretch of haunted acreage that most members of NOPD would never have to explore.

Thirty minutes later, he reached the Rigolets Bridge. After driving for exactly 1.25 miles, Jeremy observed the East Industries sign. He pulled off the highway and followed a cracked asphalt road to what looked like a defunct foundry surrounded by a high fence. A perfect place for evil. No one would suspect anyone was inside. Jeremy slowed to a crawl with the headlights out. He would need to walk through high weeds and scattered garbage to make his way to the rear of the building.

Before he left for his obstacle course, he grabbed his cell phone. It was 1:43 a.m.

*   *   *

Sandy was curled around Kayla on the lumpy Heraldson Hotel bed when her phone rang.

"Jeremy?"

"Yeah. Are you okay?"

"No. I'm a nervous wreck. Where are you?"

"There's a pen and a notepad in the bedside table. Grab it so you can write down this location."

She opened the drawer and then jotted the information, which included the familiar names of the Chef Menteur Highway and the Rigolets Bridge and something about a ladder and vent.

"Okay, now listen, if I don't call you back in sixty minutes, call 911. You know where to send the police. Say Code 3 and tell them a police officer is ... you know."

"No, I don't know, Jeremy. What are you doing?"

"Saving a little boy."

"This is crazy."

He ignored her and continued his instructions.

"Send police to our house, too. But that's not an emergency. They'll find one of the guys who broke in handcuffed in the downstairs bathroom."

"*One* of the guys!"

"The other one is with me."

"God, Jeremy. Oh my god...."

"Hey! Be there for Kayla. Everything will be ... it'll work itself out. Remember, give me an hour."

"Okay," she whispered.

"Sandy...."

"Yes?"

"I love you."

She wanted to respond, but didn't know how. Mixed feelings stuck in her throat. Then Jeremy ended the call.

The Heraldson was deathly quiet and pacing in the drab hotel room did nothing to calm her nerves. She couldn't take it anymore. Five minutes after her call from Jeremy, she broke down and made a decision. *Fuck it!* She dialed her phone. It was almost 1:48 a.m.

"Daddy! Daddy, it's me. Jeremy's in trouble. Lots of trouble and I don't know what to do."

* * *

Still in uniform, Leslie Scott sat on the couch staring at the police reports spread out on the coffee table. He went numb for a moment then roused himself. Why didn't he figure this out sooner? Especially the many times he sensed Jeremy was off kilter. The recent breakfast they'd shared near Second District revealed a jittery, distant man who was not himself.

More shocking was the depth of detail in the reports, and the long hours of surveillance Jeremy must have put in before encountering the offenders; it spoke to determination, thoroughness, and a dangerous approach to proving he was worthy. Dead men can't argue their innocence. But Scott was confident that the documents before him might provide the foundation for a strong defense of Jeremy's actions.

He rose and walked through the dark apartment. The main bedroom was spare and neat. Down the hallway he found a second bedroom with a durable cylinder lock. He turned the knob and the door opened into a small room. Reaching into the darkness, he slid his palm on the wall until he found a light switch and flipped it. He couldn't believe what he was seeing.

"Holy shit."

Two walls were covered with photos of crime scenes and people—the deceased, the abused, and the guilty whose eyes either pleaded for help or confessed their sins. Photocopied court rulings and investigation updates also commanded attention.

Where are you, Jeremy? What's your next move?

Chapter 40

Police Chief Morris Hendricks turned over in bed and reached blindly for his phone that spun in a slow circle from vibrations. He groaned when he saw the name on the ID screen. Did he not deserve a few, untouchable hours of sleep? When he answered he struggled to sweeten his voice.

"Chief Hendricks."

"Morris, this is Curtis McGuire. I'm sorry for calling. But we have an emergency. It's serious. A child is in danger and my son-in-law—"

Hendricks sat up.

"—it's horrible. I can hardly comprehend. I'm in—"

"Curtis, calm down. Whose child is in danger?"

"I don't know. I only know that Jeremy, my son-in—"

"I know who Jeremy is. Tell me what is happening?"

McGuire quickly repeated what Sandy had told him. The little boy, a snuff film that was also intended for his granddaughter, Jeremy's decision to go after the kidnappers because police would not listen to his pleas for help.

Hendricks was quite sure that McGuire was in the grip of a mental breakdown. New Orleans East? Russian porn? A fuck-up son-in-law who never should have been hired or—

"He's the Pervert Vigilante, Morris! Do you hear me? Jeremy admitted that he's the guy behind all these murders."

"Curtis ... have you lost your mind?"

"Yes! Because it's true! Now do something. Do something, Morris. Or a child may die!"

Hendricks grabbed a pen and jotted down everything McGuire recalled from his conversation with Sandy.

"We will get on this right away. I'll call you back when I know more."

* * *

"Lieutenant Bayless, Second District. How can I help you?"

"Floyd, this is Chief Hendricks. Is Jeremy Porter on duty tonight?"

"No, Sir, he used emergency leave. Family issues. Why?"

Maybe the young cop had concocted a sick ruse so that he could escape and never serve time for his crimes. Hendricks didn't know. But he was sure that whatever happened in the next few hours he would finally be free of the hapless, disastrous Jeremy Porter.

"You need to grab a couple of your officers and head out to New Orleans East. We have information that the Pervert Vigilante has been located."

"New Orleans East? But Sir, that's the Seventh District. Why not have them respond?"

"Because the Pervert Vigilante is one of your officers."

"One of my officers? Who?"

"Jeremy Porter."

"What? *Fucking Powder Puff?* Sir, I'm sorry, I just can't—"

"Believe it."

"Sir, this has to be a mistake."

"No mistake, it's him. We have reason to believe that he may be stalking his next victim. Something about a Russian immigrant. There is also the possibility that a kidnapped child will be there. I have an address and details. Lead a team. Lights, no sirens. I know the area. You'll be there in fifteen minutes."

"Yes, Sir."

"While you deploy I'll call Seventh District to get them started. I'll also have the PV Task Force meet you there. And, if you need them, I'll have Special Ops ready to back you up, depending on what you find."

"Yes Sir, but what about Porter's father-in-law and—"

"Screw family ties. Porter is a murderer. And he's armed. Use whatever force necessary."

* * *

Leslie Scott sat in Jeremy's living room, stunned by what he'd discovered and unsure of what his next step should be.

His cell phone pinged and he snatched it up, hoping it was his friend. But the text message was from command.

Alert. PV possibly located in NO East. TF members meet at SOD ASAP.

Scott jumped to his feet, secured Jeremy's documents, and rushed to his vehicle. The roads were clear as he sped back to the Special Operations Division, where he had ended his shift only an hour or so earlier.

When he entered the building, he grabbed the appropriate gear and joined other members of the PV Task Force who had assembled to listen to their supervisor.

"Listen up. We have information that the Pervert Vigilante has been located at a building in New Orleans East. Get your equipment, team up, and caravan to the Rigolets Bridge. There are district officers en route to the scene now. We will support their efforts. The on-scene supervisor is Lt. Floyd Bayless."

Oh shit! Fucking Bayless, Scott thought. He wanted to speak up and reveal all the crap the half-assed lieutenant had dished out, but held his tongue. Just *get to the scene.*

"And one more thing, we have reason to believe the Pervert Vigilante is a New Orleans Police Officer by the name of Jeremy Porter, assigned to the Second District."

Gasps and looks of disbelief spread among the cops.

Leslie Scott showed no emotion. He was strapping on his gear.

Chapter 41

The surroundings were pitch black and the air was thick with humidity when Jeremy began his trek toward the building. He didn't dare use a flashlight for fear of exposing himself. And anyway, the glare would have drawn even more of the giant mosquitoes that buzzed around his head like military helicopters, attacking his face and neck. A can of repellent would be damn handy right now, but it was not on his weaponry checklist.

What checklist? He'd been improvising all night.

After maneuvering through the shoulder-high weeds, Jeremy reached the fence surrounding the structure. The six-foot fence was topped with barbed wire. But there was no turning back. He prayed Timmy was still alive. He ascended the fence and clumsily belly-rolled over the top as his flesh and clothing were ripped by the galvanized, four-point jags.

Inside the perimeter, on cat paws, he made his way to the rear of the building where he saw the ladder Boris had described. It led to the modest cut-out some twenty-five feet up where the vent had been installed to release foul odors.

Jeremy began his climb. At the top, he carefully slipped the grating from its frame and tossed it into the weeds, far from the building, then peered through the opening. Would he even fit through? Although the interior was dimly lit, he could see Timmy, naked and strapped to a chair, but still alive. *Thank God.* A second empty chair awaited Kayla. And then he saw *him*.

The Emperor donned a flowing black robe with a hood as though he were heading to his coronation. Then he ran his artful nails through his perfect silver hair as he paced and muttered while glancing at a large gold wrist watch. He walked to the front steel door, slid open a narrow panel, and peered out. His delivery had not arrived, so he hastily dialed his cell phone and waited. When Boris didn't answer, he slammed the phone on a table top, moved back toward Timmy, and turned on a spotlight. The show must go on.

If Jeremy was to fit through the small opening, he would need to shed his vest. He pulled it off and let it fall. He wanted to take a shot but it was too risky. A miss would mean certain death for Timmy. He couldn't wait any longer. He had to make a move. He rested his head against the wall at the top of the ladder and whispered "Dear God, help me, please. I love you, Kayla. I love you very much, sweetheart."

The Emperor made one last attempt to reach Boris, then tossed the phone on a nearby chair and moved the tripod into place. He pressed *record*, saw the red light appear on the video camera, swept into position, and spoke.

"I am Emperor."

With a melodramatic flourish, the monster picked up his electric cattle prod and whipped it through the air for effect.

From his perch, Jeremy might have assumed the basic tool was standard issue on a livestock farm. What he could not know was that the fastidious auteur had pimped out his device for his own cruel purposes.

The generous blue handle grip was fitted with a lever. At its lowest, setting the shocks were superficial. Yet when pushed forward to MAX, the high-voltage/low amperage electric arc was capable of delivering a tortuous, lethal jolt.

Protruding from the handle, a long red rod ended with two sharp electrodes that looked like fangs. But even this was not nasty enough. The man had fitted the tips with an assortment of dangling live wires so that pain could be distributed to more than one patch of flesh.

Timmy's flesh. The torture began.

The boy's screaming terrified Jeremy, but it would cover his next move.

He forced his slender body through the portal; the rough edges ravaged his belly and back. Looking down he realized his landing might break his neck; it was like diving into a pool without water. But what choice did he have? When Timmy screamed again, Jeremy pushed the remainder of his body forward and then plunged twenty-five feet into a pile of refuse—scrap metal, rubble, and broken office furniture.

The crash startled the Emperor. The prod dropped from his hand. He observed Jeremy struggling in the heap of debris. He looked to the opening, saw no one else. Then he rushed toward Jeremy and pulled a stiletto from his black garb.

Jeremy, dazed from the fall, frantically reached for his firearm, but it was gone: the impact had torn it from the holster and sent it flying into the rubble.

"Fuck."

"Lose something?" said the Emperor. "What a shame."

"I'm a police officer. You are under arrest."

"I'm not sure you are capable of arresting anyone. But it was such a clever entrance—let's collaborate! We'll make a movie. An epic." He gestured toward the empty chair next to Timmy. "You'll get top billing, of course. The heroic but misguided bad-cop father of a runaway boy."

"In your box office dreams, Fuckface."

The Emperor's face darkened. "I'm an artist. There's no need to use crude language, Officer Jeremy Porter." He tightened his grip on the stiletto and slowly approached his prey.

"What have you done to my assistants, Officer Porter?"

"They're tied up at the moment."

"Ahhh … a fate you will soon experience yourself."

Jeremy tried to sit up but his lower back went into spasms and he fell backward. From this vantage the Emperor looked ten feet tall as he hovered overhead, raised his knife, and brought it down.

Jeremy blocked the blow, but as he rolled sideways the blade sliced across his shoulder. Kicking and clam-walking backwards, crying out in pain, he threw anything he could find—empty paint cans, metal scraps, desk drawers—to ward off the relentless Russian who feinted left, shifted his weight, and then moved in for the kill.

His left arm weakened from the knife wound, Jeremy began to blubber and flail. He was backed into a corner with no way out. He saw his death: pinned like a fucking insect.

"Crawl to that chair or I will slice you into pieces."

"Fuck you."

"Very well, Officer Porter. I'll take you over there one piece at a time."

The stiletto came toward him with a deadly thrust. Jeremy's hand found purchase. He slid a board over his chest just as the knife came down and stuck, impaling itself in the warped wood plank.

Enraged and unable to dislodge his weapon, the Emperor threw it aside. "I will crush you with my bare hands!"

On his feet, ready for hand-to-hand combat, Jeremy soon realized that every page in the police defense training manual would not be enough to save him. His shoulder ached and he was sorely overmatched. The Russian was a 200-pound bulldozer who easily swatted away every punch, kick, and wild claw.

Jeremy felt thick hands grab his body and lift. He floated in mid-air, then crashed against a freezer. As his body fell to the floor, the unit's door popped open and two objects fell out. *Clunk. Clunk.* Jeremy found himself beside the bodies of two dead children covered in plastic wrap. He was face to face with Benito Jackson.

The Emperor pounced again, pummeling Jeremy, who was lodged against a pile of metal. Spent and beaten bloody, the vigilante suffered a fierce blow to his head from a wooden table leg. And then, barely conscious, he felt his body being dragged across the floor and hoisted into a sitting position. His vision was so poor he assumed one eye had swollen shut or was blinded by a river of blood from his head wound.

But he could see well enough to know that the Emperor was about to strap him into the chair—Kayla's chair. Then he heard Timmy pleading.

"Wake up, Officer Jeremy, please wake up!"

Chapter 42

It was Bayless who had made the decision for the teams to meet at the Rigolets Bridge on the Chef Menteur Highway. He wanted everyone briefed before they turned down the asphalt road that would take them to the foundry.

His own troops gathered with personnel from the Seventh District. The PV Task Force caravan was still a few minutes away. Fortunately, the Seventh District sergeant was familiar with the abandoned building.

"Basically, it's a toxic shit hole. It was shut down a few years ago, and it ain't gonna be pretty once we get inside," he said.

Brock Suggs spoke up. His car was one of the first Bayless had contacted.

"We all know this is an emergency. But what kind? I'm confused."

Bayless was ready to make his extraordinary announcement; the same news that was shared earlier at the PV Task Force meeting.

"There are reasons I kept the radio chatter vague. I didn't want a bunch of ambulance chasers with police radios ambushing us with video cams. We believe the Pervert Vigilante is inside of a building a short distance from here and he may be stalking his next victim."

The officers exchanged looks. "What the—"

"Before we go in, I want you to know we have reliable information that the Pervert Vigilante is one of our own."

"What? Who?" Suggs asked.

"Jeremy Porter."

The disbelief was palpable. Many voices rose with the same response: "You've got to be kidding."

"This is not a joke, People. Get your shotguns ready now so we don't have to open trunks and make a clatter once we arrive. Brock, you take the patrol rifle."

Suggs was classified as a marksman, yet this would be the first time he put his skill to use on official business. He felt a surge of adrenaline as he leaned into the vehicle and took control of the Colt .223 with the 14-inch barrel. Attached was a Trijicon ACOG 1.5 power sighting system and a surefire grip loaded with 55g SBST, super ballistic silver tip rounds. *Bring it on. Fucking Powder Puff.* Revenge for the wrist injury he had suffered in training would be sweet. And all legal.

The PV Task Force caravan arrived, all vehicles pulling to the side lane of the bridge in orderly fashion. Leslie Scott, black as night, was among the first to hop out. The first thing he saw was Brock Suggs eagerly sighting his rifle scope. The sniper looked up and made eye contact. It was not a friendly exchange.

Scott fell in as his supervisor asked Bayless for instructions.

"Assign your personnel to the perimeter. Once we get a layout of the building, we can make any needed adjustments."

After a glance toward Suggs, Scott couldn't hold it in any longer. "Lieutenant, I have valuable information that you may need to know."

"About the building?"

"No, Sir, it's about Porter."

"It'll have to wait. Lives are in danger. We believe there's a child inside."

"I'm aware of that. But there's a cop in there, too. And you've—"

"We need to move."

"But you've already judged him. You think he's guilty," he said, pointing to Suggs. "What if he's *not*, Sir?"

Doubt flashed across the marksman's face then disappeared as a semi-trailer truck blew past the nocturnal platoon.

Bayless, unmoved, hissed, "I'm giving the orders around here, Scott. Let's move, People!"

* * *

A line of NOPD cruisers quietly rolled to the front of the foundry grounds without lights or sirens. A few yards off the road, Bayless spotted a parked vehicle in the high weeds. Suggs also recognized the car. "That's Porter's car, fucking Powder Puff, the Pervert Vigilante. Holy fucking shit."

Bayless assigned a team to check on Porter's car. He continued to the front of the fenced area and used a bolt cutter to cut the lock off the gate. The officers entered and quickly discovered that the building was a concrete fortress. The entry was a heavy steel sliding door.

"If there are no other entry points, we may need a battering ram to knock down that door," Bayless said.

The sergeant from Seventh District had a solution. "We have one. We use it for search warrants."

"Perfect. Grab it."

Bayless pounded on the door. Again. And then again. When there was no response, he gave the order to knock the sucker down.

Scott was ordered to stay with the entry team. He watched as Bayless and Suggs hustled toward the back of the foundry, while another group of officers headed in the opposite direction. The maneuver would allow them to search and contain the perimeter of the building.

At the rear of the structure, Suggs tilted his flashlight toward the ladder that reached to the opening where Jeremy had crawled in. Bayless used the radio to notify the others as Suggs lifted a police-issue, bulletproof vest from the tall grass. It was the garment Jeremy had used to protect himself in his Garden District home.

"What the fuck? It has two bullet strikes to the chest."

"I guess that means Porter is still alive."

"But why take off the vest?"

Bayless stepped to the ladder and began to ascend.

* * *

Jeremy heard Timmy and managed to open his right eye as the Emperor began to immobilize him by strapping his left wrist to the chair. He knew what was happening. Instincts kicked in. Somehow, somewhere, he found the strength to make a move. His booted foot came up fast and struck his attacker in the groin.

The Emperor keeled over and Jeremy loosened the strap from his wrist. Before the Emperor could get up, Jeremy kicked him again and again. Then he pounced but his weak punches had no effect.

The Emperor pushed him away. Jeremy flew backwards, landed against the tripod with the camera still attached, then toppled over with the equipment. Nearly out of breath and totally exhausted, Jeremy stared into the camera, the red recording light still glowing, and spoke.

"I am Police Officer Jeremy Porter. I am here to protect—"

Before he could finish his delirious comment, the Emperor was on the attack again. He kicked Jeremy on his shoulder. Screaming in pain, Jeremy scrambled to one knee. Instructor Reemer's words were loud and clear in his mind: *"Do whatever it takes to save your life. You hear me? Do whatever it takes to save your life. Pick up a hard object, bite, kick, twist, and shout. Do anything you can to defend yourself. Do what you need to do to stay alive."*

He grabbed the tripod, got to his feet, and swung for the fences, striking his foe across the face. The Emperor went down with a thud.

As he staggered back to the chairs, Jeremy loosened the straps on Timmy's wrists.

Timmy yelled, "Look out!"

Jeremy twisted away in time to avoid the electric jolt of the Emperor's magic wand.

The two men cursed and frothed as they fought for control of the deadly prod.

A lucky swipe hit the Emperor's chest, spinning and tumbling him into Kayla's chair, his body rippling with muscle contractions. The Emperor fought through the electric shocks and tried to exert muscle control, but Jeremy seized the wand and poked the Emperor's flesh repeatedly, sensing a diminishing resistance.

Moaning. That's what he would remember. Like a wounded beast.

* * *

Bayless reached the top of the ladder and observed a naked child and Porter using what looked like a cattle-prod to taunt a helpless adult male.

"Porter! Put down that weapon and back away, *now*!"

Stupid. The lieutenant believed he was speaking to a fully conscious man. Someone who could and should respond to authority. As his anger rose, it never dawned on him that the buzzing of the killer stick, blood in his ears, and the thunder of the battering ram the valiant leader had ordered might make it impossible for the Pervert Vigilante to obey rule of law.

"Put down the fucking—"

Not so much as a twitch or change in Jeremy's body posture. It was as if he didn't even hear him.

Bayless radioed to the others, "I have a vision on Porter. Repeat. I have a vision on Porter."

The responder said, "Do you want to activate SOD?"

"Negative. No time. We need to stop the threat now."

Bayless quickly descended down the ladder.

"Suggs, get up there and take Porter out. He's torturing a man and refuses to obey orders. Go!"

Brock threw the rifle over his shoulder and launched. This was it. His star was rising with each step. He knew how good he was. It was a gift. He'd discovered it during training and found it hard to explain to the other rookies: he could see the bull's eye, the point of contact, as though he were looking into the eyes of destiny.

On top, he steadied himself, sliding his boots to the widest position on the upper rungs, elbows on the concrete cutout. Then he brought the sniper scope to eye level and—that's when disaster struck.

What he observed was not a criminal or tormentor, and that rattled him, even as his vision sharpened.

Suggs saw a bloodied male individual, who barely was able to stand, confront an adversary who inexplicably wore a black robe. How many sane men dress this way?

He saw an injured police officer he had grossly underestimated.

A man with balls the size of planets who had tracked perverts, the kind of scum who deserved every rotten, motherfucking thing they got—including murder, if that's how it went down.

Fuck it.

As Suggs slid back to earth, Bayless was outraged. "What are you doing? I told you to shoot."

"No."

"What!"

"I can't."

"I gave the order!"

"He's one of us, Goddamnit! He's a *cop*!"

"I gave you—"

Suggs shoved the rifle into Bayless' hands.

"Then you shoot him! I won't fucking do it!"

* * *

Exhausted, Jeremy placed his left hand on the arm of the chair, holding the wand downward in his right hand. The two men stared at each other. With his one open eye, Jeremy knew he was looking into the face of the devil, and the devil was moving forward. He jabbed the prod to keep the Emperor at bay, and realized that at any moment he might collapse unconscious and not be able to defend Timmy.

"Officer Jeremy, can I help?"

"No, Timmy. Stay back."

His mind reeled with past events, his fall from the portal above, and quick-cut images of his shoddy surroundings. What had brought him here? How did it all happen? He had to make his body move. His body would not respond.

The ogre was regaining strength and moving to get out of the chair.

Do something, Porter. You have to do something.

Another war cry startled him. He forced his mind to focus and saw the giant man lurch from the chair, his mouth open with a fury that could swallow civilizations.

Jeremy felt himself about to tumble. Then he planted one foot behind him and lunged—sending the electrical power load down the throat of the thug, harpooning him to the back of the chair.

The constant flow of electric current rendered the Emperor helpless. His arms and legs flailed, his eyes bugged out. His bowels voided. Jeremy held the handle of the wand to make sure it remained lodged in the Emperor's throat.

Then a sharp blast echoed in the toxic chamber and Jeremy Porter, also known as the Pervert Vigilante, twisted in agony. He stared down at the thick liquid that began to flow from his chest and put his right hand over his wound. Still holding onto the prod with his left hand, he leaned onto the arm of the chair.

Once again, Jeremy looked directly at the Emperor inches from his face. "We can finish this in hell, Motherfucker."

All things were spinning. Spheres, logic, the room. Jeremy yowled and yammered. And then as he began to fall, his thumb found the amperage lever. *Fuck it*, he thought. Then he pushed the electrode to MAX.

As Jeremy hit the floor, he could not see the Emperor take his last blood curdling gasp as the surge penetrated his body.

Timmy, horrified and relieved, shouted, "He's dead! He's dead!"

Jeremy had defeated the almighty Emperor.

* * *

Leslie Scott heard the rifle shot as he and other TF team members pushed through the battered entry and rushed toward the sound of Timmy's voice.

From above, he could see Bayless shouting orders from a small opening, but with sparks still flying from the Emperor's head, no one could hear anything he said. That's when he noticed Bayless was holding a rifle. He had an angry impulse to take out the braying jackass with one shot to the head. Instead, he moved toward his friend whose body was sprawled on the floor in a pool of blood.

"Jeremy, look at me!" He snapped his fingers and patted his face, hoping for signs of life. Then he grabbed his radio mic and shouted, "Officer down, EMS on a code three. Officer down. EMS on a code three!"

As Scott called for help, a light show like no other continued. Sparks flew from the Emperor's eyes, and smoke billowed from his ears and mouth.

The sergeant from Seventh District found the hidden plug to the generator. He pulled it out and the convulsing diminished. But by then, the Emperor's head had the look of a burnt match.

Chapter 43

The stench of charred flesh choked officers as they tried to make sense of the crime scene. A TF officer wrapped his jacket around Timmy and lifted the hysterical boy to carry him out of the building.

"I want to stay with Officer Jeremy. Please let me stay with Officer Jeremy."

Scott looked up. "Son, Officer Jeremy says he wants you outside where you're safe, okay? I'll stay with your buddy."

Scott nodded to the officer who whisked Timmy away, the boy extending his arms toward his hero who lay in the toxic dust.

Jeremy groaned and his right eye barely opened.

"Hang in there, Man. Hang in there."

Jeremy's wounds were so plentiful and varied Scott could hardly assess them all. But it didn't really matter. The death threat was the rose of blood that bloomed in his friend's upper chest and left shoulder.

Bayless, you rotten motherfucker.

As police and Task Force personnel scattered to be certain the area was secure, Scott heard another radio broadcast.

"We have a code four. The Pervert Vigilante has been shot and is in custody. Again, the Pervert Vigilante has been apprehended."

Code four meant everything was under control; no other police units needed. Scott gritted his teeth: an international pervert lay burnt to a crisp in a chair yet all leadership cared about was the Pervert Vigilante. Voices cried out as the officers surveyed the scene, "Got two dead kids over here."

EMS personnel, who obviously had been alerted before Scott's code three, appeared and began to work on Jeremy. Scott gave them space as Bayless and Suggs entered the crime scene. Nearby, a police officer asked the obvious question, "Who shot him?"

Bayless, arrogant and prideful, was quick to respond. "I shot him. He was torturing this man."

Suggs bared his teeth then looked directly into Scott's eyes, acknowledging that they were now on the same team. Scott was a furnace ready to explode.

"This man? You saved this man?" Scott nodded toward the Russian corpse.

"Stand down, Scott."

"Lieutenant, look around. There are two dead children over there on the floor wrapped in plastic. "Your *victim* was about to kill another boy. Porter saved the kid's life."

"Listen, Scott, we don't torture people."

"You fucking idiot! You poor shit-ass excuse for a supervisor. Look at this police officer. He's beaten to a pulp. It would be obvious to a third-grader that he was only trying to defend himself and protect that boy!"

"You can't talk to me that way! I'll have your job." Bayless said.

Scott stepped towards Bayless until they were almost nose to nose. "No, *Sir*. I'll have *your* job."

Flustered and making a vain attempt at dignity, Bayless held his ground. "Perhaps you don't realize that Officer Porter is a killer. He is wanted for three murders. You simply don't know the—"

"Oh, you'll be surprised what I know, Lieutenant."

Brock Suggs broke away from the argument and moved toward the emergency medical technicians who had lifted Jeremy onto a stretcher.

Suggs kneeled and whispered, "I'm sorry, Man, I really am. For everything."

When he stood, Suggs looked at the grim EMT for answers. "So?"

"Barely has a pulse, Officer. I don't think your friend is going to make it."

Suggs nodded to the EMT and then stared at Bayless, who appeared ready to shout an order. Suggs beat him to it. "You better pray he doesn't die."

* * *

Captain Reed and Chief Hendricks arrived at the scene in the same car. They entered the chaos together, but it was Hendricks who confronted Bayless. "How did this go down, Lieutenant?"

"Well, I had to stop Porter from torturing this man, so in order to save a life, I shot him."

"Is he going to make it?"

"Not likely."

"Apparently, you didn't save the victim either. He looks quite dead."

As Hendricks and Reed surveyed the scene, various supervisors gathered and offered observations, hunches.

"In addition to the officer being shot, we have one adult subject DOA, two young children DOA, and another child found alive. He's outside with EMTs."

"What the hell went on in here?"

"Chief, this appears to be a makeshift torture chamber. We don't know yet how long the two kids have been dead. Both were wrapped in freezer plastic. The boy we just took away was probably going to be the dead man's next victim. Porter interrupted the plan. Just my opinion, Sir, but I think we shot the wrong guy."

Bayless snapped, "He was wanted for three homicides."

Hendricks gazed at the carnage and shook his head. His cell phone rang and Lt. Frank Styles's name appeared on the screen.

"Yes."

"Chief, I am in the homicide office. I have a brief summary for you. Earlier tonight, two guys broke into a home occupied by a guy named Eric Dietz. He got sliced up pretty bad and was left for dead. Porter found him and called EMS. The two guys kidnapped his six-year-old son, who appears to be the kid who was found alive at your location. Once the Amber alert went out we visited the hospital to interview Dietz. Apparently, he and Porter became friends and penetrated a child torture enterprise run by a guy known as the Emperor. The guys who grabbed Dietz's son also apparently intended to kidnap Porter's kid and do a snuff film with both kids. Porter must have been ready for them. Officers have found one of the perps alive and tied to a toilet in Porter's house. I've just been advised that the second man was found alive in the trunk of Porter's car at your location."

"Jesus Christ."

"It appears Porter discovered all this and worked the case alone, except for Dietz's recent involvement."

Hendricks was silent, lost in thought. He saw his career explode in mid-air, like an aircraft burdened by shoddy maintenance and enemy fire.

Styles interrupted the reverie. "Sir, are you there? Hello?"

Hendricks' stomach twisted into a knot, which worsened when he heard Styles say, "Chief, the phones are lighting up like a Christmas tree with media."

Fuck. "Frank, we'll meet you at the hospital."

"Got it. We are leaving now."

On the ride to the hospital, Hendricks made the agonizing phone call to Curtis McGuire.

"Hello, Morris. What have you found out?"

"Curtis, are you with Sandy?"

"Yes, what's happened?"

"I have bad news. Jeremy was shot tonight. He is being transported to Mercy Hospital."

Hendricks could hear Curtis share the information with his daughter and wife, and then he heard Sandy scream. Curtis came back on the phone. “How bad is it, Morris?”

“I’m not sure but it doesn’t look good.”

“But, but, how did it happen?”

“He was shot by one of our officers at the scene. The investigation is ongoing. Perhaps we can talk at the hospital.”

“Shot by one of *your* officers? Why was—”

Sandy heard her father’s comment and shrieked as she pulled up her cell phone, “What time? What time was he shot?”

“Honey, I don’t know if that makes any difference.”

“It does. I need to know. What time?”

“Morris, do you know the time Jeremy was shot?”

“No, but I’ll get that for you.”

Sandy kept staring at her cell phone and the time of Jeremy’s last call. “Oh my god, I didn’t wait for the hour. Oh my god, this is my fault!”

Curtis tried to console his hysterical daughter. “Sandy, what are you talking about? You can’t blame yourself for this.”

“Oh my god, I didn’t wait. I didn’t wait!”

* * *

The EMS unit pulled into the Mercy Hospital emergency bay. EMTs wheeled Jeremy out and hurriedly conveyed him to the awaiting surgical personnel.

Minutes later, Hendricks and Reed arrived and pushed their way through layers of media approaching the hospital entrance. The chief was tired and angry and did not like being pepper-sprayed with questions pregnant with implication—NOPD was at fault and had fucked up again.

One question shouted by a reporter hit him like a bag of cement.

“Chief, does this have any connection to NOPD neglecting child abuse cases?”

He didn't bother to answer as he stomped into the waiting area adjacent to the emergency room where Jeremy lay unconscious. The scene was chaotic as police officers were positioned throughout the room and leadership congregated in a corner.

Hendricks didn't want to be there. But it was protocol for the police chief to be present at the hospital when an officer was shot or seriously wounded. Unfortunately, this particular police officer was labeled as a perpetrator of crimes, which put the chief in a most awkward position.

Under normal circumstances, when an officer is shot, cops wait at the hospital to offer assistance or give blood. Not this time. Powder Puff had never been popular, and now that he was tagged as the Pervert Vigilante, no one could risk siding with a notorious man who might be a felon.

Yet, protocol demanded that an NOPD officer guard the recovery room of any personnel hurt in the line of duty. A cop had been assigned the operating room. But who would take the assignment if Porter lived?

* * *

Leslie Scott was determined to keep his promise to Timmy. As Jeremy was carried out of the foundry, he requested to be excused from the crime scene and sped off to the hospital, on the tail of Hendricks and Reed.

At first, the crush of amateur and professional video operators stunned him. Where do all these night crawlers come from? *Vermin,* he thought, as he barged toward the entrance, answering each yowl and complaint with a menacing gaze.

"Get out of my way."

The commotion inside was as deafening as the great outdoors. And what he witnessed from a distance confirmed his worst fears: the bickering NOPD leadership was as dysfunctional as a reality TV show. For a moment he was glad of that, though he still was overwhelmed by what he knew.

He turned to see McGuire and Sandy arrive, running toward a nurse who directed them to Trauma Room Eight. Scott followed and watched as Sandy raced down the hallway. She was about to enter the emergency room when a New Orleans police officer standing guard grabbed her by the arm.

"Lady, you can't go in there."

"Get your fucking hands off of me."

"Ma'am—"

"What are you going to do, shoot me, too?"

Scott intervened. "It's okay, Officer, you can let her in."

"Who are you?'

"Leslie Scott. I'm a member of the Pervert Vigilante Task Force. I've come from the crime scene. I'll take over now." The cop paused, unsure, so Scott lied. "Lieutenant Styles gave the order. Thanks for your help."

As the officer walked away, Sandy charged into the room. Scott followed, more to get a look at Jeremy than to restore order. The first voice of protest came from a nurse.

"Hey, you can't be in here."

Sandy heard nothing as her eyes filled with horror.

The bright lights, masked men and women, the hemostatic forceps and other surgical tools, the anesthesia machine, patient monitors and the incessant beeping of technology made her husband look like a specimen in a science fiction lab, not a human being.

"Jeremy!"

A doctor shouted, "Get her out of here. He's being prepped for surgery!"

Scott grabbed Sandy so that she wouldn't collapse. "This is the wife of the patient. She just wants to spend a few moments with him before you take him up to surgery. She'll calm down if you let her stay." He gave Sandy a stern look.

She whimpered, "I just want to hold his hand."

The lead surgeon nodded at the officer. "Okay, maybe it will help."

Sandy found an opening near the gurney, kneeled, kissed Jeremy's bloody hand, and began to cry.

Leslie Scott peered over the shoulders of medical staff. Seeing his friend under intense white light was sickening. He wanted to believe his friend would pull through. But he was a realist: seeing is believing.

Sandy held her husband's hand. "Don't you die on me, Jeremy Porter. I need you. Kayla needs you."

The fingers on his hand began to wiggle. The nurse noticed.

"Doctor!"

Chapter 44

Curtis McGuire made his way through the sea of blue and plainclothes detectives until he got Hendrick's attention.

"Can I have a moment?"

Hendricks broke away from the pack and found a space to entertain what was sure to be a very uncomfortable conversation.

"Before you begin, let me tell you how sorry we are about your son-in-law. We are hoping and praying he pulls through."

Accepting the sympathy with a nod, Curtis went on the attack. "I've called the mayor. I want a complete investigation!"

"We're still gathering all the facts."

"Why did they have to shoot him? Did he threaten the officers?"

"We are doing our best to get this sorted out."

"Well, was he armed at the time? You must know that much," Curtis pressed.

"At some point he was armed, but we haven't found his firearm yet."

"What the hell does that mean?"

"Curtis, I assure you I will get this sorted out and at that time I will tell you what I can."

Hendricks, for once, was relieved when Reed approached and interrupted with an update.

"Chief, I need you for a minute."

Hendricks stepped away from McGuire, whose anger felt like a heat wave.

"Crime Lab just notified us they believe they found Porter's firearm in the rubble. It was fully loaded and had not been fired. It wasn't his service revolver but it fits with his ankle holster. It was an antique Colt .38 caliber revolver. Looks like an old army issue but it's in mint condition."

"Does it appear to be the same type of weapon used in the other three homicides?"

"Yes, it does."

"I'll join you all in a minute. Let me finish speaking with Mr. McGuire."

As Reed left, the political insider moved in with more questions. The chief realized that the man must have overheard portions of his conversations.

"Morris, did he say something about a gun?"

"Yes. They found a gun, but it was not Jeremy's service revolver. Do you know if Jeremy owned a Colt .38? A sort of antique army issue?"

McGuire teetered on weak legs. His face went pale. He felt faint.

"Curtis, are you okay?"

McGuire turned and reached for the closest chair.

"Curtis?"

"I need to sit down."

"Do you want me to call a doctor?"

"This can't be happening."

Hendricks could see that McGuire's mood had changed from rage to fear. He looked like he might need oxygen. Dark lines made his middle-aged face look ancient. The reigning king of high-end table sets and living room sectionals looked as though he had just seen his past and future flash before him: an empire in ruins.

Or maybe McGuire was merely overcome with the chain of events and the possibility that his son-in-law might not make it through the night.

"You sit tight, Curtis. I'll send someone to check on you."

Hendricks quickly moved back to join his leadership team. Lieutenant Styles and Detective Vuong had arrived.

Vuong had news. "Chief, we've been tracking car rental activity on or near the dates of the PV crimes. We finally got a hit earlier today pertaining to the Johnson murder—where the little boy was saved?

"Yeah?"

"A gray Toyota was returned a few hours after the murder. It matches the boy's description of the rescue vehicle. Off the record, an employee told us Jeremy Porter's credit card was on file."

"Then why the hell didn't we pick him up?"

Styles intervened. "We thought it might be a coincidence. Porter would be the last person we would have suspected. Anyway, we wanted more proof. One rental doesn't make a—"

"I don't need a lecture! We've got a cop who might die in surgery because we didn't figure this thing out sooner!"

The captain stepped in. "Sir—"

"This is a public relations nightmare, Reed! Do you get that? The city is saying the Pervert Vigilante was doing our job!"

"He's a murderer, not a cop," Reed said.

"He's a goddamn hero to some."

"He is the Pervert Vigilante. A killer. He confessed to his wife, didn't he?"

"Maybe we did shoot the wrong guy."

Reed wouldn't back down. "Bayless followed orders, Sir. *Your* orders."

Hendricks didn't appreciate the reminder and would have chewed the captain's face to the bone but his cell phone was chirping, and when he looked at the ID he was not happy. *Fuck.* He excused himself and stepped away from the group.

"Yes, Mr. Mayor."

"Morris, the community is already in an uproar and it isn't even daybreak yet. I sure hope you can explain why we had to shoot Porter."

"Yes, Sir, I'll keep you updated on everything."

"And there are some reporters trying to connect all of this with the audit report regarding the sex crime stats. Are you aware of that?"

"Mr. Mayor, I can assure you that the two are not connected and I am prepared to defend our reporting system."

"I won't tolerate anyone cooking the books, Morris. Not on my watch. You know that, right?"

Hendricks felt as though he were standing in the middle of the street with concrete boots watching a bus speed toward him. How would he survive?

When Hendricks returned to his team, Reed and the detectives ended their own phone calls. "We're going to have to talk to the press soon. So let's start putting this in some type of order."

Reed began. "Bayless believed a man's life was in danger so—"

"Goddamnit, I already heard that! I want to know more about this child kidnapping enterprise and why the hell we weren't aware of it."

Styles tried to pacify the chief. "Once we heard the Amber alert go out on the Dietz kidnapping, we dispatched our detectives to the hospital. Dietz was stable and provided quite a bit of information. According to Dietz, it was Porter who found him cuffed to a toilet with both wrists slit open. A few minutes later and Dietz would have bled to death."

"So Porter saved his life."

"Yes. We listened to the 911 call and it is Porter's voice calling for EMS on a code three."

"It was then that Porter realized Dietz's kid had been kidnapped."

"Yet Porter didn't report it?"

"According to Dietz, Porter tried reporting these crimes several times. Claims no one would listen. He says Porter even went to the FBI."

"Report it to who?"

Styles looked at Reed to see if he would come clean. Even Dietz knew that Porter begged Reed to listen. Reed remained silent until probed again by Hendricks.

"Did he report this to you?"

"He ... may have said something to Tanner."

"Dexter, if there is any record of him trying to alert us about this, we are all fucked," the chief hissed. "Do you hear me? We are all fucked!"

Hendricks bit down on his fury, backed out of the huddle, and then returned, straining to control his temper. No one said a word, so Vuong stepped up and began delivering everything they knew at that point.

"Chief, we identified the children found dead in the foundry. Both were kidnapping victims. One was the Benito Jackson kid. He was kidnapped from the St. Charles Avenue area a couple of months ago. The other boy is a kidnapping victim from Thibodaux back in February."

"Christ. Go on."

"According to Dietz, this Emperor guy had a website that appeared to be emanating from Russia."

"Wasn't there a similar icon on those other computers?"

"Yes, Sir. But anyone delving into it would believe the signal was coming from Russia."

"So once they believed it was a Russian matter, they ignored it?"

"As you know, Sir, we don't pursue any incidents in other countries, especially Russia."

"Nor do the feds."

"Not likely they would either, but Porter apparently reached out to them."

The chief looked surprised. "What came of that?

"Not, sure. We are checking with the FBI."

Then the chief turned to Dexter Reed. "You know anything about this?"

All eyes turned to the captain, who swallowed hard and appeared to be trembling.

"I don't recall, Sir."

Hendricks did not like that answer so he turned back to Vuong. "Go on, Detective."

"Yes, Sir. Anyway, Dietz tells us that Porter found out that it was some type of bounce off. The signal was sent from New Orleans to Russia and then bounced back to New Orleans and who knows where else."

"Has anyone seen the videos?"

"Not yet, but Dietz tells us they are absolutely horrible. He said they are impossible to watch. This guy straps these kids to a chair and commences to slowly torture them with a makeshift electric wand. Then as a grand finale, he turns up the voltage and snuffs them. The Dietz boy was supposed to be his next victim."

"That's sick, repulsive. Who watches that shit?"

"Here's the kicker. Dietz tells us that people subscribe to these snuff films at a thousand bucks per pop."

"What did this creep do, advertise on Google?"

"No, Sir. He only allowed convicted child abusers in. Word of mouth among the sickest."

"This gets more bizarre by the minute."

The other leaders weighed in, grumbling and shaking their heads at the bizarre cruelty.

"But there's more," Styles said, and gave Vuong a nod to continue.

"The two guys who sliced up Dietz kidnapped his kid. The Emperor used these thugs to pick up kids from abusers who didn't want to go through the trouble of disposing their catch."

"So for a thousand bucks they not only have the kids picked up but they can watch them snuffed on film?"

"Correct."

"Did we get an ID on this Emperor?"

"Appears his name is Maksim Coloft. He's a Russian immigrant. Been here less than a year.

"What about the two other guys? Are they talking?"

"Both also Russian immigrants. They are asking for attorneys."

"Where are they now?"

"Both are in Charity Hospital under police guard. They are being treated for superficial wounds. Nothing life-threatening."

"What have we charged them with so far?

"Once Dietz makes an ID, we'll hit them with attempted murder, aggravated burglary, and aggravated kidnapping. In the meantime, our detectives are at Porter's wife's home. Back door glass broken, so we can also hold them on aggravated burglary, for starters. One of the guys was found cuffed to a toilet, face in the bowl.

"Cuffed to a toilet?"

"Yes, Sir. That's what Dietz said they did to him. A quick look at Dietz's phone revealed that Porter took photos of the guy and then texted them."

"Porter's idea of payback?"

"I guess. Or justice."

"Vigilante justice?"

Styles encouraged Vuong to keep going. "Tell Chief Hendricks about the Tasers."

Hendricks was reeling from too much info. *Does this fucking story ever end?* He remembered Curtis McGuire, glanced quickly and discovered him still seated in the chair, his head buried in his hands. So he gave the detective his full attention.

"The guy kissing the toilet also had been Tasered numerous times. Spent Tasers were located in the house."

"Please tell me the Taser videos were activated."

"Looks that way. Crime lab is downloading the videos now."

"Thank God. Maybe we'll finally learn something about this cluster fuck."

"As you know, the other perp was cuffed in the trunk of Porter's car. He was also Tasered."

Hendricks shook his head, both amazed and deeply frustrated. "How in the fuck did Porter uncover all of this?"

"We may want to talk to Officer Leslie Scott."

"Who is that?'

"He's the officer standing guard outside of Porter's trauma room. The Special Ops desk sergeant told us that Porter came into the SOD office earlier tonight and asked him to give Scott an envelope. He claimed it was very important. By the way, Scott is also a member of the PV Task Force."

Hendricks looked to Styles.

"Frank, you need to talk to him—and soon."

Chapter 45

The last thing Hendricks needed at the hospital was another call from the mayor. Yet moments later that's exactly what he got.

"Morris, the media is hounding me for information. They want to do a live interview for the 6:00 a.m. news. They're waiting outside the hospital."

"I know everyone wants information, but for now ... can't we send our press officer out there?"

"No, I prefer you handle this one."

The speeding bus is getting closer.

"Okay, Mr. Mayor. I'll step out."

Morris Hendricks had had an illustrious career. So many awards and accolades. He was one of the most sought after police officials in the country when the Mayor of New Orleans tapped him for the job. He relished the memory of his glory days for a moment, then looked down the hallway toward the trauma room and considered the favor he had done for Curtis McGuire.

Was slipping the political insider's son-in-law into the academy the worst mistake of his career or the best?

Thanks to Porter, three vicious pedophiles were gone, two kids had been saved, two mad men would go to prison for life, and one of the most horrendous criminals in the city's history had been executed by electricity without wasting taxpayers' money.

Good job, Chief.

Yet, somehow, as he moved through the still chaotic waiting room and exited the hospital for an area cordoned off by the NOPD public information officers, he very much doubted that the media firing squad he was about to face would see things his way. And the officers who flanked him would be of very little help once the questions started flying like machine gun bullets. It was his show. Or funeral.

"Chief, can you confirm that the Pervert Vigilante is a New Orleans Police Officer?

"Yes. We believe so."

"Can you give us his name and rank?

"I will withhold his name until we get further along in the investigation."

"Will he be arrested?"

"We are very early in this investigation."

"Was he the officer who was shot tonight?"

"A police officer was shot but we are withholding his name at this time."

"What is his condition?"

"He is in critical condition."

"Is there a reason you are not providing the name of the wounded officer?"

"Yes, but I am not able to disclose that right now."

"Our sources are telling us that the wounded officer is Jeremy Porter, the son-in-law of Curtis McGuire. Can you confirm or deny that information?"

"As I said, we are withholding the officer's name."

"Our sources have also told us that Porter is the Pervert Vigilante. Can you confirm or deny that?"

"Again, we are very early with this investigation."

"Is Porter currently under arrest?"

Before Hendricks could answer the question, the belligerent Norm Krawley, surrounded by protesters, began to shout.

"Hell no, he shouldn't be arrested. He's all we got. What the hell did NOPD do before he came along?"

"He's a hero," a woman in the group yelled. "We don't want him arrested."

"Give him the chief's job!" a third protester said, and that set off Krawley's entire entourage. They chanted and shook their fists and placards, drowning out any attempt by reporters to be heard.

Hendricks stood tall, kept his cool. As the frenzy faded, he said, "It's very early in the investigation. Our detectives are still gathering evidence and speaking to witnesses."

Krawley wasn't buying it. He challenged the media to open one very rotten can of worms.

"Ask Hendricks why all of this child abuse stuff went on without nothing being done! Why don't you ask him that?"

A reporter jumped on it. "Chief, the audit revealed that many sex crimes, including child abuse cases, were not properly followed up on by NOPD. What do you have to say about the report?"

"I haven't read the entire report but I will respond at the appropriate time."

More questions were launched, all at the same time, from different media. He felt as though he was standing in the batter's box and five pitchers were all hurling fastballs at his head.

"Chief, how was the vigilante able to carry on for so long without being discovered?"

"And how is it he was able to locate these child abusers, yet your department could not?"

"Who shot him?"

It was now officially a verbal riot. In an attempt to regain control, Hendricks began a quick summary of events hoping to bring the spectacle to a merciful and abrupt end:

> "....The officer who was shot is the alleged vigilante....he was shot by a NOPD supervisor and is in critical condition.... the officer had come across some type of perverted and abusive enterprise....

> for unknown reasons, he decided to pursue this alone and we simply cannot have our officers acting outside of the law or the guidelines of the department....there were three other suspects involved in this criminal enterprise that we know of....one was killed at the scene and two are under arrest...."

The chief finally concluded on what he hoped would be a positive note.

"Thanks to the good work of our police officers, a child who had been kidnapped last night was found alive and is safe. Once we have additional information to provide to you, we will call another news conference. Thank you."

It was Norm Krawley and his neighborhood group that would have the last word. Their hoarse chorus caught on like a brush fire.

"Free Officer Porter! Free Officer Porter! Free Officer Porter!"

Protesters stormed the speaker's podium as cops pulled leadership back into the hospital and then formed a blue wall to keep the angry people out.

Meanwhile, dawn crept over rooftops and shed humid, grimy light following a very dark New Orleans night.

Shaken, Hendricks was pulled aside by Reed.

"Crime lab just called. Ballistics matched Porter's firearm with all three homicides.

"Why am I not surprised?"

Hendricks called to Styles to join them.

"Frank, I need you to gather everyone as soon as possible and decide on the charges we'll file against all of the players."

"Including Porter?"

"Yes, but no hurry on booking him. Doesn't look like he will be going anywhere anytime soon."

Chapter 46

As daylight sparkled over the Crescent City, media coverage was endless but limited. Names had been withheld as NOPD commanders and detectives sorted through several crime sites. The foundry became a horror house of discovery, while the break-in at Porter's residence was still cloaked in confusion. The suspect's van had been towed in for evidence.

Yet, the *Times-Picayune* published a bold headline and dared to connect the nickname to a cop. "Sources who wish to remain anonymous… " That's how Jeremy Porter's picture came to be front page news.

'PERVERT VIGILANTE' COP SHOT, FIGHTING FOR HIS LIFE

The maelstrom of media interest and complexity of the investigation made it difficult for Sergeant Tanner to capture Captain Reed's ear. Before the lunch hour, he was so frustrated he barged into the commander's waiting area and told Jane he had uncovered crucial evidence pertaining to the tangled crime. Minutes later, he entered the crowded office with his laptop under his arm.

"Greg, I hope this is good."

"It proves—"

"Just show us what you have."

A weary Lieutenant Styles, Vuong, and other ranking officers crowded around the laptop. Tanner tapped "play" and a dark video began to roll. Reed was impatient.

"Greg, what the hell is this?"

"It's the Child Abuse office. And look at the time." Tanner pointed to the corner of the video where a digital timer counted minutes and seconds. "Graveyard shift."

"So?"

A shadowy figure lurched into view, then a flashlight began searching the space. Finally, it landed on the ED file cabinet and a drawer was opened. The beam was jittery as files were quickly perused by the intruder, whose back was to the camera. Reed was evermore annoyed.

"But who is it and what the hell does this have to do with—"

The man turned and placed folders on Tanner's desk. Even in the dark his identity was obvious.

"Porter," Styles said.

"Right, I see that," Reed snarled. "But what's he doing in there?"

Tanner quickly explained the day he discovered that someone had used his photocopying machine to duplicate a file. At first he thought it was sloppy work by the new detective. But his suspicions drove him to install a small surveillance camera.

"You're just discovering this now?" Reed barked.

"Captain, at first I'd fast-forward the video every morning when I got to the office. Nothing. Just hours of fuzz. Then I got busy, like all of us, with the sex crimes audit and everything, and forgot about it. This morning I decided I'd better take another look."

"But what is this telling us?"

Vuong got it immediately.

"It shows how Porter chose the sex offenders he stalked. He went right to the source. We can probably match the time on the video with Porter's lunch break. Dollars to donuts he used his free time to pilfer files. And if he was photocopying, I bet we'll find more evidence when we get a warrant to search his apartment."

"Jesus," Styles said. "I don't know whether to admire this guy or be very, very afraid. We can add theft to the list of charges. He had no authority to be in there."

"Exactly." Tanner could not contain his zeal.

The phone rang but Reed was in no rush to answer as he pondered the many layers of Porter's criminality. When he finally spoke into the receiver, the others quietly posed questions and possible scenarios among themselves, and then hushed when the captain hung up.

Reed looked to Styles. "Frank, we need statements from Officer Suggs and Bayless as soon as possible. I want you to do the interviews, okay?"

"Absolutely. What are your concerns?"

Reed hooted, "Too many to count."

* * *

Luisa Olvera wore her clean, pressed NOPD uniform as she approached the entrance of the hospital. In spite of the police guard outside Jeremy's room, she decided to take the risk of being "tainted" by associating with the so-called Pervert Vigilante. Under her arm she carried a bulky plastic shopping bag. She was nervous and lost in thought when the voices began to chant.

"Free Officer Porter! Free Officer Porter! Free Officer Porter!"

Held back by police, a group of men and women walked the sidewalk in a long, narrow circle with placards. The amateur handwriting was in harmony with the voices that sang praises for the Pervert Vigilante. Words like "hero" and "guardian" were shouted, while scorn for a negligent police force was the counterpoint.

Olvera moved toward a TV news crew that was interviewing a brassy man who stood beside the moving circle of protesters. She recognized him, for reasons she couldn't quite remember. Later she would recall that Norm Krawley was a community leader who had formed a neighborhood committee to hassle the sex offender who had landed on his street—Richard Peabody.

Olvera smiled as she entered the hospital and took the elevator to the ICU. She found Jeremy's room and her stomached knotted, afraid that she might not be ready to see him in this condition. Thankfully, the door was closed.

She staked out the territory, watching nurses and doctors buzz through the facility, before opening her plastic bag and pulling out a bouquet of flowers. She stooped and placed them by Jeremy's door, then rose to find a nurse staring at her.

"A friend of the family. They asked me to bring them up. Is it okay?"

"Sure. We'll find a vase or coffee can for them later." Stethoscope ready, she pushed into Jeremy's room.

Luisa's stomach tightened even more. Beside the hospital bed stood a bedraggled blonde without makeup who could look gorgeous even under duress.

The pang Olvera felt was not guilt: Jeremy had explained his status the first time they were intimate. What she experienced was an immediate sense of loss. How could she compete with the beautiful woman Jeremy had jokingly called the "wealthy witch?"

* * *

Investigators and police leaders met throughout the next several days, sorting through evidence and a long list of crimes the Pervert Vigilante might face.

On the second day Lieutenant Styles put Leslie Scott on the spot in front of the group. Why? The day before he'd experienced the unsettling private interviews he'd conducted with both Lieutenant Bayless and Officer Suggs. The troubling contradictions in their stories and obvious hostility between the two former friends had made him wish for a jury of peers. There was too much to untangle: the letter of the law expressed by Bayless chewed at the spirit of the law—cop loyalty and gut response—that Suggs had leaned on.

So, in the case of the formidable Leslie Scott, Styles thought it better if everyone on the team heard what the officer had to say.

"You went in without a warrant, Officer?" Styles asked.

"Yes, but I was given permission by Officer Porter. He requested that I enter the premises."

"And what did you find?"

Scott answered by opening a satchel. He'd come prepared. At his own expense, he'd made copies of Jeremy's police reports and letter. Styles was surprised and impressed.

"Sir, may I share these with our colleagues?"

Styles nodded his permission. "Please do."

Soon every task force member sitting at the long conference table had a stack of reports.

The room was initially silent as investigators pored over the findings. Slowly, hushed grunts of approval, surprise, and admiration broke the quiet. Heads shook, glances were exchanged.

Vuong appeared stunned.

"The notes are meticulous and amazingly accurate when compared to the ballistics and forensics reports," he said. "This is the first glimpse I've had that makes it clear what might have actually happened."

Others agreed and pointed to areas of the reports that could have been written only by someone present at the time of the three deaths.

Scott felt a tremendous sense of relief, even vindication.

Next, they viewed the video obtained from the Tasers Jeremy had used at his residence. To some in the room, the footage was surreal. It showed brazen and astonishingly tactical maneuvers by a cop with less than two years on the job.

Detective Telly Gikas quipped, "Jesus Christ, this guy's got balls like watermelons."

Some laughed as another investigator added, "Either that or he's on a death wish. Either way, he's my fucking idol."

A chorus of voices rose to champion the rookie who had pulled off a miracle. But Lieutenant Styles was not buying it.

"Hey. Let's not get sidetracked into the bravery aspect. We need to focus on the violations of law, of which there are many."

"True," Gikas said, "but it's clear to all of us that the two guys who tried to kill Dietz and kidnapped his kid are the same shitheads who broke into Porter's house. Dietz identified them and now we got the Taser film. So they're toast."

"So, Gike, what you're saying is we can put these guys away for life even if Porter doesn't survive," Vuong said.

"He'll survive." Everyone's attention turned to Styles, who read a text on his smart phone. "Porter's status has been changed from critical to stable."

The lieutenant waved off whoops and applause, and Scott bit down on an emotion he usually found easy to keep in check: sentiment. His colleagues were finally understanding the value of the earnest Jeremy Porter, the Accidental Vigilante.

"Okay, okay. But we still have decisions to make. I need a list of recommended charges I can take to my meeting with Chief Hendricks and the DA in the mayor's office."

* * *

Sandy entered the hospital room with bouquets of flowers. Though partially sedated and groggy, Jeremy quipped, "You shouldn't have."

"Not me. Somebody's been leaving them at the door every day. You have admirers."

"Secret admirers?"

"Not so secret."

Sandy grabbed the remote and turned on the TV. She surfed channels until she found a local station where the story of Jeremy's heroism was endlessly analyzed and debated. The coverage included Norm Krawley's band of supporters who remained in front of the hospital.

Jeremy could barely comprehend what he was watching or what had happened to him. His left shoulder had disappeared in a mass of bandages and was immobile. The pain radiated from his former rotator cuff through the upper back and chest. He didn't dare try to sit up.

A stately gentleman in an expensive suit appeared. He stood in the doorway a moment and then spoke.

"Hello. You must be Jeremy and Sandy Porter."

"Yes, who are you?" Sandy asked.

"My name is J. Howard Hartman and I am an attorney. I believe we've met at your father's events."

"Okay."

"Several times."

"Ah. Sorry. I'm a little—"

He smiled, no worries. "Is Jeremy able to communicate now?"

"Kind of."

Jeremy waved, then his eyes closed as if they were too heavy to keep open.

"This is probably not a good time."

"Sandy, if you do not already have an attorney, I want to represent Jeremy—pro bono, of course."

Jeremy's eyes opened. "What'd he say?"

"Why would you do that?" Sandy asked.

Hartman stared at Jeremy. "I have a six-year-old granddaughter."

"Are you one of the best?" she said.

"No."

Sandy's disappointment was obvious.

"I'm *the* best in New Orleans, Louisiana, and very possibly the nation."

"No thanks," Jeremy called. "I'm going to represent myself."

"Honey! Are you out of your—"

"—fucking mind? *Obviously.*" A meek smile from Jeremy put Sandy at ease. He followed with an outstretched hand. Hartman stepped close to the bed and the men sealed their deal.

"Pleasure to meet you, Sir."

"The pleasure and honor are all mine."

"I hope you realize the shit I've gotten myself into."

"I know enough."

"So how do we start?"

"I'll let the DA know that I am representing you. From this point on, I call the shots. I don't want you to make any statements unless you check with me first."

"Okay. But NOPD will want me to give an administrative statement."

Hartman grinned at his woozy client. "Not while you're on medication."

Sandy sighed, "Thank God for drugs."

Jeremy laughed then groaned. "Oh, shit, I think my arm just fell off. Oh god, that hurts."

Sandy ran out of the room calling for a nurse. Jeremy inhaled deeply.

"So, Mr. Hartman, when will I be arrested?"

"Not sure. This case is far more complex than anything NOPD has faced. You've got them scrambling for answers. It'll buy us a little time."

Sandy returned with a nurse who asked questions, checked Jeremy's medication schedule on her iPad, then administered a cocktail of bliss. Her patient's eyes dimmed as his mouth curled into a half moon. He waved and then relaxed into deep sleep.

Hartman escorted Sandy out of the room.

"Mrs. Porter, I'm fairly certain the DA will contact me if they plan to arrest Jeremy. But if not, call me as soon as you get that news. This is my card with a 24-hour cell phone number. Don't hesitate to dial. Promise?"

Sandy threw her arms around the savior's neck and began to cry. "Thank you so much. But do we have a fucking chance in hell?"

Crude language for a lady, Hartman thought. *But exactly the question she should be asking.*

* * *

At police headquarters, Styles knew he had a deep-dish problem. The more the task force pored over the evidence, the more impressed they became. How did one unseasoned officer accomplish so much carnage, and in doing so rid the city of three individuals who had committed heinous crimes?

"Come on, Folks, tell me what we've got."

Vuong said, "Malfeasance in office and obstruction of justice."

Styles held back the anger.

"*People* ... we have to consider what he did with this Ahtoh character. He was essentially imprisoned and handcuffed to a toilet. And the same with the Boris guy. He basically kidnapped the guy and locks him in the trunk of his car. These are serious crimes, Gentlemen."

"Yeah, you're right," Gikas said. "We should add cruelty to animals."

"I can't walk into the chief's office and tell him we've only got a couple of charges! He is expecting an encyclopedia."

"Okay, we'll throw in littering."

Styles cursed and paced, combing a hand through his thinning hair. He didn't like the chuckles and hoots from the assembled peanut gallery. Suddenly Porter was being nominated for king of the Mardi Gras.

"Look, I know you're all reluctant to arrest the guy. The population is calling him a fucking hero. But he broke laws, lots of them. We can't overlook that no matter how much we may appreciate his skill at terminating scum, he is the Pervert Vigilante. What if we suddenly get copy cats out there, shooting up the city?"

Vuong nodded, and took on the task of compiling all possible charges the district attorney's office might consider. His Catholic upbringing came in handy; he stood and read aloud a litany of NOPD prayers:

Malfeasance in Office
Compounding a Felony
Obstruction of Justice
Simple Kidnapping
False Imprisonment
Failure to Report the Commission of Certain Felonies
Criminal Assistance to Suicide
Intimidation by an Officer

Stalking
Theft
Attempted Murder

When "attempted murder" was intoned, Styles could feel gloom spread through the conference room. But it was the only way to protect Bayless for shooting Porter. The entry team noted that the Emperor was still alive when Porter was felled by the rifle shot. There was no evidence that Porter intentionally moved the amperage lever on the cattle prod, thus the attempted murder instead of murder. When Vuong sat, no one nodded or voiced their approval.

Then Officer Leslie Scott stood.

"Sir, I am withdrawing my name from the task force and the Special Operations Division. I'll let Commander Watts know. With your permission I'll return to the night watch in Second District tomorrow."

"Scott, why would you do this? You're ruining your career for a rogue cop?"

Scott stood motionless and considered the remarks. Then his eyes panned the room before returning to the lieutenant.

"In my humble opinion, that rogue cop is deserving of a Police Officer of the Year Award, not a list of bullshit charges. I would go to war with him. With all due respect to everyone here, I don't want to be any part of a lynch mob."

Chapter 47

Doctors were reluctant to release Jeremy despite his progress. He was stable but would require more surgery on his shoulder when he was stronger. It was Sandy who insisted he would be more comfortable at their Garden District home.

"Are you sure?" he asked.

"We'll hire a couple nurses to help out. And Kayla wants you home."

"What about Mr. Ricky?"

"Mr. *Ray,*" she chided before turning thoughtful. "Let's just get you well. And then ... we'll see."

But it was Jeremy who chose the way he would leave the hospital. He knew he'd be in a wheelchair, so he called on Leslie Scott to provide backup. "I want to meet my new friends."

As he glided through the wide entry with Sandy at his side, a roar of approval painted the air. Norm Krawley's crowd was bigger than ever, and media were present to catch it all on video for the evening news—thanks to an anonymous tip provided by J. Howard Hartman, who remained in the doorway watching and listening, eager to dominate in the court of public opinion.

"Take me closer, Leslie. I want to shake some hands."

"It's a crush, Man. You sure?"

"I need all the love I can get."

Leslie and Sandy traded glances and then, before steering his friend into the frenzy, Leslie called to NOPD officers who were on hand for crowd control. "Incoming," he said.

Crying and wise-cracking unabashedly, Jeremy reached with his good arm to high-five the neglected folks of New Orleans: the population that just wanted to feel safe in their homes.

* * *

Hartman visited with Jeremy and Sandy a few days later to strategize. District Attorney Kenneth Richards announced that he would convene a grand jury the following week. Obviously, he would be seeking an indictment on as many charges as he could. He had a long list to choose from.

"That's when you'll be arrested. So I need you to prepare for that."

"I'll get a subpoena to appear?"

"That's right. But just because you appear doesn't mean you have to talk. My advice to you is to take the fifth and not testify."

"No."

"No, what?" Sandy asked.

"No, I won't take the fifth. I want to testify."

Hartman hadn't expected this. And he was used to getting his way.

"Jeremy, as your attorney, I strongly recommend that you don't. You'll be up against one of the fiercest prosecutors in the region. And I am not allowed to be in there with you."

"I get it. It's okay. I want to testify."

"Jeremy, Mr. Hartman is a *lawyer*."

The former vigilante grinned, nodded, fully aware that one more time he was showing symptoms of being out of his fucking mind.

"Look, it's very noble of you, but do me one favor. Think about it. You don't have to decide now. And let me be clear, I can give you a hundred reasons *not* to testify, but I can't think of *one* that is in your best interest."

"I know it's expert advice. Thank you. And, yes, I'll give it some thought. But ... I need to tell my story. For once, in my own words, I need to be heard."

* * *

"We are not going to comment about anything right now. Thank you."

Hartman repeated the line so many times Jeremy thought for sure his attorney would snap and tell everyone to leave them alone. Just the walk up the steps of the courthouse felt like crossing a desert, surrounded by video cameras and shouting reporters and helicopters fluttering overhead. It was overwhelming.

He felt relieved when he could sit on the wooden bench in the cool hallway outside the Grand Jury room. Deep breaths and Hartman's assurances helped him gather his strength. He would need every drop of energy he could summon to get through the interrogation he was about to face. Yet his spirits sagged when the Grand Jury door opened and Brock Suggs appeared.

Suggs stopped when he saw Jeremy. Neither dared to exchange words. Both had been warned that all testimony was to remain confidential under penalty of law. The men locked stares for several seconds, and then the cop walked away with his legal counsel. To an onlooker, the encounter likely appeared cold, adversarial.

Yet, strange as it might seem, Jeremy sensed a change in his nemesis. Had he seen a flash of conspiratorial support in the man's eyes? Maybe. Leslie Scott told him the friendship between Suggs and Bayless had soured since the foundry incident. Rumors suggested that the two men gave very different statements to homicide about the rifle shot that had nearly taken Jeremy's life.

"Jeremy Porter."

The Grand Jury security officer called the name a second time before Jeremy stood and began his walk to persecution. His mind was flooded with images of Sandy and Kayla, and even Luisa Olvera who he suspected had left the flowers outside his ICU room. Yet he also heard the pleading appeal of his pro bono attorney, a man of great dignity and skill who was now whispering in his ear.

"Jeremy, one last time, please take the fifth. I can let them know right now. *Please* listen to me."

To Hartman's surprise, Jeremy stopped, took a deep breath, and actually smiled, as though he had been relieved of a heavy burden.

"You're a great man. I'm so lucky to know you. Thank you, Sir, for everything you have done for me and my family. But ... I never asked ... do you play tennis?"

Hartman was caught off-guard. "Uh, actually, golf is my pastime."

"Well, I used to be a pretty good tennis player. And the part I loved most was serving. I had a good serve. I could jam it down my opponent's throat. And my preacher dad probably would have called that vain or something. So I never told him, 'Dad, your son has a wicked serve.'"

"Jeremy, please tell me what tennis has to do with the grave situation you're about to face?"

"Mr. Hartman ... believe it or not ... I can't wait to get in there and let 'er rip."

The attorney, a sturdy, composed man, felt his eyes moisten. Throughout his professional life, he had been guided by strictures that he seemed born to. Yet now he willingly disobeyed, leaned forward, and wrapped his finely attired arms around Jeremy, knowing that this brave yet foolish young man was walking into a coliseum where he would be greeted by lions.

* * *

Three hours later, District Attorney Kenneth Richards was grateful that the grand jury needed a break. So did he. In fact, he could also use a stiff drink—or maybe three.

As he quickly exited the courtroom, Richards noticed J. Howard Hartman sitting on the bench but couldn't allow himself to engage.

Instead, he searched his phone for messages and then rushed to the end of the hallway, where he found Police Chief Hendricks.

"How's it going, Ken?"

"Well, Morris, he's been testifying for three hours now and there is not a dry eye in the room. I think the jury called for a break so that they could order out for more boxes of Kleenex."

"Why? He's a criminal. A rogue cop. Don't they understand that?"

"I've been in this business a long time, but I've never had to deal with anything like this. I thought you said he was a fuck up?"

"Yeah, from a staffing point of view. He was never meant to be a police officer."

"Well, he's found his calling. He's kind, he's totally believable and engaging, and he's not dodged one stinking question. He's got it all figured out and documented. When I got him to admit that he had been removed from Child Abuse after one day and therefore had no authority to stalk molesters, he countered by saying Sergeant Tanner had given him permission."

"That's ridiculous."

"Oh, yeah? Tell that to the jury. What *they* heard was how shocked Porter was when Tanner told him there were hundreds of names in the Extremely Dangerous file—and not enough detectives to cover them all."

Hendricks felt queasy, especially since the Sex Crimes Investigation audit announced the exact same thing.

Richards continued.

"And then, it's like this guy has a photographic memory, because he quotes Tanner in a way that sounds verbatim. 'If you want to spend your off days keeping track of these perverts, go right ahead. I'm sure Probation would appreciate it.' Is that true? Did Tanner say something that stupid?"

Hendricks protested. "I'm sure the sergeant was only making a sarcastic point that the section was understaffed."

"Well, whose fault is that, Morris?"

The question stung like a sharp pencil to the neck.

"And why didn't NOPD go after this Russian porn ring after Porter discovered what was going on? And the attack on Eric Dietz and his boy ... hey, don't be surprised when that victim lawyers up and pounds this city for a multi-million-dollar damage claim. We apparently totally screwed up this man's life when a false accusation about child abuse was overturned but never expunged from court records."

Richards tossed his arms upward, walked a crazy-eight formation, and began sucking in deep breaths. Hendricks gave him some space, then said, "What else?"

"Chief ... I could go on. But the point is there are so many ways Porter is making sense to this jury that— "

Hendricks felt light-headed, churlish. "Are you telling me that there's a chance the jury won't indict?"

"Listen, I can't predict anything anymore. All I can do is make my recommendations as forcefully as possible. But here's the deal." Richards shook his head, mystified, vulnerable. He hated to admit that all he could think about was how this case would likely affect his re-election campaign. "For the first time in my career ... I'm just a bit player in there. Nobody cares about me."

"All eyes on Porter."

Before responding, Richards glanced down the hallowed hallway and noticed that Hartman was now standing and staring in his direction. The DA leaned in close and whispered to Hendricks.

"Porter is a fucking rock star."

* * *

Jeremy was sprawled out on the love seat. He was not as groggy on this particular morning. With his left arm still in a sling, his mind wandered to the early days of his marriage. Things were so different then. He had not yet figured out who he was or his purpose in life. "Thanks for letting me stay here. I hope this isn't causing problems with your social life."

"Jeremy, Kayla is with my mom today. I think it's time we have a talk."

"Uh-oh, should I take my pain meds first."

His response drew a glancing smile from Sandy. "You may need them afterwards."

They exchanged a laugh.

"Jeremy, when I kneeled next to your hospital bed in the Emergency Room there were so many things I wanted to say. Knowing you were on the verge of dying, I was so scared that I would never be able to tell you what was going on in my head. I came to realize how much I love you and I was so afraid you would never know."

Jeremy felt a lump in his throat. "When they were working on me, I felt your hand grasp mine. I felt your love and I wanted to tell you how much I loved you. I never stopped loving you."

She exclaimed, "You felt my touch?"

"Yes, I did."

"I haven't been able to forgive myself, knowing you asked me to wait for an hour before I called anyone—I feel so bad that you may have gotten shot because of me."

Sandy collapsed into Jeremy's arms. She couldn't hold back the tears any longer. Jeremy could hardly believe what he was hearing. Not only had his experiences changed him, they had also changed her—in an amazing way.

"Hey, it's okay. You did nothing wrong. I got shot by an overzealous cop. It's okay."

She buried her head into his chest. "Jeremy, I'm not sure what it is. Maybe it's what you went through, or all you did for those kids, but I just have a whole new outlook—on us. I just want us to be together again. I want us to be husband and wife. I hated the fact that you left the store and wanted to be a cop but I understand now. Will you forgive me for being so selfish?"

"You're not selfish. I could have handled it better."

"Can we be together? Forever?"

"I would love to but—"

"But what!?"

"Sandy, if I am convicted, I am facing twenty, maybe thirty years in prison. I couldn't do that to you."

"Let me worry about that. We'll get through it—together."

Before Jeremy could respond, they were interrupted by the doorbell.

Sandy answered the door and returned with a FedEx box.

"It's for you."

"Who is it from?"

"It just has the initials JDD. Shall I open it?"

"Sure."

As Sandy pulled the small box apart she found a smaller box inside with a gift card.

"Read it, please."

Sandy began.

Dear Jeremy,

I am not sure if you remember me. My name is Joe Doode. We spoke a couple of times when I was on the force. Although I am no longer a police officer, I keep up with the affairs of the department. I am writing to congratulate you for your amazing courage and what you accomplished. Because of the controversy involved in your situation, I know they are not planning to recognize you at any awards function. Therefore, I have enclosed a Medal of Valor that was presented to me when I was with the department. I would be honored if you would accept it. Although you will never be able to wear it on a uniform, just knowing it is in your possession will bring me a great deal of satisfaction. I know you have an uphill battle in front of you, but know that my family and friends will keep you in our prayers. I wish you a speedy and full recovery. All the best.

Respectfully,

Joe Doode

Sandy handed Jeremy the Medal of Valor. He fixed his eyes on the beautiful medal and realized the irony: congratulations from Joe Doode.

Chapter 48

Jeremy always chose the speaker phone function when taking a call from his attorney. Privacy made no sense at this point in his life, and it was too exhausting having to explain everything to Sandy. The morning after the grand jury appearance, the couple was on the couch listening to Hartman.

"Do you want the good news or the bad news first?"

Sandy visibly tensed. Jeremy was philosophical.

"Whatever. Lay it on me, Mr. Hartman."

"The grand jury has refused to indict you on any charges."

Propped up by pillows, Jeremy stared into space, dumbfounded. Sandy screamed and cried and dropped the phone as she began to bounce on the cushions. When she picked it up, she couldn't understand why her husband was so unresponsive.

"Jeremy!"

He lingered in the moment, hoping he would always remember the sense of relief he experienced, both mentally and physically. Finally, he held one finger to Sandy's lips and then spoke into the phone. "Now tell me the good news."

Hartman continued to discover new layers of his client's shrewd wit. Jeremy wisely understood that the grand jury ruling was nothing short of a miracle, but in no way the end of his worries. A free man? Technically, yes. But—

"Yes, well, District Attorney Richards will hold a news conference later this morning. So please keep this news to yourself until then. He won't shy away from saying that, in his opinion, crimes were committed. That maybe the vigilante beat the law only because he did away with some unsavory people. That sets a bad precedent."

"I see his point."

"But now we have to prepare for the NOPD administrative investigation. You face a long list of alleged violations. And Tanner has the video of you searching the ED files."

"Stupid me."

"You must provide police with a statement and answer all of their questions. I can't help you with your responses but apparently you do pretty well on your own. At this point, you could tell them to shove it and simply resign—"

Jeremy wondered if he would ever want to go back on duty. Why? He'd just survived a lightning strike.

"Tell them to shove it," Sandy said.

Yet he'd also experienced moments of purpose that were glorious, even if they were brief.

"After everything they did to you—the rat thing when you graduated, not giving you a chance with Child Abuse?"

The world was upside down and often made very little sense. But he wasn't quite ready to walk away.

"I'll meet with them."

Hartman's mirth was evident. "How did I know that would be your answer?"

"But Jeremy ... after all they did to you?" Sandy's frustration was growing.

The attorney added, "And you do realize that if they find some of these violations to be sustained, it is very likely you will be fired."

"I hope you mean terminated. Bayless already took his shot."

Hartman smiled. "Sorry. Poor choice of words. But the point is, if they terminate you that would prevent you from being a police officer for ten years. On the other hand, if you merely resign, you may have an outside chance of returning in a few years. Need time to think it over?"

"Yeah. About ten years."

"So you would actually consider remaining on the police force?"

His dilemma had nothing to do with police work. It had more to do with his upbringing. As much as he had tried to escape his father's strictures and brittle sense of atonement, Jeremy wanted to face his accusers, come what may.

"I'll never understand you," Sandy said, her voice rising like wind. "Why will you never do one goddamn thing I ask you to do?"

"*Never?* Really, Sandy? I've been the good little husband and son-in-law for years. I went along, tried to keep the peace, rarely spoke up. If you don't understand me, maybe it's because you never really needed to. You called the shots—or Curtis and your mom. Why let Powder Puff ruin the grand McGuire plan by entertaining his opinions?"

They fell into silence. Jeremy was grateful when Hartman spoke again.

"One thing you do have in your favor… "

"Yeah?"

"The mayor won't just sit back while Chief Hendricks hangs you out to dry. Considering your popularity, he can't afford that kind of heat. It could derail his re-election."

In a whisper, "Mr. Hartman … whatever happens … thank you."

Chapter 49

The following week, Chief Hendricks was actually looking forward to his meeting with the mayor. He'd directed Internal Affairs investigators to grill Porter without mercy. The onslaught lasted several days and this time the Pervert Vigilante had no luck charming his interrogators, who recommended sustaining several serious administrative charges. The severity of the department violations could mean only one thing: termination.

Hendricks couldn't help but gloat as his car arrived at City Hall and he recalled the disappointing headlines that had appeared the previous week.

PERVERT VIGILANTE GOES FREE!

Not quite, Powder Puff.

Yet to his surprise, it was not the mayor he found waiting for him. Press Secretary Lois Stewart, an angular, tawny-haired woman of forty, led Hendricks to her office.

"My apologies. The mayor was called away. Instead, he asked me to ... well, I'd like to share some information in light of your recommendation that Jeremy Porter be terminated from NOPD."

"What kind of information?"

"Chief Hendricks, we're experiencing a deluge of commentary since the grand jury's decision not to indict."

"Well, we can't expect the media to let go of a sicko story."

He had in mind all the digging reporters had done on Maksim Coloft, a.k.a. the Emperor. The breadth of the psychopath's network stateside was horrifying.

"It's not the media we're worried about. It's the community. Our website is under water, so to speak, with demands and accusations. Our Twitter accounts are virtually under attack by neighborhood groups nationwide."

"What do they want?"

"They're using every opportunity to compare Porter's success and courage to our—in their words—negligence and indifference."

"But our statistics show improvements in several areas of crime."

Lois Stewart did not avert her eyes, choosing instead to cripple his defense with a look that said, *Come off it. You know you manipulated the data.*

"No matter what we think, Sir, Porter is a hero to nearly every sector in New Orleans. Black, White, Hispanic, everyone. Fathers, mothers, grandfathers, and grandmothers."

Hendricks was catching the drift. "In other words, *voters.*"

The press secretary didn't deny or agree, she simply plowed ahead.

"Terminating Porter will create a firestorm that we may not be able to control. It could very well be a public relations disaster that might send local and national media into a frenzy."

"If you're asking me to *not* terminate Porter, this is something the mayor and I need to discuss."

"Something lesser."

"Lesser? What do you mean?"

"A suspension. Everyone wins with a suspension."

Hendricks wondered if Lois Stewart ever smiled; her steely, pale eyes gave him the creeps. Also, he didn't like making this type of decision with a civilian press secretary who had no rank. Another thought ambushed him: the mayor had not been called away. He just didn't want to be tarred with his police chief's reversal of recommendations.

"Lois ... I'll need a little time to ... perhaps I should review the Internal Affairs notes."

"Great, I'll let the mayor know."

"But there is one problem."

"Oh?"

"Porter was out on admin leave the last time we gave the sergeant's test. Technically, if I suspend, he's still a member of the department and that means he should be allowed to sit for a make-up test."

"Hmm. Well. I'm sure the mayor would want you to follow appropriate ... procedures."

"And if Porter finishes in the top tier?"

"Procedures, Chief. What's right is right."

Chapter 50

Jeremy Porter was on top of the world. After months of tumult which included a thirty-day NOPD suspension, painful physical therapy for his shoulder, and the surprise that Sandy was pregnant with their second child, the newly appointed platoon sergeant of the Second District was reporting for night shift duty.

He'd arrived early, hoping to avoid the crush of another media circus, but the cameras and reporters surrounded him as soon as he stepped out of his Lincoln MKC SUV, a gift from Curtis McGuire. He tried to be polite, but knew better than to violate the public information officer's directive—don't answer any questions.

Once he was inside the building, he stopped to look up the stairway that led to the Child Abuse Section. Memories gave him uneasy feelings. But they all went away when he turned to discover that he was surrounded by a large group of officers who were eager to celebrate his return.

He was nearly smothered by handshakes, slaps on the back, and a hug from Officer Luisa Olvera. Then she stepped back and saluted.

"Welcome to Second District, *Sergeant*."

"Thank you. Really good to see you, Officer Olvera."

Quips and good-natured teasing diverted his attention. He did his best to keep everything business-like as he walked with his entourage toward the roll call room. Then he stopped. The entrance was blocked by a surly Brock Suggs, who saluted and then spoke loud enough for everyone to hear.

"I guess I owe you a blow job, Sergeant."

"Uh, pardon?"

Officers snorted and reeled with laughter, recalling Suggs's crude promise that if NOPD ever caught the Pervert Vigilante he would gladly pleasure the hero with oral sex.

Jeremy smiled. "How about just a handshake. I'm a little concerned about socially transmitted diseases."

"Like stupidity, you mean?"

Sergeant Porter clasped his colleague's hand and pulled close. "That's all behind us now, Officer Suggs. You likely saved my life, because I know you're a great marksman. I know what you did—or didn't do. I can't thank you enough. We're good. It's all good."

"Well, not quite."

Tension rippled through the assembled officers as Suggs broke the news.

"Sorry to report that ... Lieutenant Bayless called in sick earlier."

Jeremy had to admit that just hearing the name soured his mood. He hoped the others didn't notice.

"So, unfortunately, that means you'll have to lead roll call."

A cheer erupted and a joy Jeremy never knew he was capable of feeling shot through his senses—like a jolt of electricity.

Later, as he stood before a forest of blue, holding a stack of memos, Jeremy noticed a new recruit in the rear of the room, standing alone. Nearby, he also saw his grumpy nemesis Sergeant Finnegan, leaning back, arms folded across his chest like sabers.

"Sergeant Finnegan," he said. "Please find another chair so we can properly welcome our new recruit and invite him to join us."

Finnegan, stunned, reluctantly limped into the hallway and dragged in a chair.

"What's your name, Officer?"

"Robideaux, Sir. Daniel Robideaux."

"That's a fine name. So tonight let's start our roll call in your honor—Daniel Robideaux."

"Here, Sir!"

As Jeremy called each name, the platoon hung on his every word. After all, he was a courageous, heralded police officer, a living legend. They were proud to be in his presence, and respectful of the catastrophe he had survived. They embraced their new and trusted supervisor.

After roll call, Jeremy walked outside toward his police vehicle. The platoon officers had already ventured onto their various assignments. Only Officer Olvera and her partner remained and upon spotting Jeremy, she exited her patrol car and approached him.

Extending her hand, she said, "Jeremy, I just wanted to say how happy I am that everything turned out so well for you. I also want to let you know you are an inspiration to me—your courage, risking your life, never giving up, and taking on this corrupt system. You have reinstated my faith in what it means to be a cop. I will always treasure our friendship." Olvera felt her eyes begin to water and decided to show her friendship with a hug.

"Hey, you helped me through some very rough times and I appreciate you as well. And thanks for all the flowers. But how are you doing?"

"I'm doing well. I'm seeing someone now. It's kind of serious."

"Oh, really. A cop?"

"Hell, no! I wouldn't date a cop!"

Laughter interrupted the tears. Jeremy offered another embrace.

"I'm happy for you. I wish you the very best."

"Thank you, Sergeant Porter."

"You're welcome. Now get out there and catch some bad guys."

"Did you leave any to catch?"

They shared a hearty laugh and went on their way.

Near the end of his shift, Jeremy received a phone call from Captain Reed.

"Porter, I am on the way in to the office. I need you to wait until I get there. I want to speak to you."

Jeremy thought for a moment. *Perhaps the captain wants to personally welcome me back.* "Yes sir. I'll be here."

About thirty minutes later, Captain Reed appeared, business like, walking briskly into his office.

Captain Reed unlocked the office door. He looked at Jeremy and said, "Come on in." Jeremy took a seat in front of Reed's desk.

"How did the night shift go last night?"

"Everything went well. No problems, Sir."

"Good, because you are going to be there for a while."

Suddenly Jeremy felt uneasy but kept his composure. "No problem, Sir. Wherever you need me."

"Good attitude, Porter." Reed then placed both of his arms on his desk and leveled a direct stare into Jeremy's curious eyes.

"Porter, you may have won the battle, but you are going to lose the war."

"Excuse me?"

"You embarrassed the chief and you embarrassed me."

"It was never my intention—"

"Yes, we know all about your intentions. But the party's over. Welcome back to reality."

Jeremy sensed the hatred from Reed but after what he had been through, this was a walk in the park. "No problem, Captain. It's good to be back."

"You will be working for Lieutenant Bayless, the guy who put the hole in your chest."

"I understand."

Reed continued, " Don't even think about putting in for a transfer. And it's safe to say, your father-in-law no longer has any stroke around here so don't bother calling him."

"The thought never crossed my mind."

Reed began looking at documents on his desk. "The bad news, Porter, is that the crime stats. You know all about crime stats, don't you?"

Jeremy gave a nod.

"The crime stats show that we have an increase of crime on the weekends, so as junior sergeant, you are going to have to work weekends until I decide otherwise."

"No problem."

"By the way, your platoon members will also need to work weekends."

"They will still need two days off."

"Well, I have given some thought to that. I am going to split their days off and they will need to work all holidays. Crime stats, you understand, right?"

Jeremy realized the harassment was intended for him but Reed was going to make life miserable for the whole platoon and direct the blame to Jeremy. Jeremy had nothing to say and stared right back at his captain. He waited for the next volley.

Reed picked up another form. "Porter, I want to talk about your relationship with Officer Olvera."

"I don't know what you are talking about."

"Good, then you won't mind taking a polygraph."

"Where is this going, Captain?"

"This is called rules, Porter. Something you know little about. Supervisors cannot have a relationship with subordinates."

"Anything that happened between us occurred when I was a police officer, not a supervisor."

"Porter you were actually promoted to sergeant two weeks ago. So if you continued with this little romance up to now, that's a problem."

"I can assure you there is no romance between Officer Olvera and me. We are just friends."

"Is that right? Porter, do you realize we have surveillance cameras all around this building?"

"I do."

"So part of my job is to look at these cameras all hours of the day to make sure we are always conducting ourselves in a professional manner. You understand that, right?'

"Yes."

Captain Reed then turned to his computer and pulled up a dark video of the rear parking lot. He moved the monitor slightly to give Jeremy a view. "I made of copy of this from last night. Porter, this doesn't look like a friendly hug to me. A twenty-two-second hug is not your normal buddy type of hug, especially from someone who sent you flowers every week."

"Sir, she was simply welcoming me back."

"So did you hug everyone for twenty-two seconds?"

"Captain, I can assure you we don't have an ongoing relationship."

"Well, we don't know about that. We will need to bring Olvera in to start an investigation."

"Please don't drag her into this."

"Excuse me, Sergeant. Are you asking me to turn my head away from a possible violation?"

"No, Sir."

"Good, she will be assigned to desk duty until we get all the answers. I am afraid this could get messy."

Jeremy was bewildered. He had flashbacks of the harassment tactics from before. He thought this type of supervision was behind him but here it was, front and center. Not his courage, the admiration of his peers, nor the favorable opinion of the community could help him.

Jeremy looked down at the floor, "What can I do to make this go away?"

"If you are no longer employed, we don't need an investigation. If you choose to resign, it's over. And, I just happen to have a resignation form on my desk."

Jeremy accepted the form and at a glance, noticed the resignation was dated 'effective today.' A well-conceived plan to finally rid the department of the Pervert Vigilante—a voluntary resignation.

"I would like to speak to my platoon members before I leave. Maybe tonight?"

"I don't think that is a good idea. Probably best to make this a clean break. I'll let them know you decided on a different career path."

Jeremy signed the form and handed it to Reed.

"You are doing the right thing Porter. I'm sure your girlfriend will be most grateful."

Jeremy decided not to respond and neither man extended a hand. Jeremy walked out of the police station for the last time, broken and dejected. He looked up the stairs toward the Child Abuse Section and wondered—how many more are out there?

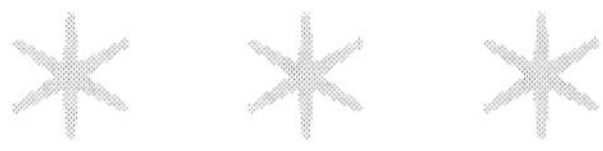

EPILOGUE

Curtis McGuire had welcomed Jeremy back to the company with open arms. And after the birth of his second grandchild—a boy—he was seriously contemplating retirement. He began to groom his son-in-law as his successor. Jeremy was given an executive's office and salary, and enormous responsibilities, yet he was always home in time for dinner. He was happy to immerse himself in his work and new life. But that didn't mean that sometimes he didn't miss being with the NOPD, which is why Jeremy was thrilled the day his secretary announced that his old friend, Leslie Scott, had stopped by for a visit.

The men greeted each other with a bear hug.

"Hey, nice digs, Man."

"Yeah. Not bad for a former vigilante, huh? So give me the gossip. I heard Hendricks resigned."

"Yes, there was no way the mayor could keep him after the audit was released. But he's not the only casualty. Quite a few supervisors are under investigation for cooking the books. Reed and Tanner are on desk duty awaiting their invitation to the grand jury."

Jeremy snickered. "I'll send them a sympathy card."

"Maybe they'll call you for some advice."

Jeremy cracked a broad smile. "Probably not."

"Actually, Reed has bigger problems. Apparently he was having an affair with his secretary and his wife caught them red-handed."

Jeremy shook his head and laughed. "What an asshole. So tell me, how is the new chief?"

"Oh my goodness, she's top notch. Hit the ground running. And her son spent some time in Fallujah, so she cut me a wide berth. I'm loving it. Won't be any cooking the books under her watch."

"That's great news. I'm happy for you guys."

"Jeremy, I know we've talked but I never really got a solid answer from you … Why did you leave the department?"

Jeremy had to struggle for an answer. "Just thought it was time."

"Come on man. One day back. All American hero. And you just walk away?"

"It's complicated."

"Whatever you say … and, hey, I've been wondering, have you heard from Dietz?"

"Yes, we have kept in touch. He and Timmy are doing well. His record has been cleared and he was recently hired as foreman of a major construction job in Lake Charles."

"That's fantastic. Good for him!"

Then Scott turned serious.

"Are you going to be home this evening?"

"Yes, why?"

"The new chief wants to introduce herself. I told her I would make the arrangements."

"What does she want to talk to me about?"

"Don't know. What time shall I have her stop by?"

"We will be home by six."

"You are going to like this lady. She is one of us. Trust me."

* * *

Jeremy and Sandy were seated in the living room when they heard the doorbell. As Jeremy opened the door, he saw a middle-aged African American woman in a navy blue suit. She held a slight smile and extended her hand.

"Hi, I'm Florence Thomas, Chief of Police."

"Hi, Chief, I'm Jeremy Porter. Come on in. It's very nice to meet you. This is my wife, Sandy."

Greetings and general introductions continued as Sandy offered tea, coffee, or hinted at a stiffer drink.

"No, thank you. I am not going to take much of your time."

Sandy believed the two of them wanted to discuss police matters so she began to excuse herself.

"I'll let you two—"

The chief stopped her. "Oh no, please, stay." Sandy sat down next to her husband, still unsure as to why the chief of police would make a personal visit. *Did Daddy arrange this meeting to show us that he already has connections with the new chief?* She would soon find out that she couldn't be more incorrect.

The chief quickly turned from her pleasant smile to a serious tone.

"Jeremy, I have read the reports involving your incident. What you accomplished is truly amazing. I offer my commendation and appreciation."

"Thank you."

"I also read the report pertaining to the manipulation of crime reports, serious crimes. Someone actually thought it was a good idea to downgrade crimes in order to convince the community that crime was on the decline."

"Yes, I also read that report. Pretty awful."

"It is a disgrace. If we can build a case against those responsible, I'll see to it they go to jail." Chief Thomas could barely hold her anger when discussing the statistics issue.

"There are child molesters running free because someone or *some people* decided not to document the incidents correctly. It makes me sick."

"But didn't you increase the number of investigators in that section?"

"Yes, I did. However, I'm not sure they realize the gravity of the situation or have the experience to uncover these atrocities." Chief Thomas paused and took a deep breath. She looked deep into Jeremy's eyes. The stage was set for the request.

"Jeremy, I want you to return to the department. I'll assign you to a special investigative unit. You can hand-pick your personnel. You will answer directly to me. Jeremy, you are the one who can track down these predators and bring them to justice. I need you. The department needs you. Your community needs you. Most importantly, we need justice for these kids who have been victimized by these monsters who are convinced they will never be caught. We need you, Jeremy."

Jeremy was stunned by the request, flattered but speechless. He began formulating an answer in his head. He would discuss it with Sandy, consider his kids, the CEO position.

For the rest of the evening and into the night, Jeremy struggled with the decision that faced him. Sandy was quiet—pensive—he couldn't figure out what she was thinking.

On the one hand, Jeremy was thrilled with the possibility of reclaiming the sense of purpose, pride, and passion that he felt as the Pervert Vigilante; he envisioned how different life would be without having to endure harassment from the former administration. On the other hand, he wondered how a return to NOPD would be received by Sandy: would she continue to love him and be proud of him, or would their marriage fall apart? He had to consider his children and the career he would be leaving behind ... again! Despite the hours spent pondering his future, it remained unclear.

The next day, as he was surveying the busy furniture store, he thought *even though it's not exciting, it provides a safe and secure living.* Then he remembered that having it all can be synonymous with having nothing.

"Mr. Porter?"

A short African-American woman looked up at Jeremy with tear-filled eyes that she dabbed with a handkerchief.

"Yes?"

"Mr. Porter, I need you to help me."

"Sure. What's wrong?"

"Oh, Mr. Porter," she cried and started to sway, ready to collapse with her burden. Jeremy quickly took her arm and led her to a sectional couch and sat down next to her.

"What is it, Ma'am?" he asked softly.

"It's my son. He's only six years old and such a sweet boy...."

Jeremy felt a familiar pang of anxiety. "Has something happened to him?"

"Yes," she whispered. "He's been kidnapped."

THE END

About the Author

Robert Sterling Hecker began his career in law enforcement with the New Orleans Police Department (NOPD). During his twenty-eight years with the NOPD, Hecker was the recipient of numerous awards and commendations including three Keys to the City, an Outstanding Service Award issued by the governor, and Supervisor of the Year. Hecker rose to the rank of captain and served as district commander before retiring from the NOPD. He is currently the police chief for the Harbor Police Department–Port of New Orleans.

Because of his experience pertaining to port security, Hecker has represented the Port of New Orleans on *Hardball with Chris Matthews* and *ABC World News Tonight*, and also has provided testimony to the congressional subcommittee on port security.

For his efforts during the Hurricane Katrina disaster in New Orleans, Hecker was named "New Orleanian of the Year" by *Gambit Weekly*, and was the recipient of several awards, including "Supervisor of the Year" by the Victims and Citizens Against Crime Organization; "Hero of the Storm" by *Southern Women's Magazine*; "Hero of the Storm" by the WDSU television station; "Meritorious Service" by the New Orleans Metropolitan Crime Commission; "Outstanding Service" by the Southern Christian Leadership Conference; "International Police 9/11 Medal for Port Security" by the

International Association of Airport and Seaport Police; and "National Service" by the New Orleans Ready Community Partnership.

Hecker prepared a video presentation describing the events throughout the Katrina Disaster, including "Lessons Learned—the Katrina Disaster." This presentation has been given to civic groups, police departments, international visitors, the Harvard Law School and various organizations across the country.

He is a member of the American Association of Port Authorities Security Committee, the International Association of Chiefs of Police, the International Association of Airport and Seaport Police, the Area Maritime Security Committee, the Louisiana Association of Chiefs of Police, and the Fraternal Order of Police.

Hecker has added novelist to his list of achievements. *The Accidental Vigilante* is his debut novel.

Made in the USA
Lexington, KY
09 June 2016